"TELL ME ... TO STOP," SAYED MURMURED

His voice was deep and husky, his face drenched in moonlight as he cradled her in his arms.

Robyn felt the strong excited beat of his heart. As his lips grazed hers her last shaky resistance evaporated, and she could only move with him as he lowered her to the warm desert sand. She shuddered from the unbearable gentleness of his stroking fingers....

Then he was holding her away, arching her back so that the moonlight shone full on her breasts, on her impassioned face. "So much for your talk of purity," he rasped. "You know quite well what will arouse a man!"

Helplessly Robyn recoiled. She was too stunned to defend herself, even with the truth—that she loved him desperately.

AND NOW...

SUPERROMANCES

Worldwide Library is proud to present a
sensational new series of modern love stories —
SUPERROMANCES

Written by masters of the genre, these longer,
sensuous and dramatic novels are truly in keeping
with today's changing life-styles. Full of intriguing
conflicts, the heartaches and delights of true love,
SUPERROMANCES are absorbing stories —
satisfying and sophisticated reading that lovers
of romance fiction have long been waiting for.

SUPERROMANCES
Contemporary love stories for the woman of today!

CATHERINE KAY

DAWN OF PASSION

A SUPERROMANCE FROM
WORLDWIDE

TORONTO · NEW YORK · LOS ANGELES · LONDON

For Egypt, whose people are the real and
enduring treasure of that ancient land.
And for Kay Mouradian, with love and thanks.

Published December 1982

First printing October 1982

ISBN 0-373-70045-8

Printed in Canada

CHAPTER ONE

THE MEDITERRANEAN SPARKLED blue far below the plane, and Robyn's heart gave a deep excited beat. Until just a few moments ago clouds had veiled everything, cheating her of even a distant glimpse of France and Italy.

Now, nearer Africa, the atmosphere was clear, and she was looking for the first time at the great sea that had been the focus of so many of her childhood imaginings. Down there the Argonauts had sailed their swift ship and Ulysses had wandered on his long quest. Dido, brave princess of Tyre, had founded mighty Carthage, and invincible Caesar had sailed to his destiny with Cleopatra.

Robyn hugged the private joy she was feeling to herself, trying to forget the large sprawling body and irritating personality of Huntley Saunders III, the Texan who sat dozing in the seat next to hers. Tightness constricted her throat for a moment while she remembered her father's warm voice saying, "One day, little bird, I'll take you to the sea of legend and to all the lands of myth and mystery." Now her father, James Arthur Douglas—whose work in archaeology was respected all over the world—had been dead for almost three years and she, Robyn Douglas, was on her way to Egypt as a representative of the university where he had spent so much of his career. Not with her father as he had promised, but with his memory.

When she was a child he had often flown off to glamorous-sounding places on archaeological digs, coming home with exotic gifts for herself and her mother and, best of all, with wonderful tales about rediscovering the past. Robyn had loved to sit near her father's big oak desk in his study, asking him endless questions. He had laughed at her flow of curiosity, until he found that her interest was real. Then gradually he had helped her become his colleague in the love of discovery and in the joy in ancient knowledge.

By the time she was ten she could classify shards of pottery into time sequences and could read a bit of ancient Greek. Much of her time as a teenager was spent in the spacious basement laboratory of their home, sorting and cataloging fragments of papyrus, helping her father with his specialty—early Egyptian and Greco-Roman writings. She often tagged along to learned meetings with him—her mother had no interest in going—and his friends soon called her the "little professor."

When she graduated from university at the age of twenty, Robyn was already expert in reading Egyptian hieroglyphics, Greek and Latin. Her master's degree came after another year of intensive study, and now she worked for Dr. Wayland, the dean of the department of archaeological studies. She was quietly on her way to a doctorate, increasing her mother's worries that she would not have a normal life.

Her father had always made light of her mother's fears, Robyn knew. She had overheard them discussing her shortly after her graduation. "There's time enough for her to settle down, Edith," he had

soothed. "Look how sweet she is, just like her name—
a small, shy, cozy bird. No one would guess what a
good brain lies in that bright brown head."

"Sesha Neheru Douglas, old maid," her mother
had replied, a touch acidically. "You stamped ancient
Egypt on her in the cradle; she couldn't even have a
normal modern name."

"Small Bird Among Flowers," her father had said
gently. "That's what she is. And after all, we call her
Robyn, don't we?"

Robyn had smiled to herself. She loved her eccen-
tric, beautiful Egyptian name....

"THAT'S THE AFRICAN COAST, all right; seen it a dozen
times. It won't be long now." Huntley Saunders
brought his jowly face close to Robyn's as he leaned
across her to peer out the window of the plane. As
usual, he managed to press against her more than was
necessary.

If he does it once more I'll have to hit him, she
thought angrily, *protocol or no protocol.*

Sitting back, the Texan yawned. "Well, old Sayed
al-Rashad ought to be damn glad to see me and my
borescope camera. It's not every day an Egyptian archaeologist gets a gift like this. Always short on cash
and good equipment over here. It won't take us any
time at all to drill into that main chamber and have a
look around with my little spy camera. Good old
American ingenuity, that's what they've needed.
We're gonna find us some valuable stuff!"

Robyn replied with a soft affirmative, not loud
enough to encourage more conversation. The man
had said the same thing numerous times on the long
flight from Los Angeles. Unfortunately, there was

good reason for her to endure Huntley Saunders of Houston. The patronizing amateur archaeologist had given a sizable grant from his inherited oil fortune in support of the dig she was about to join.

The excavation was a joint effort by her university and an Egyptian antiquities team, and the borescope camera he boasted so much about was terribly important at this stage of the work. It could be sent down through a small hole to examine an unopened tomb— or in the case of this dig, what might prove to be a hidden treasure room of ancient manuscripts. Dr. al-Rashad, leader of the project, had already dug out a small upper chamber, where some badly damaged papyrus scrolls had been found. The sealed space beneath it might contain even more significant discoveries. Al-Rashad's correspondence with Dr. Wayland in the past weeks had been growing more and more optimistic about the possibility of a major discovery.

Robyn let out her breath in a long sigh of exasperation. Her dream of Egypt did not include having the casual hand of Huntley Saunders pawing her at every turn. Surely it was just a reflex on his part, grabbing the nearest female body. She wasn't the type of girl that men usually made passes at. In fact, Robyn was quite used to not being noticed in a crowd. She almost welcomed her anonymity, especially since her breakup with John. Watching life from the outside was safer than being swept up by its uncertain fickle tides.

Cairo was still more than an hour away, but the reality of her arrival was starting to trickle through her busy thoughts. It had been only three short days before that Professor Wayland, her dear boss, had called her into his office.

"I can't make the trip to Egypt, Robyn," he had

said wearily. "I thought I could arrange things, but Joanne is worse again."

She had nodded. Everyone knew his devotion to his frail wife.

"You'll have to go in my place," he went on. "We've reached a crucial point in the excavations, and the contracts must be approved by al-Rashad immediately. You know them backward and forward anyway." He had given a dry laugh at her surprised expression. "I have to admit I'm glad it's you and not me who has to spend all those hours on the plane being civil to our great Texan benefactor."

She knew what he meant. She had sat in on department meetings about that very subject: what to do about Huntley Saunders, who stubbornly insisted on delivering the special camera to Egypt in person. Most large donations had strings attached, but this one had the man himself.

He had already violently upset the department by calling a press conference to announce his gift—and the recent finds at the dig. "We're on the cutting edge of a momentous discovery," he had intoned dramatically. "I'm supplying state-of-the-art technology, nothing but the best!"

The archaeologists of neither country were pleased with the premature publicity. Robyn understood how touchy the situation could become if the press ran news of a discovery before it had even been confirmed. It just wasn't done. None of the papyrus fragments had even been translated yet....

There had barely been time to think before the day of departure arrived. Robyn hadn't been able to coordinate her clothing the way she would have if she had had a few weeks' notice, and her bags contained mostly tried and true campus casual outfits, nothing very special.

Dr. Wayland had seen her off at the airport with some last minute instructions. "I've telexed the antiquities office in Cairo that you're coming in my place," he informed her. "No need to tell them you are James Arthur Douglas's daughter. It might make the Egyptians think we're looking over their shoulders. And al-Rashad's crew may not be ready for a young, intelligent female whose father was one of the best interpreters of Egyptian manuscripts in his day. The male thing is strong there, you know," he had said, winking.

Sayed al-Rashad was chief of the excavation and a well-respected archaeologist. He had a reputation as a fine and careful scholar. Robyn had read all his reports about his isolated desert dig near Alexandria, and she already had a healthy admiration for his work. It would be a pleasure to meet him in person, she knew.

"Just one warning—he seems to have a devastating effect on women. American women especially," her boss had continued as they walked toward the departure gate.

That little bit of gossip had been of no interest to her. She had never panted after a man just because he had a romantic-sounding profession.

And she knew how very *un*romantic archaeology could be, how slow and painstaking.

"That's one of the reasons you're ideal for the mission," Dr. Wayland had continued, smiling. "You know pretty much what to expect; you won't go gaga like my graduate students did last semester at al-Rashad's excavation. I don't know what came over

those young ladies. Maybe the desert heat.'' He handed her a briefcase and gave her a Dutch uncle hug of
farewell as her flight was called. ''Sensible girl, sensible girl,'' he murmured.

Robyn's mind had recoiled from the word. She was
grateful for his trust, but she wished he had chosen a
more sparkling description of her.

Actually, she was more than a simple courier. She
was expected to take careful notes on progress to date,
as well as make recommendations about whether the
university should continue its involvement with the
project. The decision hinged upon how valuable and
unusual the fragments already unearthed were. From
that she would have to judge what kind of discoveries
might be made once the sealed lower room was
opened.

It was a responsibility Robyn felt quite capable of
handling. And the trip gave her a chance to do what
she had hoped for since she was a child and had first
sensed the indescribable excitement of the distant
past: to breathe the same air the pharaohs had
breathed.

She thought about the home she had just left and
realized that she already felt detached from it. Her
mother and her aunt couldn't understand what this
opportunity meant to her, just as they had never
understood so many other things about her. Why
would a young woman choose to bury herself in piles
of dusty old manuscripts, writing about God knows
what in order to get a Ph.D., they were always wondering. It was as good as announcing to the world that
she was too intellectual for most of the men in it.

Only her father understood. He had taught her well
in those last years before his death, when his failing

health caused him to depend on her more and more for help with his translations. It had seemed unbearably frustrating that by the time she was old enough to travel with him he was unable to leave the confines of his wheelchair.

Robyn gazed at the golden brown desert far below. It felt good to be thousands of miles away from her mother's concern and well-meaning suggestions. Here in Egypt she wouldn't have to continually explain why the young assistant professors and graduate students she dated didn't fall madly in love with her, why there was no engagement ring on her left hand and why she didn't seem to encourage anyone enough to lead to something permanent.

Her mother and her aunt had lovingly nagged at her for dropping John Porter, a paleontology doctoral candidate who had paid a lot of attention to her. Robyn's considerable pride wouldn't let her tell them that the truth was the other way around—John had dropped her.

For a few months last summer he had made her feel beautiful and desirable, had started dreams in her heart. She could still feel a cold ghost of the ache he had left in her. One night he had been kissing her, whispering words that were almost a commitment; the next evening, among a group of casual acquaintances at a party, he had met a girl whose practiced female force had reached out and drawn him away with no effort.

Robyn had watched it happening before her eyes and had felt powerless to stop it. Trust and honor were precious to her, and she had felt betrayed. Maybe she reacted too strongly; maybe she should have been more contemporary in her standards. But she knew she would never feel the same about John. She left the unendurable party alone and went home, with shattered dreams to reflect on as she crept into bed.

John was cheerfully casual the next day when he called. "What happened to you last night?"

"I didn't feel well." She held her voice steady. If he didn't know, she wasn't going to make a fool of herself by spelling it out to him.

"I'm sorry, kid. You okay now?"

"I'm not sure."

After a silence John's voice said awkwardly, "Listen, Robyn, if there's anything you need, give me a call." It was goodbye without the formalities. "No hard feelings," he ended. So he did know.

She heard later that he was pursuing the other girl, and in the long empty days that followed she had a lot of time to think about life. John hadn't been her first boyfriend, but she had somehow counted on him. She had begun to think that maybe the pattern of her own future could fit around his needs, his career. Should she have fought to keep him, she'd wondered a hundred times since then. But at the same time she'd known there was no use trying to keep something that hadn't been hers in the first place. Part of her hurt was that she had been so eager to trust completely, and part of her realized that she was subconsciously following her mother's hopes for her. John just wasn't the man who matched her dreams.

Discomfort nettled her as she witnessed other women's stressful competition for men's attention. And her mother seemed accusatory in her own gentle way: Robyn didn't go to enough places where she would meet eligible men; she should take a cruise to Acapulco this year; she should try just a little with herself! The poor woman was at a loss to comprehend her daughter's stubbornness.

But Robyn didn't want to be part of a dance where partners were constantly changing. She wanted to love faithfully and joyfully—if such an ideal love existed in the world!

After John faded away she worked hard to pull a guard around herself. She was determined to keep her head firmly in control of her emotions. If somebody loved her it would have to be for herself, she resolved, and not because she had learned how to curl her eyelashes and laugh at his bad jokes. She was not going to be vulnerable again and trust too easily—and she had enough of her father's resoluteness to keep to that promise.

Yet in one corner of her heart there was a shadow of worry. John was gone; she could accept that now. But he had spoiled her comfort and awakened her body. . . just enough so that she would never be the same again.

"So. . ." a voice next to her was saying in an offhand tone, "it won't be all work and no play, I hope." Huntley Saunders's hand was resting just above her knee.

She looked up at him blankly, distracted from her faraway thoughts. "I'm afraid it will be all work for me. I have to earn my living." Pulling up her heavy briefcase, she placed it squarely over his soft hand and began to rummage among her papers.

After a moment he pulled his hand away and drawled, "You could be a good-looking girl if you'd use a little imagination in the right places. But then, I've heard that Egyptian men go for mousy blondes who carry a little extra poundage. It's always the plain ones who end up having a fling with the native drivers and such—you'll do all right for yourself.''

Out of the corner of her eye Robyn noticed a nasty smile on his sagging, middle-aged face. A smile of sympathy, she guessed, for a plain girl. She clamped her jaw tightly closed to keep from saying something she might regret. Without wanting to, she thought again about herself—the way a man might see her.

Her hair wasn't mousy, it was just a little duskier than honey. And she was happy she didn't have the figure of a starving model. At least she could enjoy eating three meals a day and still fit into her size twelve wardrobe. She felt sorry for her companion's girl friends and ex-wives, for he must have ex-wives. It would take an idiot of a woman to put up with him for long, no matter how rich he was.

Her father had always joked about her appearance, saying that she looked so innocent nobody would suspect how stubborn she was, or how romantic. Again she heard his voice say, ''Someday a man of real discernment will see your beauty and take you away from me, but I won't tolerate anyone less than the best!'' That had been three years ago, on her twenty-first birthday. A week later he had had his final heart attack and was gone.

While her mother drew a close circle around herself, becoming an almost Victorian type of widow in her mourning, Robyn's mind was reaching outward. The last thing she wanted was to live an isolated existence, knowing only one modern language, never traveling, ignorant of the incredible sweep that human history and thought comprised. With her father, after all, she had talked to men and women who spoke of amazing and ancient things.

It had always been a mystery to her why her father

had chosen to marry a woman of such different interests from his—and vice versa—yet her parents' love for each other had been deep and constant. Her mother had always been there when he returned from his adventures in the world outside their safe home.

Robyn had no regrets that her childhood had been different from that of other girls she knew. She had managed to feel well adjusted despite her mother's constant reassurances that she was every bit as attractive as other girls. She'd heard endlessly about how her smoky blue eyes were her best feature, how unusual it was to have such long dark lashes that made those interesting shadows over her face, and how good she'd look if she would let her ponytail fall freely in waves to complement her bone structure. And she was tired to death of being reminded of her "generous mouth."

All she cared about was that her features were reasonably regular and that when she smiled everything came together rather nicely. Certainly she wasn't plain, she reassured herself. It was irksome that Huntley Saunders could have distracted her just when she wanted to quietly prepare herself for her arrival in Egypt. As the plane began its descent she closed her eyes and tried to feel the energies of the venerable land reach up to her.

The early-evening sky was bright with fiery color when the wheels touched down at Cairo Airport. A light warm wind played with Robyn's scarf as she stepped out onto the tarmac. The breeze carried an exotic odor that touched chords of excitement in her. Somehow she had known that the air would smell this way, heavy with unfamiliar elements. There were hints of strange herbs and flowers; pungent wood smoke mixed with exhaust fumes.

Pushed along in the stream of debarking passengers, she lost track of her traveling companion. Probably, she told herself grimly, because he was trying to make a date with one of the flight attendants. But she didn't care.

Her eyes roved delightedly over the faces of the crowd inside the terminal. Drifts of Arabic swirled around her. Women whose faces were covered with veils moved past others who were dressed in the latest European fashions. Tall men in swinging robes strode by, and everywhere she looked families were being united in happy circles of activity. One man carried five ouds over his shoulder. Tied together, the bulbous stringed instruments formed a very peculiar looking piece of baggage. Another man was zealously hugging a box containing an electric fan—obviously a treasure.

Very little in the crazy cacophony of voices made sense to Robyn's ears, but there was nothing that felt alien, either. It was only later that she realized how strange she herself must have looked, standing in a blissful state in the midst of the milling confusion, soaking up every impression she could through her eyes and ears and nose.

Passport in hand, she went through customs fairly quickly. Kindly dark faces smiled at her with flashes of white teeth. The man who took her passport looked up with interest as he read her name aloud, ''Sesha Neheru Douglas?''

She smiled and nodded, but a voice behind her boomed in laughter, ''What kind of a name is that, now!''

''It's old Egyptian, Mr. Saunders,'' she answered briefly.

"Well, Robyn's a hell of a lot easier. Why all the folderol?"

"I'd think 'Miss Douglas' would be the easiest for you." If that didn't sound like an old maid, nothing would, she thought, giving the Texan a look that should have turned him to stone.

She was directed to a place where she could change her dollars for Egyptian pounds. But at the next window Huntley Saunders was angrily debating the exchange rate and threatening to go out to the nearest street corner and get a better one. Suddenly she was very tired. The Arabian nights lay out there, full of wonders and jinn, and she was fated to have this petty tyrant dog her steps. She found herself hesitating at the very brink of the world she had longed to see.

Then a distinctly American voice close beside her said, "You must be Robyn Douglas," and she turned to see a stocky, open-faced young man. "I'm Tom Perkins," he informed her, smiling. "Welcome to Egypt."

"I'm really happy to see you," she said, shifting her purse and overnight bag so that she could shake his hand. It was a pleasant surprise to be met by the university's man on the dig. She had typed the file of memos from the young Ph.D. and knew him to be enthusiastic and very thorough. He had been working with Dr. al-Rashad for over a year now, and she liked him immediately.

Tom, with the calmness of long experience, collected her luggage, then she introduced him to Huntley Saunders. After the first few patronizing remarks, Tom's eyes met hers in unspoken commentary. He helped to get the borescope through customs, after some delays about who the legal owner was—the

Egyptian antiquities office, the university in the
United States or the wealthy Texan who claimed it.

Nothing was simple in Egypt, Tom tried to explain.
"You can't make plans and expect them to work out
on your time schedule. There isn't the American sense
of urgency here, and it takes a little getting used to."

As soon as he had his hands safely on the camera he
said quietly to Robyn, "It would have been easier
without our friend here. They're very sensitive about
being pushed around."

Outside in the balmy night there was a large white
Mercedes station wagon waiting at the curb. Huntley
Saunders lumbered toward it. "Hey, that's good service, Abdul, real good." From the open back window
he called out, "I'm going in to the Sheraton for dinner
with some of the diplomatic people. I'll sleep in the car
on the way to Alex afterward and see you there in the
morning. You'd better take the 'scope." He rolled
the window halfway up, then remembered something.
"Make sure I have a whole suite at the Palestine
Hotel, will you? Last time they put me up in a
single...."

"Sure thing," Tom said, taking Robyn's arm and
walking to a nearby car. "Wait until Sayed finds out
he comes with the camera," he said in a low voice,
"and that Dr. Wayland is really a pretty girl. Glory be
to Allah!"

It was in that way that Robyn, to her consternation,
discovered that the telex system had broken down between Cairo and Alexandria. Even Tom hadn't
known that she was arriving until he checked in at the
antiquities office earlier in the day. But he laughed as
he explained casually, "The telex is always broken.
Gives zest to life, more surprises. Especially finding

you instead of our revered professor." But despite his cheerfulness, Robyn had the distinct feeling that Sayed al-Rashad would not be pleased. . . .

"First time in Egypt?" Tom was smiling. "Now is when all those pictures you've looked at suddenly get three dimensions."

They drove out of Cairo along Pyramid Road. With a tug of joy she saw the huge stone forms outlined in the distance against the dusky blue evening sky. The Middle East was already claiming her. The honking horns, the colorful crowds, the animal carts loaded with produce—everything enchanted her. And over it all came the mellow call of a muezzin from atop a minaret, crying a long prayer to Allah.

Robyn became aware that soldiers were standing guard in front of many buildings and at intersections. Large billboards and wall posters bore the faces of current political leaders.

Tom nodded toward one of the signs, written in bold red paint. "It's not quite what you're used to, is it? Poor Egypt. . . they're working so hard to create a stable situation, to improve the standard of living. It takes some doing, committing your nation to being a leader of peace in this part of the world. Old hatreds have been cherished for centuries."

Robyn felt quite ignorant of the realities of modern Egypt; so much of her attention had always been on Egypt's far past. "Do the problems here affect our archaeological work?" she asked.

"Not unless we're planning to dig near an airfield or too close to a military zone. Other than that, we're okay. There's an enduring quality to life here. Egyptians have seen many conquerors come and go, and still they live and carry on as always." He sighed. "I like the people. They have an ancient sort of courtesy, the kind that Saunders wouldn't understand. Right now they seem to be caught up in the clash of old and new, the fanatical minds struggling against the progressive ones for power. Maybe the clash won't have to bring more violence, I don't know. But there does seem to be an atmosphere of fear stirring—all around the world, not just in the Middle East, I might add." Tom gave her a rueful smile. "I guess that's why I love the past: it seems less complicated. But that's probably because I'm not living in it. Say, if you look straight ahead and a little to the left, you'll see the tops of the pyramids. And I'll stop talking."

He wove the battered American Mustang through the heavy traffic with a steady hand for a while. "Home was never like this," he remarked, moving expertly between a donkey cart and a taxi. "I inherited this car from a friend at the American University here in Cairo, who inherited it from somebody else."

Robyn didn't answer. She couldn't take her eyes off the pyramids rising from the desert cliff just ahead.

Her companion gave her a speculative glance. "I've got to stop and pick up something for Sayed at the Mena House." As he spoke he swung into the hotel grounds through big gates and drew up into a parking space. The pyramids were so close now they dominated the hotel. "If I could afford it, this is the place I'd stay." He grinned at her. "There's a nice ladies' lounge inside, and we can have a cool drink and a fast bite here before we head out for Alexandria. And on the way out I'll drive you up around the pyramids and introduce you to the old stone fellow, okay?"

"Thanks, very okay," she replied, grateful for his kind open face.

Tom left her on a mezzanine landing and motioned toward the terrace dining room where he would meet her. "Don't get lost. You might end up in a seraglio or something," he joked.

He wasn't far from the truth. The main building of the Mena House looked as if it must have belonged to a sultan of long ago. All around them were arches, latticeworks and domes that spoke of the Turkish dominance of Egypt.

As she sat having a Perrier and a large salad on the opulent dining terrace, Robyn realized she was beginning to feel unspeakably happy. Even the formidable Sayed al-Rashad and his probable displeasure didn't seem threatening anymore.

Darkness had fallen when they returned to the car. The air was fragrant as they drove through the hotel grounds, which extended far beyond the main structure. Formal gardens flashed by and a section of new buildings could be seen nestled among the trees.

"Got to hurry," Tom said. "They're getting set for the sound and light program on the hill. Before you go back to the States I'll take you to it, but for now, the ten-minute tour."

The feeling of ancient presences was strong and enfolding. Robyn was again silent as they drove up the curving road to the rocky plateau. Slowly they passed the shadowy pyramids and swung down into the little valley where the Sphinx sat. There Tom pulled over and stopped.

He watched her face with an indulgent smile. "I know how you feel. It was the same with me the first time I met him," he said quietly. "He still has impact after all these thousands of years."

The spell was gradually broken by the noise of the

crowd gathering for the show. High voices of eager tourists tore into the soft air. Beads and scarabs suddenly appeared in car's windows, held by eager brown hands, a flock of importuning faces pressing behind.

Tom said something in Arabic that created smiles and eased their way. He nudged the car through the throngs and left the area by way of Mena Village's narrow streets. Then they headed straight out the desert road to Alexandria, which, Tom said, was three hours to the north on the edge of the Mediterranean.

Robyn tried to stay awake, but the rush of warm perfumed air lulled her to sleep. The stars seemed to turn, and she dreamed of someone whose voice called to her by her Egyptian name. When she awoke they were at the hotel, and Tom was gently urging her to enter the large lobby. She stood drowsily while men at the door searched her bags. Tom helped her with registration, then escorted her to her room, where he opened a long window onto a balcony. Below she heard the sound of the sea.

"Why did they search my bags, and even my purse?" she asked through her haze of sleepiness.

The archaeologist gave her a light pat on the head. "Terrorists have been known to plant bombs in nice hotels, little one."

Her eyes flew open. "Oh."

"Sleep tight," he said, grinning.

CHAPTER TWO

ROBYN WOKE SLOWLY with a sensation of warmth across her feet. It was very hot for mid-March, her mind noted abstractedly before she opened her eyes. Strong sunlight flowed over the bed from the open balcony door, and voices mixed with the rhythmic lapping of gentle waves drifted up from somewhere below. *I'm really here!* She smiled languorously, closing her eyes again. Cleopatra's golden city....

Her mind suddenly focused when the sharp sound of banging came at her door, followed by Tom's voice. "Robyn! Are you up?"

"Yes," she answered. Her eyes snapped open.

"Better look sharp. You overslept. Himself is downstairs getting ready to leave for the dig, and he hates tardy people. You're expected to go out today, missy observer!"

"Oh, God!" she managed. "How long have I got?"

"Ten minutes, no more. I've saved you a breakfast roll." His footsteps faded away.

She dived toward her still-packaged luggage, pulling out the first pair of slacks she saw and a soft blue shirt. It was her laziness of the night before that left her no option but to wear badly wrinkled clothes on her first day, she thought in annoyance, throwing them on and dashing cold water on her face. While wriggling into comfortable sandals, she dragged a hasty comb through her brown gold hair, skimming it back into her usual low ponytail. Big anxious eyes stared back at her from the mirror. She grabbed a lipstick and ran it hurriedly over her lips. No time for more.

This wasn't the way she had planned to meet Sayed al-Rashad. She hadn't wanted to be breathless, ill kempt and, on top of it all, late. Stuffing her clipboard and notepaper into the briefcase, she flew out the door and down the curving hall toward the elevators. Hotel servants in elaborate red and gold-braid uniforms smiled at her.

Tom was waiting impatiently. Just as she ran up to him he made a lunge for the trembling elevator doors, forcing them to open. "Gotcha!" he yelled triumphantly at them. "Get in quick!"

Robyn hurried inside the vibrating lift and the doors closed with a bang. Instead of descending, however, the elevator lurched upward, with Tom cursing and punching the lobby button.

"Is it always like this?" she asked in a dismayed voice.

"This is Egypt." He gave her a look of irritated resignation. From one pocket he extracted a paper napkin that held a large white roll. Pats of butter had been stuck between its halves. "Here. You can get coffee later when we get to the site."

"Thank you. I'm not usually a nuisance," she apologized.

"You'll do all right. Just look out for the sharp eye of our leader."

The elevator jolted to a halt, and they emerged into the spacious lobby, which she had been too tired to examine the night before. Groups of tourists stood in little clusters near rows of suitcases, while a red-jacketed guide made arrangements at the desk. Obviously a bus-tour group. Near the large front windows some casually dressed people were piling a number of boxes onto a dolly.

"Come on." Tom propelled her toward them.

Robyn felt several pairs of curious eyes on her just as Huntley Saunders stepped forward and gave her a familiar wink. "Late, late!" He wagged a finger, then his attention switched to Tom. "The case with the borescope is missing. It was your responsibility." His expression was condemning.

"Hold it, Mr. Saunders—no problem at all," Tom cut in. "It's behind the telex room in a locker for safekeeping."

Robyn stood back, feeling suddenly peculiar. Some odd kind of energy seemed to be pulling at her. It was almost like a distant hum, except that the disturbing vibration was coming from inside her own body, running along her nerves. It wasn't the light-headed sensation of jet lag or the lack of food, but something else she couldn't identify.

Just then a tall man strode out of the room beyond the registration desk. He moved toward their group, speaking in a deep authoritative voice that made everyone else stop talking. Robyn turned toward the figure and found herself staring uncontrollably at a man whose face commanded her total attention.

"Mohammed, get the box of film in there... Fawzi, be sure there are two cases of mineral water... Tom, do you have the typed reference notes from yesterday...?"

The man's handsomeness was extraordinary. His

slender broad-shouldered figure had an angular grace like the men in the tomb paintings of the early dynasties. It was as if one of them had come alive and dressed himself in khaki pants and a jacket to disguise the fact that he was a son of Pharaoh.

"...and where's Professor Wayland? You were supposed to meet him last night."

Robyn jerked back to reality at the name of her absent boss. The hum along her nerves changed to an almost painful electric jolt as the man's eyes suddenly met hers. They were not Egyptian brown, she saw, but blue—very dark blue, like lapis, sparking bright flashes of intense color in their depths. They were luminous eyes, as if a hidden fire glowed inside them. She drew in her breath, unable to look away.

"And who is this?" His voice was impatient. He might as well have said, "*What* is this?"

Tom spoke for her. "This is Robyn Douglas, who has come in Dr. Wayland's place. She is familiar with all the contracts and will be standing in as observer for the university."

The man's intense dark eyes returned to her face.

"The telex got stalled in Cairo. Robyn, this is Dr. al-Rashad..." Tom finished awkwardly.

"I'm Dr. Wayland's assistant," she said in the quiet, even tone she always used in uncomfortable situations. "He couldn't come at the last minute because of his wife's illness."

There was no flicker of welcome in the man's face. "This, of course, is all I needed to complete a fascinating morning!" he said with biting irony to no one in particular. "The one thing we didn't have in our already disorganized project was a young American girl who can't get out of bed on time...and thanks be to Allah the Merciful, we now have one! Miss—Douglas, was it—I would be grateful if you would continue with your breakfast in the car!''

Leaving her stunned and speechless, the breakfast roll clutched in her hand, he turned away, calling for one of the drivers as he strode out of the hotel. Robyn felt Tom take her arm and give it a gentle squeeze. Her tired nerves rebelled, and she had to fight down the sharp words that rose to her mind. Instead she drew a deep breath.

''It's no use getting mad at him,'' Tom said softly. ''He's usually not like this. Believe me, you'll like him.''

''Humph!'' She flashed a glaring eye at him.

Just then an attractive young Egyptian woman came up with an outstretched hand. ''I am Rafica al-Wahab,'' she said in a melodious voice. ''I am the cataloger on the project, and I am very happy to know you.''

Robyn looked into her sweet brown eyes and immediately felt a little better.

One by one the others introduced themselves. There was Tom's assistant, George Lewis, a tall, thin, serious-faced young American in a cowboy shirt who was staying behind in the city that morning to get some supplies. An older member of the team, Professor Gaddabi, was Dr. al-Rashad's associate from Cairo University. In a warm voice and with slightly accented British English he made her welcome to his country, introducing her in turn to the two tall, smiling drivers, Mohammed and Fawzi.

''Do not think of what has just been said,'' he said quietly, looking at her in a fatherly way. ''Our poor friend Dr. al-Rashad has recently had problems with volunteer American girl students. And it is always tense with excavations. There is so much red tape, so much dealing with officialdom—something he has experienced this very morning.... And, of course, there was the unannounced appearance of the man from Texas with his valuable camera." The Egyptian allowed himself a slight smile. "You were a bit of a shock—the last straw, you might say—when Sayed was expecting Dr. Wayland. And you do look rather young." He patted her hand. "You will like him, my dear; he is a fine archaeologist. Perhaps difficult with women, but not impossible."

She salvaged enough dignity to answer him. "Thank you, Dr. Gaddabi, I think I understand. People at the university are often under pressure, too. However," she added with emphasis, "I do know my work."

"I don't doubt it," he said approvingly, obviously relieved that she wasn't going to make a scene.

A breezy American woman, blond, slim and about thirty, peered over Dr. Gaddabi's shoulder. "Hi," she said, "I'm Sandi Cook, the roving photographer." It was obvious, for an assortment of camera equipment hung over her shoulders and around her neck. "I'm preserving our efforts for posterity. We'd better get going before the great one spanks the rest of us."

The cargo was being moved to the loading area at the curb, and Tom walked with Robyn toward the cars. "You all right? He's not so bad when you get to know him. Better eat your roll, anyhow," he offered.

While the cars were being loaded, Robyn stuffed the controversial bun into her mouth in big bitefuls.

Huntley Saunders had obviously elected not to

help, for he was already sitting in one of the cars with
his camera. He tried to entice Rafica to ride with
him, but she made a polite excuse.

"Well, Huntley, my boy, how would you like to
ride with another Texan by way of Arizona?" Sandi
shifted her camera load with a provocative wiggle.

"Hop in," he said, with an appreciative drawl.

Under his breath Tom said, "I hope she watches
herself with that guy. Sandi's not as tough as she
talks."

"Big brother?" Robyn ventured.

"Something like that." His face was drawn into
tanned worry lines as he watched the car pull away.

With Dr. Gaddabi, he steered Robyn to a white
Peugeot station wagon, where Rafica was waiting.
When the last of the boxes had been stowed on the
roof, Mohammed sprang behind the wheel. Sayed
al-Rashad himself swung into the front passenger
seat, and they edged out of the tangle of cars parked
in front of the Palestine Hotel.

"This is Montaza Park," Tom said to Robyn, "in
case you missed it coming in last night. It used to be
the Egyptian royal family's private preserve. Over
there is Montaza Palace. King Farouk sailed from
there into exile on July 26, 1952. There's still a calen-
dar on one of the walls open to that date." He pointed out a turreted rococo building. "His father, King
Fuad, kept his wives and children in another palace
around the next turn. Convenient, but not too
close...."

They drove through the park on a road that wound
among thickets of pines and palms. There were beds
of bright flowers, and they passed a fountain guarded by four sleeping stone lions. After stopping at the

guarded high-walled gates, they eased out into the morning traffic. A long coastline curved gently ahead of them. The blue of sea and sky was dazzling. "You're about to get the grand tour of Alex," Tom laughed.

Sayed al-Rashad sat silently, reflections of sea light playing over his broad back. Robyn's eyes were drawn unwillingly to his curling dark hair. She was fighting down a dreadful feeling of confusion and irritation. Why couldn't he simply have smiled at her in a businesslike way, said something remotely civil and let it go at that? No wonder Professor Wayland's graduate students lost control of themselves working with him. First he impressed them with his incredible good looks, then he punished them with criticism. By that time they had no more self-confidence and were putty in his hands.... Robyn caught herself short. Her response to him was adolescent. Resolutely she turned her full attention to the scenes around her as the car careened along the corniche, a road that edged the long curve of the bay.

Mohammed proved to be a wild driver among even wilder ones. Honking and swerving at high speeds along the road, all the cars seemed impelled on some suicidal course. Robyn's first glimpse of the city didn't lift her spirits any. Alexandria, with its crumbling colonial—and newer—buildings, didn't offer a visitor much of a sense of serenity.

"Cleopatra slept here!" Tom joked, pointing ahead to a spit of land that jutted out into the intensely blue harbor. "This whole area used to be the royal quarter of the ancient Ptolemaic kings and queens. We might even be driving over Alexander the Great's tomb right now. It's kind of mind boggling to think that the city is built right smack on top of some of the lost treasures of history.''

Robyn's thoughts were following his own. She knew all the romantic names associated with this place—Ptolemy, the soldier-king who was half brother to Alexander; Caesar, who dreamed great dreams on the bosom of his Egyptian queen; Antony, who died with her. Euclid, Archimedes.... "And the plundered Library of Alexandria,'' she said aloud. "What a terrible loss!''

She felt Dr. al-Rashad's eyes suddenly focus on her in the rearview mirror. It was like a cold stab of recognition, and she couldn't shake off the strange feeling it gave her. She hated being so off balance with him. It was going to be difficult starting work like this.

Mohammed plunged the Peugeot into the center of the city, driving as if there were no other cars in the congested streets and squares. Adding to the confusion of the morning rush hour was every kind of cart, wagon and motorized vehicle competing with darting pedestrians for each tiny opening in the traffic flow. Once through the city and across a drawbridge over the Mahmudiya Canal, Mohammed revved the car and aimed it out onto the desert road.

Tom gave her hand a reassuring pat. "The dig's about thirty miles south of here. The Bedouin have a little village of sorts nearby. They help keep the thieves away from our stuff. You'll like the children—as sweet as angels, but they get old fast enough once they're married off. It takes some getting used to—the young girls with their babies and the fierce-looking husbands. But they're decent people.''

While Tom rambled on, Robyn's eyes drifted to

the mirror again. From an artistic point of view, Dr. al-Rashad was interesting, she had to admit. Was it the face of Hesire, the Third Dynasty nobleman, that she was recalling? The carved wood relief panel from the ruins of Saqqara showed that same kind of finely shaped head, the high forehead, the strong taut neck and shoulders.... Dr. al-Rashad seemed to have some loyal subjects in his little archaeological kingdom—Tom for one, and Dr. Gaddabi. But nobleman or not, his acid words and rude welcome were hard to forgive. Why was everyone so sure she would like him? She dragged her eyes back to the desert.

The car slowed down at a military checkpoint in the middle of nowhere. When two rumpled soldiers finally responded to Mohammed's repeated honking and waved him on, he gunned the car and laughed.

Dr. al-Rashad broke his silence. "If we hadn't honked they'd still be sleeping. The whole Libyan army could have rolled past with no trouble at all!" Robyn saw his intense eyes flash with amusement, and Mohammed roared approval.

Tom leaned close to her. "Mohammed used to drive tanks in the army," he explained in a low voice. "He's spoiling for a chance to do it again. He comes from a tribe in the Western Desert where they pride themselves on their bravery. I guess a good hot border war would be more to his liking than the tame life he leads now."

Robyn looked at the dark, almost black-skinned man at the wheel, and as she did he turned around and flashed a gold-toothed smile at her. "Libya! Phaw!" he spat, and laughed again.

The thought of living close to war was new to her. She was beginning to feel the tension of being in a land whose borders were threatened. How many other taxi drivers in Egypt were dreaming right now of steering tanks into battle. . . .

Mohammed turned the car off the road and drove across the rocky barren landscape. The sky, Robyn noted, was clear except in places where wind had stirred up the sand, giving a yellowish murky tinge. The air was getting hotter by the minute and the car was buffeted by gusts of wind.

Dr. al-Rashad and Mohammed were talking quietly in Arabic when Rafica turned to her. "The khamsin wind is coming," she said softly. "It will be a race to see who wins, Dr. al-Rashad or the wind."

"He's been working us all like a madman these past few weeks," Tom added under his breath. "Thank God for the borescope—with or without Saunders. If we can beat the khamsin we'll all be in better humor. Once the devilish thing starts blowing we can say goodbye to the work for a month or more. And if that happens we've lost our chance at getting more money for God knows how long. The funding committee meets in the middle of April. This has got to look good to them or they'll give their little pot of gold to another project. Sayed will have to go back to teaching at Cairo University and I'll be saying hello to the U.S.A. Lord, how I hate to think of a desk job in the department!"

"I know time is a problem," Robyn said. "That's why I'm here, isn't it? The contracts have to be renewed, and my report has to show just how valuable this dig is."

"You won't mind a little abject apple polishing, will you?" Tom said pitifully.

"Sorry, I can't be bought. Well, maybe for a drink of mineral water . . ."

Rafica smiled and offered a bottle of Evian to Robyn. "I hope you know that you are very much welcome to our project."

"Thanks," Robyn said with feeling. "It's nice to hear."

The car lunged over a small rise and down into a gully, where it stopped abruptly. When the dust cloud settled Robyn saw that they were in the midst of a small herd of goats, which was being tended by a girl scarcely taller than her charges. Dressed like a Gypsy in a long red-and-purple skirt, she was waving happily at the car.

Robyn's eyes drank in the scene. She remembered an old book of Bible stories belonging to her grandmother that had had an illustration of a child herding goats in the desert. . . .

Her reverie was broken by the fluid voice of Sayed al-Rashad. "Time is strange here." He had turned his head and was speaking to her. "It is almost the same now as it was in pharaonic days." His strange lapis eyes held hers for a moment and he smiled.

She stared back. Had he decided to be a gentleman, then? Or was he unaware of how rude his earlier behavior had been? "It's beautiful," she said, and felt a slight clip to her words.

"Beauty, yes—" he was serious again "—but the ways are changing and under the beauty is dirt and disease. The Bedouin no longer roam with their black tents. See over there." He pointed to a cluster of whitewashed mud-brick dwellings. "That is a permanent village, where the human refuse collects. With the vagabond life it could be left behind for nature to disperse. I advise you to take care with the children. They are very friendly, but there are diseases of the skin that are easily contracted. Some of the American students became very sorry that they had made gestures of affection to the children.''

Tom broke in, ''But Egypt is working to change things, to teach more about health.''

''*Aiwa*—yes,'' he answered. ''Thank you for defending my nation.'' He smiled again at Robyn, his face dazzlingly handsome. ''Tom truly loves Egypt, no matter how he complains about the inconveniences. Is it not so?''

''Why else would I keep coming back for more?'' A smile of open friendship passed between the two men.

They had come over another small rise of ground, where the earth was sparsely covered with low-growing desert plants. To the left, lines of shaggy Egyptian pine trees grew along a narrow strip of green.

Tom followed her gaze. ''One of the canals,'' he explained.

Ahead the desert stretched out to the horizon. They bumped along slowly, leaving the Bedouin village behind them, and drew up near a small group of temporary buildings made of rough boards and sheets of corrugated iron.

''Behold: The Dig,'' Tom intoned.

But at the same instant Robyn heard loud angry voices coming from the camp. A man, running full tilt, sprang into view from around the corner of one of the makeshift buildings. His attention was on his shouting pursuers, and he executed a faunlike caper as he jumped aside, neatly avoiding a rock that had been hurled at him. Robyn noticed that his suit was worn and his shoes were heavy.

The man stopped to pick up a stone of his own and

flung it just as a shower of answering missiles and five Bedouin men erupted into view. They came to a screeching halt when they saw Dr. al-Rashad's car, and their quarry looked around to see what had stopped them.

"Our esteemed colleague, Dr. Hassan Tarsi . . . being stoned," Tom remarked with a broad grin. Even Dr. al-Rashad had a glint of amusement on his face—mixed with annoyance—as he swung out of the car and strolled toward the battle scene.

Tom offered a rough translation of the continuing clamor. "They're accusing Hassan of shorting them on pay, and he's claiming he has to spend a lot of money to buy them food. Sayed has heard it all before, but no matter what he says, Hassan won't stop gouging the workers. Not that I blame them for getting mad—but stoning!" He gave a snort of laughter.

"I remember his name in the field notes we received," Robyn said. "He's the one who's been working for years on some Ptolemaic excavations, wasn't that it?"

"He's the one. He claims that our dig is part of his territory. His excavation—we call it Tarsiville—is over there beyond that little mound. Actually, he's jealous as hell of Sayed, who located this site by his own deductions. Hassan hadn't the foggiest idea it was here, and now he wants it. But he doesn't present a real problem. He hasn't got any kind of a case for his claim, or any influence in the Antiquities Department."

Dr. Gaddabi's scholarly voice broke in. "Our friend's story is a sad one. Dr. Tarsi is Iranian, you see. He was here as a teacher and archaeologist for one year—unfortunately, the same year that the Shah was deposed. Some of his family was killed in the ensuing developments, and he took asylum in Egypt. He got a little money from a European university with which he financed the work of digging up part of his Ptolemaic ruins. Of course, he still hopes to make 'the great find,' and his reputation along with it. But his efforts have received very little notice from our antiquities department. His excavation seems to have been an unimportant trading outpost, nothing more. Let us say that he is a brilliant man, but bitter. Not a good combination for success." Dr. Gaddabi smiled a little. "He has dreamed for years of making a great discovery, to the point that it is an obsession. Then we came, so nearby, and seem on the verge of finding a treasure. But for the will of Allah and half a mile, he would have had the fame he longs for."

"Professional jealousies can get pretty bad in this field," Tom said, as they watched Dr. al-Rashad mediate the argument. "I've told Sayed to be careful of the guy, but he doesn't seem to worry. He even gave him the title of coordinator of the dig, and lets him manage the Bedouin and some of the supplies. Hassan's bank account is too low for him to do any more work on Tarsville until he can drum up a donor to help. It is kind of pitiful."

At that moment Dr. al-Rashad's voice rose authoritatively above the outcry. He seemed to be laying down the law, looking from the Iranian archaeologist to the workers and back again.

"He's telling them exactly what their pay should be, when they are to receive it and how much money Hassan is to get for their food," Tom said. "It's official now, at least until next time."

Then Hassan Tarsi's voice rose again. He gestured excitedly, waving and pointing to an old Bedouin woman who had come up to watch the gathering. Several small children leaned against her confidingly. Her presence was dignified and she stood proudly in her long colorful dress.

"He's saying she's the local witch and that she has been poisoning the workers against him. Bahiya's pretty shrewd. She may have said a few words of wisdom to the men, but she doesn't lie."

A minute later the old woman turned and walked away, with the children following. In apparent good humor, the Bedouin men went off toward the excavation site, while Hassan Tarsi dusted off his jacket and pants.

"Better pile out and get to work," Tom said. "I'll introduce you to our erstwhile coordinator."

Hassan Tarsi's greeting was polite. He took Robyn's hand in a strong shake. His face was intelligent and determined, yet his eyes had an opaque, secretive quality. He acted as if the strange scene just past had not occurred, and the others spoke to him as though they had seen nothing. Was that the custom in Egypt—quick, painful crises and harsh words, and then...nothing?

Again Robyn's eyes were drawn to Sayed al-Rashad. He gave her a half-smile that commented silently on what had happened, and she felt an unwelcome response to him stirring within her.

She turned quickly and followed Tom and Rafica. Dr. Gaddabi accompanied her, his soft learned voice telling her about the scroll fragments that had been unearthed from the deep shored-up hole in the desert earth. As he talked she fought down a wave of loneliness for her father, which Dr. Gaddabi's personality brought into focus.

Tom was organizing a crew of men who were erecting a tall tripod of pipe in the center of the excavated room. Setting up the drill didn't look like a simple operation. The room was still being sifted through by the archaeological team, and it was obvious that the drill crew didn't understand that they had to watch where they put their feet.

Dr. Gaddabi assured Robyn that the lower chamber would be in good condition. "We are positive that it has not been disturbed. As you must know already, it was a dreadful disappointment to find so little in the way of intact papyri in this first room. It is possible that nomads at one time knew of this place and took the better scrolls to the city to sell them— either to scholars or to those who paid high prices for the incomparable fragrance of burned papyrus. God knows what priceless manuscripts were burned in the last century for their exotic smell."

He jumped nimbly down into the busy excavation site. "You see, here is where the scrolls were stored. It is only now, as we probe deeply into the corners, that we have begun to find our better scroll specimens, and precious few of those." He pointed to a row of crumbling stone niches along one wall. "We're lucky to find these last few. The nomads were probably scared off by an afreet. And that was a long time ago. That old woman you just saw is the village sheikha, or wise woman. The men wouldn't work for us until she had dispersed the afreet—the evil spirit. I'm not entirely skeptical myself," he went on, grinning at her.

"See here—" he pointed to the floor "—the way

the stones are laid. Perfectly joined so that not even a knife can be inserted between them. That is what makes us so sure that the room below us is in good preservation. Whoever stored these scrolls here, so many centuries ago, knew exactly what he was doing. We think that they used a primitive but excellent method of extracting much of the air from the chamber as it was sealed, leaving a veritable vacuum. We are standing upon a very great discovery, my dear, and our Dr. al-Rashad is to be given much credit for his perseverance.''

"Why would these scrolls have been buried here in the first place?" she asked.

He gave her the dusty smile of a dedicated archaeologist. "My dear lady, surely you know, with a father like yours!"

A warm flush started on her cheeks. "You were told?"

"I looked upon your face as we drove here," he said gently, "and I asked myself what it was that pushed at my memory. As an archaeologist I must depend upon my good memory for details, you see. Then I recalled the last time I saw my friend Dr. Douglas, seven years ago. He was talking of his family at home, and he showed me a picture of his daughter, a very young girl with serious eyes. 'Even now she helps me with my work,' he told me with pride." Dr. Gaddabi's warm brown eyes looked into hers. "I will not say anything if you do not want it known. But there are many who remember your father with love. It may be hard to keep your secret."

She smiled back, enjoying his steady energy. "Please don't say anything. Dr. Wayland felt that my father's name shouldn't overshadow the work

I'm here to do. I'm only a courier with contracts and a general observer...."

"I understand. Then this secret shall be ours until you permit. As for the scrolls and this dig—" he shook his head "—*Inshallah*, as God wills. So many ifs! If we find proof that these fragments originated from the ancient Library of Alexandria; if we find our lower room intact; if the khamsin doesn't damage the site—then your generous university will have good cause for continuing to fund the excavation. If not...." He shrugged.

"If there's anything I can do—" Robyn began.

"Oh, no! I didn't mean to sing a song of despair for you!" he protested, laughing. "This is a time of rejoicing. Now that we have the fine machine to help us, there is every reason to hope that all my ifs will become certainties. I think I am really telling you this so that you will understand some of the anxiety in Dr. al-Rashad's heart these days, so that you will not judge him from your first impression, so to speak."

Robyn wanted to say, "Certainly not, Dr. Gaddabi. I have forgotten the incident at the hotel completely and find him a charming gentleman," but she couldn't. They stood for a few minutes watching several young Egyptian students from Dr. al-Rashad's university classes at work. With soft brushes they were painstakingly flicking the earth away from each piece of papyrus.

As they watched, Rafica came up to them with an earnest expression on her face. "May I now show you the work I am doing with the cataloging and packing?"

Dr. Gaddabi bowed slightly as she left with Rafica, and the two women made their way toward the ramshackle buildings. Without wanting to, Robyn's eyes searched out Sayed al-Rashad. He was helping to push one of the metal pipes into place, and she noted the grace of his body even in stressful effort. Definitely Third Dynasty, she mused to herself.

Rafica unlocked the door of the wooden shed and left it open to allow fresh air inside. The close little room they entered smelled of warm earth. Large tables of rough boards ran along two walls. Some partial scrolls were piled on one table, with sheets of thin plastic foam separating them. Bits of earth were still clinging to their brittle, ragged edges. A second table held trays of papyrus fragments partially sorted into a series of numbered shallow wooden boxes nearby. More of the soft plastic sheets stood in rolls in one corner of the stuffy, dusty room, and a single light bulb hung overhead.

"It's not much of a laboratory, but it's all we can afford," Rafica said. The Egyptian woman showed her the record books containing the catalog numbers of each piece, and the fine-tipped pens that were used to put matching numbers on the fragments themselves. "I am far behind, as you can see. They are bringing them to me faster than I can handle them. The papyrus is so fragile that it cannot be dealt with in haste."

"Could I help?" Robyn said, noting the worry on Rafica's face.

"Would you? I would be so grateful! *Shokran!*" A smile of relief made her eyes sparkle.

"Don't thank me, Rafica. I am grateful to be in Egypt, and I'd be glad to help."

Rafica's delicate brown hand came out to clasp Robyn's, then she pulled it away with shy dignity.

"Forgive my forwardness, but you cannot know the depth of my concern that I would fail in my obligations to Dr. al-Rashad."

"I count on you to tell me what I must do, and to explain things about the dig. I promise you I will be a good assistant," Robyn said. In the back of her mind she felt sorry for Rafica and her fear of al-Rashad's anger.

"Rafica!" Tom's voice came from the direction of the excavation.

"I must go." She smiled. "Maybe you can look around some more, and I will call you when we're ready to begin. *Aiwa!*" she called, and ran toward the dig.

Robyn walked out into the hot sun and turned her face to the soft breeze. Fine particles of sand hung in the air and gave the scene around her an almost blurry effect, as if it were being seen through a filtered lens. Then Huntley Saunders's complaining voice punctured the peace, sounding like that of a plantation boss.

She didn't turn around to watch him; his loud words told her exactly what was happening in the excavation.

"I didn't come all the way out here just to be told I had to stay away from the action, al-Rashad! It's my hard cash that's making this possible, and I expect to be listened to when I tell you something. . . ."

Dr. al-Rashad's answer was brief and cool. "Talk all you want, sir, but unless you wish to slow down our already delayed work, I would advise you to stay out of our way."

"We'll just see about that. Your superiors won't like to hear this, not one bit!"

"My superiors, Mr. Saunders, have given me complete control over this dig. Now, if you will excuse me, I must return to work.''

Robyn couldn't help giving a silent cheer for Dr. al-Rashad. She might have expected problems between the two men. In Dr. Wayland's hurried last-minute briefing, he had left the matter of her exact responsibility unresolved. Was she supposed to keep Huntley Saunders out of harm's way—out of Sayed al-Rashad's hair—or should she stay out of the conflict entirely? Her instinct told her not to do anything until she understood more about what was going on here. She planned to include those questions in her telexed report to Dr. Wayland tomorrow—if the telex system was working.

The drivers, Mohammed and Fawzi, were sitting in the shade of their cars, and Sandi was busy taking close-up camera shots of the area where Tom and Rafica were working. Robyn felt relieved to have some time alone to get the feel of the dig site. If Dr. al-Rashad wanted her for anything, he would have to ask her, and nicely.

She strolled past the buildings. In one there were more rough tables and benches, probably used as a cooking/eating area. Shade stretched invitingly along one side of the building, and Robyn stepped into it gratefully. Small desert plants grew close to the ground, she noted, with tiny purple flower buds along their creeping stems.

The soft sandy earth was irresistible, and she sat down. Hugging her knees to her chest, she rested her head against them, reaching down for a handful of warm soil—Egyptian soil. She was touching Egypt, was breathing the air that held such ancient memories. It was magic earth!

Her eyes followed the little erratic dust swirls near

her feet, and she began to see something taking shape within—a picture, blurred at first, but coming into sharper focus. It was a familiar sensation; these pictures used to come into her mind occasionally when she held one of her father's artifacts, as if she had suddenly dropped into the ancient past as a spectator.

This time a group of weary men struggled across the desert, their donkeys laden with huge double baskets. Other men were digging in the earth, moving great slabs of stone into place. Their eyes kept scanning the horizon, as if they were afraid of being discovered. Some of the men had the faces of scholars. Robyn knew the look; her father's had been the same. They were hiding their most valuable scrolls, which came from the library in the great city. There, however, war and religious strife threatened to destroy the wisdom that they all held dear.

Drowsily, Robyn watched them wrap their scrolls with haste and bury them in the prepared place. She saw them stand for a long moment gazing at where their finished work was now concealed beneath the sands. When she drifted off to sleep, the pictures followed and became dreams. She watched as the donkey caravan left the hidden place and slowly moved away, back toward the troubled city....

CHAPTER THREE

A HUSKY WHISPER awakened her. "Lady! Lady!"

Robyn raised her head from its cramped position on her knees and found herself looking into a dark, weather-beaten face. Sharp dark eyes looked out from its wrinkled depths and wispy gray hair straggled from under a bandannalike head cloth. Age could not obscure what had once been beauty.

The woman sat on the sand before Robyn like a heap of colored patches. Her wide skirt and heavy blouse glowed with colors and her face rolled the wrinkles into a delightful smile. "*Kuwayyis*—it is good," she said with satisfaction, touching her breast, lips and forehead in a gesture of greeting. "*Salam-sitt.*"

Robyn looked into the steady powerful eyes. She was not completely free of the numbing effects of her warm nap and her dreams.

"True dreams," the old woman said with a nod of approval. "I read sand for you. Can my Ingleezi? Is understanding?" Her voice had a compelling timbre; there was a charm in it. Quite unreasonably, Robyn trusted her.

"I understand," she answered, as her head began to clear a bit. "You are the woman with the children. I saw you earlier when the men were arguing with Dr. Tarsi."

The wrinkles rearranged themselves into lines of disgust. *"Abu'gurân!"* she hissed. Her opinion was obvious. *"Aiwa,"* she continued, "I live in village—there. I know someone is to come—you!" A sudden long finger pointed at Robyn. "Stars say time for to remember."

She smoothed the sandy earth between them. "Take in hand...handful," she commanded.

Robyn wondered what she was supposed to pay the old woman. The extraordinary eyes before her snapped with amusement. "True sight not for sale. Gift to you, not to me."

For a moment despite the hot shade, Robyn shivered. All of this felt like a continuation of her dream, and yet it was more than real. Her mind had just been read without effort.

The woman reached out and took her hand, and somehow there was comfort in her touch. "No afraid, *sitt*." She seemed to search for words. "All person can see in mind. Have to understand how. I born to knowing how."

Robyn looked into the wise old eyes. "I'm not afraid."

"Kuwayyis." She looked at Robyn's young white hand against her own dark one. *"Letif*—pretty. Take sand, give to me."

Robyn scooped up the soft earth in her fingers. "Give me!" the voice rasped sharply. She hesitated a moment, then let the sand fall into the upturned wrinkled palm.

The woman took the earth and raised it to her broad forehead. A crooning, wavering sound came from her lips. It was an ancient vibration, Robyn knew, something the women of the old temples might have sung to call to their gods.

Smoothing the sand in front of her, the old woman let the contents of her hand fall slowly in a spiral pattern, moving toward a center. The last grains fell and she held her palm down, passing it back and forth above the spirals.

"El hamdu li-llah." Her voice was low. She spoke on a droning note, "Small bird among flowers...." Swiftly her finger stabbed down in the middle of the pattern. "Why you hide names belonging to old ones? More better to you than bird of cold rosy breast. Here—this land—is home of heart...by destiny."

Robyn drew in a shaky breath. Was the old one still reading her mind? The droning voice went on. "Father of you walks to protect. A smile has he to the blue-eyed god." Her voice dropped lower. *"Muktir!* Danger!" Her eyes flashed at Robyn. "Courage, small bird! Dreams make truth. Not turn from love. You not to hear lies. To you all shall be knowing. Old ones give treasure to true hands. No more time for hide knowing...."

Her voice wound down like an antique phonograph losing power. "Sister of destiny," she wheezed, "you choose. Two roads for you, only one road happy. Sand is true destiny. Wind blows for good...."

Silence moved around them, except for the distant voices at the dig and the soft breath of the desert wind. A heavy sigh shook the colorful heap of the old woman's body. *"Subhân Allâh."* Again her smile broke through the wrinkles. "Have quiet heart.

You bring good luck, lady. I, Bahiya, your friend.''
She grasped Robyn's hand and looked earnestly into
her eyes. ''I not witch! I do no evil. *Ya, Ibn Awa!*
Jackal Tarsi no like I can read his heart!''

Bahiya gave a shake to her dusty garments and
stood up in a quick motion. She had surprising supple-
ness of body. She scuffed her foot over the patterns of
the sand reading and Robyn rose, also. Bahiya's eyes
smiled. ''I keep watch, *sitt*.'' She turned and strode
away, graceful and upright, the vivid patterns of her
skirt swinging around her tall figure.

Robyn stood gazing across the desert, her mind
trying to adjust to the strange words. How had
Bahiya known her father was dead—she had said as
much—or that her own real name was Egyptian?
And what did she mean by a blue-eyed god? That
part had sounded like a fairy tale.

But the old woman seemed to know so much! As
James Arthur Douglas's daughter, Robyn had heard
enough about such folk knowledge not to scoff too
easily. There were things old cultures handed down
that were beyond modern comprehension: things in
the blood itself, true links to the distant past.

The warnings were clear, but what was she supposed to do about them? Destiny...danger. She gave
herself a mental shake. It was only a sand reading by
an old Bedouin woman! ''Sensible girl,'' Dr. Wayland had called her. Well, the sensible girl would pull
herself together and be useful. Her dreams and imaginings had never yet turned out to be helpful. Still,
there was something about this place—the desert, the
winds—that made it easy to drift into its spell. Maybe
that was what had made the American students lose
their composure.

Tucking her speculations away for the moment, she walked back around the building. Dr. al-Rashad and some of his workers were still struggling with the drill-rig frame. Huntley Saunders, she noticed, was sitting sulkily on the sidelines, watching.

Rafica called for her. "Do you want to work now?"

"*Aiwa.*" Robyn answered.

The woman laughed and clapped her hands. "Soon you will speak Arabic like an Egyptian."

In the workroom Robyn sat down on one of the hard stools. Rafica showed her how to carefully lift a papyrus fragment with gauze-padded tweezers, shake the earth from it gently, mark it with a tiny number and record it on the lists. It was then laid on a spongy plastic sheet in one of the shallow boxes.

"The challenge we have," Rafica explained, "is trying to keep the fragments of one scroll separate from those of another. It will make the reconstruction work at the museum much easier if we do. Sometimes the age difference or artwork in the margins gives us a clue, but we still have hundreds of tiny pieces that are not so simple to work with. Don't hesitate to ask me for help if you have difficulty."

For a while the two of them sat companionably at work. From time to time Rafica glanced over at Robyn's trays and gave a satisfied nod. "You look as if you were used to handling fragile things. What good fortune that you are here," she said. "I have been so worried. Dr. al-Rashad has put such effort to this project...." She got up from her stool. "I see you have no problems with this. Now I must go and supervise the materials being uncovered. You can see why I have fallen far behind in the cataloging."

"Don't concern yourself about me. I'll be fine," Robyn called after her.

Once alone, she savored the sight and touch of the papyrus, and the odd, delightful aromatic smell of antiquity. Who had written these scrolls; what did they tell? Was some lost play of Euripides passing through her fingers, or a history of Egypt written by a scribe of the old temples? She longed to unroll one of the more intact scrolls, just for a glimpse of what might be in it. With an audible sigh she returned to her cataloging, even though tantalizing words and phrases caught her eye. Some of it she recognized as early Greek.

Footsteps moved behind her. She was expecting Rafica. "How frustrating to be handling these treasures," she said, "and not to know what's in them."

"I agree," said a dark velvet voice. Robyn swung around. Sayed al-Rashad stood there, a tiny cup of Turkish coffee in one hand and a paper bag in the other. "I remembered you had nothing but that abominable breakfast roll this morning." He placed the cup beside her and opened the bag, which looked to be full of cookies. Perching himself on Rafica's stool and offering the bag to her, he asked, "Am I forgiven?" The fine lines of his lips lifted in a slight smile, but his eyes were serious, probing into hers.

An unexpected whirlwind tingled along the edge of her nerves. His manner had caught her off guard.

The smile on his lips reached his eyes. "I think I must apologize to you. I was without doubt a brute this morning. My only excuse is that I was wearied with problems. And when I expected Dr. Wayland, I received instead our difficult Texan friend, as well as an unknown lady who looked too young and too in-experienced to be anything but a handicap to my work. I was too thoughtless to remember that you also had reason for weariness. You were admirably restrained at my provoking behavior, and now you are helping here just when it is most needed. Rafica says you are an excellent worker. How can I thank you?''

His warm voice flowed around her, its vibration almost like a tangible caress. "I'm sorry I'm not Dr. Wayland," she said, glad that her voice seemed normal. "I can see that Mr. Saunders and I were a shock to you." She held her eyes steady and looked into his.

"If I had been capable of thought, I should have known that Dr. Wayland would send me only a qualified person. It is my good fortune that it is a lovely lady." His glance was admiring. Then he chuckled. "I think I can say to you that, grateful as I am to Mr. Saunders for his generous financial support, I find it hard to accept the fact that he will be with us."

His easy charm relaxed her nerves. "I've just spent twenty-eight hours traveling with him," she said.

His dark brows went up. "But no wonder you are exhausted!"

". . . and he told me at least twenty-eight times how lucky you were to have him and the borescope."

"Only once an hour!" He began to laugh and Robyn joined him. "Praise Allah, I can speak my mind to you. May we be friends?" He held out his hand and she gave him her own. He turned it over gently, studying the delicate garnet ring that her father had given her long ago. "You should have lapis. In Egypt it is the stone of kismet—destiny. They say it will bring you back to Egypt, just as the alexandrite will teach you about love.'' He lifted her fingers to his lips and brushed them with a light kiss.

Robyn felt herself start to blush and tried to will it to stop. He looked up, releasing her hand, and saw the pink glow. ''In America,'' she said quickly, ''we're not used to hand kissing. I blush over all kinds of silly things.''

''I see,'' he said with amusement.

She couldn't tell him the truth—that her body's reaction to the firm touch of his hand had taken her by surprise. To her dismay she blushed deeper.

He reached across and took a cookie from the bag. ''I think I'll have one, since it's the dessert for lunch that I've stolen.'' He pushed the coffee cup nearer. ''Drink, before it is cold.''

Obediently she picked up the little cup and sipped its dark sweet brew. ''It's good. Thanks for bringing it.''

''You like it? Then you will be happy in Egypt,'' he teased. And then his face grew serious. ''I must tell you something that I am concerned about. The drill rig we are working with is too heavy. It may cause the floor to cave in. Tomorrow I must find another way to make a clean hole for the borescope camera. Perhaps with a different kind of drill or with a crew that is not so clumsy. The stones may be thin enough that we can use a manual drill and not have to use water to cool it. Flooding would be the worst thing we could do to a collection of priceless papyri. I don't know. I have become almost too tired to think well lately. The winds come chasing after my efforts like old Bahiya's evil spirits.''

He sighed and looked intently into her eyes. "I'm convinced that these scrolls originated in the Library of Alexandria, yet I have no proof, not enough hard evidence. If I had proof I would be able to proceed without worry. Our grants depend upon it...but of course you know this."

"Maybe if some translation were done," she offered. Somehow she couldn't tell him of her knowledge of ancient writing—not yet.

"Unless the library was specifically mentioned in a scroll, there would be no real proof. The papyri could have come from other sources."

"What would be proof?"

"In the ancient libraries the scrolls usually had identifying tags with the name of the library or the owner. Sometimes there were numbers referring to a library catalog, or simply the name of the work itself. Often these tags were small ceramic discs affixed by leather to the scroll. If luck is with us we will find a tag with the name of the Alexandrian library. I should not trust to luck; I should say *Inshallah*, which you will hear frequently in Arab countries. If Allah wills it."

Robyn sat bemused, listening to the flow of his rich voice. He had a very slight soft accent, and his words wrapped her in a feeling of excitement and peace, of belonging and loneliness together. "We will find something," she heard herself say with conviction. "But even without proof of the source surely this is a wonderful find. The fragments I have seen so far are very old, I'm sure, old enough to be of interest to scholars...."

"Undoubtedly, but today money doesn't come easily for excavations unless the discoveries are great ones. Hold your faith, my friend, that we get proof. And learn to say with me, *Inshallah*.'' He ran a graceful dark hand through his dust-flecked hair in a gesture of weary frustration, then looked at her intently for a moment.

She turned her eyes to the boxes on the table, afraid of his deep blue gaze. "Well, I must get back to my work,'' he said, standing up. "Oh, I nearly forgot my reason for coming here. We must go over the contracts and discuss Dr. Wayland's ideas immediately. Are you too weary to do it tonight?''

"I'm not too tired,'' she answered, a feeling of pleasure starting to steal over her. "When do you want to work?''

"Mohammed will drop Dr. Gaddabi and me at our apartment, then take the rest of you to the Palestine. I will have him come back for you at seven-thirty. We can dine at the Santa Lucia restaurant in the city, and then work later at the hotel. I wouldn't ask you to slave for me on an empty stomach.''

"It's very kind, but you don't have to take me to dinner—''

"Robyn,'' he cut in, "you must allow me to do it and not object. I desire that there should be friendship between us. Otherwise, I would have to eat with Yussef Gaddabi, and I know him only too well.'' He smiled. "All we would do is worry together about the dig—tiresome matters that are not compatible with good digestion. You, I do not know, and I want to hear about your life and the university—and Dr. Wayland. Besides, this shall be a small compensation for the twenty-eight hours of Mr. Saunders.'' His smile was gentle. There was no doubt of his sincerity. She was beginning to see why the others had said she-would like him. And that was all it was going to be—liking, she reminded herself.

"I'll be ready," she replied simply, looking up at the tall length of him.

"Until then." He picked up the empty cup and the bag and went out the door with quick, lithe movements.

Rafica passed him on her way in, then looked questioningly at Robyn.

"He brought me coffee and a nice apology for this morning." Robyn's eyes dropped down to the numbers in her notebook.

The other girl looked at the open doorway and said under her breath, "I knew he would. He is not an easy man to understand. He can be as kind as a saint or as harsh as a devil, and he is always driving himself, never allowing rest. I sometimes wonder what it is he is really searching for...."

Robyn's pen stopped writing for a moment. She could hear the throbbing beat of her heart and tried to think it back to a peaceful rhythm. She almost wished Sayed al-Rashad hadn't apologized, hadn't looked at her with those penetrating, disarming blue eyes. Almost.

ON THE DRIVE BACK to the city, Robyn worked to hold her racing emotions in check, but it wasn't easy. Her treacherous mind kept sneaking away from the conversation going on in the car to fabricate images that were, to say the least, out of order. Such things as Sayed al-Rashad leaning across a candlelit table, his hand holding hers, that odd blue fire burning in his eyes.

Fawzi was their driver this time, a short grinning

man with gaps where teeth should be. Tom, Rafica, and Dr. Gaddabi were also in the car with Robyn; Dr. al-Rashad had decided at the last minute to return to Alexandria with Huntley Saunders.

At one point Tom effectively drew Robyn's attention away from her inner imaginings. "Sayed's got to calm that guy down," he said. "Saunders was planning to talk to the Antiquities Department on his own, to demand that they translate the manuscripts immediately so we'd know if they came from the library. As if we had a pile of scrolls ready to be opened and read! He was threatening to go to the top, maybe to the president himself, dropping big names like bombs. I shudder to think...."

"He knows nothing at all about archaeology," Dr. Gaddabi sighed. "He could make trouble for us. These things are delicate."

"What does *Abu'gurân* mean?" Robyn asked after a short silence. All eyes swung around to her.

"Where did you hear that?" Rafica's expression was startled.

"Someone said it today. I didn't know what it meant, except that it wasn't a compliment. I thought it might apply to our Mr. Saunders."

Fawzi exploded into laughter. Even Dr. Gaddabi couldn't help a chuckle.

"My dear Miss Douglas, you mouth will have to be washed out with soap," Tom admonished, wagging a finger at her. "It means 'father of dung,' and it does have a certain affinity to our great benefactor."

"Who said this to you?" Rafica pressed.

"The old woman from the village, Bahiya. She was referring to Hassan Tarsi."

"It is hard to say which man would be more

worthy of the title,'' Dr. Gaddabi said with a grin.

"You talked with Bahiya?'' Rafica was serious.

"I was resting behind the dig house in the shade. She came and read the sand for me. I didn't think it could hurt.''

"I like the old girl—she's sharp,'' Tom said, looking as if for confirmation to Dr. Gaddabi. The older man nodded. "She's a friend to Sayed, a remarkable woman, although I won't let her read the sand for me. How could I be seen listening to a village *fazza'a*—a scarecrow, I think you say. My reputation would be in tatters. But she probably knows more about our dig than we do.''

"What did she tell you?'' Rafica asked. "Forgive my curiosity.''

Robyn was reluctant to tell everything. "Oh, she just said it was destiny for me to be here. She seemed to think things would go better. I got the idea that she wished us luck.''

"Good.'' Dr. Gaddabi smiled. "I'd like to have her blessing. She can stir up trouble with the Bedouin if she wishes.''

Robyn grew silent once again. Bahiya had spoken of love and lies, of two roads to take....

A jolt of the car broke her reverie. They were already in the city, letting Dr. Gaddabi out at the apartment he shared with Dr. al-Rashad. Robyn peered with interest at the old building, hoping... what? To see a dark handsome face at a window smiling at her? Dr. Gaddabi waved the car off, and Fawzi threaded another suicide course up the corniche to the hotel.

Her fourth-floor room was a cool place of peace, but Robyn couldn't settle down to rest. If she drifted off, the dreams that were waiting just beyond consciousness would start to flow again. She still felt the touch of Sayed's lips on her hand and gently stroked the place with her fingertips. *I should have outgrown this,* she thought.

The soft air of the balcony beckoned her, so she went out and leaned on the railing. Below the hotel was a narrow strip of beach and a pier. Slow shallow waves washed the edge of the small bay; her eyes followed the curve of beach around to a peninsula, where a decorative bridge arched over to a tiny island. Just below Robyn's balcony, several small birds were fluttering around the masonry niches. As she listened to their happy twittering, some sense of reality started to relax and clear her mind.

I'm just overwhelmed by Egypt, she explained to herself finally in relief. She smiled at the thought of herself as a typical wide-eyed tourist, done in by the glamour of foreign travel. She was becoming a living, breathing cliché!

And no doubt Sayed al-Rashad used his caresssing personality with women as a matter of habit—except when he was frustrated, as he had been with her this morning. A good night's sleep should put things into perspective.

She showered the ocher dust of the desert from her hair and skin and put on the pink silk shirtwaist dress that she had tucked into a corner of her suitcase. Most of the wrinkles had fallen out with the steam from her hot shower. After first drawing back her hair into a loose coil, she decided to let it fall in its natural waves instead. A short string of pearls at her throat and a quick spray of perfume satisfied her that she was upholding the dignity of the university, with just the right touch of softness.

A tap came at her door. It wasn't even seven yet. When she opened it she found Sandi outside, dressed in a magenta peasant skirt and blouse. Her bare feet were squeezed into spike-heeled sandals and her neck was gleaming with silver bangles.

"Hi, what are you doing for dinner?" she asked breezily, stepping inside. Not waiting for an answer, she went on, "You've got more space than I have. Of course, I'm piled up with equipment." She sat down on one of the twin beds. "Our Texan friend was going to take me to the yacht club for dinner and dancing, but he stood me up. I don't know whether I should buy his excuse of having to meet some VIP's or not." She ran her eyes over Robyn. "The dining room here is okay if you don't mind having the same menu every day. I thought we might go into Alex and see what's doing."

"I'm sorry, I can't," Robyn replied. "I'm going out for dinner, and then later I have to work."

Sandi gave her a long look. "Three guesses it's with our glorious leader. He knows how to soften up the help so they gladly work themselves silly for him."

Robyn hoped her visitor wasn't going to continue on the subject of Sayed al-Rashad. She didn't want to hear any more about the man—and yet she did.

"I guess you already noticed that Sayed's hot stuff with women," Sandi was saying cheerfully. "He knows how to use his natural assets to good advantage. He's one of he few archaeologists who have a talent for prying money out of rich people and universities. They all think he's great.

"And he is, don't get me wrong," she insisted. "Not like poor old Tarsi, who has to scrounge for every piaster. It's all a game, only you never win unless you know how to hold hands with rich society ladies whose husbands sit on the boards of universities. I'll have to admit, I wouldn't mind holding hands with Sayed. I'd follow him anywhere!"

She paused to light a cigarette, blowing the first puff out the side of her mouth. "Hope you don't mind, but I can't give up the habit. I did once, for a week, but my willpower is lousy. Anyway—" she took another drag of her cigarette and grinned at Robyn "—these Egyptian men are really something. I've never felt like such a beauty queen in my life, not even when I was working in Turkey, and that's saying a lot!"

Robyn felt herself tensing up as Sandi talked. "I have contracts and business from the university to go over with Dr. al-Rashad," she replied quietly. "His invitation is only courtesy to the university representative, and I agree, he does seem to be a colorful character." She smiled weakly.

"Do you have a boyfriend back home, or are you among the available?" Sandi asked bluntly.

"Nobody special, but I'm not really interested in being available, either." Robyn could almost see her mother's frowning face.

"That's hard to believe." Sandi stood up and looked around for something to use as an ashtray. "Is Sayed picking you up?"

"No, Mohammed is."

"Can you give me a lift as far as the San Giovanni? It's a good place to eat, and there's a hell of a good-looking manager at the hotel desk."

"Sure. Be ready at seven-thirty. But now I've got to get some papers organized before I go." Robyn could feel that her co-worker wanted to ask more questions, but she walked her toward the door anyway. When they reached it, Sandi turned to face her once more.

"If you can stand more advice, I'd say take it easy with Sayed," she said seriously. "I don't understand just what gives in this religion here—about women, that is—but all around the world men will take what they can get and forget to say thanks." She looked at Robyn wryly. "But two can play that game. Women are—" she waved her hand in frustration "—stupid sometimes. They settle for what comes along. And then men expect them to be grateful! Listen, I'm talking too much. Just watch it with Sayed, okay? He's used to getting what he wants, and that's no lie. See you later." She left in a swish of magenta.

Robyn watched her go. She didn't want to make sense of Sandi's hard-edged remarks, but she had heard them anyway. Distractedly, she tidied up the room, in case they should work at the little coffee table, and laid out the contracts. Then she stood for a long time at the windows, watching the bay change colors. On the hotel terrace below, evening cocktails were beings served.... For some reason the thought of Cleopatra entered her mind. What really happened in the palace by this restless sea? Did the ancient queen ever find the joy of total love with her Caesar, a man of such unpredictable energies? Or had she wept for a love that never was, betrayed by the primitive search of her body?

Suddenly Robyn felt very untried. What did she really know about the rules of love in this bigger world? And why wasn't she drawn to Tom Perkins instead of Sayed al-Rashad?

It was almost seven-thirty, and tension filled her heart. It wasn't that she was expecting anything—no intimate hand holding, no low whispers.... She shivered in the warmth of the room, telling herself not to be a fool.

With a stern face she looked into the mirror one final time, then gathered up her scarf and bag.

Sandi was already in the lobby when she got there. She was joking with Mohammed, whose desert-chieftain's face reflected the satisfied expression of a male who knows he is attractive. Robyn remembered John's face at that terrible party. It had taken on an identical glow of self-pleasure under the admiring gaze of that other woman.

Mohammed let them into the back seat of the Peugeot, then began the wild drive along the cor-niche. Robyn gripped the door handle and watched the swaying bunch of artificial fruit that hung from the rearview mirror. A Koran in a velvet box sat on top of the dashboard. She hoped it would serve its function and protect them. With a series of honking tattoos, Mohammed executed an especially breath-taking passage between two cars. His eyes met hers in the mirror and he winked.

He dropped Sandi off at the San Giovanni, a beachfront hotel partway into the city, and continued on toward the center of Alexandria. Once alone with him, Robyn avoided the driver's eyes. He asked a few polite questions about her family, and she replied briefly.

"My father had four wives, and I have fourteen brothers." There was pride in his voice.

"And sisters...?"

"I don't know, we never counted."

They turned away from the sea just past a monument in a small park and crawled through heavy traffic for several blocks before stopping in front of the Santa Lucia restaurant. A very thin doorman welcomed her with a wide smile, and the bustling headwaiter bowed her the rest of the way in.

Sayed al-Rashad was waiting at a window table. He rose when she came toward him, and his heart-turning smile had its usual effect. It took an effort for Robyn to relax, to put down her purse gracefully while his eyes, very dark in the candlelight, were watching her. But they were steady, she noticed. No spark of masculine force flowed from them, and her contrary heart was disappointed.

"I hope you were able to rest." His warm voice sent a little frisson of feeling along her spine. "I have blamed myself for not sending you back to the hotel earlier, but Rafica was so overjoyed to have help...." His hand touched hers briefly. "I have already ordered for us. They are specialists here on the grilling of fish."

"Thank you, Dr. al-Rashad." How dull and uninteresting she sounded. "I'm glad to work, and Rafica is a lovely person."

"*Aiwa,*" he agreed. "And now that you are in Egypt you must have a lesson in Arabic. First, my name is Sayed. Can you say that?"

She blushed again, the warmth starting at her throat and spreading over her face. "Sayed," she said tentatively.

"Good. How simple to learn. Dr. al-Rashad is reserved for my students and my enemies." As in a

game, he began to name things on the table, waiting
for her to repeat the words. Her awkwardness and
the scarlet tide on her face retreated, and she was
soon laughing while she tried to imitate the throaty
sound of *kh* in the Arabic word for lettuce, *khass*.

"Or khamsin," Sayed said, frowning. "The wind
is gathering in the desert. I can feel it, like electricity
in my nerves. May Allah grant us time."

His talk returned to his work and the excavation.
Together they dipped crusty pieces of rolls into dishes
of taheena while she heard the story of his search for
the scrolls. Fine white fish *en brochette* was a
delicious accompaniment to his fascinating tales of
little-known archaeological discoveries in Egypt.
Robyn forgot her apprehensions in the sheer pleasure
of his company. She forgot that he was a dangerous
man who took women lightly.

She was content to listen to the deep tones of his
voice, tones that gave her such a feeling of comfort.
She longed suddenly to tell him about her father,
knowing that the two men would have understood
each other. Before she could decide what to do, however, he was giving her a lesson in archaeology,
describing things that it would be useful for an intelligent beginner to know—various methods for
digs, for example, and about protocol among archaeologists.

Robyn knew all of it already, of course, but now it
was too late. How would he react if she told him who
she was? He was making every effort to be kind, to
orient her to his problems. It would only cause both
of them embarrassment.

At one point he looked up at her quickly, a dark

light in his eyes. "The university should have stopped that disastrous press conference!"

The sharp statement took her off guard. "What? Oh. . . Mr. Saunders announced it before anyone else was told. It caused quite a furor in the department, let me assure you."

"Have you any idea what it did to us here?" He ground his teeth in vexation. "For days I had reporters crawling over the excavation, accusing me of hiding the news of the discovery from them. I finally had to direct them to Hassan Tarsi's dig and tell them that his work was far more interesting than mine! By Allah the Infinitely Patient, I do not understand the American use of public relations schemes. I'm not in the business of creating media events!"

"We were all unhappy about it, Dr. al-Rashad," she said defensively.

"The time it took to undo your Mr. Saunders's careless words—"

"I'll have to object," Robyn interrupted. "He isn't *anybody's* Mr. Saunders. There was just nothing we could do to stop him. Unless you wanted to do without the borescope camera. . . ."

He smiled. "Perhaps you are right, and I should make another apology. My second today, something that has never happened before. And you have gone back to calling me Dr. al-Rashad. I trust that does not mean we are enemies. I would feel very grieved." He gave her a dazzling smile that she felt down to her toes. "No more talk of my work; it only puts me in a malignant humor. And it is a good thing you are not knowledgeable in archaeology. I feel more free to express myself upon the subject without fear-ing contradiction. You are the type who would gladly contradict me, I suspect, if I made a mistake, hmm?''

She flushed under his condescending tone. ''I'm not really that type at all,'' she protested. ''And when you say I don't know much about your work, I—''

''Shh. I didn't mean to make light of your expertise in your official capacity. Of course I respect your knowledge of the contracts and your acuity as an observer. It's just that I'm relieved to talk with an American woman who doesn't fancy herself all-wise about Egyptian archaeology and papyri. I was almost overwhelmed last winter by your fellow university ladies. They came to give assistance on the dig and ended by following me everywhere I went, hanging on my every word and trying to demonstrate how very advanced they were in their understanding of my work. I shan't go into details, but it was quite inappropriate, and I requested that Dr. Wayland send me no more archaeological neophytes. He is a fine man, your boss. You are fortunate to be working for him.''

''Yes, he is,'' she managed to say, appalled by the position he had just put her into. What could she say to him now? His adamantine mind certainly didn't want to be told that Dr. Wayland had sent him someone who really *did* have expertise in his field of specialty.

''But I have done all the talking and no listening,'' he was saying. ''What a boorish dinner companion you must think me.'' His eyes had softened. They had become so warm and probing, so familiar to her heart's deepest memories....

Noticing the sudden change in her, he reached his hand out to take hers. "What is it, little Robyn? Is there a problem?"

Having his face so close to hers made her want to lean closer and put her cheek against his firm amber skin. No man had ever made her feel this way before—so audacious, or so at a loss. And he was still waiting for an answer.

"Why should there be one?" She tried to summon a bright tone, but even to her own ears her voice came out sharp and brittle. His expression changed and the warmth that had been in his eyes withdrew.

Robyn felt a dreadful pull in her breast. Why hadn't she said something else to him, in a soft flattering voice? *Don't be a fool,* she told herself for the second time that night.

They sipped the delicate strawberry-cream dessert drink in silence, except for Robyn's effort to say that it tasted good. Sayed's smile was polite, remote. He called for the bill and paid it without comment.

His Fiat sports car was parked near the restaurant, and they walked to it quickly. He swung into the insane traffic, driving with demon energy. Robyn held onto the seat and was silent.

It was after ten o'clock when they reached the hotel. Together they went up to the fourth floor, where he took her key and unlocked the door, making a point of leaving it wide open.

"Don't worry, I won't compromise you." His voice was almost brusque as he sat down at the small table and started reading the contracts. When he had finished she joined him, and in her best business manner read him her notes from Dr. Wayland. They plunged into paperwork, her shorthand flowing swiftly over the pages as Sayed dictated letters to the university and memos for amendments to the contracts.

At one point she looked up from her concentration to find him watching her. An admiring smile had begun in his eyes; he had come back from his cool retreat. "You are an excellent worker," he said quietly. "No wonder Dr. Wayland values you. But there are shadows under your lovely eyes. I think I am pushing you—it is one of my faults. They say that my career has been built on the battered bodies of my workers, over whom I have trampled mercilessly." He laughed. "You must promise to tell me when I am acting like a slave driver of Pharaoh, hmm?"

The knot in Robyn's solar plexus began to untie itself and she felt a glow of pleasure at his praise— she hoped it wasn't a blush. "I'll tell you," she promised. He had the ability to reel her in whenever he wanted to, she realized. Sandi's blunt advice intruded for an instant, but she tried to push it away.

He finished dictating, finally, and reached for his briefcase. "That would seem to be the end of our business tonight."

"I'll type the notes tomorrow and leave them for your approval," she replied, shutting her notebook. When he stood up, he held out a hand to draw her to her feet. His other hand rested lightly on her shoulder, then his fingers traced the line of her cheek, leaving a wake of delicious response.

"You puzzle me." His eyes held hers. "You don't fit neatly into any category of woman. That is not to be taken as an insult or as criticism. But surely you can't be completely satisfied being a very efficient secretary." His eyes moved to her lips.

Robyn dropped her own eyes and waited, feeling powerless to move. The old story of the bird and the snake went through her mind. Only this time Robyn, the brown bird from the north, was caught in the spell of the kingly cobra. How had this poor little bird strayed so far from the safety of home?

His finger outlined her mouth with a silken touch. "Your lips look as if they had not been kissed with real passion. . . a pity." Smiling briefly, he turned on his heel and was gone.

Robyn stood there trembling. She waited until his footsteps faded down the hallway, then pushed the door shut. Catching a glimpse of her face in the dresser mirror, she touched her lips—her "generous" lips. *Am I so easily read,* she wondered. Why did he say such things to her? It was almost as if doing so amused him.

She stood for a time listening to the waves below her balcony. Tired as she was, sleep was far away, and she pulled out her portable typewriter. She might as well work; at least she would show him that she was indeed an efficient secretary.

After an hour everything was ready for Sayed al-Rashad's signature. Then she slept.

CHAPTER FOUR

ONCE AGAIN THE BRIGHT SUN awakened her. It was early, but for no good reason a sense of joy, almost of anticipation, was in her heart. She dressed in khaki pants and a much-washed cotton shirt of pastel colors. A little tune escaped her lips as she pulled her hair tightly into its band and pinned it into a spiral blond knot. It would be less likely to acquire so much dust and grit if it didn't flop around.

Her breakfast was brought in by room service, and Sandi drifted in with it. She was dressed in her habitual eye-catching colors, braless and good-humored. "Thought you might be sleeping in... after last night," she greeted, a gleam of curiosity in her smile.

"I stayed up late to type all of Dr. al-Rashad's memos, but I feel fine."

Sandi helped herself to a breakfast roll and honey. "Then it really was work?"

"Of course." Robyn smiled back, damned if she would say more.

"Well—" the photographer gave her an up-and-down scrutiny "—you sure look no-nonsense in that outfit. I didn't mean for you to go off men completely—just to be careful. Say, do you want to go into Alex? I've got a pickup assignment from a gal who's doing a feature article on ethnic jewelry for

Town & Country. I've got to shoot some pictures in the suqs, but you're welcome to tag along. We can shop around afterward.''

"I'd love to see the market, but I have to be at the dig today," Robyn said regretfully.

"Okay, you say when and we'll go. I know the city. It's kind of confusing the first time."

Robyn finished her coffee and put the typed pages into a folder. She was putting them in her briefcase when Sandi said, "You haven't asked me how my evening was." She didn't wait for an answer. "It was a bust. The guy already has a wife, maybe two. My luck. Don't mind me," she said, grinning, "I'm just frustrated because I can't get Tom to give me the time of day. When I'm around him I get the feeling that I'm talking too loud or something. It's depressing."

Robyn reached out to give her hand a quick, comforting squeeze. "What if I gave you some advice for a change? Tom isn't a lost cause. That's just my observation; I wouldn't write him off so soon."

At her words, Sandi's face lit up like a little girl's.

ROBYN, RAFICA, AND TOM were the only passengers in Mohammed's car that morning. Dr. Gaddabi and Sayed were staying in town to arrange for a better drill and would come out later.

Rafica pointed out more places in Alexandria that might be of interest to Robyn. A tall red granite pillar from the first century B.C. stood all alone in the middle of a vacant lot behind a rundown apartment building. A Roman amphitheater had been found almost intact when a pile driver for a new high rise accidentally smashed into solid marble one day. These and other odd bits of antiquity were scattered among the everyday lives of modern Alexandrians.

They spoke about Egypt, and Rafica's patient voice reflected the age-old adjustment of her people to the problems of life. Tom left them to their talk while he checked out long lists of equipment. The borescope—and Huntley Saunders—would not be at the site that day because there was no chance of a drill hole being dug for at least another two days. Sayed had apparently made it clear to Saunders that the borescope was the possession of the university. The little detail had not been well received by the gentleman himself.

"I can't figure out the guy," Tom said. "Sure, he gives umpteen dollars to the university so that they can buy the camera, but he gets plenty of praise from the academic higher-ups, he gets his fat tax deduction and he still has to have more! What does he want us to do, chisel his name in the sandstone?"

"Ego," Robyn sighed. "It comes in all sizes and shapes, and ours happens to be named Huntley Saunders III."

When they arrived the site was quiet. There was already a basket of scroll fragments by the door of the workroom. Rafica was in and out, and Robyn stuck to her cataloging until her back was tight with fatigue. When lunch was called she was glad to stretch her tired neck. The heat today was stronger. Gusts of reddish dust blew along the desert horizon.

Rafica had been working in the dusty niches of the excavated room all morning, watching to find any identification tags that might link the papyrus scrolls to the ancient library. She had commented earlier that it was very strange to find no tags with the fragments, as if they might have been purposely removed at some time. The fact was a puzzle, she had said. If only some small proof could be found! She had clasped her hands expressively. "That is why I must now watch each one as it is uncovered."

She reappeared outside the workroom door and washed the dirt from her hands and arms, using water that had been brought from the canal by one of the Bedouin children. Several of them worked doing odd jobs for the crew for a few piasters.

"It's getting worse in the hole," she announced. "The shoring is working loose and some of the niches have collapsed from the vibration of yesterday's efforts to set up the tripod. I know some things have already been damaged in our haste. This is not the way Dr. al-Rashad likes to excavate." She looked up into the blowing, sandy sky. "It is the fault of the wind spirits, old Bahiya would say. The old woman has eyes that see far, but I don't want her to look into the future. I would rather not know." Her face was suddenly melancholy.

Robyn handed her one of the box lunches. "I guess it's best not to know what will happen next," she agreed. At the same time she remembered the sand reading from yesterday, the potent force of Bahiya's voice. . .and Sayed's gentle fingers stroking across her lips.

They walked a little apart from the men and found a snug spot by a scrubby clump of bushes. There, leaning against two discarded cases of Evian water, they ate quietly.

"I can't get used to the idea that Egypt is mostly desert," Robyn said after a while, her eyes roaming from horizon to horizon.

"They say that Egypt is like a beautiful lotus plant, alone in the midst of emptiness. The Nile starts like the roots of the lotus, far to the south of our land. It flows toward the sea in a long green stem until it reaches upward to bloom in a glorious flowering at the delta." Rafica's voice was like a storyteller's, soft and faraway. "And for all these thousands of years the Nile—our beautiful lotus—has fed us and given us life. My people used to sing to the river god, whose name was Hapi. There is a hymn from the Eighteenth Dynasty that I have always loved...." Rafica closed her eyes for a moment, then started to recite:

O Hapi, thou appearest in this land and thou
    comest in peace to make Egypt to live.
Thou art the waterer of the fields which Ra hath
    created,
Thou givest life unto all animals,
Thou descendest on thy way from heaven.
Thou art the lord of the poor and needy.
If thou wert overthrown in the heavens, the gods
    would fall upon their faces and men would
    perish....

"I learned it when I was a child," she said, as if to herself. "It tells how very long my people have looked to our river for sustenance. The Nile has been our father and mother and we its grateful children, no matter who has claimed ownership of Egypt: the ancient pharaohs, the Hyksos, the Persians, the Greeks, the Romans, the Arabs, the Circassians, the Turks, the British. No matter—the Nile has opened its bosom to all without selfishness."

"How very lovely, Rafica. I will never again think of the Nile without seeing a great lotus in my mind."

"*Aiwa*. We have been finding ways to live with our great parent river so that all of its children will have enough fertile ground to till. It is a problem that we seem never to solve perfectly." Her face was set in lines of weariness as she spoke.

"But the Aswan Dam—"

"A blessing and a curse. Now we can control the flooding of the Nile, but the rich silt that used to arrive with the floods and spread over our land, giving nutrients to the soil, no longer comes to us. We now have more diseases from the water because it grows sluggish in the canals and is not allowed to be cleansed each year in the great washing up of floodwater."

"I understand, I think," Robyn ventured, hesitating to offer an outsider's opinion. "I wonder why we humans always tamper with something that nature has tried to balance?"

"Because we have no choice sometimes. How does a nation feed forty million people—and three-quarters of a million new mouths each year—from a fragile strip of fertile land never more than fourteen miles wide, except at the delta? People become desperate to find new ways. They think maybe Nature was not so wise, and then they come up with shining new technology and experiment upon her."

"And then it is too late to go back to the way things were in the first place. . . ."

"*Aiwa*. I love my land and my people. I am a villager myself, from the dark, moist earth of the Nile Valley, and I am sad for the farmers who now have to buy chemicals to feed their crops, when before the river gave them all they needed. And yet the farmers now have more land to till and electricity in some of their homes.

"It is a time of terrible decisions and changes for

us. Our traditions and culture are strong. We do not want to imitate other cultures, to become another America or West Germany or Japan. We are Egyptians." Rafica reached into her large shoulder bag and pulled out a head of fresh romaine lettuce. "Try some of these leaves dipped in the sesame paste."

Robyn gratefully accepted the lettuce. It was delicious and cooling, much more tasty than the hotel's box lunch of bland boiled chicken and white rolls.

After a while Rafica looked up and smiled. "I suppose you wonder why, with all these problems in our land, we are sitting out here in the wind scratching a hole in the desert to look for old scrolls."

"I might have thought you would train for a medical or technical career."

"The truth is, our universities are training agricultural specialists and engineers in greater numbers than there are jobs for them. Many graduates become taxi drivers. When I entered Cairo University I was given very good advice by a man I respect deeply. He said that when the technological revolution comes to Egypt in full force, the most important thing you can train yourself for is to preserve the old cultures. This revolution will come like a khamsin, clouding everything that we used to revere, confusing the minds of the young people. My service to my land would be great he told me, if I studied the past and found ways to convey its wisdom to the future. I have not regretted listening to that very farsighted man."

"Was he your father?"

Rafica's face darkened for an instant, then she smiled slightly. "No. It was Sheikh Sayed Abdelaziz al-Rashad." She watched Robyn's reaction. "You are surprised at the name?"

"I guess I am," Robyn replied, trying to imagine Sayed as an Arab sheikh and managing only to think of Rudolph Valentino. She felt silly immediately.

"Dr. al-Rashad and his family made it possible for me to have an education when other girls in my village were taking the traditional path of early marriage and motherhood. I thought I should tell you, since Dr. al-Rashad would not speak of it himself. That is why I would do anything to help him with his work."

"But isn't education free for everyone in Egypt?" Robyn was remembering the crash course in Egyptian culture she had received from a guidebook.

"In a way it is, but very few girls take advantage of it. Before the overthrow of the king, Dr. al-Rashad's family used to own our village and several others. When the wealthy families had to give up their holdings, Dr. al-Rashad and his father helped the new small landowners of our village learn about economics and modern farming methods. After the death of his father, Dr. al-Rashad became our sheikh, a mark of honor and respect."

Sayed, a sheikh. What an intriguing contradiction. A man of wisdom who inherited a tradition of service to his people, a man whose very fingertips could arouse fire within her. Robyn tried to keep that sweet sensation at bay, but it shivered along her spine. She pulled herself back to the conversation. "I'm glad you told me, Rafica. In the two days I've been here I've managed to find out how completely ignorant I am. I think I know more about ancient Egypt than I do about the more modern culture and traditions."

"Tradition can be a hurtful thing," the young woman answered in a whisper. Her eyes filled with tears and she turned her face away.

"Rafica, did I say something wrong?" Robyn asked in alarm.

"Oh, Robyn, I have to talk to someone!" She dabbed at her eyes with a handkerchief, then reached into her purse and pulled out an envelope. "Please forgive me, but I have been holding my problems inside for so long. It is such a tangle and I don't know what to do...."

Robyn put a comforting hand on her shoulder. "If I can help, I will," she said sincerely.

"No one can help." Rafica bent her head and wept quietly for a moment, then raised her heavy dark lashes. "I'm ungrateful. Here I am with everything I could hope for—an opportunity to learn, a good job—but I have managed to make it all seen unimportant. This is a letter from someone close to my heart—from Karim." She opened the folded letter and spread it out on her lap.

"You are in love with Karim?"

"More than I thought it possible to love. But I am standing on a knife's edge between my family's traditional belief that a daughter must obey them in everything, and my own desire to marry a man not of their choosing."

"But surely they will understand...."

"My father has arranged a marriage for me with my cousin Mustafa," she said in a trembling voice. "I am expected to marry him this summer. It was arranged when I was a child. My father has great debts to his brother, debts that can only be settled by this marriage. I hardly know Mustafa. He has been studying at al-Azhar, the Islamic university in Cairo. If my father cannot clear his debt to his brother it will dishonor him. And if I do not marry soon, my two sisters will not be able to be married. If I cannot marry Karim I—'' Her voice broke.

"What does your mother say about it?"

Rafica looked at her forlornly. "My mother has no influence. It is the business of the men in a family to arrange marriages. She can only sympathize, and tell me that I should never have left the village in the first place. Maybe she is right. Tradition is still too strong for one person to oppose it. But Karim...." She wept quietly once more.

Robyn felt confused. She couldn't accept that this bright, educated, modern young woman could not choose a life that suited her. "Tell me about Karim if it makes you feel better. I really do want to understand."

"I know you do, but I'm sure you cannot. I mean no offense, it is simply the truth. Karim was a student at Cairo University. He has his certificate to teach and he will be a very fine teacher. He is presently serving his three years in the army, as all Egyptian men do. I haven't seen him for six months, and then last night at the hotel I received this letter. He is coming home for a few days of leave and he wants to see me." She crumpled the letter in her hand.

"Will you see him?" Robyn asked softly.

"That is what I don't know. The more I see him, the more I go against my family and all that it stands for. I am cutting myself off from them forever. But I can't lose Karim. The only thing that keeps me from flying into a million pieces is this work and my sense of duty to Dr. al-Rashad."

"Rafica, nothing is hopeless," Robyn said in a positive voice. "Someone should talk to Dr. al-

Rashad. If he is the sheikh of your village he may have some influence.''

The young woman looked up in alarm. ''No! It is not his concern—only mine.''

''You can't mean that.''

''Please. I shouldn't have said anything to you. I'm sorry to have spilled more tears and involved a friend.'' She stood up quickly and walked back to the excavation.

Karim's letter had dropped to the sand and Robyn picked it up. She felt futile and inept. What could be done to relieve Rafica's anguish? Her eyes followed the beautiful flow of Arabic script in the letter, and even though she couldn't read the words, a feeling of love and yearning seemed to reach up to her from the paper.

Instead of returning to the workroom immediately, she searched out Tom, who was taking a break in the shade of one of the buildings. He listened to her story and shook his head. ''There isn't a thing you can or should do, Robyn, believe me. I feel just as bad as you do, but this isn't our country. These things have roots that go back centuries.''

Robyn fixed him with a baleful eye. ''I can't believe you can stand by and watch that poor girl suffer, when a word to Sayed might change everything for her.''

''Come on, Robyn, don't put me in that position.''

''Well, will you say *something* to him? Rafica is your colleague. Do you want the project to suffer because she can't think straight, because she cries herself to sleep at night?'' She had decided to appeal to Tom's practical masculine side.

''I can't promise anything,'' he said uncomfortably. "I'll see if the right time presents itself. Sayed doesn't need another problem, you know...."

Spontaneously she stretched up to kiss his cheek. "Thanks, Tom. Just a word—it could save her life."

"Okay, okay," he said, grinning. "I'll talk to you later."

THE DAY WORE ON. Robyn spent all of her time bent carefully over the long table with her tweezers and pen, trying to put her whole mind on the task instead of on the complications that had suddenly grown around her like mythical dragon's teeth. Two days ago she had been worried only about doing a decent job with the contracts, and about keeping a safe distance from Huntley Saunders.

It was late afternoon when footsteps crunched on the threshold. She turned to see Hassan Tarsi standing in the doorway. He entered uninvited.

"Good afternoon, Miss Douglas." His smile was ingratiating as he glanced at her lists. "How fortunate we are to have your help."

She looked at him noncommittally. "I'm enjoying the work."

"Ah, but I find it wonderful for such a young and lovely lady to be in a position of trust to a great university such as yours."

Robyn's uneasiness was growing. What did he want? Beneath his patronizing expression his eyes were harsh with disappointment. A sort of pity moved her to smile in a more friendly way. Obviously he was an intelligent man. Maybe he did truly believe that this excavation and its contents were rightfully his.

"I hope when you report to your superiors in the

United States you will give a fair, unbiased account of this project," he was saying. "Of course, for some time I suspected the existence of these—" He waved his hand at the sorting trays with their precious fragments. "Unfortunately, I am a poor professor and do not come from a family that wields influence. I cannot raise funds easily. But I have managed to discover a significant Ptolemaic settlement by my own efforts." He shrugged. "Who believes me when I say that I think it was a winter villa belonging to the great Cleopatra? Nobody. I have found clusters of small rooms that could have been the servants' quarters. And next I will find the grand villa itself... when I have the funding. I have discovered two wells already. To find the foundation stones of Cleopatra's villa will be a great contribution to world knowledge, don't you agree?"

"Of course," Robyn felt compelled to say. She looked away from his intense black eyes, wishing that he would finish what he had to say and leave.

"Thank you. And when you speak to your university, to Dr. Wayland, would you tell him of this? I am writing a paper about my work. Will you give a good word for Hassan Tarsi?"

She picked up her pen, pretending to return to work. "I will be happy to take him your report. His specialty is papyrus manuscripts, but he is always interested in new findings in Egyptian fieldwork."

"You must come out to my excavation. I will take you. Soon I might even find another hidden room full of ancient writings there. Then your Dr. Wayland will want to come here personally to see me." He reached out and plucked a large curled section of a scroll from the top of the uncataloged pile. Spreading it flat, he ran his eyes over the dim writing. "Demotic script," he said. "Early Ptolemaic period."

Robyn held her breath as the papyrus made small crackling sounds. The scroll fragments were extremely delicate; should she ask him not to handle them? But he was an accredited archaeologist, she argued.

She watched with horrible tension as he rolled it up carelessly and set it back in place, only to pick up another and treat it in the same casual way.

"Ahh, Greek," he purred. "I can hardly wait to begin translating. Who knows what treasures are written here." He waved the ominously rustling scroll.

Robyn's lips were open to protest when Rafica came in with a tray full of dirt-encrusted papyrus. She eased her precious burden down onto the table, then looked pointedly at the scroll still in Hassan Tarsi's hand.

He set it down with deliberate slowness. "Good day, Rafica."

She nodded without a smile.

"It has been a pleasure to speak to you, Miss Douglas." Nodding his head to both women, he turned and left.

"What was he doing here, handling the papyrus like that!" Rafica exploded.

"Thank goodness you came in. I was just going to say something to him. But he's supposed to be an archaeologist. He was saying how eager he was to begin translating—"

"Translating!" Rafica looked up in amazement. "He won't be translating. Dr. Gaddabi, Dr. al-Rashad and a team of specialists will do that." She shook her head. "He had some other reason for coming in here. He knew you were working alone."

"Well—" Robyn smiled wryly "—he did ask me to send a good report about him to Dr. Wayland."

"Merciful Allah, we must speak to Dr. al-Rashad about this. I do not trust that man. If he comes again...." She stopped and thought for a moment. "Tonight I shall make a sign: Scrolls to be touched only by permission of the catalogers. What a nerve! Isn't that the expression you say in America?"

Rafica looked at Robyn and her voice dropped. "I hope you can forget my unseemly emotions during lunch. My parents are not monsters with hard hearts. They love me very much. In Islam a woman always has the right to refuse a marriage. I am afraid I sounded to you like a fool."

"Don't say that, Rafica. Love must be a very difficult thing when it isn't the way everyone around you had planned."

"My parents were very liberal to let me go to the university. They tried hard to think of my best interests, and of course Dr. al-Rashad helped to explain things to them. It is still difficult for them to imagine how I could be happy and fulfilled away from the protection and traditions of village life. When I wept, my tears were not only for myself, but for all of my family. How can we all be happy? Only if Allah wills it to be."

"*Inshallah,*" Robyn said softly.

"How quickly you learn. There is another word: *bukra*. It means, perhaps...someday. That is the only answer I can give myself, *bukra*. Someday the puzzle of my life will be made clear to me and there will be no more questions. That is why I do not want old Bahiya to tell me of the future. To see it ahead of its proper time would be too difficult for me to accept.''

Her expression changed to a no-nonsense one. "Now, no more wishful thinking for us. We have another hour of sorting before the cars come for us. Dr. al-Rashad must have been delayed in the city. I'm sure he's very frustrated. The first drill was supposed to be sufficient for the job, but you saw how crude it was. It may take days to find a better one that is available. But we shall put the time to good service, won't we?''

"Aiwa," Robyn answered in her best tourist Arabic.

EVERYONE WAS TIRED and grimy with fine ocher dust when they got out of Mohammed's car at the Palestine Hotel. "Why don't we get cleaned up and have dinner together in a first-class restaurant somewhere?'' Robyn suggested. "I'm dying to sample some Egyptian cuisine.''

Tom shook his head. "I don't have the strength for another run back into town.''

"Then let's eat here in the hotel. It can't be too bad.''

Rafica begged off. "I'm not terribly hungry, and I have food in my room that I share with Amina, my roommate. Have a nice dinner.''

Tom's eyes followed Rafica as she walked away. "She shares a room with one of the hotel maids, a friend of hers. The budget doesn't give her more. She's too proud to say she couldn't afford a meal in a fancy restaurant, and it wouldn't have done any good to offer to pay for her. She's very sensitive.''

"I should have thought..." Robyn began, then stopped in confusion.

"You were just being an American. You can't help that." He grinned. "Well, that leaves just us. I'll see if I can find Sandi and make it a threesome. Meet you in the lobby at eight."

Robyn was dressed and ready a little before the hour, so she wandered around the large sprawling lobby of the hotel. The gift shop was in a small building at the other end of the hotel gardens. She made a note to herself to browse through it on the first free day. For now she strolled through the maze of easy chairs and couches, then noticed the darkened nightclub beyond. Waiters were setting up long tables nearby and bringing huge trays of food. Her mouth watered at the array of hors d'oeuvres, artfully arranged delicacies that must have been prepared for a very expensive party.

At exactly eight o'clock she was standing in front of the open doors of the hotel dining room. A moment later Tom arrived, checking his watch. "Right on time, except for Sandi. Let's look in the bar."

A few steps away and down a short stairway the cocktail lounge was buzzing with people, mostly Western businessmen, Robyn guessed. Sandi was finishing a glass of Stella, the Egyptian beer, when they found her sitting alone in a booth. "Don't tell me, I'm late," she said, with self-conscious toss of her light blond hair. "Sit down for a second, there's something I want you to see."

Tom gave a quizzical look. "What's up?"

"I would have been on time except that Huntley Saunders was walking in. I didn't want to bump into him—for reasons I won't go into—so I stayed awhile. Then in walks Hassan Tarsi and sits down with him. If you turn just a little you can see them at the last table over there.''

Tom turned his head slowly, then swiveled it back. In the dim smoky corner the two men were bent intently over their drinks. They appeared to be in animated conversation.

''I shudder to think what they might have in common to talk about,'' he said in a grim voice. ''Hassan can spin a pretty good story when he's around money. I suppose I'll have to talk to Saunders and find out what our colorful colleague has been saying to him. One more thing to worry about.'' He heaved a deep sigh.

''Just thought you should know.'' Sandi smiled at him. ''Come on, let's get out of here and have some dinner.'' She linked arms with both Tom and Robyn, and they left the lounge together without looking back at the two men.

In the dining room they were given a quiet spot away from the tourist groups. ''After a while you start feeling like you belong here and all those other Americans and Britishers are aliens,'' Tom said. ''Then, when you see tourists breeze through with their eyes out on stalks, trying to take it all in, you feel sort of sorry for them.''

''If it's Tuesday, this must be Egypt, right?'' Sandi quipped.

Tom flashed his boyish grin at her. ''I'd hate to have to do it that way. I've been here more than a year and there's still so much to see that it could take a lifetime.''

''Oh, oh, he's hooked. See those glazed eyes, Robyn? Tom's an Egypt junkie. Poor guy!''

"Right you are, m'dear. And you will be, too, if you stay here a few more weeks. I've watched you taking pictures of the Bedouin children and the desert scenery."

Sandi looked pleased that Tom had noticed her. "It would help a lot if I had somebody to explain the history to me," she said, her large green eyes turned in Tom's direction. "I've got some terrific photos, but my captions aren't so hot. Look at this one." She pulled a color slide from her handbag and held it to the light. "I took this shot the other day on Nebi Daniel Street. Looks like I aimed at a pile of junk, but close up you can see all kinds of goodies—an old pillar, a stone archway that's blocked up." She handed it to Tom. "Do you know what it is?"

"Sure." He held it up so that Robyn could see it, too. "That's one of the sites that might be part of the ruins of the great library. Nobody knows. The sheikh of the mosque next to it told Sayed that his building was constructed over an ancient place of learning."

"What's being done about it?" Robyn asked.

"Well, you can't just take a pick and start digging under a mosque. A lot of people are happy enough just to know the tradition and let it go at that. There are two or three other places near there that could have been the site of the library. Who knows, maybe all of them were. Alexandria was immense in the old days, with colonnades that stretched for blocks, gardens, a university, medical laboratories—the works."

"You paint some pretty good pictures with words," Sandi said jauntily. "If I showed you some of my proof sheets and slides, could you give me a little help with captions? One of these days I'll be submitting some of them for a photo story on this place, and I don't want to sound dumb.''

"Hardly dumb," Tom said, laughing. "I'd guess you have more brains stored in that blond head than you let anyone know about. You're kind of like a good dig—lots of levels. That didn't sound right, did it?''

"What a romantic!" she teased. Glowing from Tom's approval, Sandi was enjoying her dinner, Robyn knew.

"We're not exactly alone tonight," Sandi said a moment later, pointing with a forkful of roast beef. "Glorious leader is here with friends.''

Even from halfway across the room Robyn recognized Sayed's face and gestures. He was sitting with five or six other men, all dressed in business suits. There were no women with them, a fact that somehow made her very happy. She watched him with a feeling of long familiarity. She knew exactly how he was smiling, how his eyes were commenting on the conversation with that vivid flash. . . .

Sandi cleared her throat. "Robyn, I've got to turn in early. Tom, too. Want to have an escort up to the fourth floor?" She winked at Tom.

Robyn looked away from Sayed's table, not caring how transparent she was at the moment. "I was thinking of having a last cup of coffee. Thanks, anyway.''

"All right, honey, but remember. . .if a man gets to be thirty-seven and nobody's snagged him, there's not a lot of hope.'' Sandi took Tom's arm and started toward the lobby.

Without the protection of her co-workers, Robyn suddenly felt conspicuous. She was sitting directly in the line of Sayed's vision, and as she sipped her tiny cup of thick Turkish coffee she lowered her eyes. She knew the exact moment when Sayed discovered her there, for she felt his glance. She barely had time to take a breath before he was standing beside her, smiling.

"How fortunate for me, Robyn. I was just telling my friends about Dr. Wayland and the university's partnership in our work, and here you are, right under my nose! Let me introduce you to some of the members of the Alexandria Archaeological Society." Although she demurred, he took her by the hand and led her to his table. Robyn knew it was useless to object.

Half a dozen pairs of welcoming eyes were on her as Sayed presented her. "This is Miss Robyn Douglas, special observer and assistant to Professor Wayland. A very important member to have at our excavation."

The names went past her in a blur as she nodded her head politely and smiled. Then Sayed was saying his goodbyes to the men and was walking with her out of the dining room. "I want to show you something," he said cheerfully. "You may never have another chance while you are in Egypt...."

He guided her into the lobby area, where a crowd of people in formal festive attire was milling around in front of the nightclub entrance. "This is the second night in a row that you have saved me from business talk. Those men are friends from long years past, but dry as the antique dust they love so much."

Robyn looked down at her green wraparound cotton skirt, her white tailored blouse and flat shoes. "Dr. al-Rashad...Sayed, I'm not dressed for this," she stammered as his intention grew clearer. He was leading her right into the midst of the well-dressed crowd.

"Nonsense," he replied playfully. "A wedding reception is to be enjoyed. Don't you hear the tambourines? Listen." He pulled her forward, where they could see a procession starting to form. The tambourines—there must have been a dozen of them to make such an unearthly rhythmic din—were coming nearer from somewhere in the depths of the hotel, and the women in the crowd began to give a wild piercing cry, their tongues vibrating against their palates.

The hair stood up on the back of Robyn's neck as she strained to see what was happening. Clapping and tambourines and cries welcomed the bride and groom, who were almost swallowed up among the parting waves of guests.

Reality started to lose its form in her orderly mind. She couldn't believe she was actually seeing this—a troupe of elegantly robed Arab men marching ahead of the bridal party, playing a deafening wedding tune on huge bagpipes. By the time belly dancers with tambourines joined the procession, pastel-gowned bridesmaids walked sedately past carrying white candles as tall as they themselves and the bride and groom entered, looking like classic decorations on an American wedding cake, Robyn's senses were close to being overloaded. She found herself in the midst of sounds so strange and compelling that she lost track of Robyn Douglas, the controlled, reserved American girl with the complicated thought processes.

When Sayed's hand reached for hers she gave it to

him willingly, and his gentle strong touch sent another kind of excitement through her body. It felt so good, so right, to have him close beside her, with his warmth and his penetrating presence reaching around her as if to say, "You are home with me, where you belong. Egypt is your land now, my little bird."

They stood wrapped together in the almost unbearable loudness of the celebrations, while the wedding party made its way slowly into the nightclub. Finally the doors closed to outsiders, and a Middle Eastern orchestra replaced the bagpipes, the ululating women and tambourines.

Sayed turned to Robyn. "The rest of the evening belongs to the bride and groom and their families. I knew there was to be a reception tonight, and I was afraid I would have no one to share it with me, least of all my archaeological dinner companions. What you just saw is a segment of the moneyed Egyptian society—living partly in modern Western style and partly in the traditions of the past."

"It was amazing," Robyn said, still caught by the spell of what she had witnessed.

"Perhaps you will be fortunate enough to be out one evening in the city when a street wedding is taking place. You will never forget it. It is as if you were suddenly lifted up and taken to another century. At such a wedding you would be most welcome as a stranger, and you would have difficulty refusing their enthusiastic hospitality."

He walked her to the elevators and waited until the door slid open and she was safely inside. "An early day for you tomorrow, Robyn. Oh, and if you want to telex Dr. Wayland, I will be glad to do it for you from the antiquities office in Alex. The hotel telex won't be back in order for another day at least.''

Robyn thought he was going to kiss her hand, but he didn't, instead giving a slight bow and a half-smile as the elevator door shut between them. She wouldn't be giving him her telex message for Dr. Wayland, she knew. She wanted to ask the delicate question of what her relationship with Sayed was supposed to be—professionally, of course. On the personal level she knew what was happening to her and she couldn't—or wouldn't—stop it. But she had to! She was starting on the long heady slide toward falling in love, and at the bottom there was nobody to catch her. What was it she said to herself yesterday? Work, be pleasant and don't be a fool. *Then don't be,* she cried at her pulsating nerve endings as she stepped out of the elevator at the lonely fourth floor.

She didn't look in the mirror as she loosened her hair from its tight green ribbon. Tears were too close to the surface. *You* are *pathetic,* she berated herself. Oh, why hadn't the drill been working right the first day so that the borescope camera could take its pictures and they could find out once and for all what was down in the lower chamber? She could have packed up her notes and contracts and been on her way home by now. And where was the self-contained woman who could hardly wait to experience the mystique of old Egypt? Wishing she could control the mad jumble of her emotions, that's where!

CHAPTER FIVE

SHE WOKE the next morning very early. Sometime during sleep and dreams she had managed to lay a cloak of calm over her nerves. She was looking forward to a day of hard work and mental exercise. Now that she had finally recovered from her jet lag, she knew she would have better control of herself.

The day passed in intensive work with Rafica at the cataloging tables. George Lewis, the young assistant she had met the first morning, was helping with the painstaking unearthing of fragments. He was a silent man, busily writing in his dig journal as he perched on the precarious sandy edge of the square hole. Sandi was climbing cheerfully all over the excavation like a wagging dog, taking pictures of the work in progress.

Dr. al-Rashad and Dr. Gaddabi were both absent. Rumor had it that they were in Cairo on business, probably tracking down a new drill. Sayed hadn't mentioned it to her, Robyn realized with disappointment before she brought herself up short. She would definitely have to stop thinking about him.

Near midday there was an unusual discovery in the deepest niche. George, Tom and Rafica appeared together at the door to the workroom with something cradled tenderly among them. It was a matted, crushed mass of parchment, which had become lumped together over the long centuries and was now crackling alarmingly as it was carried to the table.

"It's vellum, all right." Tom peered through a hand magnifying glass and looked up smiling. "Well, girls, good luck. Don't tackle it today. I'll bring some chemical spray to use on it tomorrow." He examined the large brown mass again. "My God, it's dry. But it hasn't rusted away into dust like a lot of the parchment." He pointed to a fragment that stuck up out of the main body of it. "I thought so. See there—that's Greek." He frowned thoughtfully, scratching a sandy hand through his rumpled brown hair. "Do you suppose. . . ?"

The eager faces of the others made him stop and smile. "What I thought was. . . ." He tantalized them by pausing once again. "Well, everything's been papyrus so far, and now it's parchment."

Sandi came to the door. "You're too fast for me. I want to get a shot of that thing. What is it?"

Tom assumed a professorial air, but his eyes were alive. "Do you remember your history? About the big rivalry between the great Alexandrian library and the equally large one at Pergamum in Asia Minor?"

All heads nodded except Sandi's.

"Sometime in the second or third century B.C., the Egyptians slapped an embargo on the sale of papyrus to Pergamum, which caused a hell of a problem. No paper to make copies of books or to carry out business and contracts! So, *voilà*, the Pergamenes found a substitute. They invented vellum, using the fine-grained skins of sheep and goats. Now, if you're following this, the next part of the puzzle comes in. Marc Antony was trying to impress Cleopatra some years later. When he conquered Pergamum he confiscated their great library and sent the scrolls—and all that vellum—to the Library of Alexandria. One of the world's most valuable gifts of love.''

He paused and grinned at his expectant audience. ''Do you suppose this could be a scroll from the Pergamum library, which found its way to Alexandria? Keep sharp. Maybe this could give us our clue to the origins of our scrolls.''

A shiver of hope stirred in Robyn's chest. That dark matted heap of two-thousand-year-old skins might be the single most important thing in the entire project. It seemed fantastic. What would Sayed say when he found out?

She had to admit that it would make her happy to be able to put real proof into his hands. And after that there would be so much money available for his dig that he could work for years, searching out other storage rooms of the ancient Library of Alexandria. All because of this ugly brown heap.

Rafica brought them all down from their heights by taking a clean soft cloth and covering the mound of vellum. ''We'll start tomorrow.''

''What are you doing, honey,'' Sandi drawled, ''keeping the dust off it?'' She winked at Tom. Rafica laughed and they went back to work.

All day in the hot little room Robyn's thoughts played around the dust-encrusted mass of manuscript lying under its white cover.

Her hands weren't steady today. Her mind flew too easily in all directions. There were mysteries all around her—in the parchment, in the wind, in the sudden disarray of her personal life. She noticed that the hieroglyphics on the fragment she was holding in her tweezers were clear enough for easy reading. It was part of a priestly hymn to the god Ptah.

O Ptah, First in Wisdom,
give me of your understanding that I may not. . . .

The cracked edge of the papyrus ended the ancient
plea. A picture of Sayed came to her strongly. "Give
me of your understanding that I may not..." she
whispered, "be foolish."

Rafica came back with a tray of small pieces of
vellum sifted from the site where the larger mass had
been found. They worked until they heard the others
securing the excavation outside. Large tarpaulins
were being placed over the sides of the hole to protect
the niches from wind and from the wild desert dogs
that looked for shelter at night. The wobbly fencing
that surrounded the area of the excavation was pulled
together at one corner and locked.

Just when it was time to leave, Huntley Saunders
drove up with his white Mercedes and his driver, Abdul. Rafica was displeased. "Now we must stay until
he decides to go," she whispered.

He walked around for a while, talking with Tom
and George. From the sounds of the loud conversation that drifted toward the little workroom, he was
trying to impress them with his knowledge. Finally he
bustled over and called out greetings from the doorway.

"Fine work you're doing, Miss Rafica, Miss
Robyn." He leaned over a sorting tray that contained
part of the day's efforts. "Aha! Very professional.
Did something of the same myself, only it was shards
of pots and bits of Incan gold, at one of the digs
I was on in Ecuador. That's South America, little
lady." He threw the information at Rafica, who
nodded, a pinch of irritation around her soft
lips.

"We're leaving now, Mr. Saunders." Her voice was gently matter-of-fact.

"Go right ahead. I'll just poke around here for a while. I'll close the door tight when I leave." He reached to pick up a cataloged fragment of papyrus.

"Please don't handle that!" Rafica's voice had a new edge.

"Listen, little one, I've got a right to be here. I'm no dumb tourist."

"The scrolls are my responsibility, and I'll stay until you are ready to go."

"Okay," he responded, shrugging. Robyn took the fragment from his plump fingers and laid it back in place. "Well, I must say, you're good little mother hens. How many scrolls would you say we have?"

Rafica gave an expressive glance at Robyn. "We haven't any complete scrolls. We have parts of a large number of them, and when we get the fragments in order we may have a few complete ones. These pieces of manuscript have been badly damaged, probably because the scrolls were originally put into the chamber in haste. That's why we hope the lower room will be full of better-preserved scrolls."

Huntley Saunders nodded. "If it's true, we can claim a find to challenge Tut. Well, I guess I can't hold you up any longer. Let's lock up the stuff. It's lucky everybody's honest. Collectors would pay a pretty penny for even a few of these fragments."

He strolled out of the room. Rafica waited until he had driven off, then turned on the outside night lights and locked the workroom door.

They rode silently home in Mohammed's big station wagon. Sandi sat by Tom and seemed to go to sleep partway through the drive. Her curly blond head dropped against his shoulder. Tom smiled. "The poor kid's run out of steam." He adjusted his body so that her head rested more easily. George was asleep spread across the far back seat.

Robyn's thoughts moved unwillingly toward Sayed. Every car sound during the day had started her hoping that he had come. Even the provocative discovery of the parchment had only lifted her spirits for a time. She was still angry with herself for being so finely tuned toward his presence. "It's got to stop," she muttered.

"What did you say?" Rafica turned her sad dark eyes toward her.

"Nothing."

A wisp of a smile crossed Rafica's face. "You are tired, my sister."

Robyn pulled herself together. "I'm going to eat in my room tonight. Will you join me as my guest, Rafica? Please?"

Rafica regarded her questioningly. "All right, I'd like that. Too often I have an appointment with loneliness."

"And that's one thing we won't talk about. Let's have a positive-thinking evening!"

Over dinner they kept away from uncomfortable subjects, except to dissect Huntley Saunders. "I cannot trust him," Rafica concluded. "We must be doubly careful with the workroom."

They laughed over the bits of Arabic that Rafica tried to explain, enjoying the feelings of sisterly affection that enveloped them. Rafica left early and Robyn slept. In her dreams Sayed was always walking swiftly away from her while she called after him.

SAYED WAS AT THE DIG in the morning, examining the
site with a new drill foreman from a Cairo engineer-
ing company. He waved a greeting to the group and
turned back to his business. Robyn envied Rafica,
who could go down into the dig where he was standing. She stuck to her work and had finished sorting
two trays when Sayed entered the hot cluttered room
with Tom and Rafica.

"So we have a find." Sayed nodded to Robyn and
lifted the cloth from the brown pile of parchment. He
blew out a surprised breath. *"Ya salam!"* He turned
to beam at all of them. "Praise to God,—it's wonderful!" He touched the crisp mass of material with gentle fingers and looked at the chemicals Tom had
brought. "That should be good."

Then he sighed expressively. "I wish I had time to
help with this, but I trust you, dear ladies. Your nim-
ble hands will bring these words to life again. But let
us get the other things cataloged first."

He clapped a hand on Tom's shoulder. "I know,
you want to find a clue. But have patience." They
went back to the excavation again.

"How can he wait?" Robyn said. "I'd be halfway
through it by now."

Rafica laughed. "We in Egypt know how to control our hopes. Remember the Sphinx. We are well
used to patience."

The day moved faster than the day before because
Robyn could see Sayed's graceful figure at work in
the distance. At the noon break old Bahiya appeared
with her troop of children. Sayed greeted her respectfully and gave some sweets to the children. She had
something on her mind and stood purposefully, looking from Sayed to Robyn, her deep-set black eyes

glinting. She gave a laugh and nodded her regal head toward Sayed.

"*Alim.*" Her long finger pointed at him, then swung around to point at the dig. "*Maktába qadim.*"

Tom leaned over to Robyn's ear. "She called our esteemed leader a learned man. Now she says, 'Library of the ancient ones.'"

"*Ya rit!*" Sayed smiled.

Tom translated again, "I wish it were!"

Bahiya's face lost its smile. "*Tabt.*" Her hand pointed down. "*Muktir!*" Her eyes were on Sayed's face, almost beseeching. She switched to English. "Here is danger, wise man. . .not to lose your treasure!" Her eyes came around to Robyn. "*Letif*—listen to heart. After moon, tears, but only if not see clear. Not be afraid. You find answer in wind, *sitt.*" She turned with a colorful whirl of her long skirts and strode away, the children following silently in her wake.

"She likes you, Robyn." Tom put a friendly hand on her shoulder. "She called you pretty—did you know?"

"She did? That makes my day." Robyn laughed to cover her tension. Behind Bahiya's words had been something powerful. What did she mean this time—tears and moon and wind? And heart. And the warning again, just like in the sand reading, but this time directed to Sayed.

She caught Sandi watching them. Tom's hand was still lingering on her shoulder and she moved away from him. Tom was kind and reliable and like a brother. Pity for Sandi and irritation at the complexity of human emotions tightened her stomach.

After a quick bite of lunch they scattered to their various jobs. Rafica worked silently at her table for a while, then looked up with a serious face. "I wonder how the old woman knew about our hope for a link to the library. And why did she speak of danger to Dr. al-Rashad?"

"She probably picked up some talk."

"I suppose, but I have a strange feeling about it. Do you have any idea about the things she said to you?"

"No," Robyn lied, "it's just standard fortune-telling talk."

"Maybe." Rafica went back to work.

They made good progress in the afternoon. Robyn's eyes kept returning to the pile of parchment with the same feeling of anticipation that she used to have as a child when her father brought her a treat to unwrap—especially when it was something from his travels.

Rafica followed her gaze and laughed. "You should be an archaeologist. You have the natural curiosity of a scholar. Just think what we may discover in the parchments."

They finished the day's work, and had just covered everything carefully when George stuck his head into the doorway. "The cars will be late. You have forty-five minutes to amuse yourselves." He gave a little laugh at his weak joke and disappeared again.

Rafica looked unenthusiastic. "I'm tired of bending over the tables. How about walking to the hill to look at Dr. Tarsi's excavation?"

"Will he be there?"

"Don't worry, he's teaching today. Only lizards and sheep to greet us."

"Fine."

Robyn swung into a fast walk beside Rafica. She wouldn't let her eyes stray to the dig where Sayed and Tom were bent over something of interest.

When the small rise in ground dropped off again, Robyn saw below them a little valley and the outline of foundations and walls dug out of the sandy soil. They walked through the exposed foundations while Rafica pointed out where doors and windows had been—even traces of small rouned tiles where a decorative floor mosaic had been.

"There were wells in the old days, and here was an avenue of palms," Rafica said. "The wells must have made it possible for the gardens to be beautiful. You know that Dr. Tarsi thinks it belonged to Cleopatra."

"Do you think it did?"

Rafica shrugged. "She did have hideaways."

"Isn't it a bit small for a palace? Or maybe she played at being a village girl, like Marie Antoinette did."

"Or brought her lovers here." Rafica's eyes twinkled.

"Better than that, she might have cooked *foul* and *aish baladi* for Julius Caesar, and that's why he fell in love with her," Robyn said. "You see, I remember your lesson in Arabic."

They were laughing together over their mixed-up vision of the past when Sayed's voice suddenly reached them. "So this is where I find you."

Rafica was serious at once. "Oh, I'm sorry. Have we kept you waiting?"

He approached with long easy strides, and Robyn's uncomfortable heart gave a leap of joy. How beautiful he was, moving so lithely against the tawny cream of the desert sand—like a great lion pacing across his territory. "No, no. There's no problem," he answered Rafica. "The cars haven't come. Tom told me he saw you go this way, so I came along. To find...what? Two houris in a forgotten paradise, perhaps?" His smile made Robyn blink in the delight of it.

He looked around. "So, Rafica is showing you Hassan's little dream. I haven't been here for a while. He's found a few more walls, I see."

"Was it really Cleopatra's hideaway?" Robyn had to ask.

He shook his head with a rueful smile. "I'm afraid not. She could command much more than this. It's probably just a remnant of a small country estate. There is evidence of a tiny settlement, and what looks like a sand-filled canal. It might have been a way station for caravans." He turned and started back toward his own dig. "Come, I want to show you something." There was a playful light in his eyes.

"Aiwa," Rafica's voice urged Robyn. "You will like this."

They walked to the top of the hill from a different direction, and Robyn could see that several other ancient walls made an enclosure just below the rim of the embankment. Sayed went into one square area that had once been a room and sat on a section of crumbled wall. Rafica crouched down near him, while Robyn stood wondering what was so interesting about this bit of desert hill. She could see Sayed's excavation from where she stood—the great find of scroll fragments so close to Hassan Tarsi's painstaking little dig site. No wonder the Iranian was disgruntled.

Rafica had picked up a shard of pottery, one of a large number strewn around the area. Then she and Sayed were both leaning over scratching at the loose soil. "Ah," she exclaimed, picking up a gleaming bit of something from the earth. She held it on the palm of her hand toward Robyn. It was iridescent in the sunlight.

Robyn leaned close. It was a small broken piece of ancient glass, glowing with prismatic color.

Just then Sayed plucked another larger piece of glass from his mini excavation. They both laughed at Robyn's surprise.

"We call it the glass factory," Sayed said. "Undoubtedly it was a store that sold glass, and maybe manufactured it, too. Get yourself a shard of pottery and dig for treasure." He offered her his own jagged piece. "Come here by me. It seems to be a good spot."

She took the shard and their fingers touched briefly, sending signals of pleasure rippling within her. Sitting on the wall next to him, she began scooping in the earth, so conscious of Sayed's nearness, of his strong hand moving in the loose sand, that she could hardly concentrate. Then a quick gleam of blue green radiated up from her own little trench.

With a quick breath she pulled it out of the embracing earth. It was a delicate curved handle, about an inch long. "Look!"

Sayed took it from her hand and held it to the sun. The light from it illuminated his eyes even more than usual, making them glow with changing flecks of blue. "Some lovely lady's perfume bottle—at least the handle of it. Not bad," he added, smiling.

Rafica found another fragment and then there was

silence except for the scraping of their improvised trowels. Robyn was aware that Sayed had changed the rhythm of his digging and was driving his little tool deeper, using his left hand to probe for something. Then her own efforts showed another sparkle of color—this time a round button of glass with a broken stem. No doubt a bottle stopper.

Sayed said softly, "I'll trade your two pieces for one of mine. Are you willing to take a chance?" He held something in his closed hand. Rafica stopped digging to watch. "Your two...for my one," he urged.

"Should I, Rafica? All right," Robyn whispered, holding out her two bits of glass.

"Close your eyes." He laughed tantalizingly.

She obeyed and felt him take the pieces from her hand. Then something else was placed on her palm and Sayed's warm hand closed over hers. It was a smoothly shaped small tube of some sort, but Sayed still held her fingers closed with his own. He couldn't have realized the effect his firm touch had on her. She didn't move.

"Now you can look." His voice was teasing and indulgent as he released her hand. She opened her eyes to see what she held, and was delighted.

"Oh," she exclaimed, as excited as a child, and held it up for Rafica to see. The tiny glass bottle was perfect except for a slight nick at its rim. It was filled with earth and encrusted with a grayish material, through which a flash of iridescence showed.

Sayed took it from her hand and with his thumbnail flicked off a piece of the gray film. Underneath was a swirled pattern of color within the glass itself. He flicked off another piece. "The rust of glass," he said, handing it back. "You can clean it later. Rafica can show you."

Rafica's delicate brown hand reached out and took the sparkling little object. "I believe it is a tear bottle—or maybe a perfume vial," she said slowly.

"Hmm," Sayed's voice purred, "a tear bottle! According to the sheikha it was moon, then tears... and after that, wind. But we seem to have changed the order."

So he had paid attention to old Bahiya!

Rafica gave the vial back to her with a tinge of concern on her face but with no comments.

"You bring luck, Robyn," Sayed went on. "I haven't found anything but broken pieces here for a long time." He put a strong finger under her chin, lifting her face from her contemplation of the tiny bottle. "Are you pleased with your gift?"

"My gift?" She suddenly realized that it hadn't been a game—he had given her the bottle. Bright color flooded under her skin, drawn there by surprise and by the penetrating energy of his eyes so near to hers. "I...I thought..." she stammered. "Is it really for me? How wonderful!" She held the bottle to her cheek, absorbing the essence. This was something that had come to her straight from long ago, from out of the Egyptian earth.

Rafica and Sayed smiled. "It is yours now." Sayed took her hand and closed her fingers around the vial again.

She made a strong effort to keep her emotions in line. The natural thing would have been to move her other hand over his, but she didn't dare. "Thank you. If I could have chosen any gift, it would have been this."

He released her hand and said to Rafica, "Do you think I have now made up sufficiently for my poor conduct when Robyn first came?"

Serious brown eyes met his and Rafica said in her soft voice, "A gift given from a true motive is without price."

A sudden thought flashed into Robyn's head. "Isn't this part of Dr. Tarsi's dig?"

"No, this is part of our dig and this is the first place I excavated a little, soon realizing I was in the wrong spot. But we discovered the glass." Sayed smiled. "Don't worry, I am entitled to a few things, and so is your university. But I would not report you for picking up some of the innumerable shards of pottery that lie all over this area, and small pieces of glass come under the same heading. As for Hassan, he doesn't know about the glass. We've found only scraps, as I told you. Keep your tiny memento with an easy conscience."

Robyn sighed. She would cherish the luminous little bottle forever. The earth inside it was part of the joy. She put it to her nose and thought she could detect a faint flowery perfume.

Just then a horn blast sent its ragged sound toward them and there were distant calls from the camp. "Tom needs me to load up the equipment and make a last inspection. Come as quickly as you can." Sayed stood up and sped toward the camp with a long, easy gait. So might Pharaoh's trusted messenger have run, his supple feet touching the sand lightly, Robyn thought. In the distance Sayed's loose white shirt over khaki cotton trousers gave the illusion of a short robe.

"We'd better move, too." Rafica dropped her

piece of broken pottery and stood up. The two glass pieces that Robyn had dug up lay on top of the wall where Sayed had left them. While Rafica retied her scarf, Robyn pulled her own off and put the two blue green bits into it. She couldn't resist picking up the pottery shard that Sayed had used, and her own, as well. She wrapped the precious vial in one corner of the material and folded the whole collection into a little package.

She would always feel the warmth of this Egyptian sun and sense the strangely soft desert breeze. Always she would see Sayed's strong fingers on the shard he had used. Whenever she wished, these small things would bring back that moment of joy, when he had put the bottle into her hand and held it there.

Rafica turned back toward the dig and Robyn followed. The Egyptian woman's face was shadowed by some tension, and partway back she spoke hesitantly. "My sister, I must say something to you. Sayed al-Rashad is a fine man, a kind man. He is on top of his field of work and very well respected. But he is now nearly forty years of age and has not married. This is not usual for a man of Islam."

Robyn felt her own body grow tense. She took breath to disclaim interest in him, but Rafica gestured almost impatiently. "Let me finish, Robyn," she said, and stopped walking. Robyn stopped beside her reluctantly. "There is much you don't know about Dr. al-Rashad—his mother, for instance. She is English and very charming and elegant. You surely have noticed his unusual eyes, which come from her."

Robyn's heart felt constricted, as if it wanted to ward off any incoming hurt.

Rafica continued, "His parents were widely known for their devotion to each other. When his father died ten years ago, Dr. al-Rashad drew even closer to his mother. It was correct for him to take on the responsibilities of the family, but life at the family home near Cairo is very private and it is not easy to become a part of it."

Robyn immediately envisioned a cool, dignified, unapproachable matriarch with lapis eyes that were used to showing disapproval. She was no match for such a woman, and she would not wish to enter where she wasn't wanted. She shivered in the warm air.

"People who know Dr. al-Rashad well are aware of his...his reputation. Women are all drawn to him, and if he is only a little kind they follow him like sheep, or maybe I should say like purring cats with claws." She sighed and went on. "He is amused, a little flattered, but mostly annoyed by it all. He does have women friends who come and go. They are usually beautiful—what you would call of the jet-set sophistication." She looked with deep concern into Robyn's eyes. "I see him being attentive to you, my sister, but I hope you keep your heart cool. It is best. Truly, it is best." She turned away abruptly and started trudging through the sand again.

Robyn hurried to catch up, her mind aching with a kind of shame. Was she so obvious that Rafica could see it? Sayed had played with her feelings expertly today. No doubt he was trying to be gallant to the university observer, to make up for a bad start. It was good politics. A glass bauble would be enough to keep her adoring and docile, she realized. She was probably not the first woman to be given one.

Again she regretted her earlier mistake. She should have told him that she had knowledge of archaeology, that she had the academic credentials to back that knowledge up, instead of letting him believe her to be just another troublesome amateur, another of Dr. Wayland's American girls. What a consummate master she was at handling things, she thought drearily as she got into Fawzi's car with Rafica and George. Sayed had already left in Mohammed's car with Tom, Sandi and Dr. Gaddabi.

Robyn quickly calculated what time it was in California. It would be early in the morning there, not too early to place a call to Dr. Wayland. It shouldn't be necessary for her to stay much longer in Egypt, she reasoned unhappily to herself. The contracts were all approved and signed; she had taken notes on the status of the dig. Tom could easily relay any news of importance via telex. Who could tell how long it might be before Sayed's drill finally made its little hole and the borescope camera got its pictures of the sealed chamber? It could be weeks—and that would be too long, much too long.

Her shadowed face discouraged any conversation from Rafica or George, and when they reached the hotel Robyn walked immediately to the telephone switchboard behind the lobby.

"I want to call the United States," she said urgently.

The young woman at the switchboard looked sympathetic. "I'm so sorry. There is a twelve-hour wait. I will ring you in your room when it is possible."

Robyn's momentum came to a screeching halt. "No, don't. That won't be necessary," she said to the waiting face. "I'll place my call later."

"The telex is not working, either, miss," the operator said helpfully. "Maybe tomorrow things will be better."

"I hope so. Thanks." Robyn turned slowly and walked toward the elevators. She wasn't going to run away. There were bigger things at stake here than herself.

While she waited for the erratic elevator she decided what she should do and why. She would put her relationship with Sayed back on a dignified footing where it belonged. How naive of her to think that he was anything more than what he was...a man of another culture trying to draw the best from the people who worked for him.

There was no time like the present to start all over, she sighed to herself. Forget the silly dreams and see the cold truth. Whatever was going on inside her overactive imagination, the world obviously saw an unexceptional-looking young woman who blushed at everything and was obviously inexperienced in using her feminine equipment to good advantage. Hardly an enchantress who could speed a man's pulse just by the touch of her hand. She would leave Sayed to his own way of life and get on with her own, she decided with an emphatic nod of her dark blond head.

CHAPTER SIX

THE TELEPHONE BESIDE HER BED rang just as her alarm went off.

"Good morning, miss," the operator's voice said. "There is a message for you from Mr. Thomas Perkins. He left the hotel very early and wishes you to know that there is no work for today. He suggests that you may use the day for your own pleasure."

"Thank you, operator. Was there anything else?"

"Yes. Mr. Perkins regrets that you will have to hire a car yourself, as the regular drivers are unavailable. He left an envelope of tourist information for you at the desk. Good day, miss." The voice rung off.

She sat up in bed and stared at the telephone. Her resolve had survived the restless night; there would be no surrendering call placed to California. She smiled at her small victory and pulled her briefcase onto her lap.

Her work was in terrible disorder because of her distractions and her fatigue. This morning she felt newly vitalized, and she had days of notes to catch up on. At least Sayed would never be able to fault her thoroughness; every *i* would be dotted, every observation duly documented. She was determined to make the case for additional funding so convincing that no committee could refuse it.

Carefully she filled in the dry details of the dig—the number of significant scroll fragments, the vellum, the number of workers, the problems with the drill. It was a far cry from what her sentimental aunt called a "heart diary." With her pen at rest, she felt a wave of nostalgia come over her, almost as if she was already looking back on this whole Egyptian interlude.

In a way she wanted to record every thought and sensation, not to let memory fade any of the beauty or the confusion of heart that had flowed through her every day—even if it hurt her to recollect it. Sayed's disturbing blue glance, his graceful strong body, the exciting vibration of his presence no matter what mood he was in—she wanted it all to be imprinted on her memory forever. And Egypt itself—the wonderful faces of the people, the color of the sunset sky, the sound of the soft waves on the shore, the vital life that grew from the dark moist earth. When she was old, would all of this be relived like a tiny gem of experience, one that had promised so much and had gone nowhere?

With a stab of frustration she gripped her pen and went on putting the dull details into her work journal. She should be grateful for a free day so that she could gather her dignity and composure and meet Sayed again from a new position of strength. Tomorrow would be soon enough.

When her work was done, Robyn wandered out onto her balcony, enjoying the soft warm breeze from the water. Below, sunbathers from the hotel sprawled beside their umbrellas on a walled sandy strip and anglers dropped lines from the small pier. All at once she was impatient to explore the city.

She dressed comfortably in a soft dusty-blue sleeve-less dress with flat walking slippers, her hair pulled back into a ponytail and held with a matching ribbon. Downstairs the lobby was noisy with tourists as usual. Robyn ate a quick breakfast of coffee and rolls in the dining room. None of the crew was there, and she wondered if Rafica had taken this day to meet Karim. Did everything between men and women have to be painful? The rhetorical question had no answer. She picked up Tom's envelope of maps at the desk.

At the curb outside, the bustle of taxis was confus-ing. It had always been so simple to have Mohammed waiting there with his Peugeot, but now Robyn was beset by a swarm of eager drivers who competed with good humor for her fare. Using sign language and her handy traveler's guidebook, she was able to strike a deal with one driver, who promised to take her to the Greco-Roman Museum for seventy-five piasters. The other drivers returned to their cigarettes and gossip, out of the corners of their eyes alert for customers.

The driver started out through the shaded roads, and had almost reached the imposing wall at the en-trance to Montaza Park when the old taxi lurched. A sighing sound signaled a flat tire. He pulled over to the roadside and got out. All around them were grass and blooming flower beds.

"I am sorry," he said in careful English. "I change the tire. You wait."

While he worked busily with his tools, Robyn strolled across the lawn and admired the flowers. From out of nowhere a brown hand held out several pink and blue asters, and she looked up into the benevolent face of an elderly gardener.

"For you, lady." He smiled with a flash of gold-filled teeth. He watched as she admired his gift.

The sun was growing hotter, and she felt its warm fingers exploring her head and shoulders. The gardener tried to talk to her with bits of English and Arabic. "Ingleezi?" She shook her head. "Ameerica?" She nodded. *"Aiwa,"* he said respectfully, reaching out to shake her hand. *"Kuli en nas hum ikhwan*—all men brothers!"

A car swerved down the road from the hotel and drew up with a sudden screech beside her. It was Sayed's Fiat.

"What is happening, Robyn?" He caught sight of the driver laboring with the ancient-looking jack. At the same time the gardener burst into Arabic, punctuated by wide gestures.

"He says you're stuck," Sayed informed her, chuckling. "Where were you going?"

"Into Alex. I haven't seen much of it except at breakneck speed." Robyn heard the note of complaint in her voice, but couldn't help it. She really didn't want to see Sayed right now, for she hadn't made up her mind how she was going to handle him. "I was going to the museum and maybe walk to some of the old places in the city."

"Hop in." Sayed laughed again. "Better me than another flat tire. I won't bite," he assured her when she hesitated. "And I'm going to the museum myself; a happy coincidence." He noted her disbelief. "It's true! I want to get a book from their library. And...I have a meeting." His eyes sparkled. "Make up your mind, little one, I can't wait all day!"

"All right, but I've got to pay the man." She drew out her purse but Sayed forestalled her by tossing a folded bill to the driver, who had been watching interestedly. The two men exchanged a flow of rapid Arabic.

"He knows who I am," Sayed told her, grinning, his white teeth gleaming with the sun's reflection. "I told him you are a scholarly lady from the States who is working on my dig. Get in and try to look like a scholar." He revved the motor while Robyn scuttled forward and climbed into the sporty little Fiat. She had never seen Sayed so lighthearted and playful.

They drove away amid the *salams* and smiles of the driver and the gardener. The police at the gate gave them a respectful wave. For the first few minutes they drove in silence, merging with the traffic along the corniche that edged the bright blue bay. Robyn took a long deep breath. Dr. al-Rashad didn't make it easy for her to start implementing her sober resolve. Here was the blue sky and blue sea, the neat white car and the firm dark hands of Sayed on its wheel.

How could serious misunderstandings possibly exist between them? If only time would bend, she thought, and they could ride like this forever... everything happy and just right. They could go back together through the barriers of time, visitors in history. She heard Sayed's voice, "A piaster for your thoughts."

Robyn shook herself. "I was just thinking about time travel," she said unguardedly.

"A good subject." His deep caressing voice set a soft shiver vibrating in her solar plexus, like the strange humming feeling she had had the day she first heard his voice. That awful day.

"And what about time travel?" he asked.

She slanted a look at him and saw his fine lips curved in a slight smile. "I was thinking, wouldn't it be wonderful if we could drive toward the city and suddenly things would be the way they once were. Maybe when Alexander first saw the bay, and then perhaps as it was when his general Ptolemy was building the city. I'd like to see what it was like here when Caesar fell in love with Cleopatra. . . ."

She heard him chuckle and could have gladly eaten those last words. Over the noise of traffic he said lightly, "I think I have surprised a romantic in you, efficient Robyn. I'm glad to see you're not all notes and typing, cataloging and observing." When he noted her rueful expression, for a moment his hand reached to enclose hers. "I shouldn't tease, should I?"

His hand returned to the steering wheel and his face grew serious. "I confess that I often have similar thoughts. I think every archaeologist is tantalized by that opaque veil of time, behind which he or she longs so much to see. Maybe someday one of your technically brilliant fellow Americans will invent a camera that can see through the veil and give us a clear picture of the past." He gave a sharp sigh. "What I wouldn't give to see the great library as it was; to walk through its doors and meet Euclid teaching a class, Archimedes working on his hydraulic pump." He turned his head and gave her an open look. "You see, I am not without my own dreams."

They smiled at each other and a spark of shared affinity glowed warmly in the air between them. They were silent again while Sayed maneuvered through a honking traffic jam, and then they sped along the seaside road. There were crowds of people on the beaches and in the rows of brightly painted concrete changing rooms that lined the waterfront. Men and children played in brief bathing suits, but the women sat fully dressed under their brightly colored umbrellas.

"Don't the ladies swim?" A thread of disapproval was obvious in Robyn's voice.

Sayed answered easily, "Oh, yes, but modestly, my friend."

"Humph. It wouldn't be much fun to be all wrapped up in wet cloth."

"This is Islam, my dear; women are expected to be modest. It makes for a better society."

Robyn looked at the tight revealing bathing suits of many of the men. "And what about the men?"

"What about them?" he said smoothly, a deep blue twinkle in his eyes. "A man doesn't want his women displayed for the desires of his fellows."

She smiled a little. "I'm not criticizing your ways, it's just that American women are used to more freedom."

"I know that very well, but are they more happy?" His voice was deep and soft. "It's not easy for a woman to move alone in the pursuit of fulfillment. Should not society and family play a helpful role toward this end?"

Before she could answer he went on, "Take, for example, our friend Sandi. Does she receive happiness in her sexual encounters with men? I think she longs for something better; and I regret to say that the women students from Western nations who come here to work are more like men in their personal aggressiveness."

Robyn couldn't think of a good answer, so she remained silent. Again his warm hand touched hers. "Don't be upset. I have met many fine women in your country and some silly ones; it is the same everywhere. If a woman wants to play the fool, then the rules of Islam can only try to make her pathway more difficult."

"But I have read that you stone women who have committed—"

He swung suddenly off the corniche and onto a small road, stopping Robyn's words in midsentence. "I have never stoned a woman in my life!" His eyes were teasing again as he reached over to put his arm across the back of her seat. "If we were in our time machine, where do you think we would be?" he asked.

He had brought the car to a halt near a little statue, in an area planted with dusty trees. A high chain fence and a gate barred the view to what appeared to be a jutting finger of land extending a short way out into the harbor. It looked like a military installation, with radar discs and other large antennas.

She recalled Tom's quick remarks about the old royal sector as they had sped past on her first day. "I think I know where we are." She didn't know how vividly bright her eyes had grown as she scanned the long curve of the harbor. "How sad that nothing is left. This is Lochias Point, isn't it? And the palaces of the Ptolemaic kings were built on it. And over there—" she pointed to a long peninsula at the western end of the harbor, where small boats bobbed against their moorings and a fortresslike building loomed "—that's the Pharos island. And that building is where the wonderful lighthouse used to be." She said it all on one long, eager breath as she suddenly comprehended the pattern to the city. All these days in Alexandria and she had never given herself the time to stop and really look at it—the way it had been laid out by Alexander the Great twenty-three hundred years before.

"Too bad we can't blow the veils of time away, isn't it? But Cleopatra might not like to find us sitting in the middle of her ancestral palace."

"Is this the very spot?" Robyn was ready to be swept into the romantic possibilities. She peered down at the ground as if she might really see something that wasn't there.

His smile deepened. "Yes, all around us. The sea has claimed some of it, but we know most surely that it was here the kings and queens lived and loved and died, sometimes horribly and sometimes in joy."

Sayed put the car into gear and raced out into traffic again. "How much do you know about this city?"

"Past or present?" she asked.

"For instance, do you know that this harbor has a name? It is the Eastern Harbor, the historic and ancient arc around which the original city was built according to Alexander's dictates. Beyond this harbor is another, which has a beautiful Greek name, Eunostos—the harbor of happy return. It is that one that became the principal center for shipping in modern times, after the Eastern Harbor became too shallow and cluttered with the debris of centuries. When Alexander came here he found one great bay perfect for ships, and a long thin island just offshore—Pharos. He built a causeway to connect the island to the shore, bisecting the harbor." He turned to Robyn. "Can you forgive my pedantic conversation? I am too used to standing before a classroom of students and declaiming my vast knowledge.''

Robyn had to laugh at his beseeching eyes. She could have forgiven him almost anything at that moment. ''We aren't going to the museum, are we?'' she asked as the car continued along the coast.

Sayed just smiled and kept driving. They passed a large and beautiful old mosque, drawing up to the curb when a call to prayer began to fall in mellow cadences from the loudspeaker atop the mosque's minaret. Sayed looked intently at Robyn and his quiet voice echoed in English the words of the muezzin. ''*Allahu 'Akbar.* Only God is great....'' She sat spellbound by the melody of the ancient devotional phrases and their translation. When the last long note faded she had to blink away tears of emotion.

A flicker of tenderness moved over Sayed's face as he watched her. With a gentle finger he caught a tear on her cheek and wiped it away.

''It is so beautiful,'' she whispered, a little abashed to be showing feminine weakness. ''Were you...I mean, wasn't it necessary for you to pray?''

''You expected me to leave the car and prostrate myself on the street, facing east?'' he said indulgently. ''It is left to us to answer the five daily calls to prayer in our own manner and as best we can.'' He started the car and drove along crowded streets where the buildings were older and the atmosphere was not as modern as the rest of Alexandria. They passed a small yacht harbor and a long seawall. ''And you are correct, the museum is back in the center of the city. I am taking you on a short tour of the oldest part of Alexandria. That's the yacht club down there and we are now on Alexander's causeway, which through the ages has grown very broad and solid.''

He watched as she leaned close to the car window, taking everything in with her eyes. "You are a most satisfying sightseer, Robyn, and I am glad I found you stranded in Montaza Park."

Robyn felt a rush of pleasure. "You are very kind to do this. It's wonderful to see things with someone who cares about...." All at once she was undone by the clear gentleness in his face and the light of his smile. "I mean...it's not so much fun to see things alone that you've always dreamed about. My father promised to take me here someday."

"You are saying that I am a substitute father—so be it."

She couldn't read his smile, but it seemed to have changed until it was merely polite. "But I didn't intend...that is, I'm very happy you're with me...," A blush was sending a hot wave up her cheeks.

They were moving along a narrow road with the sea on one side and a high gated wall on the other. Above the wall appeared the giant stone sides of a fortress tower. "Don't explain," he said. "I'm not sure you know what you mean, and perhaps I don't know what I mean, either." He stopped the car and left the motor idling. "That is what is left of the Pharos lighthouse."

With her eyes she followed the tower upward as it loomed against the brilliance of the azure sky.

"It has had a long and stormy past, this place," he said, with more meaning in his voice than those simple words implied. Then he put the car into gear and executed a quick turn. "I'm afraid we have to leave. Another day I can show you more. I find it easy to forget time because I'm happy when I'm with you."

The little car threaded its way back through streets

teeming with traffic, people, goats and dogs, until they were again on the mainland.

Robyn hugged those last words of his as if they were precious jewels: "I'm happy when I'm with you."

"If you are free for lunch, I will take you to a very special place after I finish my meeting at the museum. Are you free, Miss Douglas?" he asked in a playful voice.

"I'd love to, but I don't want to interfere with your work."

"Consider it an order, then, from the chief of your dig," he said with a smile. She relaxed a little in the warmth of his mood and smiled back. They sped through squares, past monuments to modern heroes of the land, and finally drew up in a parking area in front of a long white wall. Behind the barrier was a building with classic pillars at its entrance. The Greco-Roman Museum.

Sayed's face became their entrance ticket at the door, and he hurried her across a columned walkway, through a garden filled with ancient statuary and into the museum office, where he introduced her to several smiling members of the staff.

"I have a meeting," he said briefly. "They'll look after you." She watched his tall back disappear into other offices. Almost at the same moment an old man came in with a tray of tiny cups steaming with the thick Turkish coffee that Robyn had come to relish.

She accepted the offer of a tour by two of the staff members, a young man and a large, older woman. The museum was filled with treasures, many of them standing in the open, inviting a secret touch. Robyn felt obligated to admire the particular objects that were pointed out to her, but her eyes could hardly take in the variety of wonderful things collected there.

They swept her through rooms of Byzantine and early-Christian artifacts and back through time to the founding of the city. A huge mosaic of a helmeted woman—the spirit of Alexandria—gazed from a wall with a fierce vital glare.

In other rooms there was ancient glass glowing with luminous colors, reminding her of her own tiny tear vial. She hung over display cases full of gold and silver coins etched with the faces of Ptolemaic kings and queens.

Busts of Roman emperors masquerading as Egyptian pharaohs looked stolidly out of agate eyes, and Julius Caesar, too proud to be anything but the greatest of the Romans, smiled ironically from his marble bust. And there was Alexander—wild, strange Alexander with his classic face, his shock of curling hair and poutingly curved lips.

It was not the grandeur of the kings that was as catching to Robyn's heart as the little inscriptions of love on fragments of stone or papyrus. In one case a broken wooden comb lay beside a small panpipe, its ancient fragile reeds never to make music again.

She was taken up a spiral metal staircase to the museum library and shown a book that Napoleon had commissioned his engineers and artists to illustrate when he temporarily controlled Egypt. The large pages were dotted with a brownish mold, but the pictures were still clear enough to see. Napoleon's book showed the Egypt of 1800, with Alexandria a mere sand-covered ruin by the bay.

More coffee waited downstairs, and a note from Sayed. His swift flowing writing was decisive and energetic.

Robyn, I must go to the University of Alexandria at once to see representatives of the Antiquities Department. Our friend Saunders has opened his large mouth again and I have to repair the damage. I will discuss this with you later. Forgive me for not waiting for you. You will find Hosni, an honest taxi driver, waiting for you outside. He is fully paid and tipped, and will go where you instruct. Thank you for this morning.

Yours, Sayed

Robyn shared his exasperation. How could Huntley Saunders be so dense? She felt like sending him home to his oil wells like a naughty child, but she still didn't know what the university and Dr. Wayland expected her to do in this case. They certainly hadn't planned on having their chief donor behave so outlandishly. This time there was no doubt in her mind that Dr. Wayland would have to be called.

She thanked the museum staff for their kindness and found Hosni in his cab at the foot of the museum steps. Back at the hotel again, she placed a call to Dr. Wayland. This time her head was clear and she knew exactly what she wanted to say to him. While she waited for the connection to be made she reread Sayed's note. It was full of his presence and she impulsively held it against her heart. Something of the warm feel of his hand seemed to touch her from the paper. With a rush of good sense she stopped herself just as a picture of his finely cut lips and his amber skin crowded into her mind. *What a wonderful lover he would be,* a familiar little voice whispered in her ear before she had her guard up.

Her call came through quickly, and Dr. Wayland's sleepy voice sounded close by. "Robyn, what's going on? I'm sure you're not waking me up just for fun."

Rapidly she outlined the problem with Huntley Saunders.

"Damn fool!" his voice said explosively. "Well, my girl, you're the representative of the university— my stand-in. I give you full authority to do what you think best. Tell our adolescent donor I know about his stupidity and that I'll publicly deny anything he says if it's out of line. What does Sayed say about it?"

"He's very angry. I suppose we will both confront Mr. Saunders."

"Good. By the way, how do you like him? Sayed, I mean."

"He's..." she hesitated, "he's a fine worker under very difficult circumstances—and I like him. He's cooperative and knows what he wants. Everybody respects him, but I guess you know that. He's a nice man and a fine scholar."

She heard Dr. Wayland's chuckle. "Then you're not head over heels in love with him as yet, eh?"

"Of course not!" she said indignantly.

"That's good, m'dear. Now don't get nervous. You can handle yourself—with that Saunders fellow, I mean." He chuckled again. "What did Sayed say when he found out he had a young woman and not an old professor on his hands? I heard my telex didn't make it past Cairo."

"He. . . wasn't pleased. But he thought it over and apologized."

There was outright laughter on the other end of the line. "That's a first for Sayed. Apologized, eh? Well, it looks like I picked the right deputy. Does he know you're on the way to your doctorate?"

"No!" she grated. "And he doesn't know of my specialty on manuscripts, either."

"And he doesn't know about your father?"

"That's something I should have told him on the first day. It would have saved misunderstandings." She was sounding severe and primly virginal again, she knew.

"Do what you want; you're levelheaded. Now, don't hang up yet. What's the status of the dig?"

The connection started to fade, then came back again. Robyn raised her voice. "There are—or were— quite a few scrolls, but most of them are in fragments. It's slow work getting them out of the earth. I'm helping Sayed's—Dr. al-Rashad's—assistant, a dear young Egyptian woman who is a graduate student from Cairo University. We're numbering the fragments and doing the best we can before we send them to Alex. The equipment is very limited, and so is help, and the khamsin winds are building up—more each day."

"Any clue to the old library yet?" His voice took on the eager note of the dedicated searcher into the past.

"The fragments are mostly in Greek, some demotic script, and a scattering of hieroglyphs. From what I can see it's a collection of a lot of things, literary and scientific. I'm not quite as swift with the Greek—

they had careless handwriting then, too." A seven-thousand-miles-away laugh rewarded her little joke.

"Sounds good. I've read Sayed's latest report that just arrived in the mail. My God, it took three weeks to get here! He told me about the condition of the excavation in detail—the worn basketry and leather wrappings around the scrolls. . . all that. But no clues yet. . . ."

"I saw one small fragment that reads 'Apollonius,' and then a pi symbol. The rest is torn away. I thought it might be something."

"Could have been the scholar Apollonius of Perga, the geometer from the library," he sighed, "but Apollonius was as common a name as Robert or William. Too bad!"

"I know," she said in frustration.

"Keep looking. I'm sure you feel that funding should continue."

"Of course!" She heard her voice rise in tension. "It would be terrible not to go on now. . . and dangerous, now that the place is known. We haven't determined anything about the lower room except that it sounds hollow and there's a well-cut smooth stone floor with a seam down the center where two big pieces fit together. Working space is tight, and Dr. al-Rashad hopes the new drill will make a clean hole for the camera to drop into."

"I see. Robyn, I want you to write me a dated letter about all this. Make it good and exciting, and tell how unusual it is to find any papyrus fragments at all, let alone a few reasonably intact ones. You know how to word it. I have a donor on the string and it would help. Saunders won't play such a large part in this if we can get other financing. By the way, give my best to Sayed. Handsome dog, isn't he?''

''I'll write,'' she said in a sensible voice.

''Don't let Saunders get you down, m'dear. Help is coming from other funding sources. If we only had a proven link to the old library it would be easy. Well, keep me informed. I envy you!''

A click ended their conversation, and Robyn set the phone down. Her stomach still felt tight, and even Dr. Wayland's sympathy and granting of authority didn't help much. She still had to deal with Huntley Saunders somehow, and if she handled it badly he might make trouble for Sayed and the university. He could hire the best lawyers to make sure he got his way.

She wanted to talk to Sayed first. There was nothing to do but wait. Restlessly she roamed around her room, finally sitting down in one of the black leather chairs on the balcony to watch the waves in the bay and the activity on the narrow sandy beach directly below. The balmy sea air urged her into a light sleep, which was broken by the telephone's sharp ring. She hurried to answer.

Sayed's deep resonant voice spoke into her ear, making a shiver of pleasure ripple through her. She was getting used to her reaction and tried not to acknowledge it.

''Robyn, did Hosni bring you back in one piece?''

''Yes, thank you. He was very nice.'' How stilted she sounded, she observed with irritation. She took a deep breath to bring up Saunders's name, but he spoke first.

''You read in my note about our problem. That man is doing everything possible to ruin our work.

He will make us the butt of the press again. I've already had inquiries from *al-Ahram* in Cairo, and from American TV. He is claiming that we have found great lost manuscripts, written by famous names of antiquity. He is taking credit for the finds, of course.'' The angry vigor of his emotions flowed around her.

"I'm so sorry," she said defensively. "I didn't think he'd go so far, especially after his first press conference back home. It's really terrible...." She hesitated to say more, out of a nagging fear of Sayed's anger, but she had to. "I've already talked to Dr. Wayland," she said, her throat tight.

"So, and what did he say?"

"He was very unhappy. He told me that I had his authority to deal with Saunders—along with you, of course."

There was a brief, chilly silence and Sayed said, "Yes, you are the university representative. I'll phone Saunders and ask him to meet with us after dinner. I'll be dining with friends at the hotel and we can meet at the conversation pit in the lobby at nine o'clock."

"I'll be there." She tried to sound businesslike, but she didn't want him to think her ungrateful. "And thank you for a lovely morning. I really enjoyed the museum. Everyone was so kind...and the Pharos...." She was chattering and knew it. Sayed's quick sigh was audible.

"No thanks needed, Robyn. My pleasure, of course." His voice was politely brusque and her heart sank like a stone. "I'll be waiting in the lobby at nine."

"I'll be there," she repeated, and heard the sound of his receiver going down.

Angry tears burned her eyes. She had sounded like

an idiot, a silly chattery female. No wonder he'd been silent for a moment when she told him about getting Dr. Wayland's authority. She should have handled it better. It was like asking Sayed to see an authority figure in a pleasant child. The outside package was wrapped all wrong—in a female body, she thought, and too eager looking, too unsophisticated and. . . . "Oh, damn!" she exploded. The little brown birds on the balcony were pecking at crumbs she had spread out for them earlier. Her mind was flapping here and there like their whirring wings.

So he was going to have dinner with friends. Immediately an image of a svelte Egyptian couple and a beautiful dark-haired woman flashed into her head in full technicolor. They were having dinner with Sayed, laughing together like old friends. The woman was smiling at him from deep liquid eyes, and her slim hand with painted nails rested on his sleeve.

I can't believe myself, Robyn thought grimly. *The man is decent to me for half a day and I'm acting as stupid as Dr. Wayland's students.* Hadn't Rafica's words meant anything at all? They should have been enough to deflate her rampant emotions. Her father had always said she was creative, she thought, smiling ironically. How true. She was creating herself right into a mess of disappointment when she should know better.

She went into the bathroom and splashed cool water on her face. She wasn't pleased with the reflection that looked back at her from the mirror. The expression was still hopeful. The big smoky blue eyes were too sensitive. Even as she admonished herself a stab of jealous curiosity moved through her mind. Maybe she should dress and go to dinner in the dining room. The place was large, but most of it could be seen from a side table. At least she would see who was with him. . . .

That line of reasoning ended abruptly as she marched herself back into her room and lay down on her bed. She would force herself to concentrate on a book about demotic script in the Middle Kingdom, which Dr. Wayland had given to her for reading during the flight.

Her nerves jumped at a sudden ring of the phone. She reached for it expectantly. Perhaps Sayed had changed his plans. Perhaps. . . . She drew a deep breath to steady her voice. "Hello?"

"Hi, there, Robyn, honey," Huntley Saunders purred.

Her hackles rose and she lurched back to unwelcome reality. "Hello, Mr. Saunders."

"Is that any way to greet a friend, darlin'?"

"Why are you calling?"

"All business, eh? Okay, Miss Robyn, I just got a call from old Sayed. What do you know about this nine-o'clock meeting? I haven't got a clue, but I didn't like his tone with me."

"I don't know," she said, hating herself for being a coward.

"Listen, honey," he drawled, "I just happened to see you driving by downtown today in a little ol' white Fiat, sittin' next to Sayed just as plump as a plum. What do you think of that?"

"I'm sure Dr. al-Rashad will tell you what he has on his mind."

"I can't wait. I just got me a heavy date at nine. I'm two doors down and I'm comin' over to get to the bottom of this right now." The phone slammed down.

Robyn ran to the bathroom and dashed a comb through her hair. It hung loose, making her look even younger than she was. She gazed at the wide-eyed face in the mirror. "You're in for it now," she muttered, putting powder on her slightly red eyelids and dabbing lipstick on her mouth.

A rat-tat of knuckles sounded on the door and her guest strolled in, holding two glasses and a bottle in an ice bucket. "No hard feelings, Robyn. Brought us a little treat. Old Huntley's not such a bad guy, you know." He winked. He set his bucket on the coffee table, sat down on the couch in front of it and began to work on the loosened cork of his bottle of Dry Sack.

Robyn made sure that the door was left wide open and sat stiffly in the straight chair opposite him.

"Come on, Robyn, you look all pinched up on that chair. Be a sport and have a drinky-poo with ol' Uncle Huntley." His nose had a slightly pink blush and so did his soft sagging cheeks. This was obviously not his first drink of the evening. He eyed her with a teasing gleam. "Close the door. You're not my type, sweetie. Your hair's prettier down, though. I have to admit you're easy on a man's eyes. Real cute, in fact." His gaze faltered when she didn't move. "Aren't you goin' to close the door? Those room servants slip up and down the hall in their red pantaloons all the time."

She pulled herself together. It was now or never. She looked into his moist eyes. "Please don't pour a drink for me, Mr. Saunders. And I am leaving the door open because this is a Muslim country and they don't understand the freedom of a man coming into a woman's room. I value their good opinion, although no doubt they're used to foreign ways."

He laughed and his eyes narrowed. "You are a prim one! Well, if you don't want a drink, you're the one that's missin' out. Now what the hell is the hornet under ol' Sayed's saddle about? He practically ordered me to meet you both tonight. He's forgettin' that he's indebted to me for his little dig, and I didn't like his manner—not one bit."

A rush of dislike for the patronizing male on the couch gave her courage, and she spoke as she thought her father might have done under the circumstances. "I have talked with Dr. Wayland this afternoon. I informed him of the serious leak of information about finds at the dig. Not only that, the information is false, giving the impression that we have found scrolls written by famous people of antiquity. Someone has told the press that you are in charge of the excavations, as well. You know how unprofessional and unethical it is for such things to be said. The big Cairo newspaper, *al-Ahram*, as well as television reporters from the States have approached Dr. al-Rashad, and he is justifiably angry."

"So that's it!" He took a gulp of his drink and swished it around in his mouth while a bellicose expression hardened his face. "Listen, that guy al-Rashad doesn't have a prayer to find out what's in that room below if he can't use my borescope. Besides that, I've planned to give more funding. But I'm not layin' out another red cent if I don't get credit for it. Put that in your Dr. Wayland's ear!"

Righteous anger stiffened Robyn's backbone and brought sparks to her eyes. "We know that you're the one who is leaking this false information. Dr. Wayland asked me to tell you that he is prepared to deny all of your statements to the press and disassociate the university from your actions completely."

The face opposite her was growing redder by the moment, but she rushed on past his spluttering. "You must realize that since the borescope was bought from the fund for the excavation—contributed to by you and by other donors—you are being given credit for it only as a courtesy. I remember writing a letter to you from Dr. Wayland suggesting that such an instrument would be helpful in the dig. It was bought by the university, and you took charge of it only for the flight, if you recall."

"Well, I'll be damned! You're a little nip of a shrew. Who do you think you are?"

"I'm the university's representative, with authority to speak to the press here and make you look silly, Mr. Saunders. I'm sure you've been to parties, drinking out of your private flask and showing off. I can apologize to the press here for an American who is misinformed and incompetent—you." She held his sagging eyes with her own indignant ones. "One more word to the press about our project until it is properly announced, and I will go straight to the media here. Dr. Wayland will silence it at home."

A change came over his face and a wide false smile beamed at her. "You're a spunky kid. Hell, I may have talked a bit about the dig here and there—social chitchat—but the press boys got it all screwed up."

"You'd better not talk any more nonsense. This is a serious matter."

"I can always take my little ol' borescope and go home," he offered in a childish voice.

"It's not your borescope, remember?"

"Okay, but maybe I won't give any money for next year—"

"That's your privilege. Shall I call Dr. Wayland and say that you agree not to talk about the dig until permission is given?"

He assembled his features into an expression of amiability. "You're real pretty when you get mad, honey. Come on, no hard feelin's; Huntley's a good boy." He pushed his bulky body up from the couch and came around the table. Before she could move, his big perspiring hand was under her chin and his wet lips had planted a kiss on her surprised mouth. He chuckled, "That wasn't so bad, was it? Kiss and make up, that's what I always say."

She pushed away from him. "You had better leave immediately."

He was stretching a heavy hand toward her shoulder when a smooth voice cut him short. "I agree with Miss Douglas. You had better leave her room immediately." Sayed stood in the doorway.

The Texan's face twitched. "Well, well, I thought we were all meeting at nine," he leered, looking from Sayed to Robyn. "Guess you had other ideas first."

"Since we're all here, we might as well meet now." Sayed's voice was harsh and the blue coals of his eyes burned deep. "My dinner guests are late and I came to have a word with Miss Douglas about how to deal with you, sir. But I heard her say already precisely what I would have said, with this addition: if you plant any more lies in the news media I will have you barred from the dig and will tell the press why. I'm sure the international news services would find it interesting, especially since your family's company does so much business in foreign countries. I am willing to have you stay on as a silent observer, Mr. Saunders, provided—''

''How long have you been eavesdropping?''

''Long enough. Your words were audible down the hall. Do I have your promise?''

''Sure, sure. Don't make such a fuss. You know how a story gets taken out of context—just rolls up and keeps goin'.''

''Yes, and that's why it must not start. Do you understand?''

He nodded. ''We've got a little spitfire here. Who would have expected her to be so hot?'' He gave Robyn a sexy look, then winked at Sayed, but a shiver of ice went through Robyn at the spark of venom under his words. He was an enemy now.

He went out the door without taking his cocktail paraphernalia, and Sayed entered the room, where he turned a closed face to Robyn. ''I thought we were to confront him together—''

''I expected to, but he came to the door and said he couldn't meet us. He started demanding to know what it was about. He...he'd been drinking, and one thing led to another.''

''From what I heard, you handled the problem well, but you should have refused him entrance. It was unwise. And the liquor....'' He waved an impatient hand at the bucket and glasses.

''He brought it, but I wouldn't drink with him.'' She gestured to the unused glass.

Sayed's face softened a little. ''*Aiwa*. The man is a cur. But you left yourself at his mercy. What about the kiss I witnessed? If I had not appeared you would have had to struggle while he tried to use male persuasion on you. Could you have stopped him?''

She didn't see how vulnerable her face was at that moment, framed in its soft honey-dark waves of hair. "Of course I could have stopped him!" There was rebellion in her voice. What did he think she would have allowed? She wasn't an utter weakling.

"Please do not try to negotiate without me again." He paced restlessly to the balcony door and looked out at the night stars. She gazed at his erect back and broad shoulders silhouetted against the darkness. He was an ancient prince from the Old Kingdom, come to tantalize her with his vital energy and challenging maleness, even though he stood before her in a finely cut creamy linen suit and spoke to her of twentieth-century things.

He turned around to face her. "We'll see what he does. He is against us now. I called Dr. Wayland just before I came here, to verify his message to you. He told me to take care of you. But that's a lot to ask when I can't count on you to cooperate with me." His tone was fatherly and sent unreasonable irritation through her. Did he think she'd been lying to him when she said she had Dr. Wayland's authority? She wanted to say something to oppose his position as patriarch, but the cool blue of his eyes silenced her.

"I have friends who move in the wealthier circles of society. I will speak to them and alert others to our problem benefactor." He looked at the gold watch on his sun-dark wrist. "My dinner guests probably wonder where I am." He reached out and gave Robyn's shoulder a light pat. "Don't worry, you told him the truth. But you must stay away from him. His kind of man will find ways to bring a woman down to his level when he is thwarted." Again his fatherly tone grated on her nerves.

"I don't want anything to do with the man." She tried to hold his eyes with hers but he wasn't to be held.

He nodded and moved toward the doorway. "Until tomorrow, then. And you had best get rid of that." He waved at the bucket in passing. "Good night." The words washed across her with curt impersonality.

He closed the door behind him, leaving her with a feeling of frustration. He hadn't really understood what she was trying to do with Saunders. Suddenly the sight of the bucket and glasses infuriated her. She grabbed them up and strode the short distance down the hall, setting them by Huntley Saunders's door. "Let him fall over them," she muttered to herself, and stalked back to her room.

Her appetite had vanished. She had no desire to go into the dining room alone anyway, not now. Sayed could have dinner with all the exotic females he wanted, it was none of her business.

She undressed and showered and wrapped herself in her robe. The balcony was welcoming, and so was the gentle whisper of night air. The soft swish of the sea in her little bay and the flicker of the bright eternal stars began to soothe her. *I really am here—in Egypt, where I've always wanted to be,* she thought. *These are the stars that Cleopatra saw, and the same breeze that blew around the royal palaces on Lochias Point.*

Then why was she feeling so miserably lonely, when she had so much to think about, so much history to revel in? She held up her empty hand and looked at it, and a few hot tears blurred the starlight. *Just a warm hand and a gentle touch—that's all I want, no more. Someone with whom to share the wonder of this ancient land.* It was an almost audible voice inside her head that spoke.

She shook herself distractedly. She hadn't realized what a strong and stubborn streak of dreaminess she was afflicted with. At home it was never this bad. *But I didn't know Sayed al-Rashad then,* the voice explained.

A knock came at the door. She stiffened and it came again. After another second's hesitation she called out, "Yes?"

"Room service."

She opened the door and a smiling old man wheeled in a white-covered table. "But I didn't order—"

His face crinkled into a smile. "The gentleman did."

"What gentleman?" Her defenses were quickly rising against another onslaught from Huntley Saunders.

"The professor doctor. He say you have hard day; maybe not eat. You must have nice soup and salad." He set about whisking the silver covers from a steaming soup bowl and a plate topped with a crisp-looking salad, then he drew up a chair and held an open napkin out to her invitingly. With a little lift of heart she sat down and he grinned. "I come back to see if you want sweets or coffee."

She tasted the creamy vegetable soup and buttered a roll. Sayed did care. Maybe this was his way of showing approval. She sighed. *Maybe I don't understand Egyptian men—or is it just that I don't understand men, period.*

Another peculiar day with Sayed, another day of resolve, hope and misunderstanding. Tomorrow had better be an improvement, she thought, and set about ordering her thoughts for the coming day. The drill should be arriving anytime, and Sayed would be fully occupied with setting it up. She would have her hands full in the cataloging shed with Rafica and the manuscript fragments.

The fragments. She smiled to herself, thinking about the dark, dusty heap of vellum that fairly throbbed with possibilities. Something important was inside that dismal, timeless wad. She was certain of it, as certain as she had ever been about anything in her work with her father. The prospect of tomorrow took her thoughts away from herself, and she felt considerably better by the time she finished her small dinner.

The old waiter came back with a piece of light sweet pastry and a tiny cup of dark bitter coffee. "Big party downstairs," he said with a twinkle. "Nobody miss a little *Om Ali raisin kek*. Name of *kek* means 'mother of Ali.'" He left his gift on the coffee table and rolled out the dinner cart, waving away her thanks. His kindly smile was perceptive. "When sleep, forget trouble, and new morning sun show everything much clear."

CHAPTER SEVEN

ROBYN HAD BEEN WORKING diligently at her long table since the crew's arrival early that morning. She had already posted her letter to Dr. Wayland, knowing without doubt that it was going to help him pry money out of his prospective donors. She ate her lunch alone, then got back to work, feeling a kind of satisfaction to be doing her job well.

Rafica was hard at work at the dig and hadn't offered any explanation about where she'd spent her free day. Her mood was hard to fathom—cheerful on the surface, but with a shadow of misery buried beneath.

In the early afternoon Rafica suddenly appeared in the doorway. "Look what has been found!" Carefully she held up a disintegrating woven casing that still contained part of its scroll. Even as she mothered the scroll onto a sorting tray, a piece of it dropped away. "Look!" Rafica picked up the torn part delicately.

Along the bottom of it a picture had been painted. The artist had used the established style of old Egypt, but there was a flowing grace to it. This picture was less angular in its lines, Robyn noticed. "It's like the move toward naturalism of the Amarna period," she exclaimed. "How beautiful!"

Rafica gave her a thoughtful look. "You have studied that period?"

"Yes. I'm working on a paper about it at home."
Robyn stopped herself. "Just something that always
interested me," she added evasively.

"The painting is so unusual." Rafica held the curling piece gently on the table and both heads bent over
it. "It seems to be a canal with trees, just as in
modern times," Rafica said. The stylized trees did indeed line a canal; flowers and grasses grew on the
near bank, and among them a delicate feminine
figure was kneeling. Her arms were raised toward a
glow that was like blue sunlight, making a path of
color toward her.

Robyn was entranced. The tiny figure was like
hope itself, waiting for fulfillment to come. "How I
wish that this one could be read," she said with feeling.

"*Aiwa.* There is a wonderful story here, I am
sure." Rafica worked with the loose and torn edges
of the scroll, gingerly wrapping it and its almost
nonexistent casing in a sheet of soft plastic foam. She
took a quick drink from the bottle of Evian water on
the table and retied her head scarf. "Wish more
luck," she called back from the doorway, then headed back to the dig.

Robyn returned to work, but the picture on the
scroll stayed in her thoughts like a remembered romantic scent. It brought to the surface an odd feeling
of anticipation.

A sudden hot gust of wind pushed hard against the
door of the workroom. It slammed shut, disturbing
the tray of small papyrus pieces on Robyn's tray and
moving the new scroll precariously close to the edge
of the table. She had just reached over to reposition it

in its wrappings when a second heavy gust of wind swung the door open again. The scroll dislodged itself from its plastic and, to Robyn's horror, started to unroll in front of her, as though opened by an invisible hand.

She looked down at the beautiful flowing script on the papyrus and knew it immediately. It was the everyday writing style of old Egypt, the demotic script. Fascinated, she bent to study it. The long hours working with her father had engraved the ancient language in her mind. She had not forgotten. Automatically she reached for a fresh sheet of paper and began to read and copy. The urge was too great, the situation too strange. She had to find out what it said.

. . . I rose before dawn to wait by the canalside,
     hoping he would pass as he sometimes did . . . .

Oblivious to anything but the words, she wrote on:

He who is my destiny—
he comes like Horus, the blue-eyed god in the
     morning light.
And who am I that I dare to hope for his gaze
as he walks with his thoughts among the golden
     lotuses. . . .

Bahiya's old and wrinkled face flashed into her mind, and then the faraway voice of the ancient lovesick girl came to her. She felt painful tears cloud her eyes.

How can I speak my love to him?

The poignant whisper enfolded her:

... he is as far above me as the sky,
and I am no more to him than a small bird of the
morning at whom he smiles.
I would fly above his head to shelter him from
the sun,
and spread my wings over his breast to shield
him from harm...

A crease in the papyrus had made a line illegible.

... and I will take courage and stand in his path.
I will beg from him one favor—that he shall kiss
me once
so that I shall remember one taste of joy forever.
Mother Isis, who loved the golden king, Osiris, take my hand....

The next lines were hidden under the fold just beyond sight.

"What are you doing!" Sayed's angry voice shattered her concentration. She gasped and looked up
into his eyes. They were smoldering blue coals, just
as they had been the first time she met him. "You
have no authorization to unroll and tamper with
these. See what you have done!" He picked up the
torn piece that was partly visible under the scroll.

She stood to face him, her face crimson with the
sting of undeserved guilt. "That isn't true. It was
already torn. Rafica will tell you!" She struggled for
composure under his heavy stare, then her head went
up. "It fell without warning and unrolled in the
wind. It was accidental and I was not tampering!"

"What is this?" He shot a long arm past her and picked up her translation. He started to read, leaned over to look at the papyrus, then turned sharply toward her. "How did you...?"

"I meant to tell you...I'm really sorry. My father taught me, and the words just leaped out at me...."

He stared at her. "Douglas? James Arthur Douglas?" he said slowly.

She nodded.

"I can't believe this! Why didn't you say this before? He was my first teacher when I studied at the University of Chicago." He stood silent for a long moment, probing at her with his eyes. She felt sick. This was the Sayed whose powerful mind would stand for no foolishness, no games.

"I don't understand you, Robyn. I am confused—forgive me." He watched her unabashedly, without saying anything, while she wished she could turn the clock back to the moment when she should have told him all about herself. She felt like a schoolgirl before a teacher, not knowing what punishment to expect.

Suddenly he spoke again. "You must have been amused when I explained things about archaeology that you probably knew when you were in high school. There must have been a good reason for your coy charade, Robyn. Don't you think I deserve an explanation?"

"I...."

"Just tell me why!"

Her mind wavered and she rushed ahead in an effort to stop his penetrating glare. "Dr. Wayland thought it was best—after all, I'm a woman. And my father's reputation—and this was a Muslim country where women...." She sputtered to a halt.

"What you're telling me is that you and Dr. Way-land are full of ignorance, that you don't have the least understanding of our Islamic society in relation-ship to women. Was I supposed to reject you because you are a woman of some learning? By Allah, what kind of a pompous idiot do you think I am! It doesn't upset my masculine pride that you have a sur-prising knowledge of an ancient language. What does bother me is that you were not honest about it! Are you honest about other things, Robyn, tell me that?"

Robyn's eyes had dropped to her hands. She stood turning her ring around on her finger. She could gladly have sunk into the desert sand. She didn't feel like challenging him because he was probably right—she had been dishonest.

There was silence, and she was relieved for a mo-ment from the force of his emanation. She had not seen the smile that moved across his face briefly while he watched her. She raised her eyes to find him read-ing her translation.

" 'Mother Isis, who loved the golden king, Osiris, take my hand,' " he said softly, his deep voice mak-ing music of the words. He looked up from the paper, directly into her eyes. For a magic instant there were no veils between them. His eyes held hers, seeming to draw her close to him, then she took a shaky breath and the spell broke.

"This is excellent, Robyn. You have caught the spirit, the emotion and the poetry." He laid her paper on the table. "Now we had better get this scroll safely boxed."

Deftly he rolled up the brittle papyrus in the cushioning foam sheet, tucking the torn section in-side. He picked up a pen and numbered the corner, noting it in the listing and adding in parentheses, "the scroll of the blue-eyed god."

Robyn felt a peculiar yearning as it disappeared into its box. How did the story end? Was it like Cinderella, or the king and the beggar maid? Or did the blue-eyed god pass her by, perhaps with a careless kiss, and go on his way? She watched the graceful movement of Sayed's hands as they worked with the scroll, wishing that she could feel their touch and hating herself for it.

"I can see that it is an extra temptation for you with your ability to read the demotic script." His voice was remote again. "I will accept this as an accident, but I will not tolerate any effort to unroll or to read the papyrus."

"I will do my job," she said, feeling that she should address him as Dr. al-Rashad.

"See that you do. By the way, how much do you read. . .hieroglyphics, as well?"

She nodded.

"Hmm. And ancient Greek, perhaps?"

Her yes was just a whisper. He was like an inquisitor. Instead of pride in her knowledge, he seemed to want her to feel guilty about it. "And I read Latin, too," she said, needing to push against his arrogance and condescension.

He ignored her tone. "I should have guessed when I first saw your name of the hotel register. How unperceptive of me not to think of the ancient Egyptian words 'Sesha Neheru.' Surely no one but my old teacher would call his child 'small bird in flowers.' Has anyone else connected you to your father?"

"Dr. Gaddabi."

"And was sworn to secrecy. Allah give me patience! Well, the incident is closed, Robyn Douglas. Get on with your work.'' He turned on his heel and disappeared into the bright sunlight, leaving no warmth behind him.

She looked at her workbook with unfocused eyes. It would have been better if she had never come, had never met Sayed. *Who am I that I dare to hope for his gaze as he walks with his thoughts among the golden lotuses....*

The scroll of the blue-eyed god sat in its box, a subtle power flowing from it. Robyn longed to defy Sayed and read the rest of the story. The sand prophecy hovered very close to her mind.

Rafica came into the room with a few large fragments of papyrus. ''We're going to stay here tonight. That is, if you wish to.'' She smiled at Robyn's expression of surprise. ''It is not so bad. We have cots and pillows stored away, and Dr. al-Rashad has brought extra food and blankets. We have done it before.''

Part of Robyn wanted to stay, to experience the desert night. Another part said, *Get away—you don't belong out here.*

''Are you sure I'm supposed to stay, too?'' she asked.

''You are to work with me, starting early, my sister. We must finish the numbering and sorting tomorrow, if possible, so that everything can be taken to Alex for storage at the museum.'' She gave a dismal look at the large pile of still-uncataloged papyrus fragments. ''If the drilling machine comes too soon we will not be finished with our excavating, so it is best that we stay.''

''I think I'd like that,'' Robyn said. ''We can work

in the cooler hours of the morning, and I can tell my friends at home about my romantic night in the Egyptian desert.'' She made a face at the dusty, miserable-looking workroom.

Rafica laughed softly. ''How much better to imagine romance than to truly know it,'' she said quietly, turning away from Robyn to examine the newest fragments.

''Oh, Rafica, I'm sorry.''

''It is nothing, my friend. I am not the first woman to have this problem, and I shall not be the last.'' She sighed heavily and smiled. ''See, we will set up our cots here and maybe we shall have dreams from the scrolls. Think of all the words waiting to tell us their tales.''

THEY WORKED UNTIL SUNSET. Rafica said nothing more about her meeting with Karim the day before, but her silence spoke volumes. Robyn tried not to wonder where Sayed would be sleeping this night. During the day he had been pleasantly polite the few times she had glimpsed him, but his entire attention was on his work. By late afternoon the air outside glowed red with the swirling particles of hot dust.

George stuck his head into the workroom and announced dinner, such as it was. His uncomplicated midwestern face brought Robyn back from her musings. She and Rafica offered to help him set up the dinner tables and to fix the food. The entire crew was staying, including the drivers and Sayed's Egyptian students. Hassan Tarsi had not appeared at the dig all day, and neither had Huntley Saunders. It was better for Sayed's nerves that they didn't, Robyn felt.

George was busy heating a kettle of *foul* on a large

electric plate. The dark bean mixture would become
the filling for the round wheat pocket bread that was
called *aish baladi*—the bread of the people. Sliced
tomatoes and onions, and dishes of sesame paste sat
ready for the pocket bread. George gave one of his
rare laughs. "Just watch that you don't eat swarms
of gnats and mosquitoes with it!" He stirred his kettle, and Robyn put the Evian bottles on the tables.
Except for the French mineral water, she knew, this
was a meal that had been enjoyed in the Middle East
for thousands of years.

Several strong lights were illuminating the dig area,
and the silhouettes of Tom, Sayed and the students
moved in their beams. George raised his voice in a
kind of Wild West yodel, "Come and get it!" and the
men from the dig washed the dust from their hands in
a bucket of water.

The meal was eaten quietly. Robyn hadn't experienced nighttime in the desert before, and she sensed
an almost tangible peacefulness flowing over everything, a silence that had deep meaning in it.

Sayed was sitting with Tom and the students; the
drivers sat on the earth, speaking Arabic and laughing. Rafica, George and Robyn sat at a small table
formed from two old oil drums with a rough board
across the top. Robyn's ears were tuned to listen for
Sayed's deep voice. He was speaking Arabic, also,
but even though she didn't understand his words, the
sound of his warm resonant tones soothed and excited her.

Rafica asked for the bread by its Arabic name and
Robyn handed it to her. *"Shokran,"* Rafica said.

Robyn remembered the correct reply, *"Afwan."*
She looked up to catch Sayed's eyes on her. A swift

smile slanted the corners of his fine lips. One more language for you to learn, his eyes said, but there was an intimate flash of joking in them. She felt color rising into her cheeks.

Clouds of mosquitoes were starting to crowd around the unshaded light bulbs that lighted the table area. ''Better turn them off and let them buzz around the dig lights,'' Tom suggested.

They cleared up the dinner swiftly. Sayed went to the hot plate and managed to brew tiny cups of Turkish coffee for everyone. In the soft darkness they sipped the aromatic concoction wordlessly. Occasionally the dull flash of a match lighting a cigarette revealed a face for an instant, and a kind of serenity settled over them.

Someone in the Bedouin village began a wailing song, the minor cadences drifting on the warm wind. Drowsy bleats of sheep punctuated the flow of darkness, and the stars came down to the horizon with a diamond shine that made shadows on the desert land. For the moment the winds relaxed their gentle but insistent pressure and the night air was clear.

Tom slapped at mosquitoes and grumbled, ''To bed! Climbing under the covers is the only way to get away from them. I'm going to turn in.''

Good-nights were brief and general. Rafica and Robyn went to their cluttered shed, where two canvas cots waited to be unfolded and set up. Rafica brought out heavy blankets for mattresses, and others for cover. At least there were pillows with soft cases. They washed in a fresh bucket of water, slipped off their shoes and tried to find some comfort on the cots.

Rafica was soon asleep and snoring lightly, but for

Robyn sleep stayed just out of reach. From where she lay she could see the box that held the scroll of the blue-eyed god, and her mind played with the possibilities of the ancient love story that had been so briefly opened to her. Wasn't she in the same predicament? *Who am I that I dare...* she said the words again to herself. Finally she found an uneasy sleep, where confused dreams flowed back and forth from the far, far past to the present in a swirl of images.

Suddenly she was wide awake, as if a voice had called to her. She sat up, staring into the darkness as if to see who had spoken her name—her Egyptian name. Rafica still slept deeply.

Maybe one of the dream voices had become too insistent, Robyn explained to herself. She had gone to sleep much earlier than normal, and now she had had her usual amount of rest.

The little room was stuffy, and a faint tinge of dawn was showing through the grimy windowpanes of the shed. Turning and twisting on her hard cot was futile at this point, so she quietly rose, careful not to waken Rafica. Shoes in hand, she eased herself out the door.

Cool air blew against her hot body, and she filled her lungs with the sweetness of it. Last night's bucket of water was on the step. She splashed her face, drying it with tissue from her pocket. Her small comb tumbled to the ground, and she shook the sand off of it before she used it on her hair.

The sky glowed indigo blue and the morning stars were bright against the whisper of dawn light. The air felt heavy with mysterious energies. Robyn's heart began to beat unevenly. She felt a peculiar sense of anxiety for which she could find no reason. That odd hum started vibrating along her nerves and a strange urgency pushed at her.

She walked quickly away from the sleeping camp, feeling as if she had done this a hundred times before. Her heart was racing, expectant. The dark line of trees in the mid-distance beckoned to her. With light steps she almost ran across the desert earth. As she came close to the trees she could see a gleaming sliver of water. It was the silent canal.

Dusty pine trees with long needles lined the path along the steep banks. Dry growth tufted here and there, and nearer to the water green patches of tiny flowering plants and feathery grasses began to show color in the growing light. On the edge of the bank she sat down among the flowers, waiting.

Across the canal a herd of sheep and goats was wakening. Some came down to the water to drink and looked over at her with patient eyes. Expectancy grew in her heart, and with it the dawn burst into vivid glowing colors that were reflected in the still water. When the sun came above the horizon Robyn wanted to call out a greeting to the ancient god. She was no longer held in the present, but was floating with the energies of time itself.

Long fingers of sunlight flowed between the trees, and out of the light strode the figure of a man. His white robe took on the sun's color. He was moving rapidly along the path with the light at his back.

Robyn sat immobile, watching him. He was part of the dream, the one for whom she waited. He stopped, looking down at her, blue fire stirring in the depths of his eyes. Words moved through her mind: *He who is my destiny—he comes like Horus, the blue-eyed god in the morning light.*

Because she could not do otherwise, she rose to her feet, her eyes still locked with his. He reached a hand to her and drew her up to the path beside him. Her hand warmed in his. The ancient words of the scroll were still speaking in her mind.

Sayed's beautiful voice answered her. "Small bird of the morning." His smile was part of the dawn light. "Will you kiss me once so that I shall remember the taste of joy forever?" He placed her hand against his breast and his free arm went gently and firmly around her. His eyes gazed into hers intently, then his smiling lips came down and closed on hers. She stood in a blaze of delight, where time and space dissolved and there was nothing but his strength holding her. The touch of his lips was a promise and a homecoming.

She stayed enclosed in his arms until he released her, steadying her with his hands on her shoulders. "One taste of joy forever," he whispered. "I won't forget that kiss."

The energy around them was changing; the dream was blowing away with the dawn breeze. She drew back from him and watched a flight of birds settle on the branches of a pine tree. His fingers reached to draw a gentle line along her cheek. "Why are you here?" he asked. She tried not to read a deeper meaning into the question.

"I couldn't sleep. The scrolls in our workroom seemed to have voices."

She saw that he was dressed in a long white galabia, the lines of it emphasizing the breadth of his shoulders. His feet—long and narrow like the ancient tomb carvings—were thrust into thong sandals. Who was he, really, she wondered shakily.

"And one scroll in particular?" he asked in a soft voice. "Is it not strange, small morning bird, to find ourselves part of such a tale from out of time?" He brushed her hand with a caressing touch of his lips. "Forgive me, but I had to play it out. There was no way not to kiss you."

She nodded. "I don't know what made me come. I think I was expecting you."

"Let us say that something called to me, also. I felt the need to walk in the dawn. Come, we had better go back. They will miss us." His eyes looked at her with a serious and speculative gaze. "I seem always to be asking forgiveness. Will you forget my hasty words when I found out about your father yesterday? I respected him very deeply and obviously he taught you well. He would not object if we were friends, I am sure, and I most certainly need to know that you do not judge me ill." His hand rested on her shoulder, to the detriment of her composure. "You and I will have to be clear with each other, Robyn. There is a storm brewing over the excavation. Our findings are a precious heritage for the whole of humanity. They must not be brought to light in the glare of jealousy and anger, or stupid ego. I need your help."

She looked into his intense lapis eyes. "You have it," she promised.

They walked in silence back toward the dig. Once he smiled down at her wordlessly, his eyes telling her that he, too, was puzzling about the pull of energy between them.

Robyn wrestled with her thoughts, but could find no simple explanation for all of this. She loved him; that was the truth. What he felt for her she could not imagine.

The words of the scroll came again: *Mother Isis, who loved the golden king, Osiris, take my hand!* She hurried to keep up with his long strides. He had forgotten her, his mind already on the real business of his life. She sighed and followed him into the camp.

Only Tom was awake, his brown hair disheveled from sleep. He noted their arrival with a quizzical expression. "Hi," he said, and went back to washing in his water bucket.

CHAPTER EIGHT

RAFICA WAS TACTFUL and said nothing when Robyn entered the workroom. "I couldn't sleep," Robyn said lamely, starting to fold her bedding and cot. She tried to force herself to function normally, but anyone who saw her face would know that something much more than insomnia was at work in her.

What had just happened out by the canal should stay there, her mind rapidly decreed as she shivered helplessly with emotion. If she let herself believe in its reality she would surely lose it, but if she remembered it as a dream—her personal dream that Sayed had walked into for one indescribable moment—then she would never lose it. With that settled she reached for her notebook and pretended to be fully involved in her lists of numbers.

Rafica put a light hand on her shoulder. "Aren't you having breakfast?"

"Oh...yes. I wasn't thinking about it. Sure, I could use a cup of coffee." She kept her eyes away from Rafica's perceptive ones.

"I'll bring you something. Maybe you would prefer not to go outside again...."

The morning quickly turned hot. Flies and tiny buzzing things were thick in the shed and they made suicide dives into Robyn's and Rafica's hair. Robyn accepted Rafica's easy silence gratefully and forced her brain into concentrated work.

By noon Tom reported that the drill crew hadn't yet arrived as scheduled from Cairo. The excavation was finally cleared and prepared, but precious time was being lost because of this latest foul-up. On top of that, it had been two days now that Hassan Tarsi had been absent from the dig without explanation.

"Hassan was supposed to have made the final arrangements for the drill crew's arrival today, and where is he? Where is everybody?" Tom thrust a hand through his dust-colored thick hair. "Sayed just left in Mohammed's car to see if he can track down Hassan in Alex."

"I'm so sorry about this," Rafica said grimly. "I know what it means to Dr. al-Rashad. He cannot tolerate disloyalty or inattention to duty."

In a swift mental picture Robyn saw Sayed's blazing cobalt eyes. There was no doubting the intensity of his reactions. If only she knew what was in his proud mind—what words of hers might move him to wrath or to tenderness. . . .

"I worry that he expects too much of the people around him. But, then," Rafica sighed, "he never expects more of others than he is willing to do himself. I cannot help but admire him . . . with a small amount of fear, also."

Robyn nodded her head in agreement. "I'm just as happy that Dr. Tarsi stays away from here altogether."

"But he is being paid to take some of the minor problems from Dr. al-Rashad, and for that reason I wish he were here."

Tom clapped his hands. "How about lunch? I can

heat up last night's *foul* in a jiffy and tantalize your palates.'' He was trying to lighten the mood. ''Your regular chef, George, is in Alex picking up some parts for the spare generator, so I'm afraid I'm it.''

The dig was essentially at a standstill, silent and very warm. The dry air was full of sand particles that found their gritty way into everything. Sayed's handful of students made their own circle for lunch, behind the work shed and shielded from the wind. Tom, Robyn and Rafica sat around an outdoor table and speculated on Sayed's situation with the dig.

''I think Hassan bothers him almost more than the drill not being here,'' Tom said, as he chewed his pocket bread and bean mixture. ''Sayed hates deviousness, and he hates disrespect for the integrity of an archaeological site. He calls Hassan's kind of work 'rape and pillage archaeology,' because he goes to town with picks and shovels, destroying as much as he saves. Even if he did find Cleopatra's villa—or whatever the heck he thinks it is—he probably wouldn't know how to preserve it long enough for the press to get good pictures.''

Robyn was curious. Sayed had never explained how he happened to start his search right here, so close to Hassan Tarsi's site. ''Did Dr. Tarsi really think he was going to find something from the library, too, in his villa digs, or was it just because Sayed was looking for the scrolls?''

''Who knows what was in his Byzantine little mind,'' Tom answered, shrugging. ''If it weren't for Sayed's acute sense of the land, this site would never have been found, no matter what Hassan says. Sayed spent years searching for the remains of the library, following clues in obscure writings, and mostly using his sharp intuition. It's almost uncanny. The reports make it sound very scientific, but I was there when he made his first test dig—in the place he calls the glass factory. He sniffed the air like a desert animal, as if he could actually smell the presence of something out of the ordinary, something that wasn't originally part of the landscape. I won't forget the look on his face, like he was seeing something that no one else could see. . . . ''

Huntley Saunders chose that moment to arrive with his Mercedes and driver. Robyn could have evaporated him with a look.

"My, my," he said, grinning, "I'd hate to think I spent all that money just to have everybody layin' around doin' nothin'. Miss Robyn, Miss Rafica, how are you girls today?" He made a little bow. His white cotton leisure suit was wrinkled and his body perspiration showed through it.

Tom stepped forward to meet him. "We spent the night out here, Mr. Saunders, and Dr. al-Rashad's in town tracking down the drill. We're pretty much finished with the top room. All we can do now is wait. Want some lunch?" He handed a dripping brown portion of stuffed pocket bread toward Huntley.

"Thanks, but I had a big night over at the yacht club," the man drawled. "We had us a fine Texas time! I'm not gonna eat again for a while. Y'all should have been there. You, too, Miss Robyn—loosen up your gears a bit. Sure a lot better than sleepin' like a native with the insects." He wiped his sweating face with a large white handkerchief and looked critically around at the camp. "Well, no use wastin' my time out here. Tom, you sure my borescope's under lock and key? I can't tell you what it'd do to my bank account to have to buy you boys another one.'' He smiled insincerely and ambled off to his car.

"Oh, by the way, Tom," he shouted back, "Little ol' Sandi won't be comin' out today; she wanted me to tell you. Treat her nice, will you? She didn't have a lot of sleep. Y'all take care!"

"Bastard," Tom said through clenched teeth. He walked away toward the excavation.

Robyn and Rafica went back to the workroom. "Poor Tom, poor Sandi," Rafica said softly. "Why is love so hard to understand? Must we hurt each other without being able to avoid it?"

Tears stung in Robyn's eyes. Why, indeed, she thought.

SAYED ARRIVED EMPTY-HANDED. No Hassan Tarsi, and no drill. He had a long conference at the dig hole with Tom. Robyn could see their frustration even from a distance as they turned their faces into the wind to assess the khamsin situation.

It was late afternoon when George returned, bumping over the rocky road in a dust cloud, the station wagon full of equipment. Dr. Gaddabi was with him. They made a beeline for Sayed and Tom, and all four men stood in a huddle, conversing seriously.

After a few minutes Sayed came to the open door of the workroom. "I'm sorry to interrupt, ladies." His voice had a tight tone. "I have news that the estimable Dr. Tarsi has filed a complaint with the Antiquities Department about the validity of the university's permit."

The words hung in the stifling air like evil portents, and seeing Sayed's pained face, Robyn ached with empathy. "This could shut down the dig for days—

weeks—while the department takes time to investigate.'' He sighed and shook his dark head in exasperation. ''The whole situation is so delicate...the general
stressfulness of the times, the politics. Cooperation on
an international project is difficult enough, and there
are already adverse reports concerning Saunders. You
know, Robyn, that my government routinely checks
on people who come here on archaeological, film or
business projects. Now I am told that a new investigation is necessary, some sort of clearance of credentials.''

He pursed his lips and let out a sharp breath. ''I
have to let them know that Saunders has no power
over the university's commitments and, especially, no
deal with me concerning any antiquities. You will have
to go to Cairo with me in the morning, Robyn. We
must see the people in charge of the situation. It is the
only way to free up the dig.''

A flash of delight swept through Robyn's being. To
be with him for a whole day! She schooled her face in
composure and nodded. ''Of course. When do you
want to start? The file of contracts and letters is all in
order.'' She had managed to find her efficient tone,
and Sayed's face relaxed a little.

''Good. I knew I could count on you. We'll leave
early to be in Cairo before midmorning.'' Suddenly he
smiled at her. ''How early can you be ready?''

''Whenever you wish.''

''Hmm.'' His eyes teased her for a moment. ''I
don't want to pace the hotel lobby waiting for a lady
with a breakfast roll.''

''When?'' she repeated indignantly, hoping that
Sayed knew she was teasing him back.

''Six o'clock.''

"At six o'clock," she said in a businesslike voice.

"Then get to bed early." He turned away to walk with Dr. Gaddabi again. Their serious faces told Robyn how worried they were.

That evening at the Palestine things were quiet. Robyn washed out some of her work clothes, amazed at the amount of reddish earth that had accumulated in them.

Sandi wandered past her door and talked for a while. "Just thought you'd like the latest bulletin on romance in old Egypt," she said with a sarcastic laugh, and lighted a cigarette. "I really blew it this time. Tom must think I'm Mata Hari or something, the way he bit my head off downstairs in the lobby. I'm supposed to know what Mr. Terrific from Houston, Texas is up to about Sayed's dig. Tom was really mad, as if I was a buddy of Huntley's."

"You might as well come in, Sandi," Robyn said. "Maybe I can help make sense out of it for you."

"Don't bother. The idea that Tom would give me a second look was just a laugh. He's mad as hell at me, that's what!"

Robyn couldn't believe Sandi was so dense that she didn't know what her dating other men was doing to Tom. "You may be older and more experienced in this department," she said with some firmness, "but you didn't help things by spending the evening with Huntley Saunders. I thought you didn't like him, anyway."

"I don't, but I was bored. If I sit around in my room I just wonder where Tom is. So I let the old guy take me dancing. It wasn't even fun. But at least he doesn't make me feel like I'm some kind of a disappointment."

"Don't you think you're exaggerating just a bit?" Robyn insisted.

"Tom's the type who wouldn't bring anything home to mama but a wholesome little piece of apple pie smothered in whipped cream—and no cheese." Sandi prowled around Robyn's room restlessly.

"And how are you getting along with our handsome leader? Don't tell me he hasn't made your heart disco yet. If he hasn't, you'll be the first American gal on record." She eyed Robyn with curiosity. "Any special reason why Huntley is saying little nasties about you and Sayed? For a shy gal you must have lit into him like a rattlesnake. He's real sore about something. I told him to shut his trap. You'd better tell Sayed to watch him."

Robyn nodded. "He already knows. We're going to Cairo tomorrow to straighten things out."

"Hmm—well, that kind of business could turn out to be a pleasure. I wish Tom would take me on one of his fast runs south, but no such luck." She smiled with somber eyes.

"A lot can happen in Cairo with a good-looking gal and a guy like Sayed. I've seen him look at you, and I've watched you look at him. I'm a photographer, remember? I notice things."

"Sandi, that's just nonsense, and you know it," Robyn stated firmly.

"Whatever you say." She picked up an archaeological journal from Robyn's pile of books. "Can I borrow this? Maybe I need a new image. I ought to know a little more so I can talk to Tom." Her dreary, unprotected face made Robyn's heart tighten with sympathy.

"Of course," she said, nodding.

"I'll get it back to you." Sandi stopped at the door and looked back. "So many things are up for grabs in life. Don't miss what you can get." She flipped a hand in farewell.

Robyn set her alarm for five in the morning, then had to read herself to sleep. Impossible dreams of Sayed chased across her slumber, and it was after a restless night that her little clock whirred her awake. The opal light of sunrise glowed on the little bay, and she went onto her balcony to breathe deeply of the balmy air.

Even if Sayed was only being a pleasant male, one who couldn't resist responding to the attraction in a woman's eyes, even if Rafica's warning was right, it would still be a day with him to remember.

The phone shrilled in her room and she hurried to answer. Sayed's voice said briskly, "Good, you're awake. Better pack an overnight change of clothes. We might have to stay on to complete our business. I've ordered the hotel to pack us a breakfast. It should be waiting at the desk. Will you be ready at six?"

"Of course."

He chuckled and rang off.

Overnight! Her mind was in a whirl as she rushed to find something to wear for two days—something that was at least clean and fresh looking. Would she spend her evening alone, or with him, an unbusinesslike thought intruded. She grabbed her flight bag and packed quickly, throwing in her night things. She hesitated, and then added a short silk skirt and a soft ruffled beige blouse. The pearls went in and her high-heeled sandals.

She dressed carefully for the day in a cool cotton dress of muted lime green with delicate pink piping

and covered buttons. Its gently flared skirt was graceful, and the stitched design of pink at the neck was
simple but flattering. A pink tie flowed out of the
rolled collar and fastened into a soft bow. She decided
to wear the tiny rose-shaped earrings that her father
had given her on his last Christmas with them. Cairo
might be terribly hot, and she packed her best and
coolest day dress, a sundress, really.

In the mirror she congratulated her image. Cool and
sensible; pretty, but not showy. And definitely feminine. She had drawn her hair back in easy waves into a
knot fastened with a silver clip. The antiquities people
would see a professional representative of the university.

She stuffed a change of walking shoes and her
makeup into the last corner of the bag, then she was
ready. Her honey-colored cashmere sweater, old but
good, went over her shoulders, and a book to read in
her handbag.

Downstairs the lobby was vacant. The day staff was
just coming on duty, and she spotted two pink card-
board boxes on the main desk. "Yes, these are the two
morning meals ordered by the professor doctor," said
the sleepy clerk.

The hotel clock said quarter to six. She decided to
wait on the wide covered porch area outside and, with
her hands full, headed for the big swinging glass
doors. Just then someone pulled them open, and
Sayed's hand relieved her of the boxes. His sparkling
white Fiat sat at the curb with its top down.

The overnight bag and food boxes went into the
small back seat while Robyn dropped down onto the
comfortable cushions in front. She hoped her face
didn't reveal how excited she was, and she was glad

that Sayed couldn't hear her heart's pounding rhythm. Her eyes followed his lithe figure as he went swiftly into the hotel again.

In a moment he came out with a thermos in hand. His stride outlined the ripple of muscles in his graceful strong legs. He had the body of a well-trained athlete. His shirt of rough woven cloth was tucked into a flexible belt with a silver buckle, which topped his smoothly tailored amber-toned slacks. She had already noticed a matching jacket in the back seat. A dark blue scarf, loosely tied, showed inside his collar.

Sayed slid into the driver's seat, and she caught a light scent of sandalwood. His freshly shaved face creased into a teasing smile. "I'm amazed. We're ready to go and it's not even six yet. You are a remarkable woman, a jewel above price." He put the car into gear and drove at high speed along the roads of the park and onto the corniche. She sat contentedly beside him. Somehow there was no need to make small talk and simply sharing this beautiful morning with him made her happy.

He threaded the car through the early traffic, turning in an easterly direction across the city. "We'll be going by the delta road instead of the desert highway," he said, his eyes on his driving. "I thought you would enjoy seeing the ancient breadbasket of Egypt."

"How wonderful!" Her eyes were shining as he gave her a satisfied smile. "I was afraid I wouldn't see the delta before I left for home."

His hands tightened on the wheel. "Have you a deadline on your return ticket?"

"No. It was left open, depending on the circumstances and what the borescope shows."

"Good." His hands relaxed as she watched, fascinated by their supple strength. Again she thought of the prince of the Third Dynasty, and the aristocratic men's long hands she had seen in so many tomb paintings of the Old Kingdom.

Another thought urged its way into her mind. How would those hands feel against her body, intimately seeking to bring her pleasure? A tremor began deep inside her and spiraled through her nerves. She sat silently, in the grip of this strange feeling. Never had she felt such intensity of longing. Even with John's reasonably ardent kisses, her body had not signaled a response like this. In fact, a certain unwillingness had made her sometimes brush aside his groping hands. She was amazed at her present thoughts, amazed and distressed. *Sayed hasn't even touched me,* she thought. *What's the matter with me!*

She concentrated on the green lush scenery they were rushing past and gradually her taut nerves settled down a little. Sayed was talking about the history of the land. The flat green fields stretched away on both sides, punctuated by the tall masts and arching sails of the feluccas on the canals. The warm black earth was moist and rich where plows drawn by big lumbering water buffalo were turning it into planting rows.

Sayed suddenly pulled the car off the road into the shade of a clump of sycamore trees beside a canal. Across the water a blindfolded donkey creaked a huge wooden waterwheel as it plodded in a circle. In their cool bower, set like a scene from faraway ages, they had breakfast. Rolls and butter, salty native cheese slices, foil-wrapped triangles of Laughing Cow cheese from Switzerland, several of the thin-skinned, bright-colored Egyptian oranges.

The rich sweet aroma of green growing things, tinged by the wood smoke of breakfast fires in nearby mud-brick houses, made Robyn sniff the air with pleasure. Sayed smiled and poured a cup of hot fragrant tea for her. "That's the morning smell that takes me back to my childhood." His eyes moved lovingly over the fields to the green horizon.

"Very early I would run out of our home on the farm, through the lettuce and the cabbages and down the street into our village." His voice was full of tenderness. "Even though I would have my breakfast later, I knew that my friend Ahmed was waiting. He had a small teahouse, with two iron tables and ten metal chairs, of which he was very proud. He would hand me a cup of strong tea with sometimes a pinch of spice and a cube of sugar—or maybe with water-buffalo cream and anise seed. In another country he would have become an innovative chef."

He smiled at the distant picture in his mind. "Later, the men would sit on the chairs and oil drums, drink tea and coffee and play games. They would smoke their water pipes, sometimes made from a glass fruit jar and bamboo reeds. But that first cup of tea of the day was like nectar, and old Ahmed's smile made me feel that the world was made up of friends. It was only when I had grown a few years older that I discovered that there were also enemies." He sighed and came back to the present.

Robyn had been listening with her heart, seeing the supple boyish figure in its white galabia running on the soft moist earth. She could almost see the smile of Ahmed and taste the hot goodness of his gift. Sayed turned toward her and saw the expression drifting over her face. His eyes flickered with response and for a moment smoky blue eyes looked deep into potent lapis ones. Sayed broke the mood. "Your childhood must have been much different," he said softly.

"Yes, our garden was a small one in our backyard, but we did grow lettuce and radishes and beans in summer, and we had an apricot tree and a fig. I used to fight with the blue jays for the first ripe fruit."

"Ahh, *mish-mish*—that's the word for apricot. How well I know how they taste hot from the sun. And the joy of breaking open a round green fig all honey sweet...."

She nodded. "...and fight with the bees who want to taste it, too."

His hand moved to hers in a brief warm touch. "So, we do have some shared childhood memories. Since I have a captive audience, I shall tell you more about mine." He laughed. "I remember the feel of the soft mud of the canal as my bare feet sank deliciously into it. And picking a head of the tall lettuce—what you call romaine—out of the field to wash it at the village well. I would walk home eating its sweet green leaves. It had a magic taste of vitality."

"I know," she interrupted easily. "Rafica gave me some of hers the other day. I've seen the carts full of lettuce on the streets of Alex. My mother would die if she saw me eating fresh greens here. She's certain I'll poison myself with some dread foreign bug."

"But you must take care. In every country there are microorganisms that the local population is used to—that cause them little harm—but travelers from other places are not." He smiled warmly at her. "When I first studied in the United States—when your father was giving his special class at the University of Chicago—I was sick for the first few weeks. It was the chemicals in the water—they weren't what my body expected."

He gathered up the fragments of their breakfast, which Robyn had barely tasted. Her whole attention had been absorbed in him. "We can leave the scraps under the trees for the birds."

He got out of the car in one smooth motion and went to scatter the crumbs. She sat watching him, fascinated by the sense of contained power that his body movements expressed. Another shiver of delight tumbled through her, and with it a kind of terror. He was too close to her now; the stories of his boyhood were too intimate a sharing, and she felt her hold on her emotions slipping disastrously.

"I can't fall in love; it's impossible!" she whispered, while the sight of his tall figure against the great spreading tree wrenched at her with an irresistible joy.

The branches of the sycamore drooped near them like a leafy shield, and lines from Omar Khayyám came to Robyn's mind. Along with the words of *The Rubaiyat*, she remembered a painting that had hung in Dr. Johnston's house. One of the older widowed professors, he had become a friend of Robyn's when she was young. She had often sat entranced before the picture, which illustrated the great poem, while her father and the elderly professor talked.

Dr. Johnston's dry old voice with its hint of lost resonance came back to her now, "A jug of wine, a loaf of bread, and thou beside me singing in the wilderness— Ah, wilderness would be paradise enow...."

The picture had shown an Arabian couple sitting beneath a sycamore tree, sharing wine and bread. How strongly she had dreamed herself into that picture, until she could smell the pungent, exciting odor of the sycamore and taste the bread and wine. Always in her reveries the next step should have been to look up into the eyes of a man—but she could never quite do it, even though she loved him. She knew that she loved him.

Now, having Sayed come toward her was like déjà vu. This was the man and the place. They had had their bread together, but what of the absent wine? Her common sense said, *Muslims don't drink.* And she wrestled with the painful symbolism that struck at her heart: the wine of love was missing. How could she share with Sayed what he had not brought with him?

There was tension where her heart should have been. As Sayed slid into the driver's seat, she was afraid to raise her eyes to his. Just as with the picture dream, her gaze would reveal too much.

He sat for a moment, breathing in the scent of the tree, then said softly, "I love that fragrance of sycamore." When she didn't respond he turned to her. "You are very silent, Robyn." It was a question.

"I was recalling a picture that I loved as a child, an illustration for *The Rubaiyat.* It had a sycamore in it, tall and ancient like this one."

"Ah, yes, I have seen such illustrations. Let me guess the verse." There was warmth in his voice. "'A jug of wine, a loaf of bread, and thou beside me singing in the wilderness....' Wasn't that it?"

She nodded, keeping her eyes down.

"Oh, Robyn—look at me." There was a little laugh of tenderness in his words, and his gently insistent hand turned her face toward him. "Would the wilderness be paradise if we were together there?" He gave a soft shake to her chin. She didn't dare to look at him, but sat there mutely. The hand raised her face to his and butterfly kisses touched her trembling eyelids, then came down lightly to her lips.

It wasn't a passionate, demanding kiss, but through her mouth, which couldn't stiffen under his no matter how much she wanted not to respond, its warmth explored her heart. He took his time, smoothing his lips tantalizingly back and forth against her own. She felt his newly shaved beard rasp excitingly against her tender skin, and the heat of his tongue tip asked deeper entrance.

A quivering blend of love and fear shook her body. She drew her lips from his slowly, hating to break the contact—but she had to!

"Please... please," she whispered, "I didn't expect...."

He lifted his head away from hers. "What didn't you expect?" His laugh was a purr in his throat. "Shouldn't we have asked for a taste of paradise for ourselves?"

His eyes stayed on her while she wondered if he really wanted an answer to his question. Then he let her go and matter-of-factly turned on the ignition, driving swiftly away from their quiet canal with a sure, deft ease.

His sudden practical attention to the road and to his driving confused her. Did his kisses mean nothing at all? Was he only playing a game that she was too unsophisticated to understand?

She would make no reference to what had just happened. To say anything would only give emphasis and importance to it. The next few minutes were devoted to schooling her eyes and face into some discipline, and stilling her rapid breath and pulse. He must not suspect.

Sayed was the first to speak again. He began to reminisce about his studies in the United States with her father, and his admiring memories brought back the excitement of her own early life with him. She was glad that he knew her secret at last, and that they could talk freely of the things they shared in common. To have heard from his lips the words of Omar Khayyám made old Dr. Johnston's recital seem pale by comparison. The words belonged on the lips of a man of Islam.

Before she realized what was happening, Sayed had practically drawn out her life's story. She couldn't stop herself from telling him of the long hours she'd spent in the basement workroom at home, and about the indulgent laughter of her father's colleagues when he had brought her with him to lectures. Her quiet description of her efforts to learn the old languages revealed her love for the ancient voices that spoke through the fragments of papyrus and vellum.

"So...now I understand better why Dr. Wayland trusts you. You had a privilege to have such a father and such a love. You were his precious, bright little bird—Sesha Neheru, his pride."

She nodded, unable to talk for a moment, choked with an aching lump in her throat. His warm hand gently touched hers again. "We must talk more about the scrolls. I see that you have inherited your father's loving curiosity for the old ones." He looked at her with an open, easy expression, like a dear and comfortable friend. "Maybe, if we can get appropriations to start soon, you can help with translations. The one you did on our scroll of the blue-eyed god was excellent."

"I would love to try." Her heart raced with hope. To be near him longer, to share at least in this impersonal but exciting meeting of minds, would be something to cherish in the long cool years when the sun of Egypt was only a memory.

Sayed pointed across orchards and fields toward the east. "Rafica's village is over there—and our farm, which is shrunk to a small area. Most of the land now belongs to the people, which is as it should be. But old Ahmed is still in his teahouse. One day I'll take you there. Would you like that?"

Her expression answered him and made him laugh. "What a satisfactory companion you are, all wonder and excitement," he teased.

She felt a tinge of distress. Did he still think of her as a child, a learned but naive student? On impulse she said in a serious voice, "Did Tom speak to you about Rafica's problem?"

A swift sharp glance rewarded her question. "Yes." He looked straight ahead, concentrating on the road.

She gathered up a shaky courage. "Is there anything that can be done to help?"

He gave her another look, in which irritation seemed suddenly to blend into a cool impersonality. "Don't meddle into affairs that you know nothing about. You don't understand the necessities of Rafica's family and what is expected of women here in Egypt."

Rafica's sad face appeared in Robyn's mind, arousing her determination. Sayed was so high-handed. How could he be unwilling even to discuss the problem? "I know how deeply unhappy Rafica is. Doesn't anyone consider love in marriage? You have helped her to get her education; you're the sheikh of her village. At least you could talk to her father!"

Blue blazing embers sparked deep in the somber

eyes that looked at her now. "It seems that she has told you a lot. But you don't really understand. Has she told you what a blow it would be to her family if she refused Mustafa? Has she told you that he is a good man who would treat her well, and that he is not uneducated?"

"She hasn't been unfair to him, but she loves someone else," Robyn stated. How could he be so unfeeling, so brutally practical?

"Has it occurred to you that love—so-called love—is a very unsteady emotion? Look at your society, where women are free to pick and choose, to be appraised and handled by any number of men!" His foot went down hard on the gas and they sped around one of the large two-wheeled donkey carts that were busy in the morning traffic on the delta road. The tiny donkey drawing the tottering load of carrots shied, and its driver called out a stream of Arabic curses that faded into the distance as they raced down the narrow highway.

"Do you understand what being a sheikh is?" Sayed's voice was still sharp. "A sheikh is a man who can give counsel, learned to some extent—or he is a member of a family in whom trust has been put for a long time. My father was considered a sheikh, and I have tried to walk in his very wise footsteps." He sighed and the irritation seemed to empty out of him. "If I interfered, her father would say to me that Rafica's education is a detriment to her if she can't act as a woman should." His face smoothed into a polite but determined smile. "We will not discuss this further, Robyn."

Rebellion surged within her while sharp retorts pressed at her lips. The uncompromising look of his profile almost silenced her. "Maybe Mustafa would like another woman for his wife. Or is he free to choose even if Rafica is not?" she said in a low, persistent voice.

There was a heavy silence while the car flew along. Robyn felt terrible. She hadn't helped Rafica at all, and Sayed's indictment of American women gnawed at her sense of justice. "There are lots of happy marriages in my society, and all women are not as you describe."

"Of course." His voice sounded politely bored.

She tried to get a grip on her irritation and on something else rising in her. She wanted to argue, to hit at him, to break his wall of masculine security—to get him to look at her as an equal, deserving at least of discussing the subject. Or did she just want to have him truly notice her?

She was almost shaking by this time, trembling and trying not to let him see it. The worst of it was that his attitude, no matter how at odds with hers, didn't diminish one bit her fascinated admiration for him. She sat with her hands clasped on her purse, wrestling with the knowledge that part of what drew her to him was his strength. Did women truly want to be ruled by a man? Her mind swerved from angry rebellion to the exciting thought of being held and protected by Sayed's superior strength.

The car slowed suddenly while Sayed swerved to avoid a donkey, which pranced across the road with its naughty back hooves kicking in glee. In hot pursuit, oblivious of all else, was its master, rope in hand and the hem of his long, awkward galabia gripped in his teeth. The morning light outlined the man's thin legs and pounding feet, and brought out sparks of devilry from the frolicsome donkey's rolling eyes.

Sayed straightened the car on the road and drove along beside the canal, following the uneven contest. He began to chuckle as the donkey tantalized the man by stopping and then speeding on again. When Sayed's laugh grew deep and full, Robyn tried to maintain her irritated mood and failed. Her own laughter bubbled up irresistibly. The donkey decided to swerve off across a field, and the two disappeared into a clump of trees.

Sayed speeded up, still chuckling. "This same scene must have been played out since the days of Osiris. Do you remember the animal papyrus in which the donkeys, baboons and lions all have naughty gleaming eyes and play the parts of men?"

"Yes, I saw it once when the original was on a loan exhibit at our museum."

His hand came out, loosening her tight fingers from her purse and enclosing them in a sweet weakening warmth that sent a melting heat and excitement to the roots of her being. "Don't frown anymore, Robyn. I want you to be happy today. I have been unforgivable, but forgive me anyway." He raised her hand to his lips and kissed it lightly, giving it back with a smile. She had to smile back. "That's better. Could you peel one of those oranges in the box and share it with me?"

She obeyed him and stripped off the skin from one of the large tangerinelike oranges. Its segments were juicy and easily separated, giving out a fresh, tangy aroma.

"You will have to feed them to me," he said. "I must concentrate on the road now. Traffic is heavier and the animals and carts are a hazard."

She selected a plump orange segment and put it to

his lips. He leaned forward a little and his lips touched her fingers softly. She withdrew her hand swiftly, trying to still the sweet pleasure that the contact sent flowing through her nerves.

"Delicious." He gave her a quick smile. "Have some."

She ate a segment. It was tangy and sweet. His glance asked for another and she fed him again, hating the blush that she knew was beginning to glow in her face.

"It is the ambrosia of paradise, and I am being fed by one of the lovely rosy-cheeked handmaidens of the blessed." A gentle laughter was in his words. "Few men are able to experience the delights of Allah's heaven before their time. Why am I so fortunate?"

She fixed her attention on the orange and quickly stuffed a piece into her own mouth to avoid having to answer.

She heard an amused sound emerge from deep in his throat. "I won't tease anymore. Give me another piece."

She fed him the rest of the fruit, willing her hand to be steady.

"That was good," he finally said. Again his swift, devastating smile unsteadied her. She put the remains of the fruit away and brought up the subject of the contracts, asking sensible questions in a businesslike voice.

Sayed answered in kind. They discussed the problem of Hassan Tarsi and of Huntley Saunders—in detail—until at last she felt more in control of herself.

They had come past miles of flat green country and lush crops. Now the desert was growing more apparent again and the ragged outskirts of the city were in view. Robyn was completely fascinated by the variety of sights and sounds. A small smile lingered on Sayed's lips, as though he enjoyed her pleasure. Yet not all of the sights were beautiful. Poverty showed itself in many ways and Robyn's heart twisted at the sight of children and old people sitting in the dust, of forlorn, aimless stray dogs and cats.

Sayed's voice spoke to her thought. "My people are timeless, having survived many armies and conquerors. We are dependent always on our rich land and mighty river, but we grow in population and there is not enough productivity. We are moving into the modern world painfully, as all ancient and agrarian societies must do." He sighed. "There is so much to do, and so many stresses move around us. Yet we are a noble people, good at the core. The racial strain of the mighty old ones of Egypt has been blended into many other strains, but it always absorbs and tempers them with reason and wisdom. We are a far more stable people than many, and we must work for the future. . . ."

She looked at his fine face and saw the nobility that he had spoken about. She had seen it in the faces of the people in the fields and in the cities. "You will be builders of the future. The work of this special land is not finished." She heard her own voice ring with the passion and love that she had learned from her father. She was surprised to see just how very deeply she felt about Egypt herself.

Sayed braked to a stop at an intersection. His face was serious as he turned to her. "Thank you, my friend. Would you like to help the birth of the future Egypt?"

"Of course!" she said quickly. What did he mean?

Her mind leaped at possibilities: a job in Egypt, help in translating the scrolls, research with Sayed, or maybe...? But she couldn't let that enticing hope swamp her common sense. *He won't fall in love with me just because I love Egypt,* she told herself realistically.

Sayed was quiet again as he maneuvered through the heavy midmorning traffic. Robyn was having her first real look at Cairo since the brief nighttime drive from the airport with Tom. Her senses were busy savoring the fascination of the noisy, bustling city. As usual, Sayed seemed almost amused by her reaction to things, and she knew he glanced at her from time to time from the corner of his eye.

She turned to watch the progress of a great two-wheeled cart loaded with chairs whose French-style shapes were painted bright gold and upholstered in imitation petit point. Finding an indulgent smile on Sayed's lips, she felt very young. "I love to see things. It's fun," she said on a note almost of defense. "I haven't traveled much, but my father used to tell me incredible tales. If I had been born a boy I might have made travel my business."

"Hmm. You do not have the woman's desire for a home and family?"

"Not just for a safe place and babies, only with a man I could truly love. Then we would share ideas and work, and give opportunity to our children." She stopped, and bright color lit up her face under his gaze.

"So, you would be a helpmate to a man. Should you blush for such a fine desire?" His breathtaking smile shook her composure even more.

"I want to live to use my mind, to make some kind of contribution to the world's knowledge."

His eyes crinkled with humor. "No doubt you will, daughter of James Arthur Douglas. But what if some man came to sweep you off your feet, what then?"

"That won't happen!" she protested, too loudly, she knew.

"Hmm." He honked at a taxi and vegetable cart in his way and drove boldly through the narrow channel between them. "Did you know that the Prophet's first wife was a businesswoman? She advised him and even financed him while bearing him six children," he said seriously.

She shook her head slowly. "If she was so liberated, why...."

"Yes, why? The Prophet said that women were to be able to pray in mosques, that they should have the final say concerning whom they marry. It is possible for a marriage contract to specify a monogamous relationship."

"Then Rafica could—"

"She could, small bird, but the weight of long tradition is heavier and more difficult to work with than the words of the Prophet himself, on whom be peace."

Just then she didn't feel up to challenging him again about Rafica, and she lapsed back to silence, feeling guilty toward her friend. If only Sayed didn't have such power. He emanated a decisive male energy that was both intimidating and attractive, and she disliked herself for such weakness. The difference in their backgrounds was like a wall separating them. If she had been dealing with Tom she would have spoken again about Rafica's cause. She couldn't accuse Sayed of being unreasonable, yet there were deep convictions, limits to his tolerance that she didn't understand.

Sayed wove the car past a clanging tram. The vehicle was hung with riders whose galabias flapped in the wind caused by the motion. They laughed good-naturedly as Sayed bumped over the track in the middle of the road, so close to the tram that one fresh youngster leaned out with a grin to say, *"Baksheesh!"* to Robyn.

They turned into a parking area in front of an imposing old columned building that had a wall and a garden in front of it. Sayed drew into a tight parking spot and gave the attendant some money. "The Museum of Egyptian Antiquities." He motioned toward the building. At the other end of the parking area was the multistoried, modern Hilton Hotel—old and new architecture jostling for space in the crowded city.

Robyn squeezed out of the car and joined Sayed. Just inside the gate of the museum's garden she paused, looking up. Sayed gave her an inquiring glance and she said softly, "It's just as my father described and as I dreamed about. The 'Magic Place,' we used to call it. Many times I went to sleep imagining that I was here. I walked up those steps, and inside I knew just what to expect. To the right is a big statue of Alexander and to the left you can find artifacts from the Old Kingdom." A sudden feeling for her father flooded over her, and she felt tears prickle into her eyes. Quickly she ducked her head so that Sayed wouldn't see—but he had.

She felt his warm hand enclose hers. "Don't weep, little bird. Surely your father is happy that you are here."

She nodded, not able to speak yet, and his strong hand moved her gently forward. "I'm sorry," she said, after she pulled herself together. "It's just, well,

I always expected to come with him. Really, I'm very happy. I'm about to do something I have wanted to do for many years.''

Sayed smiled. ''You'll not be disappointed, Robyn. And don't forget, you're not alone. I'm here.'' They went up the stairs and into the cool halls of the old building. ''First we must go to the offices and meet with the antiquities people.'' Determination sparked from his eyes.

In the offices they were ushered into an old room with a few bare wooden chairs, a desk and bookshelves. Two pleasant-looking men rose to greet them. As Sayed made the introductions, Robyn felt the speculative scrutiny of dark assessing eyes. She stood up straight and looked at them calmly.

They were courteous, speaking mostly to Sayed, but in English for her benefit. A copy of Hassan Tarsi's letter of complaint was given to Sayed and her to read. In it he accused the university of making a secret deal with Sayed for some of the more valuable finds. He said that the chief sponsor of the dig, Mr. Huntley Saunders, was dissatisfied with the progress of the work and that he suspected underhanded dealing. Mr. Saunders charged that he had been asked to vacate the dig so that Sayed could carry out his secret arrangements. Dr. Tarsi recommended closure of the site until the truth could be determined.

Sayed handed the paper back to the officials. ''What is my reputation as an archaeologist?'' His voice was mild.

''You are considered top in your field.'' The answer came with a smile.

''Then what possible reason could I have to jeopardize my respectable position? I am a man of means and do not need secret funds.''

One of the men cleared his throat uncomfortably. "Dr. Tarsi says you are obsessed with the fame that would come if the scrolls are of importance, especially if they can be traced to the ancient library at Alexandria."

The other man remarked quietly, "He says that this man Saunders is willing to swear that you have been insulting to him and have threatened his reputation and that of Dr. Tarsi. We had no choice but to investigate. It is a delicate matter, Dr. al-Rashad...."

"And what is Tarsi's reputation? He is well-known to you as a difficult man, one who is not careful in his methods."

Robyn's mounting irritation reached a boil. "May I say something, please?" Three pairs of masculine eyes looked at her as though interrupted, but they deferred to her courteously. She drew a smile to her lips and looked into the waiting eyes. "I have been sent by my university as an observer, since we are in large part financing this dig. I am here in place of Dr. Wayland, the head of the school's archaeological work. I want you to know," she said with measured dignity, "that before we left the United States there was much trouble with Mr. Saunders, who wanted a disproportionate degree of personal publicity for the money he donated."

She took a steadying breath. "He was told then that the university would not tolerate such action. He insisted on coming to Egypt anyway, and he is not the sole financial sponsor of the dig. Several other large grants have been given, and even larger ones are pending if we can see into the unopened room below the present excavation."

She smiled again at the listening faces. "In my opinion, Huntley Saunders is a self-seeking egotist who, unfortunately, has money. I have spoken to Dr. Wayland and he supports my view.'' She paused. "I don't like to speak against my countryman, but Mr. Saunders has been talking irresponsibly. I have given him my views and Dr. Wayland's about this." She looked at Sayed. "Dr. al-Rashad heard my words to him and added some of his own, which were to the point. Mr. Saunders was violently angry, but clearly in the wrong. His accusations in this matter are purely malicious and unfounded.''

Robyn knew that she might be overstepping, but her momentum was pushing her to say everything that Sayed couldn't say to the men. "As for Dr. Tarsi, he is intelligent, but deeply jealous of Dr. al-Rashad's project. It is what he wishes he could have done himself. Dr. al-Rashad has been more than patient, and even helpful to an untrustworthy man." She saw that she had the full attention of the chief investigator and spoke to him directly.

"I have just sent in my report to Dr. Wayland. I am not unqualified to make judgments. My father was James Arthur Douglas, whose work and love for Egypt I am sure you know. He was at one time, in fact, Dr. al-Rashad's teacher. For myself, I am well-acquainted with the dig and its contents. I read hieroglyphics, demotic, Greek, and Roman scripts, and I have been helping to catalog at the excavation. I believe that the find is already one of great importance and that much more is to be found. Dr. Wayland has been informed about the Tarsi jealousy and the ego problem of Mr. Saunders, and he and I both have unqualified trust in Dr. al-Rashad's ability to carry on the work in the most correct manner.''

She paused for breath while slight smiles touched

faces of her audience. "You are men of great experience in this field, and I know that I really don't have to explain to you further. The whole problem is one of pitiably foolish human emotion, from two insecure and somewhat unscrupulous individuals." She smiled again, and was relieved to see genuine smiles returned.

"Thank you, Miss Douglas." The chief gave her a look that was no longer man to woman, but colleague to colleague. "I could wish that I had as competent a defense for myself in my professional problems. Dr. al-Rashad could not as easily discuss his own associate or your American donor without being thought prejudiced, so it was good that you came forward to speak for him," he said respectfully. "I think that we can dismiss this complaint as groundless."

He rang a small bell on his desk and a staff member of the museum entered, carrying a tray of steaming coffee. "Please—" the chief motioned "—I am happy that we can have coffee together as friends while we finish up the routine business. We will want to see the university contracts, if you please, and there will be papers to be signed by you, Miss Douglas, as university representative, and by Dr. al-Rashad."

The chief turned to Sayed and engaged him in a discussion of the dig. Robyn opened her briefcase and brought out the contracts and correspondence, including a copy of her report to Dr. Wayland. She was glad now that she had written it with such enthusiasm. There was a discussion with an occasional question in her direction, but she tried to fade into the background with her tiny cup of coffee.

Had she taken over too strongly? Would Sayed resent what he might regard as interference in his plan of defense? His face had told her nothing. Yet, somehow she felt good. She had, in a way, saved the dig, and she didn't want to think Sayed's masculine pride was so tender that he would resent her help.

Finally the men concluded their business. A copy was made of her report to Dr. Wayland. Sayed read it carefully, handing the original back to her with a steady look that didn't seem to be withdrawn. She gave him a small smile and he returned it, unknotting the lump in her stomach.

The officials wanted Sayed to go with them to the Antiquities Department offices nearby in the city on other business. They all stood up, and Sayed moved to her side. "Well done, Robyn." His voice was low, almost a whisper. It carried more feeling than his simple words.

"I regret having to leave you now, but what better place for you to spend time, hmm? If you are hungry, the Hilton is close, as you saw. It has a good coffee shop. I'll come back for you before four o'clock. Be near the entrance then."

"But this is my magic place, remember?" She smiled. "I'll be happy." She left the office with the men. The Antiquities officials said goodbye with real warmth, and Robyn watched Sayed's tall figure disappear with them through the entrance doors.

CHAPTER NINE

THE HOURS SHE SPENT in the great halls of human treasure were enchanted ones, and Robyn forgot everything but the excitement of seeing the marvels of antiquity. Tutankhamen's lonely jeweled sandals touched her more deeply than the gold and pomp of his funeral regalia. There were moments when she would have loved to share her feelings with someone, but she knew somehow that her father was near her in this haunted place of the past.

The textiles and manuscripts drew her like a magnet. She hung over a case containing an ancient marriage contract, and her heart began to soar once again. Absorbed in the delights of discovery, she forgot her hunger and her weary feet.

Four o'clock was suddenly upon her and she hurried to the entrance. Moments later Sayed arrived, whisking her out into the hot sunlight and the jarring noise of the city. She was silent as they drove away from the museum.

"Were you happy in your magic house?"

She smiled. "I'm not back here yet, I'm only up to about 100 B.C. All of this traffic and all these buildings must be unreal. Are you a dream, too?"

He laughed. "Did you have lunch?"

She shook her head.

"Just what I thought! I have phoned my mother. She will have a good tea waiting."

Robyn came down to earth with a thud, and her hands were suddenly as cold as ice. How could she meet the formidable, aristocratic Madame al-Rashad? Sayed said nothing more. They were leaving the city core, entering an area that was more residential. Villalike homes were enclosed by walls that also surrounded gardens and trees. Robyn sank into herself, too nervous even to put on lipstick.

Sayed gave her a quizzical look. "My mother isn't a dragon, Robyn. You will like her."

"I'm sure I will," her voice piped insecurely.

Sayed's face broke into a broad smile. "Is this the decisive young woman who spoke so eloquently this morning?" He reached into his breast pocket, drew out a small box and set it in her lap. "Well, aren't you curious?"

She opened the lid that had the name Ismael Fikri, Jewels and Antiquities. On a bed of pink cotton lay a tiny blue lapis figure surrounded by a gold chain. She picked it up with eager fingers, a sound of pleasure in her throat. "It's Ptah, the god of Memphis. How beautiful!"

"It carries my thanks for your invaluable assistance today. Everything is cleared now and we need only to sign some things tomorrow." His face softened as he watched her turn the tiny, ancient stone figure on its gold chain, her eyes shining.

She gave him a serious look. "I only did what seemed right. I'm sorry if I talked too much, but the whole situation made me so mad. Dr. Tarsi and that poor excuse for an American! They can only bring trouble for us."

"I agree." He turned into an open gate in a high wall and stopped the car near a hedge of flowering shrubs. A massive, square white-plaster house sat behind a wide porch with carved wood pillars. Several tall shuttered French windows faced out upon the porch, and an open door led invitingly to the inside. Robyn was reminded of the early-Spanish architecture of California.

Huge pots of blooming marigolds guarded the few shallow steps to the porch level. Sayed's hand at her elbow urged her up the steps and into the house, where she found herself standing in a lovely, airy room. An attractive native Egyptian rug covered a large area of the floor, and comfortable cushioned wicker chairs surrounded a round table set with a white linen cloth. The centerpiece was a crystal bowl of yellow roses. A silver pot on a silver stand was steaming over a candle flame and fragile china cups and saucers were waiting next to it. At the sight of the silver plates filled with tiny cakes and sandwiches, Robyn felt a sudden pang of hunger in her stomach, easing her nerves a little. The setting was gracious and welcoming, not at all like the stiff tea table of an English dowager—or what Robyn imagined a dowager should be like.

Sayed's hand tightened on her arm, and she looked up to see a tall, thin woman standing in the open doorway. The woman's face riveted attention. The smile was full of light like Sayed's, and the eyes were a bright clear blue, youthful and alert despite the soft lines of aging around them. Her waving silvery hair was piled up on her head and she wore a flowing gray caftan stitched around the neckline in silver. This was a woman with the ease of an aristocrat.

She came forward with a graceful motion, her welcoming eyes on Sayed. He left Robyn and held his mother close for a moment. Robyn saw the flash of diamonds and emeralds on the delicate hand that lay on his shoulder. Then a very English voice exclaimed, "How happy this makes me, my darling." The woman drew away from him and turned to Robyn, holding out her hand. "And you are Robyn Douglas. I am so delighted you have come, my dear."

Robyn couldn't help relaxing in the warmth of her smile and under the kindly touch of her hand, which was holding hers in a comforting clasp while the vivid blue eyes searched her face. "I met your father several times when he was working in Egypt. I imagine you were very young at the time, but I can see him in you, especially those serious eyes filled with dreams and endless delighted speculation." She laughed gently. "But you will want to freshen up before tea. Wafah will show you to your room and Famy will bring your bag."

A sweet-faced young woman appeared in the door. "Please to follow me, *sitt*." Robyn went through a large and beautifully furnished living room in the wake of Wafah, noticing the great stone fireplace, which she thought must be unusual for Egypt. Inviting-looking sofas mixed easily with stiff, finely carved furniture inlaid with mother-of-pearl. Robyn quickly looked around the room. Fascinating bits of antiquities and modern handcrafts were everywhere, and abundant bowls of flowers. Traditional Egypt and the style of Western Europe lived together easily here. The soft yet brilliant tones of beautiful Oriental rugs warmed the polished floor.

Other rooms could be glimpsed through wide

doors as they passed. They walked up a carpeted
stairway to a second floor, where Wafah led her into
a large bedroom that faced the east. Here, too, were
tall French windows, leading to a balcony. Wafah
showed her a modern bathroom tiled in blue and
lilac, with the dark slate-colored stone floor that
seemed to be the custom in Egypt. The bathroom in
her hotel room had the same slate floor. "Tea will
wait your coming." Wafah smiled and left.

Robyn wandered around the room for a moment,
curious to see everything. A double bed of heavy wood
stood against one wall. The low bedposts were carved
sphinxes, and the headboard had intricate and graceful inlaid designs. A sheer mosquito net with an embroidered edge was gathered against the ceiling above.

There was a peaceful energy in the room. The bed-
spread and curtains were of supple Egyptian cotton
in a pattern of mauve and soft blue stripes; a love
seat and an elegantly feminine armchair were
upholstered in blue, accented by lavender pillows.
The room-sized rug was a dark blue violet. In fact,
blue was everywhere. On the wall hung one of the
beautiful woven tapestries of Egypt, a village hand-
craft that Robyn had admired since her father had
brought one home many years before. Against its
creamy background blue birds perched on a tree with
green and violet leaves.

Luxury and comfort spoke from every part of the
room, but quietly and without ostentation. A large
watercolor of an English landscape hung on another
wall, showing oak trees and a lake and the thatched
roofs of a village in the distance. Robyn wondered if
the woman downstairs ever longed in secret for her
cool homeland.

The doors to the balcony beckoned and Robyn stepped out into an Arabian Nights atmosphere. The whole balcony was surrounded by a carved lattice-work of flowing design. Small shutters of various sizes and patterns hid away, but did not entirely obscure, the view into the large walled garden below. There palm trees grew around a fountain and a pool of lotuses. Such a balcony could have belonged to the harem of a caliph.

So this was Sayed's home. No wonder he had a self-assured manner, with such a background.... Yet there had also been the boy who ran in the lettuce fields at the delta farm.

Halting her thoughts, she went into the bathroom to splash cool water on her face and renew her makeup. She didn't trust her present mood. The desire for a home like this with Sayed must not even start its insidious entry to her mind. She shook herself like a small ruffled bird and pulled her dress into shape in front of a tall mirror.

Looking at the bed again, a sudden thought occurred to her—one that should have been obvious. Just then a light knock sounded on her door. She opened it to find a smiling boy in a galabia. He handed in her overnight bag and went swiftly away—Famy, no doubt. She had been right, she was to spend the night in this charming room. Despite the warm air, she shivered slightly. Already she knew that her memories of this place were to be bittersweet. How could she stay one night and not wish it were longer?

She hurried from the room and from her realization. From the living room she paused to watch Sayed and his mother deep in conversation on the porch, their chairs close together. The woman's loving hand was on his arm and he covered it with his own hand. His face was softer and more gentle than Robyn had ever seen it, making him look younger.

They both looked up at the sound of her footsteps on the polished floor. Sayed rose with a smile and seated Robyn beside his mother. As if by magic, Famy appeared with a wonderful big English china teapot decorated with a traditional pink cabbage-rose pattern.

Madame al-Rashad gave a fond pat to its shining curves. "It is my firm conviction that tea must be brewed in proper china. I always detect a taste of metal from a silver pot. Sayed thinks it's my imagination, and maybe he's right. I never notice it with coffee, even though it is often made here in brass pots that haven't been scrubbed out for years." She gave a little chuckle. "Of course, the English are known for idiosyncrasies, my dear—dreadfully irrational, but stubborn."

"My mother would agree with you about the tea," Robyn said. "It's not just the English. She believes in china, too, and I'm sure it tastes better when brewed in a proper teapot."

"There, I have support!" Madame al-Rashad exclaimed.

Sayed answered her I-told-you-so voice with a futile wave of his hand and a laugh.

"Now, let me guess," she went on, raising the pot and pouring part of a cup of very strong tea. "You will want hot water to dilute it, and lemon rather than cream. Do you care for sugar?"

"You've read my mind, Madame al-Rashad," Robyn laughed, enjoying her airy wit. "A small spoonful of sugar, please."

Appreciatively she sipped at her fragrant cup, savoring the delicious sandwiches and cakes that Sayed set before her on a dish.

"She had no lunch," he was explaining. "I left her at the museum and she became so entranced that she forgot to eat."

"Ahh." A gentle hand patted Robyn's knee. "A true lover of the past. My son tells me that you are the representative for your university and that you work closely with that charmer, Dr. Wayland." She smiled at Robyn. "You are so pretty and so young to hold that responsibility, yet I hear you were able to impress the heads of our Antiquities Department very well today."

Robyn felt a glow in her heart. So Sayed had already told her. "I only spoke the truth to them."

"It is a wise woman who does not dissemble." The clear blue eyes held hers steadily. "You know, my dear, I have never regretted leaving London society to marry Sayed's father—partly because truth seems to have become somewhat of an outworn virtue there."

Sayed leaned forward in his chair and spoke quietly, a deep loving note in his voice. "My father once told me, find a woman who lets you see her real self before marriage, not after. He was fortunate in his choice." His eyes looked into his mother's with unconcealed love.

Robyn felt an urge to say, "But your father was able to know your mother as a person before their marriage. In arranged marriages this is not so possible, is it?"

Madame al-Rashad's perceptive eyes moved from Robyn to Sayed and back again. "I take it that you are referring to marriage arrangements here. It's true that certain marriages are arranged and others are prevented because of prejudices and customs. The arranged marriage is most often seen in the villages." She paused, and her eyes went to Sayed. "Sayed's father and I loved one another, and because I was English I was expected to be a bit. . .different," she added, smiling.

"But the status of women is gradually changing around the world, isn't it?" Robyn pursued the subject.

The older woman looked at Robyn with interest. "Is there some particular incident that you don't understand?"

Robyn nodded and Sayed patiently outlined Rafica's problem of loving one man while promised by her family to another.

"Oh, dear, that sweet child. How miserable for her. The family is a kindly one, too." She looked thoughtful, and Sayed's watching eyes were speculative.

"Don't," he said, as if warning her not to interfere.

"Whatever do you mean?" Her face became bland and innocent, then she veered swiftly to another subject. "I do believe that modern women are becoming more honest. There are so many careers possible for us now, and we must meet men on an equal basis—not with the old way of indirection and acquiescence, but with our own inner strength."

Sayed's deep voice broke into her flow of words. "Relationships between men and women have to be based first on honor. A moral standard cannot simply be talked about, it must be lived. That is why in

Islam we try to protect women, perhaps because men believe that most women will surrender themselves under the proper persuasion.''

"I don't think that's true," Robyn retorted sharply, her irritation rising. How could this man seem so much at ease while he had such power to stir her reactions? "Lots of women aren't so susceptible. And what about men? They pursue advantage unfairly and then blame the opposite sex." A pink flush made her eyes seem larger and prettier.

Madame al-Rashad's expression was a little tense, then it relaxed. In an unconcerned voice she said, "My dear, don't pay any attention to my son, who is now posing as a worldly cynic. Ever since he was a child he has enjoyed giving a little stir to conversations. Like his father, he has an unabashed belief in his own considerable attractiveness. His problem is the need to experience more failures.''

She laughed at Sayed's disgruntled expression. "But that's only the outside male shell. Underneath is gold, pure gold." She put out her delicate ringed hand to Sayed and he enclosed it in his.

Robyn felt the warmth of their love, and she was lonely sitting at the edge of the comforting fire that would never be hers. No sooner had she let herself feel this than the conversation moved to more general subjects, allowing her easy entrance to them.

"And do be a friend and call me Daphne, would you?" Madame al-Rashad said at one point. "Formality merely serves to separate people.''

Robyn was grateful. It wasn't long before she knew that Daphne al-Rashad was deeply engaged in social work, health and education. She had interests in almost every kind of human activity.

Robyn's mind wandered happily in the agreeable setting. The charm of the big house was its timeless peace, she decided. It might have been the home of an Egyptian noble of old days, and there sat the descendant of one of them, she was sure.

"Do many families in Egypt trace back to ancient times?" she asked.

Her question brought a brief silence to mother and son. Then a twinkling smile came to Daphne al-Rashad's face, while Sayed sighed and raised his eyes to the lotus patterns painted on the ceiling of the porch.

"You have opened a door that will not be easily closed," he said, as if to a fat pigeon on a rafter.

"Pay no attention to him. How delightful, my dear, that you have hit upon my hobby. Yes, some of the families can trace back beyond the days of the caliphs and Alexander and the Persians. The threads are tenuous, of course, but I have some scraps of manuscripts handed down in our own lineage. I'll show them to you this evening." Her face was alight like that of a delighted child.

"This evening I intend to take you both to dine at Kasr el Rachid at the Meridien Hotel," Sayed interrupted.

"Lovely," his mother exclaimed. "Then we must take Robyn to the tower for the view from the observation platform. I'm positive you haven't given her a moment's rest to be a tourist."

She turned to Robyn. "It's beautiful by night—or day. You can see as far as the other pyramids beyond Saqqara." She rose, still smiling, and Robyn and Sayed stood up, also. "You don't know what a treat it is to have company. My daughter lives in Saudi

Arabia with her husband and my younger son is still at Cambridge. And this rascal is always traveling about or digging in the sand.'' She placed a loving hand on Sayed's shoulder. ''Robyn, you would probably like to rest for a while. When shall we be ready, my dear?''

''We should leave here about eight-thirty.'' Sayed put an arm around her straight shoulders. ''I have some phone calls to make and a few things to prepare before tomorrow. I'll be in my study.''

Robyn said impulsively, ''If you need typing done I'd be happy to help.''

''Good. Now rest, small bird, and I'll call you later.''

His mother's eyes had a speculative twinkle. ''What is the small bird, my son?''

''I didn't tell you...'' Robyn answered swiftly. ''My father loved the old languages, as you know. He named me in ancient Egyptian—Sesha Neheru.''

''Small bird among flowers,'' Sayed translated. ''Robyn for short, and for convenience,'' he said, smiling at her. ''I'm afraid I've been teasing Miss Douglas, but she does suit her name, don't you think?''

''Hmm—yes, indeed. Surely you aren't embarrassed by your charming name?''

''Not really. In fact, I love it, except that most people can't read hieroglyphics and don't understand ancient Egyptian....''

''And you do?'' Madame al-Rashad asked, her fine eyebrows raised.

This time Sayed spoke first. ''Hieroglyphics, demotic, Greek and Latin.'' Robyn felt at a loss. The list sounded so terribly pedantic and scholarly.

"But how delightful. Your father taught you, no doubt—of course he would have done. I remember his enthusiasm." She looked at Sayed. "You didn't tell me how truly accomplished she is."

"I knew you'd find it out very soon."

Madame al-Rashad put a light arm through Robyn's. "Come, we will rest and then talk more." She yawned delicately and walked Robyn to the stairs. Sayed turned away to his study.

Robyn didn't feel in the least like sleeping, but she obediently followed her hostess upstairs. At her door she was suddenly the recipient of a gentle, enfolding, fragrant embrace, and she felt a light kiss on her cheek.

"Later I want to talk about Rafica," the older woman said in a low voice. "I'm sure you can tell me more of this than Sayed. I'm so very happy you are here. Rest well." She continued down the hallway with a graceful motion to her tall slender body, and Robyn went into the blue bedroom. Her mind was buzzing with questions and anticipations.

Thank heaven she had brought the silk skirt and the dress sandals. Someone, undoubtedly Wafah, had unpacked her case for her. She looked at the skirt and ruffled blouse. They were plain, but nice. The skirt was a soft tone of amber, matching her sandals and tiny evening bag. The ruffles on the blouse didn't look too crushed. They made dainty rows around the wrists of the flowing sleeves and gave softness to the V neckline.

She remembered the jeweler's box still in her purse and took out the lapis Ptah pendant to hold against the blouse. It would look lovely with the sandy beige color of the fabric. The small blue god seemed to tingle in the palm of her hand. Sayed's energy was in it and she shivered with the potency of it. Sighing, she dropped it in the box again and prowled restlessly around the room.

On the balcony she opened one of the many small shutters and gazed over the walls to the east. Out there once stood the ancient temple city of On. She remembered the story her father had told her at bedtime about the Bennu bird that flew up from its flaming nest, renewed with life; the Greeks had called it the phoenix. Now there was nothing left of the old holy place but an obelisk and a few walls to mark the site of the proud priests and the temple of Ra, the sun god.

Robyn's thoughts came back like a magnet to Sayed; a subject from which they were never far away. She could imagine him in the garb of an ancient nobleman, a wide collar of lapis, gold, turquoise and malachite over his dress of fine pleated linen. She pictured him strolling by the pool in a long-ago garden, much like the one below. His strong hands plucked a pure-white perfumed lotus and held it out to her.... She closed the shutter with a snap and turned her back on it. "Don't, Robyn Douglas!" she said aloud.

With determination she took a shower in the pleasant bathroom and set her travel clock by the bed. Rest would be impossible, she knew, but she lay down anyway. The soft warm air and the deep comfort of the bed's smooth linen sheets gradually soothed her to sleep.

A light knock at her door woke her. Wafah entered at her sleepy response. "I bring a message from the Sheikh al-Rashad."

Robyn blinked; that meant Sayed. Wafah's voice continued, "I am to say, *sitt*, if you will dress ready for dining, he would be happy for your help in his office in one hour."

"Tell him I will come."

"May I bring you refreshment? Is there anything you wish, lady?" Wafah's face was earnest.

"Thank you, but I don't need anything. And thank you for unpacking, Wafah."

A wide smile broke across the pleasant dark face. *"Afwan, sitt."* She went out the door.

Robyn's stomach tensed with excitement. She had an hour to prepare, and knew she would enjoy it. Fantasy took over again and she dreamed that this was a real date with the man she loved. The practical part of her mind grumbled protests, but she was determined to treat herself to the forbidden delight of her imaginings. She wanted to remember this forever—this stolen hour in this lovely room, with the lotus fountain singing softly in the garden. If she dared to look down from her balcony she would see the handsome prince still there in his linen robe, caught somewhere between past and present, and real only in her imagination.

Her hair had curled loosely after its steamy shower, and she pulled it into a relaxed knot on top of her head. There was already a soft flush on her cheeks and the pupils of her eyes were wide and dark with anticipation. A touch of eye shadow and mascara made them more vivid. Sayed had never seen her looking elegant and well dressed. It would be a secret pleasure to watch his face when he first saw her. The amber skirt and soft sash tied gracefully over the blouse, and she pulled the ruffles into attractive curves around her neck and wrists. The lapis Ptah hung in the hollow of her throat like a tiny caress. Her old honey-colored cashmere sweater would have to do for a wrap. She touched herself lightly with perfume and, taking her evening bag, opened her door onto a deserted hall.

Downstairs she hesitated—which way to go to find his study? A short wide hallway led out of the living room, and she heard a rustling of paper from a door to one side of it. With her footsteps silent on another colorful rug, she peered into the room. Sayed looked up from a large desk that was mounded with papers.

"Oh, there you are." His factual voice shriveled the last remnant of the dream. "Forgive this mess." He waved at the confusion on the desk. "The typewriter is over there."

A small table in one corner overlooking the garden held the waiting machine. His hand held out a sheaf of papers to her. "I need a good copy of these. As you will see, there are corrections to be made."

She went to the typewriter in silence and sat down to her work. His voice followed her. "You don't know how much I appreciate your help, Robyn."

She turned, meeting his deep eyes steadily. "It's my pleasure. If we had more time I could do a little filing for you." Her eyes appraised his cluttered desk with the cool look of an expert secretary.

"Hmm. So I've been caught in my own litter like a rat in his nest of scraps." His voice again held a light teasing tone.

While she lined up the first piece of paper in the machine her mind was storming rebelliously. *Not one word that you look nice! That should tell you what he feels!* Her fingers flew, spurred by irritation. She would show him how efficient she was. There was no conversation, only the sound of her typing. Once in a while she raised her eyes to glance at the garden, glowing with color in the long rays of afternoon light, but she worked steadily and soon the pile of finished papers was almost complete.

As she rose to hand them to him he smiled gratefully. "This has been a great help. I'm nowhere near your speed and accuracy." He stood up and opened one of the tall windows. "Come out into the garden. I want you to see something."

Reluctance and desire battled within her. How could she go into the romance of the sunset garden with this cool and potent wonder of a man? But her feet took her through the door and she felt his firm hand urging her toward the lotus pool.

Her breath caught with delight as she saw the lotus flowers up close. White and creamy, or blue and vivid, their thick fragrant petals stirred memories of graceful ancient ladies painted on the walls of tombs, each hand holding just such a perfect flower. Now, floating in the pool among their leaves, the lotus blooms seemed to glow with their own light.

"They are never changing. Are they not lovely?" Sayed's voice made her look up to catch a smile of pleasure on his lips. "I knew you would find magic in them." He leaned over the water and selected a partly opened blue bud, pulling its stem with a swift snap. His fine hand held the blossom out to her, and she took it with a shivery sense of wonder.

"To match your Ptah, sweet Sesha Neheru."

His voice as it spoke her name stabbed with an agonizing pleasure, and her hands tensed until she almost crushed the cool lotus stem. Her dream came flooding back, and it frightened her to have so little control over it. A delicate painful whisper ached into her heart: *Who am I that I dare to hope for his gaze as he walks with his thoughts among the golden lotuses. . . . He is as far above me as the sky. . . .*

With an effort of will she pulled herself back to the present. Sayed's eyes were on her face. "Where were you, small bird? Did you fly away into the past? I couldn't tell if it was with joy or sorrow."

Surprisingly, her voice sounded normal. "I guess I fell back into time. I've seen pictures of ladies holding lotuses so often, and now here I am holding one—a real one!"

He laughed gently. "How much you are your father's daughter. But now we must find my mother or we will miss our reservation at the Meridien." He hurried her inside, where they found Madame al-Rashad just coming downstairs. She was elegantly simple in a soft blue floor-length dress, a loosely woven stole to match.

"There you are, my dears. How delightful you look, Robyn. It's a pleasure to see *you* in a proper suit." This to Sayed, who straightened his peacock-blue tie and adjusted his heavy silk suit over broad shoulders while he quirked an eyebrow at her in pretended offense. She had another stole over her arm. It was like a small cape of smoothly brushed wool, creamy and thick. "I brought this, Robyn, because it becomes very cold at night on the tower. I think your light sweater will not be enough protection." She dropped the soft warm cloud of wool over Robyn's arm and drew her sweater off her shoulders in one decisive motion. "We'll leave the sweater here. Now, let us go."

Sayed gave Robyn a wink. "*Maktoub*—it is written."

"I am not bossy," his mother said in a tone of finality.

"The stole is lovely. You are very, very kind," Robyn said sincerely, and Sayed laughed quietly deep in his throat, reminding her of a contented leopard.

Sayed disappeared for a moment, then brought a blue sedan around from behind the house. Madame al-Rashad smiled with satisfaction. "The Peugeot is much more comfortable than Sayed's little contraption."

The car sped through the balmy darkness toward Cairo. In the distance the pyramids at Giza were bathed in illumination, bright cameos against a dark velvet sky. Whispers of turquoise light lay along the western horizon and the stars were glowing like opening flowers.

Even at night the swift traffic of the city was befuddling to Robyn's sense of order, but Sayed was a master driver and soon they were drawing up to a large circular building near the river—the Meridien Hotel.

The evening became an enchanted blur from that point on. Robyn tasted many exciting dishes of Eastern cooking at the elegant restaurant's lavish buffet, while the sinuous beat of Egyptian music enfolded her. Daphne al-Rashad and Sayed outdid themselves tempting her with treats, until she was surfeited by sensation and was glad to sip at a tiny cup of bitter Turkish coffee.

Outside once more, away from the luxury of the hotel, the pungent odors of the East flowed over them. Sayed drove across a bridge and stopped at the foot of the tall Cairo Tower, which looked like a long-stemmed modern mushroom. An elevator propelled them swiftly to the observation place at the top of sixteen stories.

Robyn gasped appreciatively at the view that spread around her. Sayed came over and stood beside her, pointing out various landmarks. The Mohammed Ali Mosque was luminous on the Citadel, rising out of the old city, and other great mosques thrust their minarets upward from every section of Cairo.

The wide smooth breast of the Nile curved its way to the sea, shining in the light of a three-quarters rising moon. The sky seemed to have a light of its own, a living quality.

"No wonder the ancient ones used the symbol of a sky goddess arched overhead with stars adorning her body. The sky is an actual presence here," Robyn said softly to Madame al-Rashad.

"Out in the desert it is truly alive. The stars are like the watching eyes of Allah's angels," Sayed said out of the darkness.

Robyn was glad for the warmth of her shawl, and for Sayed's mother, whose gentle hand held hers while she pointed out the hazy shapes of pyramids to the south.

"I never tire of Egypt or of this amazing city." Her voice was soft in Robyn's ear. "I remember those nights with Khalid, Sayed's father, when we went into the desert at Saqqara. We would sit together on the sand with the ancient Step Pyramid behind us, among sand-covered hillocks that were surely unexcavated tombs. I often sifted the earth through my fingers and found tiny beads, and once an amulet of blue faience—a Horus eye. I still have it." She sighed with remembrance and went on. "It was the night when I found the Horus eye that Sayed was conceived. No wonder he loves the past." A whisper of a laugh touched her words.

"That night we sat near the edge of the desert cliff, overlooking the palm groves where old Memphis once lay behind her white walls. The breath of palms and other growing things came to us, while below on the canals the caravan birds called into the living night and the stars glimmered with the breath of Nut, the sky goddess. At least that was how Khalid described it." She turned her still-lovely eyes to Robyn and tears glinted in them.

"I loved him, my child, more than my life, and I miss him as though he had left me only yesterday. He was a man to trust, full of the power of a generous heart—a unique being to whom my destiny is bound forever." She looked at Sayed, who gazed over the city lost in thought. "He is the fruit of the splendor of love—my dear son, who is so like his father."

She added in a practical tone, "My son Kamal in England is like me." She put her hand on Robyn's for a moment. "Choose love, Robyn, even if the choice brings pain. It is better than safety and it takes bravery to recognize it."

She turned to Sayed. "It's chilly. Let's go down now."

THAT NIGHT Robyn sat down on her bed, her mind racing and far from sleep. She had put the wilted lotus in water. Somehow she would preserve it—press it dry and keep something of its beauty to haunt her memory.

Sayed had given a brief good-night, kissing his

mother and brushing aside Robyn's thanks for the evening. "It's a pleasure to show things to one who enjoys so much, isn't it?" he said to his mother.

"Enthusiasm is a gift to be cherished, my dears. How I tire of the so-called sophisticated women who make life a game of acquiring sensation," she had said, looking directly into his eyes as if they had spoken of this subject before.

As Robyn was settling into her fairy-tale room, a light knock came on her door and the handle turned to admit Madame al-Rashad.

"I've brought you a hot drink that is typical of Egypt." She raised a small tray so that the two glasses on it could catch the lamplight. The steaming liquid in them glowed ruby red. "It is called carcady, a tea of a special plant that is soothing and aids the digestion. I thought you may have eaten unusual things this evening that you are not used to."

She set the tray on a small table and sat down in one of the armchairs without invitation. After all, it was her house, Robyn thought. She couldn't help liking Daphne al-Rashad.

As if in echo to her thoughts the soft English voice said, "I like you, Robyn."

She smiled and Robyn did, too. "You work well with Sayed. I can see you have an easing effect on him. He carries such a lot of burdens, here in his family and in his work." Her eyes watched Robyn's face carefully for response.

"I can see he is a very responsible man."

"Yes." Then Madame al-Rashad made a startling turn in the conversation: "Haven't you wondered why he hasn't married?"

Robyn's nerves jumped at the candor of the question. "Why, no," she lied.

A tiny smile dented the corners of the older woman's fine lips. "Then you'll probably be the first woman in his adult life who hasn't done so." She shook her head slowly. "Actually, *I* don't know why, and I'm his mother! He certainly doesn't lack for women, but he seems untouched by them—except sexually. After he returned from studying in America he had an almost cynical veneer about women, especially foreigners. I suspect that there was one who led him on rather far and then cut him off."

She slanted her blue eyes at Robyn, whose color was increasing with each revelation about Sayed's past. "I would like grandchildren before I become too old to enjoy them. And the family needs to grow. Al-Rashads have always contributed to the energy of Egypt."

She took a soft leather notebook from the tray. "These are the manuscripts I told you about, giving proof of the family's continuity. Come, try your carcady."

Robyn drew up a chair to look at the book. "Here," Madame al-Rashad urged, "open it on your lap and examine it." Some of the pages were clear plastic, protecting scraps of papyrus and vellum. Other pages contained listings of names in Arabic. There were notations and translations, all neatly typed.

One fragment of very old papyrus read:

In the tenth year of the glorious reign of Ramses, the son of Seti, a son was born to Ra-Sa-Ded, friend to Pharaoh and chief counselor to Pharaoh's house of books, and his wife Lady Kepri.

Other fragments still held the name Ra-Sa-Ded. There was one in demotic script from the third century B.C., and another in Greek noting that the family of Xenios Rasaad held a grant of land from Ptolemy Philadelphos. The family was obligated to pay taxes of grain, lettuce and onions, so much per *aroura* of cultivated land, and a certain portion of gold to the royal treasury.

"That land is the same as our present farm," Madame al-Rashad said. "Of course we have better records after the seventh century A.D.; I am now used to calling it C.E., for the common era, since Egypt is not largely a Christian land."

"This is wonderful," Robyn exclaimed.

"Sayed thinks it is foolish to believe a name from the time of Ramses the Great would be connected with our family, but Sayed's great-grandmother was still alive when I married his father. She was terribly old—no one was sure just how many years—and she was still clearheaded. She gave the fragment to me and told me that family oral history confirmed it. Unfortunately, she died before my Arabic was good enough to get the full story." She sighed. "I never could get Khalid to take an interest. Such a pity!"

They drank the pleasantly aromatic carcady in silence. "Would it appeal to an American to be part of such a long tradition, do you think?" Her eyes probed curiously at Robyn.

"It's fascinating. I don't see why it shouldn't be true." She gave a little laugh. "In the United States we take pride if our family came over on the May-flower from England, just a blink of time ago." She hesitated, then went on, "The first time I saw your son, Madame al-Rashad, I was reminded of the face of a nobleman of the Old Kingdom.''

"Ah. So you have seen it, too. Khalid had the resemblance, also.'' She patted Robyn's hand. ''Do you think you might stay on in Egypt for a while? You've seen very little as yet. If you should decide to stay, you are very welcome to make this house your home base. I miss my daughter. It would be a pleasure for me to have you as a guest, my dear.''

"How kind, and how tempting.'' Robyn's thoughts raced. What would Sayed think? With a sigh she changed the subject to Rafica and her troubles.

"I don't care what Sayed says.'' Daphne al-Rashad's eyes sparkled when she had heard Robyn's version of the tale. ''I am going to get to the bottom of this. I'll go to the farm for a few days and just happen to visit the village.''

"That gives me hope. I've come to love Rafica. She deserves happiness,'' Robyn replied.

"And what do you deserve, my dear? What about happiness for you? I see a sadness in you that should not shadow your youth.''

"I'm not sad—not really,'' she evaded. ''I miss my father, who was my best companion.''

"And what about young men?''

"Well, I'm not an exciting beauty. I'm just an average, pleasant girl who frightens men off because I'm always talking about things that happened thousands of years ago. I don't enjoy football games, and besides, I'm not good at competition like some women.''

"Ah! Let me tell you, Robyn, that you are very charming. You have no false pretenses, your mind and your accomplishments are very fine. I think your self-assessment is dreadfully mistaken in every respect.''

Robyn looked into the older woman's bright eyes. ''Thank you. It's nice to be told something like that.'' Suddenly she laughed. ''Huntley Saunders, the obnoxious man who has been such a problem at the dig, said it was always the plain ones like me who had flings with the tourist guides and cab-drivers....''

''What an awful person! I suppose you had set aside an attempt on his part to be more friendly.''

''He had made a halfhearted pass,'' Robyn agreed ruefully.

Madame al-Rashad rose and picked up her book from Robyn's lap. ''I'll let you get some sleep. That son of mine will run you ragged with his business tomorrow, no doubt. He was really very pleased with your help this morning with the Antiquities Department. I'm glad he has met an American like you. His attitude toward women is, perhaps, a bit unrealistic, his search, perhaps, one for perfection that would be hard to find in any one woman.''

She leaned down to give Robyn a delicate kiss, then picked up the tray. ''Sleep well.'' She went out the door, her pink peignoir trailing behind her.

CHAPTER TEN

THE HOT CARCADY DRINK worked its soothing spell, and Robyn slept deeply. In the morning she went to her closet and found her tan cotton sundress. It was low-necked, but modesty would be preserved by a long-sleeved mauve overblouse, which was embroidered around the V neck with tiny mauve flowers. Even though old, the ensemble was in good shape and cool. The heat of the Egyptian sun, so much more penetrating than that of California's, was already setting a wavy haze over distant hills.

She was glad that she had at least bought some good-looking canvas walking shoes before she left home. The tan espadrilles were not heavy or clumsy; more than ever before in her life she didn't want to appear unfeminine.

Her few belongings were quickly packed, and the lotus was wrapped in some paper guest towels. It would somehow find its way intact for the final plane ride back to the United States. She went to the balcony to look one last time at the garden and its entrancing pool. Her fingers touched the carved shutters lovingly. This was part of the little paradise to which her memory would return again and again.

The breakfast table was set on the eastern terrace, shaded by a trellis of green vines, with oleanders in huge pots blooming white and scarlet. A tree covered

with large blooms of a deep golden pink stood beyond
the trellis. Bees sang in the sunshine and a beetle waddled along the nearby path, leaving a fascinating
calligraphy from his shiny black legs.

Robyn had the garden to herself for a few minutes,
and she reveled in the color and joy that seemed to
radiate from the plants and the earth itself. Her heart
lifted from the sadness that had been like a tiny persistent ache inside her. She would enjoy this day.

Words from the *Kasidah* of Haji Abdu el-Yezde
came into her mind. She could still see the small blue
gray book in her father's hands. So often she had
pored over those small gems of poetic wisdom, learning them by heart. It seemed right to remember that
distant voice in this Middle Eastern garden. The words
echoed her own unspoken lament:

> Why meet we on the bridge of Time—
> To give one greeting and to part?

She looked up to find Sayed gazing down at her.
"In the past again, small bird? Where have you flown
this time?"

It was hard to meet his sunlit face, so bright was the
beauty her love saw in it. "I was remembering some
poetry about gardens that I used to know."

Daphne al-Rashad came out into the sun, her step
light and youthful. "Do you like it here, my dear? To
me a garden is a place where troubles have no entrance."

"Your garden is such a place."

"All the work of my mother, on whom be peace,"
Sayed said, as he moved to kiss her offered cheek.

They ate breakfast unhurriedly, chatting about the

trees and flowers. Everything held an unreal quality, and Robyn resisted the thought of leaving. Her heart seemed to cling to the trees and the limpid lotus pool, and when it was finally time to go she had to wrench herself away.

Madame al-Rashad enclosed her in a warm, fragrant hug. "You must come again, Robyn. Think about what I said."

Robyn's thanks felt inadequate on her lips. She could have wept. She straightened her back and marched to the car with Sayed. Famy had already put the bags in the trunk and now stood beside the car to speak a goodbye in soft Arabic words.

With Sayed's usual swiftness, they drove toward Cairo. "What did my mother say?" He kept his eyes on the road.

"What?" Robyn couldn't decipher his tone.

"She told you to think about what she had said."

"Oh. She suggested that I might want to stay longer in Egypt—to see more of the country after the dig is closed for the season. She was kind enough to offer your home to me as a place to stay. Of course I wouldn't impose on her generosity; and anyway, I must go home, even if I haven't seen all I'd like to."

He turned his eyes toward hers. They were charged with the blue light that she found so startling. "And would you like to stay in Egypt? Have you a sense of ease here, or is it all just colorful and strange?"

She hesitated for a moment, then answered honestly. "I feel I belong here—more than I expected to. Things are not so convenient here as at home, and they are different—as you say, colorful and strange. The pace of life is not the same. The suffering is more noticeable, both with the people and the animals."

She felt she could say these things to him, since he wanted an honest answer. And she really did love Egypt.

"Then you are not fearful of the turmoil of change that is sweeping us toward a new destiny?" He gave her another penetrating look. "There are deep stresses in Islam that must be resolved. Egypt has chosen to take a path of moderation and peace in the world. Such an effort always draws out violence, as we have seen."

"But stresses are worldwide, aren't they? We all have to start to understand better about human needs and feelings. That's why I love the past. My father always said it could teach people how to deal with the future." Her eyes turned to his intent profile, and she saw a smile move over his beautifully defined lips. "Even in university too many students, unless they are history majors, don't know much about what humanity was doing before the First World War. They know a tiny bit about Napoleon and Julius Caesar and Alexander the Great—maybe George Washington. But the past isn't real to them. Few of us in America know the history of Islam, I'm sorry to say. I think that's why the discovery of Tutankhamen's tomb hit at our imagination so hard. Suddenly there were tangible things, objects of everyday life. The past had become real."

There was no reply from Sayed for a moment, and Robyn wondered if she had sounded too pedantic. But she had only spoken her own deepest thoughts.

"You amaze me, Robyn," he said at length. "There are so many things hidden behind that gentle face of yours. I agree with your opinions of the past and present. I think you understand why I desire so urgently that those scrolls we have dug out of the earth be from the ancient Library of Alexandria. I want people to see how human growth and knowledge can flower in an atmosphere of peace and encouragement, and how vulnerable our hard-won progress is to the forces of destruction. That was a library built to last forever, with its hundreds of thousands of scrolls and its incredible influence on science and thought. And yet, after only six hundred years or so, it was nothing but a pale shadow of itself. The great books were gone, burned or taken—or hidden. And it took hundreds of years for mankind to reawaken from the Dark Ages and rediscover the lost knowledge. We must not have another Dark Age, Robyn," he said passionately. "The free flow of the written words of man must never again be stopped."

He drove in silence for a time. Robyn was burning to talk about the library, but her mixed feelings—of love and of awe at his powerful energy—kept her mute. She was angry with herself for her shyness.

Sayed spoke again on a surprising new note. "How is it, Robyn, that you are wise and capable in some things and yet seem to have remained unsophisticated in others? Surely in your country, where men and women are so free together, you are not an innocent."

His tone was probing and not especially pleasant. "I don't know what you mean by innocence," she said tartly. "Of course I go out with men at home, if that's what you are asking—" he gave her a quick look with narrowed eyes "—but I do have my own standards of behavior. I am not obliged to follow society's permissiveness."

"Hmm, I see." His foot pressed hard on the accelerator and he screeched around a lumbering donkey cart, once again leaving braying and cursing behind him.

He didn't see at all, Robyn fumed, and here he was, judging her for something he knew nothing about. She felt defeated, although they hadn't really been fighting. It was his attitude toward women that she found so irritating. Surely Daphne al-Rashad would not have put up with a husband who patronized and judged her, or did she know the secret of handling Egyptian men?

She tried to take her mind off of his powerful presence and turn it to the sights and sounds of the city. It would be nice to feel angry at him, but the best she could do was to try for a cool and businesslike manner.

They arrived at the museum again. Inside, a secretary told them that the papers to be signed wouldn't be ready until afternoon. Sayed's face went dark for a moment, then he did some phoning, obviously pressing for speed, but without success.

Robyn felt in the way. When he looked at her with frustration written on his face, she said, "If there are things you need to do, don't concern yourself with me. I'll enjoy the museum and walk around the city, do some shopping. I'll meet you back here whenever you say."

His eyes flickered with a slight smile. His good humor seemed restored. "Across the street to the left, where all the trams are, you'll find some good shops. Small antiquities and gifts. Meet me here at noon for lunch." He waved away her look of protest. "I'm not taking a chance on your missing lunch again. Didn't anyone tell you that thin women are not to the taste of Muslim men?" he teased lightly. "I'll take you to see the Mohammed Ali Mosque and for a look around the city. By then the papers will surely be here. I'll use my time this morning to make sure we have our drill firmly committed for tomorrow's work at the dig.''

Outside the offices Sayed left her to drift around the museum again. It was early, and the busloads of tourists hadn't begun arriving. She was able to stand for a time before the cases of ancient jewelry, marveling at their perfection, and visit King Tut's treasures without being jostled.

Then she went outside and had to fight off the urgent but polite offers of hopeful tour guides. She regretted that her light-colored hair branded her instantly as a foreigner, when she really wanted to fade into the background and pretend that she truly belonged here.

She made an escape across the busy street with its loaded trams and followed an avenue that angled across the city. She was delighted when, a few blocks later, she found bookstores. She browsed for an hour, finding volumes in English, French and German, as well as Arabic. She would teach herself Arabic as soon as she returned home, she vowed. Somehow she felt that she must understand the subtleties of the Muslim world, not just in translation. *And,* the little voice commented truthfully, *you want to be able to meet Sayed on his own terms, not as a foreigner.*

Inside the stores the familiar jumbled piles of used books and the neat shelves of new ones made her feel at home again. Finally, loaded down with irresistible purchases, she struggled back toward the museum. It was hot and humid. The darkened shady interiors of the shops in sight of the museum drew her in.

She sat down with a sigh and sipped the complimentary mint tea served by the proprietor while she hunted through dusty boxes of ancient coins. She couldn't hide her pleasure at finding a silver coin of Alexander the Great, and one of Ptolemy Soter, the founder of the Greek dynasty of kings in Egypt. She had always loved Ptolemy, since he was the one who had started the Library of Alexandria around 300 B.C.

For her aunt and mother, and for friends, she bought some modern jewelry with ancient designs. The Alexander coin would be for Dr. Wayland. She would have it set in a key chain for him.

Time had flown, and she rushed back to the museum, to find Sayed seated on a bench in the garden by the entrance. He rose with a smile. "Let me help you, my little donkey. Such a burden in so short a time of shopping," he said. "The papers have not yet come, so we will have to drive home after dark. We can have dinner by the pyramids and you can see them by moonlight—a full moon, it seems. Doesn't that do something for your romantic soul, small bird?"

In the car he approved her choice of books, especially a big volume full of wonderful Greco-Roman portraits done on the lids of sarcophagi. "You chose well," he said, nodding, "but you haven't thought about how you will get them home. I'll send them through the university as official business. It will save you problems on the plane."

Lunch was at a garden restaurant hidden deep in the old city between high walls. Birds in reed cages called to one another from a high trellis and the food was delicious. Sayed deliberately drew her into conversation. They talked about Alexandria and the library; about the *fellahin*—the village people; about the stresses of searching for antiquities. He soon had her laughing at his amusing tales of his own experiences.

Her nervousness began to ease, but it was still hard to look for very long into the blue depths of his eyes and remain cool. The slight accented stress of his voice pronouncing her name sent a shiver along her nerves. Sometimes she lost track of what he was saying, just enjoying the vibration of his deep tones. She tried to draw his every movement, his every statement into her memory so that she would lose nothing.

They drove to the Citadel and entered the beautiful Mohammed Ali Mosque after covering their shoes with protective slippers. The quiet of the great echoing place with its lovely play of light and shadow soothed her—except when his hand, guiding her to see some special beauty of carved marble, sent her senses into a riot of response. Why should the smallest touch make her hunger for more, she wondered unsteadily, as if she couldn't survive without it?

There was a stairway leading to a carved pulpit. It was a special place, he told her. "If you walk under the stairway it will bring the fulfillment of a wish."

They walked toward the small passage and Sayed stood smiling, waiting for her to step through the carved screening. Suddenly her heart cried out its wish into her mind: *Let him love me!*

He was watching and she tried to look nonchalant. "Did you wish?"

"Yes." She felt the tide of hot blood in her face and he laughed.

"I hope it comes true," he said softly. He bent to kiss her upturned face—swiftly, as he might have kissed a child.

Her knees signaled weakness and her breath seemed

trapped in her throat. *I love him,* she thought painfully, *and I always will.*

After wandering in the neglected garden of the mosque they leaned over the parapet to look down on the roofs of old Cairo. In the far distance the pyramids raised their tawny sharp forms on the desert plateau, and just below were the Arabian Nights rooflines of the old city. Farther on, near the Nile, growing clusters of high-rise buildings formed a modern skyline.

Robyn was terribly conscious of Sayed's warmth beside her as he leaned close to point out special areas of the city. The effect of his tall body on hers was disconcerting. His slightest contact sent fiery messages of pleasure into her nervous system. *This can't go on,* she ordered her stubborn flesh.

Back at the museum the papers were signed and approved. It was after four o'clock. Sayed was obviously happy, and when they got back to the car he tapped the manila envelopes that contained the new agreements with an approving finger. "This will keep Hassan Tarsi in line," he said with satisfaction, then turned to her with a smile. "I promised you the pyramids, if my memory is correct."

He moved the Fiat out into the honking turmoil of Cairo traffic. "But first I think we will go out to Saqqara. I feel like relaxing before I go back to the sour faces of Tarsi and Saunders and have to decide how to proceed with them." He headed westward along the broad double Pyramid Road, with its green center strip of hedges clipped into pyramid forms.

Robyn said nothing. She would have gone anywhere with him. This was a blessed gift, having more time to spend with him. He hadn't consulted her wishes, but somehow it didn't matter. She wanted to see Saqqara. How often she had pored over pictures of the Step Pyramid enclosed by its sacred area of high walls.

"This time of the day is the most beautiful." Sayed's voice had a tranquil tone. "If I were an artist I would always paint when the sun sends its long shafts of light to enhance the colors of the world." He looked lovingly across the flat green fields, now covered over in places with homes and apartment buildings.

Robyn could see the love of his land in the gentle set of his mouth, and her heart echoed it. There was a warmth in the land itself that reflected into the eyes of the people, an eternal caring and patience and creativeness. She longed to speak of it to him, but a kind of fear stopped her. Suppose he thought she was just angling for his attention and favor? His changes of mood baffled her, kept her from letting him know her as she really was.

He was an enigma, and she was desperately swimming in an uncertain sea of emotions, trembling with each look or touch or word of his. She had to stop herself, had to accept his offerings for what they were: isolated gestures of friendship only. She would have that, at least, to remember. Maybe she could correspond with him on archaeological subjects. Maybe Daphne al-Rashad would write back and forth with her. That way she could find out what was happening in Sayed's life, at least obliquely. It was a tiny bit of hope and comfort.

His voice interrupted her thoughts. "Why such a sad face, my friend?"

"I guess I was wishing to see the way it was long ago; you know how I am."

"We can't bring the past back, but we can go forward into the future. May Allah grant that the best of our wonderful heritage will help us toward a worthy tomorrow."

The sun was slipping fast toward the horizon as they drove through the gate of the Saqqara area. The guards knew Sayed and gave greetings. They walked among the beautiful walls and temples of the Old Kingdom period. Sayed showed her into tombs with walls exquisitely colored, delicately carved, where the daily life of a prosperous land was pictured.

Bats flew with high-pitched clamor from the quiet of the tombs. He led her to the cliff edge to look down at the palm trees of ancient Memphis. "Here I was conceived, or so the story goes," he said with a laugh.

"No wonder you sometimes look like the nobleman Hesire in the carvings." Impulse pulled the words from her.

He smiled, taking her hand. "I will remember that compliment, Sesha Neheru. I can't think of one that could please me more." He kissed her hand and released it. "We must go. The light is fading and I want to drive you to the Great Pyramid at sunset."

She sat covering the tingling hand that he had kissed while the car sped along a road near a busy canal. Little brown children splashed in the water as they bathed big white water buffalo and donkeys released from their day's burden. Geese and chickens gossiped along the banks.

The pyramids of Giza loomed in silhouette against an orange sky, and the smoke of cooking fires rose from the whitewashed houses in the villages. Large estates were hidden behind flower-covered walls and fences. Men walked in groups or sat around little tables in front of one-room coffee shops.

Mena Village, just below the brooding Sphinx, was full of dust and motion. Its narrow winding streets hid homes behind high dust-colored walls. Sayed wove deftly through the traffic, animal and human, and aimed the car toward the Sphinx. The great face was in shadow now, but its presence was full of power.

"He is our grandfather," Sayed said in a quiet voice. "At a certain time of year all the marriages in these villages are celebrated at one time so that the brides can walk in procession around the Sphinx. It is a charming ceremony and may have long roots in ancient days." He eased the car to a stop along the curving road.

In its hollow of sand the Sphinx crouched patiently, lost in the meditation of eternity. Robyn felt something of its ancient peace soothe the disturbance of her spirit. Sayed slid the car into motion again, and they drove around the Great Pyramid and down another curve to the greenness of the Nile Valley again.

Taxis waited at the gates of the Mena House hotel, sitting in the midst of its lush lawns and flowers. Darkness was closing in quickly, and Robyn looked back to see the face of the Great Pyramid illumined by floodlights.

Sayed turned the car to the left onto a narrow road that paralleled a canal. They were moving through cultivated farmland. The sweet damp scent of growing things filtered through the more acrid aroma of wood fires and what almost seemed like spice.

The silence between them was not awkward; it held companionable feeling. Little lights from farms twinkled out of the darkness here and there. Sayed stopped the car off the road, beside a wall and a lighted trellis gate. On the curved top of the gate was written La Rose.

"This is a pleasant restaurant. I hope you will like it." He slid easily from the car and came around to open her door. Inside, a large area under vine-covered trellises accommodated many tables with white cloths and bowls of flowers. The floor was hard-packed earth, and pots of flowers bloomed everywhere. An efficient headwaiter took them to a table at the end of the outdoor room, which overlooked a wide canal.

Moonlight was disputing the soft lights and the candles flickering on the tables. The bright moon image shimmered in the canal waters, and a small farmhouse could be seen on the far side of the canal. There, in the dim light of a fire, two great white water buffalo lay at ease and a camel sat folded on his jackknife knees. While Robyn watched entranced, a small child in a long robe came to put its arms around one of the buffalo, leaning against the great bulky shoulder. Both child and animal seemed unaware of the audience across the canal. Robyn turned to Sayed with a smile of delight.

"So you *do* like it," he stated, his face beaming one of his heart-disturbing smiles at her. "I enjoy this more than the Mena House or the Meridien. And the food is very good."

"The entertainment is wonderful, too." She waved her hand at the scene across the water. "Where else could it be possible to eat dinner and watch a scene out of the Old Kingdom?"

The headwaiter arrived at their table and Sayed ordered for them both. There were the usual bits of vegetables and toast to eat with taheena, the tasty sesame seed paste, and *babaganoush*, a spicy eggplant dip. *Gambari*—large shrimp—followed, grilled with herbs, and then rice with a thick green sauce that seemed to be made of finely cut up stewed leaves. It had a strong flavor that startled Robyn's taste buds at first, but which she found delicious as she ate it.

Sayed watched her take more sauce and looked amused. "You are a true Egyptian. That is called *thalokhia*. It is usually served in private homes, and people have secret recipes for it handed down in their families. My friend the chef knows I enjoy his particular mixture, so he makes me a special dish. To most visitors it is an acquired taste."

"I've always liked to try different food, and I do enjoy eating. Unfortunately, perhaps."

His eyes looked her over with a twinkle "Why unfortunately? You have a sweetly shaped body. As I told you, men in Egypt don't admire bones that stick out, as they do in Europe or America."

He stretched a hand across the table to touch her cheek. "Surely you are used to compliments?"

Her pride rose up as swiftly as her pulse. "Of course."

"Then you have had many compliments, is that what you are telling me?" The blue sparks in his eyes probed hers. "Are there no restrictions put on you by your family concerning men?"

She began to tremble inside. "You've asked that before."

"I am serious. I am trying to understand you, Robyn."

"What's to understand? I don't believe in sex as an appetite to be satisfied, but as a particular joy to be experienced with someone very special." The words came out baldly, partly because she hated to sound so unsophisticated with him and partly because he kept bringing up the subject.

"Only someone very special, and not necessarily your husband? Then you exercise the right to choose what you will do sexually?"

"Yes."

"And you believe that a woman can mingle with men freely? Without the protection of society in case she should fall prey to the persuasions of an experienced man? You do not think that a woman needs to be protected from herself?"

Her irritation flared dangerously. "I believe that women can be self-responsible, but I don't think this conversation is, er, worthwhile."

"Then you don't believe that a man can seduce a woman against her will."

She gave a long-suffering sigh. "No."

He withdrew into silence and Robyn picked nervously at the remains of a dish of vine-ripe tomatoes. Surely some of the sophisticated ladies that rumor said he was partial to were not strangers to calculated seduction. She felt dreadful. Whatever she said was wrong. She didn't know how to deal with men, especially *this* man, with his quicksilver temper.

A welcome interruption to their heavy silence came with a dish of *mahala biya*, a luscious rice pudding dessert. Sayed began to talk about the dig and the need for haste. "We must have *haz*—luck," he said brusquely.

The pleasure of the evening had disappeared for Robyn. The full moon was now covering the canal with liquid silver, but the flow of its romantic light flooded her with distress. What had been so warm and exciting was now cool and impersonal again. The rice pudding seemed too sweet, too full of the taste of pleasure. Its plump raisins and bits of fruit should be the food of lovers on a night like this, when everything in nature spoke of love.

A carawan bird called on a long fluid note, and tears gathered under her eyelids. The pudding sat heavy in her stomach and she felt a little ill.

"Shall we go?" Sayed's polite voice asked.

They left the restaurant to the kindly goodbyes of the waiters. Sayed turned the car back along the way they had come. "I enjoyed La Rose very much," Robyn ventured into the silence.

"Good." Sayed gave her a slight smile that held out warmth again. "We will visit the Sphinx by moonlight." It was almost a command, yet there was more than that in his words.

Her heart began to beat with anticipation. At least she would see the pyramids in this rich silvery flood that was streaming across the quiet land. What better memory than to be with this beloved, maddeningly inexplicable being in a magic world? She knew, despairingly, that her love for him was deep in her soul and that the roots of it could not be torn out without pain to her.

The car wound up the curved road to the desert plateau again. The Great Pyramid loomed like a glowing wall against the starry sky.

"Ahh, the sound and light program is over and most of the people are gone." Sayed slid the car to a smooth stop on the flat area that surrounded the pyramid. He uncoiled his long legs from the car and came around to help her out.

She stood looking at the vast angular building. The strong simplicity of its lines seemed to vibrate with force. She was drawn to its silent strength; perhaps all the stories about its mysterious energies were true.

There was a sense of peace and eternity in its very stones.

It pulled urgently at her until she found herself crossing the pebbly ground toward the huge stone blocks of one corner of the pyramid. Rough places made easy steps to climb the first tier of worn stone. She put her hands against the great squares of the second tier and leaned her cheek against it, feeling a startling warmth under her hands. The stone was still full of the sun's heat, and it felt like a warm being at rest—alive and somehow intelligent.

She turned away from the towering wall of masonry and collided with Sayed. He was standing close to her, his eyes bright with moonlight.

"It's a strange feeling, isn't it?" His arm had come around her as she bumped against him, and she drew in her breath sharply. Her body was signaling delight again. He was still holding her close to his side. He bent his head to look into her face. "You felt how warm the stone is. . . ."

"Oh. . . yes." She gathered her wits. "It's. . . it feels alive."

He laughed softly, pulling her against his strong body in a little hug that set her heart thudding in erratic rhythms. "Just what I thought you might say. You are an original, Robyn Douglas. You can be trusted to come up with none of the usual reactions." He jumped to the ground and helped her down behind him.

Out of the dark moon shadows an old man and two younger men materialized. "These are the night guardians," Sayed told her. There were solemn handshakes all around. The old man drew a tiny blue imitation scarab from his robe pocket.

"For you, lady." He put it in her hand. "You love Egypt." It was a statement, not a question. "Good luck!"

"Aiwa." Sayed took up the conversation in Arabic. Obviously he was giving Robyn an impressive status, because three pairs of eyes beamed respectfully at her.

"Lady professor," the old man said, "I am a poor man, but it would give me pleasure to give you tea at my home."

Sayed laid a gentle hand on the old man's shoulder. "My friend, I want to show the lady Khafre's pyramid and look up at the face of our grandfather in the moonlight. We must then drive to Alexandria tonight. May we be honored to come to your home another time?"

The old man smiled and gave an acknowledging bow. "Come, I will take you to the guardian."

As they walked down the curving road toward the Sphinx, their guide kept turning his face toward them, his smile broadening each time. He broke into a series of delighted chuckles while unlocking the gate to the fenced area around the Sphinx. "To look close at great face is most lucky, lady...hee, hee! Good for bride to come here—is good for marriage and make many babies...hee, hee!"

Robyn was grateful that the moonlight hid the rush of scarlet to her face. Sayed said nothing, looking unperturbed. The friendly old fellow drew back into the shadows with the perceptive kindness that Robyn had noticed to be characteristic of Egyptian people.

Together she and Sayed walked forward, to stand between the huge front paws of the lion body. "Now what are you thinking, small bird?"

"I was thinking about the prince who had a dream

here, promising him that he would become Pharaoh if he cleared away the sand from around the Sphinx. And it all came true. I think this is a good place to have special dreams.''

Sayed's hand took hers with a gentle pressure. ''And what would you dream about?'' She felt his warm breath close to her face.

Her hand, beyond her control, trembled slightly in his. ''I . . . don't know. Maybe how to find a real clue to the library. I'm not the kind of woman who dreams for impossible things.''

She was pleased to have turned away his question easily. She feared he was testing her again with questions that had hidden meanings, and she couldn't give him more ammunition to judge her harshly. *I want him to care,* her thoughts whispered drearily. It was so ironic to be standing drenched with moonlight, hand in hand with the man she loved, and yet to have this awful sense of loneliness and frustration.

''Will you make a wish?'' His voice had lost the warm invitation that had vibrated through it a moment ago. ''Or was your wish at the mosque sufficient to your needs and desires?''

She didn't want to answer him. Drawing her hand free of his she joined her palms and made a small bow, then looked up at the great far-seeing face above her. She couldn't possibly feel frivolous about this. In the holes of the shadowed eyes a look of patient compassion seemed to send strength to her, and she spoke to them. *Let me understand love,* her heart whispered. *Let some bit of love for me be in his heart and memory. Give me as much of him to remember as possible. . . .*

''Have you asked for marriage or for an exciting

lover? It's hard for a man to imagine what a woman wants."

She made no answer and he turned away. They climbed up the path to the road again, after shaking hands with the old man. Sayed set a brisk pace across the flat stony desert earth toward the second pyramid.

They walked close to the immense pile of stone. Against the white disc of the moon it seemed vast as a mountain. Robyn looked back at the Great Pyramid and the crouched and sleepless Sphinx. Even though the pyramid next to them had been built by Khafre, son of Khufu, whose wisely powerful face commanded attention from his green basalt statue in the museum at Cairo, it could not rival the mystery of the marvelous energy of the great one, the first pyramid.

Sayed said nothing, and Robyn was loath to break the silence of the place. He put an urging hand under her elbow and moved quickly again. They went around the western side of the Great Pyramid and Sayed stopped abruptly. He stamped hard on the ancient paving, and a hollow sound answered from the earth beneath his foot.

"Below where we are standing is one of the ancient sun boats, not yet excavated," he said, sounding like a guide. "We know of several others nearby. The one that was found was in perfect condition. It was assembled recently and put on display in a special building. But it is no longer on view, due to problems with deterioration. It is difficult to keep a proper and stable environment for something that has been hermetically sealed for thousands of years." In the moonlight he gave her a quick apologetic smile. "I'm sorry you won't be able to see it. It is removed from public view and protected until the problem is solved, but without doubt it is one of the most beautiful things I have ever seen.''

Not waiting for an answer he hurried her forward again. There were still a few people wandering around or sitting on the broken edges of the pyramid. Robyn wished that she could find a stone niche and sit in it all night, absorbing the feeling of peace that flowed from this amazing place.

They reached the car and Sayed handed her in. He pushed a button and the car's top folded down. ''I'm so glad we won't shut out the night,'' she said delightedly.

He started the car, causing a flap of night birds' wings and disturbed cries. The engine sounded a harsh note into the ancient energies of the area.

He turned the car onto a road that Robyn knew curved down to Mena Village, but instead of continuing toward it he took another road that led westward over a series of small undulations of the bare desert.

Soon a small hollow and then a low hill put them among dim shapes of excavated tombs, and finally the desert stretched its tawny moon-white space outward to infinity.

Sayed drew the car to the side of the road, slid out and came to open her door. He said nothing, only extended his hand to help her out. She stood looking up into the starry sky washed with moonlight. Dark shadows obscured Sayed's face, but she felt the heat of his body near her in the night.

It was growing slightly cool and a soft wind blew like a touch against her hot cheeks. She moved a few steps onto the sandy soil and then, growing brave, walked toward the uneven horizon, not looking back to see what Sayed was doing. She wanted the warm darkness to enfold her, wanted to be absorbed into the starry bowl of the heavens and the earth, as it would be possible to be absorbed in love.

She stopped and looked up at the stars, now seeming to wheel in vast measured circles in the sky. There was a sound like a deep harmony, heard more by the mind than by the ear, humming around her. Suddenly the depth of the sky was an endless space into which she could fall, clutching at the moon's bright path.

She remembered how it had been as a child to look up into the deep sky, leaning against her father's loving arm. "Don't worry, I won't let you fall," he would say softly. Now her head whirled and she swayed with the starry rhythms.

Then a strong arm came around her and she was drawn back against a firm warm body. Almost without thought she leaned against him, and then she realized what was happening. A shiver of delight and fear rippled its yearning way through every nerve. His arm tightened against her trembling, and she felt his soft breath stir the tendrils of hair at her neck, then the exploring heat of his lips against her shoulder.

She had to break away immediately or be lost in the joy of his touch. She stiffened and said in a shaky voice, "I was dizzy for a moment looking up. I was pretending I could see the sky goddess, but I'm all right now."

His strong hands whirled her around to face him. "Don't talk so much, and don't flutter so. You ran into the desert to be caught." His voice was very deep and rough. One hand cradled the back of her head and the other caressed a line of fiery response along her spine, pressing her against the wonderful strength of his body.

She saw his lips moving toward hers while the moonlight drenched his face in silver. She couldn't turn away with that urging hand tangled firmly in her hair, and she wanted more than anything else in life to have those beautiful lips touch hers once more.

All her reason fled and in its place was a need for fulfillment, an urgent desire to experience the touch and taste of him, to be drawn into his vitality.

His lips touched hers gently, and then insistently. Her shaky last resolve made her try to hold her own lips closed against the fire of his exploring tongue, but they failed to obey her and she found herself dropping into a deep space of pure blissfulness while her lips opened to him.

All her love and need rose like a flood and she was kissing him back with a thirst that could not be denied for another moment. Her hands against his chest felt the strong excited beat of his heart, then slid upward to fasten eagerly around his neck. She explored the crisp softness of the hair behind his ears, and the wonder of touching him set off thundering waves of delight that almost deafened her.

He murmured deep in his throat and his lips slid down to the soft hollow between her breasts, while his hand started an electrifying path, pushing apart her blouse, expertly releasing the three small buttons on the bodice of her sundress. The cool air stirred against her skin and she felt her nipples grow taut. His hand gently stroked the fullness of one breast and then the other as he worked to free them completely. She shuddered from the unbearable gentleness of his stroking, and he gave a low, silent laugh that had the sound of victory.

"Please," she whispered weakly, in spite of her

fierce desire to have him take her. Her hand moved down to cover his, making a feeble attempt to stop his fingers from their excruciatingly pleasurable play with her passion-hardened nipples.

"Tell me you want me to stop," he breathed, as he untied the thin straps of her dress and cupped her breast upward for his lips and tongue to find. His breathing was rapid and impatient, and the passionate virility of him flowed over her, arousing more need, more desire... until she was helping him to push away the loose bodice.

Her head was swimming and she couldn't say the words that would stop the onslaught of his potent force. She could only move with him as he drew her down slowly to the warm sand of the desert floor. The weight of his hard body pressed against her and she had no will to prevent his hands and his lips from their determined path of discovery.

Soft moans of impatience came from his throat as he reached the impasse of her waistband. It was almost too much to bear. She wanted, almost more than breath itself, to strip away everything that separated their bodies from the promise of fulfillment.

The first alarms began to ring through the paralyzing joy of his touch. He must not go further... this was much too far already! But her heart wailed from its little paradise, *let me have just one moment more— one last kiss!*

In a final moment of clarity she knew without any doubt what she had to do, and it was the most painful thing she had ever forced upon herself. She took a deep and trembling breath to push him away from her, releasing her hands from their eager hold of him. In the same instant, before she could execute her withdrawal, he suddenly straightened and seized her arms, gathering them in back of her.

His eyes were open and shadowed. She knew instinctively that this was not an act of lovingness or even raw passion. He said nothing, but held her from him, arching her back with the steel strength of his hands, turning her so that the moonlight shone full on her breasts and her flushed face.

Fear flew through her body. He was hurting her. Sayed smiled sardonically, looking from her shocked eyes to her lips to her breasts with a deliberate stare, like a jaded pasha surveying the goods in a slave market.

"So much for your talk of purity," he hissed with a fury that was tangible. "You know quite well what will arouse a man, and you would have gone with me as far as I desired. What a disappointment you are!" He ground his teeth and gave her a sharp shake.

She couldn't meet the mocking smolder of his eyes, and she turned her head away helplessly. The rush of her own blood surged deafeningly in her ears. His unleashed anger overwhelmed her and she despairingly realized that his misunderstanding was complete. There was nothing to say to him, no words to express her feelings at that horrible moment.

He saw tears well up in her eyes and let go of her, so suddenly that she fell back roughly onto the sand. "Cover yourself!" he ordered. Her hands reached to pull the bodice of her dress back over her throbbing breasts as she rose slowly to her knees.

If she could have folded up into a tight ball and rolled away she would have. Instead, the weight of his denial pressed her down and she sat like some archaic figure, head lowered in her hands, while uncontrollable sobs shook her to the core of her heart. The angular desert pebbles cut into her knees, but her flesh was numb.

Sayed stood a few feet away from her, outlined against the glow of distant Cairo. His hands hung at his sides, balled into fists, and his head in profile was bent.

She heard his long sigh and then he turned toward her. "Come, Robyn." His voice was patient. "To learn a lesson is a good thing. Crying won't help. We have to drive to Alexandria now." Then he quickly changed his tone, "You act as if you had been raped. What happened was because you wished it. Don't think you can manipulate my sympathy by tears."

He strode over to her and lifted her sharply to her feet. His piloting hand steered her to the car, where she huddled down into the seat. The sobs were silent now, but her mind still wept.

He drove the Fiat back toward the city at reckless speed. The imperturbable Sphinx still sat gazing eastward and the three pyramids were silent presences. Was it only a while ago that she had been so happy here? It seemed like another lifetime. And the worst of it was that she still loved him, in spite of what he had just done to her.

She quietly pulled herself together, at least outwardly, and wiped at her tear-salted face with one of the little wet towels that her mother had given her. "Those foreign places are bound to be dirty," she had said with a finicky tone. "Goodness knows where you might find yourself, dear. Be sure to always take one of these towelettes in your purse."

Sayed drove rapidly, his eyes on the road. Anger began to rise in her at the indignity—the unfairness—

of his treatment. There was a cynical cruelty in him that she couldn't fathom. She ventured into the thick silence, ''I was going to stop you—''

''Good.'' His eyes didn't leave the road. ''Just don't forget that men will take what is offered, but that they dislike accomplished teases. You probably know that already.''

She was unable to say more. To call it teasing was to make it ugly and hateful, as if she had planned it! Tears were hot in her tired eyes again, but she refused to let them flow.

A quick look at Sayed's set face brought back the yearning. She wanted him still, with every rushing beat of her heart. John had never kissed her as Sayed had done; this was entirely different. What she had thought was passion, perhaps even love, was only a childish colorless nothing compared to the drowning ecstatic response she had felt tonight.

She should despise him, sitting there with his lips set in stern judgmental lines and his expression cold. He had put her in the wrong and humiliated her, but only because *he* had been the one who called a halt to passion when she should have. He would never believe that she had tried. It made all of her talk of virtue seem laughable. And then to weep in front of him!

She looked away and tried to stop thinking. The moonlight was beautiful, making the long road a silver ribbon at the edge of the shadowy desert. To the right the Nile waters gave life to the land. Long rows of windbreaking trees flourished, protecting fields of crops. On the left the desert stretched out into a pale infinity. They passed a group of camels standing silhouetted on the horizon.

A few hours ago she would have asked about them,

but now the silence was not companionable. And worse, the waves of masculine virility that were part of Sayed reached out to her and she still longed for his arms—now more than ever. She needed his comfort, even though he was the one who had removed it from her.

Sayed stopped at one point and put up the top of the car. He didn't ask for her help and she didn't offer it. Little gusts of wind were blowing fingers of misty sand across the road as they neared Alex. "The wind begins again, *Inshallah*," he muttered, and drove with more tension.

Finally Robyn gave up all thought and dozed off, her body turned away from Sayed in the soft car seat. She woke to a bump and sudden braking. They were crossing an area overgrown on each side with reeds— part of the ancient lake of Mareotis that lay like a barrier between Alexandria and the desert.

"Some sheep were in the road," Sayed said briskly, swinging the car to full speed again. "And, no, nothing was hurt."

The lights on the outskirts of the city were coming into view, and Robyn knew that she had only a few more minutes to endure her painful situation. Her head was swimming and she longed to fall into oblivion in her own bed at the hotel.

"Perhaps I should apologize—from your point of view," Sayed said evenly. "But frankly, Robyn, you were to blame. I wish I understood the confusion of the American women I've dealt with. I have to look at facts, my dear." The endearment pressed like a freezing knife into Robyn's heart. "I have seen how vulnerable women are to men's needs." A challenge sparked in his eyes.

She drew breath to object, but he gave her a silencing look. "I thought that there could be a new woman—one who could be trusted to love a man of her choosing and his, trusted to be honest and not to shame. I think I was hoping for too much."

Her lips opened to dispute his outrageous statement, but he interrupted her. "No need to talk about it, Robyn. We cannot solve this problem. You have your standards and I have mine, and they do not meet in harmony. I should have realized it sooner and spared both of us this unpleasant scene."

That was the last straw. "You are impossible!" she fumed. "Blind and lacking in perception! Look at your mother and father—they chose each other, and your mother wasn't even an Egyptian. Look at my parents, and a lot of other true couples—Dr. Wayland and his wife, whom he dearly loves!"

"Hmm. Of course my father was certain that my mother was untouched and he made sure of her happiness. As for others, I don't doubt there are happy marriages in Egypt and the United States. But this discussion is useless. When our parents were married the climate of sexual permissiveness was far different."

Robyn sat up straight. Words exploded from her. "You know nothing about me! If I should tell you that I am 'untouched,' as you call it, I am more than sure that your rigid mind would reject what I say!"

He was looking at her with a penetrating attention and she plunged on. "It is unjust of you to draw conclusions, unfair of you to say that I went into the desert to tease you. My God! A psychologist would say that something was wrong with *you*, not me! I was simply overwhelmed by the beauty of the moon and the stars, and I never expected you to try to take advantage of me in such an ungentlemanly way." She stopped a moment at the thunderous look growing on his face, but he said nothing, merely studied her as she went on, "I must admit, to my shame, that the setting drew me into a kind of romantic unreality. It was so different from anything I have known, and then I suddenly woke up from the spell of it, to find what? That you were going far beyond what I would have expected from the protective friend I thought you were!"

A strange expression was on his face now.

"I am aware," she said more softly, "that Muslim men want their women to be virgins. I can agree to that desire as a good one, but does your honor of women extend only to women of your own faith? Am I fair game because I don't belong?" She was shaking, and clasped her hands together to keep them steady. "Or was this a test to see if I was acceptable?" She turned her eyes away from him, to watch the passing outskirts of the city.

"You think it was a test?" he repeated slowly. "Perhaps it was, and I was prepared to let you fail it. For myself, I will want a woman who has not been explored by other men." He gave a short, futile sigh. "But you are right—my understanding of you is difficult."

"Then don't punish me in the name of some disillusionment in your own life."

He turned sharply toward her with a steely look, and then a slight quirk of a smile moved on his lips. "So be it. We all have devils hidden deeply in our hearts, is it not so? Let this experience show you how fine a line protects innocence from disaster."

He turned his attention to the intricacies of Alexandrian traffic, which seemed to be heavy no matter what the hour of the day or night. Sayed's set profile forbade more talk, and Robyn agreed with him on that—it was futile to try to make him budge from his point of view, no matter how mistaken he might be.

They drove the long curve of the corniche while the moon made magic gold and silver paths over the sea. Just being away from the desert made her start to feel a little better. The clear ocean air wiped away the memory of the heady desert fragrance, but it was still a night for lovers.

So might it have looked when Cleopatra stood at her palace window, secure within the arms of her bold Caesar, the conqueror of the world and of her heart. Angrily Robyn shut away the picture. What a child she was!

Her heart beat heavily. This was the disastrous end of her unbridled dreams. Would she never again sit beside Sayed, alone with him, sharing the joy of a moment when they both understood something and didn't need words to express it? A shiver of coldness, a lonely dreariness, shook her.

They moved past the high walls of Montaza Park and pulled up to the impersonal presence of the Palestine Hotel. When they did, Sayed came to help her out of the car, carrying her overnight case through the swinging glass doors.

She held out her hand for it beside the elevator doors. "I enjoyed seeing Cairo." She swallowed at the hard lump in her throat. "Thank you for your time. I hope the new agreements will make things easier. Good night." If that sounded to him like a recorded message, then fine—that was the best she could do under the circumstances. She turned away and punched at the elevator button, trying to restrain tears.

"Good night, Robyn; no thanks needed. Let us forget the rest." Sayed's tone was so odd that she looked up at him again and surprised a puzzled and speculative expression in his eyes.

In her room she flung her bag onto a chair and set about unpacking with all the pent-up energy she couldn't fire at Sayed. She found herself staring at the remnants of better moments—the fading lotus from the magic garden and the jeweler's box that held the lapis Ptah pendant. She felt like sending them back to Sayed, but that would be too dramatic, as if she were breaking a relationship. *A relationship.* Tears started flooding again.

How could it have happened this way? She was the one who should have stopped the growing excitement. If she had, there would be no question of virtue and he would have drawn away immediately. *And probably be angry at me for* that, *too,* her mind shouted. She was glad she had not been keeping a heart diary; instead of a happy ending there would be this murky mess.

At last she got into her nightclothes and climbed into bed, punching the damp pillow under her hot cheek. She didn't know exactly how she should act for the remainder of her time in Egypt. She didn't have much practice as a fallen woman, but she was not going to let Sayed make her run away.

On that she slept.

CHAPTER ELEVEN

IT SHOULD HAVE BEEN A DAY to celebrate: the crisis with the antiquities office was resolved and Sayed was firmly in control of the excavation once more. The drill had arrived at the site while they were in Cairo, with the crew ready to begin this morning.

By some stroke of kismet the most severe winds had held off their attack, and it seemed a sure thing that today or tomorrow would bring the answers that everyone had waited so long to know. Even Huntley Saunders had a cooperative tone in his languid voice for once. In the lobby of the Palestine he was checking the borescope equipment, ready to shepherd it to the dig in his Mercedes.

Robyn had been turning over in her mind what to do. She was past the point of running home with her tail between her legs, another victim of foreign travel and romantic delusions. Dr. Wayland would never hear of her failure of character and will.

"Too soon old—too late smart," he liked to say, and the old saw ran around in her mind that morning. For her it would not be true. Sometime during the night of heavy sleep and dreams she had had a sudden infusion of wisdom that straightened her backbone, her resolve. . . her dignity. It didn't matter what Sayed did or said anymore. He had cut himself out of her life permanently, unforgivably. She wouldn't dream of asking for another dose of humiliation, and the little bird wasn't going to hide in the flowers waiting for his next move.

She purposely joined Tom and Rafica in Mohammed's car, knowing that it would pick up Sayed and Dr. Gaddabi in the city on the way to the desert. She was going to teach him a lesson about American women: they were strong even in defeat. Her jaw was clamped shut and her eyes had lost their shy little-girl look. If he wanted honesty he would have it.

"Anything the matter?" Tom asked, after a long silence from her as they drove. "You look like you could eat glass and it wouldn't bother you."

"I've just done a little thinking, that's all," she answered tersely.

"Not about the excavation, I'll bet."

She didn't answer, and Tom and Rafica looked at each other in understanding. Sayed greeted them all briefly and sat in the front seat with Mohammed for the rest of the drive to the dig. Dr. Gaddabi took the far back seat, where he proceeded to work on some papers.

Robyn willed Sayed to look at her in the rearview mirror so that she could meet his eyes squarely and steadily. Instead, he turned around to speak. "Today will be the day, my friends...*Inshallah*." He didn't look at Robyn. "Tom, we'll need one last check of the site to make sure it is cleared of papyrus fragments. You too, Rafica. When the drill crew starts working, anything that is still in the earth will be trampled. I trust Sandi is in the other car. If we ever needed accurate photographic records, it is today!"

"She's there," Tom answered. "I made sure of it."

Sayed turned back to the papers on his lap and said nothing further while Mohammed maneuvered the car over the rough desert terrain. Robyn had become an invisible passenger. *Look at me,* she mentally commanded him.

As the dig came into sight over the last low rise, the car was quickly surrounded by a group of gesturing Bedouin workers all talking at once. Mohammed stopped the car and Sayed got out.

"Oh, God!" Tom said. "They're saying that someone came in the night and wrecked the drill motor and the generators. Sand in the gas tanks...." He sprang from the car to join Sayed.

Dr. Gaddabi stayed behind. "Vandalism. Someone is desperate to stop our discovery. Someone with a vengeful nature."

"Who?" Robyn demanded. "Hassan Tarsi?"

"Perhaps, but there are others who would enjoy seeing Dr. al-Rashad lose his reputation," he mused thoughtfully.

"Devils!" Rafica burst out. "Let me find them and I will not be lenient!"

Dr. Gaddabi put a comforting hand on her shoulder. "Pray it is only the machines and nothing else. They can be fixed."

Sayed returned to the car and Mohammed drove the rest of the way into the camp. "Rafica, the papyri must be checked at once. I'm sure the Bedouin had nothing to do with this, but it was someone who knows our work well. With the generators down there were no lights here last night, and there won't be lights again tonight."

"We should have taken the cataloged fragments into Alex before this," Rafica moaned. "I blame myself for not being better organized."

"Don't," Sayed said curtly. "You have worked as hard as you could. It was my responsibility to protect the finds."

Huntley Saunders ran up to the car in a rage. "I've given enough money to prevent such a thing! Your superiors will hear about this, al-Rashad!" He banged the car door with his fist. Hassan Tarsi was with him, but it was hard to know what emotions were visible in his shining black eyes.

"Come," Rafica said to Robyn. "We have to examine the workroom. I'm afraid of what I may find there."

The door was still locked. "It appears to be undisturbed," Rafica remarked with relief. Inside, after a quick examination of the trays and fragments, Robyn and Rafica assured themselves that nothing had been vandalized.

"But something could have been taken out of here," Robyn said, looking at the piles of uncataloged papyri that still waited in the larger boxes. There were several large scroll fragments that had been among the last to come out of the niches in the dig.

"If only we had worked faster," Rafica complained to herself. "Then we wouldn't have to guess what has been taken. Everything would have been safely at the museum by now!" Her face was shadowed with self-accusation.

"How could we have? Look at all the work we've done as it is."

Tom appeared in the doorway. "What news?"

Robyn looked seriously at him. "We can't be sure. At least nothing was destroyed. It wasn't just petty vandalism."

"That's what Sayed and I thought. It was someone

who at least respects the stuff. He's probably sold it in the black market and it's halfway around the world already, in some rich guy's collection—that is, if anything *was* taken."

"Are you as disgusted as I am?" Robyn asked.

"You're lucky you aren't outside where the commotion is. Saunders is squealing like a stuck pig, as if he was personally insulted by the loss of the generators and the drill. He's just like a kid who expected to have a party and someone ate the cake first. Sayed's taking it pretty well, though. The drill foreman is driving us into Alex to find another motor. You'll have to hold the fort; we probably won't get back again today."

"There's lots for us to do here," Robyn said, opening her notebook on the table. "I don't know if we should take the time to track down every cataloged piece or just forge ahead with our work. I'd really rather forge ahead."

"Sure," Tom agreed. "Oh, and would you do me a favor and make sure Sandi goes in your car on the way home this afternoon? I don't want to worry that she's with that jerk Saunders. There's enough going wrong as it is."

"We'll look after her," Rafica smiled. "Mr. Saunders will go home alone, I promise."

"Thanks. Just one more thing—that guy's looking for someone to blame for the damage, so he's making some pretty weird accusations. Sayed isn't paying any attention to it; just thought you should know."

"What do you mean?" Robyn called after his departing back.

"Nothing much, just being a little too loose with some names."

"Whose?" she insisted.

"Yours, Miss Douglas. Didn't you know you were a vandal before you became a university observer? Don't let it bother you. The guy's rotten all the way through. See you later, and wish us luck." He shut the door after him, leaving Robyn speechless.

Rafica's cool hand came out to cover hers. "My sister, let it go. Your rude countryman is not worth the thought. Now, let us get to work. This trouble has been a sign to us that we must be attentive to our duties."

"That terrible man!" she spluttered.

"The ego of such a one cannot tolerate being slapped, and I suspect that you have done this, is that not so?"

"You're right, Rafica. I should have expected him to hit back. Will you go out and tell Sandi we'll take her home? I might run into Huntley Saunders, and I don't trust myself not to lose control and hit him in his fat smirking face!"

THE WIND WAS SOFTER NOW than it had been on previous days, and the air sparkled with a cooler breeze. Robyn could almost imagine that nothing had happened here to cause her distress. The little workroom was an island of calm where Robyn and Rafica worked steadily over their tables. Robyn tried not to be bothered by the outlandish accusations.

Rafica looked up at her once as if she read her thoughts. "Most archaeological sites are damaged at one time or another," she soothed. "It was almost to be expected. We have been fortunate, really. The black market for antiquities is a big one. Nobody seems to love historical treasures for their own sake anymore, only for the money.''

"Well, nobody is going to take our scrolls, Rafica, not if I have to defend them with my own body." Robyn's blood was boiling again with the outrage of it all.

"Don't be rash, my sister. We do the best we can and then no more. We must trust to God. In a few minutes we will lock the door behind us and say *Inshallah*. It will be well guarded tonight.''

"*Inshallah,*" Robyn repeated. "I'll try to remember that.''

SANDI WAS GRATEFUL for the invitation to ride home with Robyn and Rafica. "It gave me a good excuse to keep out of Huntley's hot hands," she piped cheerfully, as she settled her camera gear around her in Mohammed's car. "I really wanted to be with the girls. I guess everybody's going to the formal banquet tomorrow?''

"What banquet?" Robyn asked.

"Didn't Dr. al-Rashad tell you?" Rafica said apologetically. "It is to honor the university observer—which is you, of course. It's all part of the politics of an international archaeological effort. Officials of Alex and the archaeological society arranged it with Dr. al-Rashad.''

"Why was I the last to be told?" she asked with a sharp edge to her voice.

"Hold it," Sandi said. "You were the one who just spent the last day *and* night in Cairo with him. Don't get mad at us.''

"I'm sorry. So much happened that it must have

slipped his mind," she backpedaled. "I'm really sorry."

"Anyway, I haven't a thing decent to put on my back, and I'd love some company shopping at the suqs later," Sandi went on. "The galabias in the suqs are cheap and sharp looking. We can have a bite at Pastroudis—that's a fancy bakery and restaurant that's been here forever. Let's all go, the three of us. How about meeting me downtown at seven? I have to see this woman from *Town & Country* for a few minutes first, and then I'll stand under Mohammed Ali's statue in the square. You can't miss me. I'm the one that doesn't have the bronze tan!" She laughed at her own joke.

Rafica smiled. "I would love to go with you both, but I must stay in my room to await a telephone call this evening."

Robyn caught her eye for a moment and knew that it was from Karim. She had a quick pang of irritation to think that Sayed had refused to do anything to ease Rafica's situation. That should have been a clue to his entire character, she thought acidly. If she had been more alert she would never have been subjected to the horrid scene at the pyramids.

She shuddered involuntarily as she remembered the degrading moment of Sayed's fury. But her body kept on remembering his pleasurable touch on her bare breasts, the delight of his hard body pressing against hers, the dizzying intensity of his urgent, penetrating kisses. "Seven o'clock under Mohammed Ali," she forced herself to say. "I'll be there."

At the hotel she didn't want to go to the emptiness of her room, to start thinking in the same punishing circles that she had the night before. She wandered out into the hotel gardens and found the little gift shop open. The proprietor eagerly brought out trays of jewelry and loose stones to tempt her.

"I'm not a tourist," she said in explanation, apologizing for not having a lot of money to spend in his shop.

"That's okay," he grinned. "Look anyway. No charge for look!"

She picked up several lapis stones and admired the depth of the blue color. Flecks of gold were buried in them like points of light in a midnight sky. She had seen Sayed's eyes look like that, she recalled bitterly. She held one of the loose alexandrites to the light and saw its red purple glow against her hand, thinking of Sayed's words about kismet and love. He had made them into meaningless words for her.

She backed away from the tray of stones and browsed among the more typically touristy objects: fake scarab necklaces, silver Bedouin ankle bracelets, brass trays inlaid with awful profiles of Nefertiti. She felt safer with these, and bought several postcards with photos of the hotel and the coastline of the city. Her mother would appreciate having a card from her.

What would she write, "Dear mother, I'm having a wonderful time—wish you were here"? She set her lips into a grim smile as she left the shop and found a table among the pine trees in the garden. There she sat with her postcards and pen to write:

Egypt is everything I hoped for...and more. I can't begin to tell you all my impressions of it *(how true)*. I'm going to find you some good

Egyptian cotton so that you can make yourself a
new summer suit and be exotic! Don't worry
about me, I'm just fine. I'll probably be home
before you ever read this, but just in case....

Love, Robyn

That would keep her satisfied, Robyn knew,
checking her box at the hotel desk for messages.

"There is a lady waiting for you, miss," the clerk
said, pointing to the lounge. Puzzled, Robyn looked
toward the sunken area near a large darkened fireplace, where she could see the profile of a dark-
haired woman seated in one of the comfortable
chairs. "That is the lady," the clerk affirmed.

"Who is she?"

When the clerk shrugged his shoulders Robyn
started toward the lounge, wondering if she had the
patience to deal with a reporter or another official
from the Antiquities Department. As she drew closer
to the woman Robyn dismissed both possibilities.
Her hair was styled too elegantly for either profession, and the chic veiled hat that perched on top was
certainly not standard garb for a business conference.

Robyn slowed her pace before taking the final
steps into the woman's visual field. Clever brown
eyes turned quickly at her approach and the woman
stood up. She was tall and smiling, but the smile was
artifice, something out of *Vogue* magazine. The
manicured hand was cool as it came forth to shake
Robyn's.

"I'm so happy I found you in," the stranger said
smoothly. "I am Aziza Atef." When Robyn didn't
respond to the name the woman arched a sleek eye-

brow. "Didn't Sayed tell you I would be calling on you? The naughty man!"

"I'm afraid I don't. . ." Robyn said cautiously as she removed her hand from the cool grasp.

"I told him days ago that I wanted to meet the university's representative. Do have some tea with me." She motioned for a waiter, then smiled again at Robyn. "I assumed that you were an older gentleman—very experienced and scholarly—and when I was told that you were hardly old, nor even a man, my curiosity was piqued."

Robyn's guard went the rest of the way up immediately. There was something reptilian in the way this woman's eyes moved over her. "Perhaps Dr. al-Rashad didn't tell you that I am a qualified observer for my university. My youth and sex have nothing to do with my ability to function professionally, Miss Atef."

"I am a widow, Miss Douglas, but you must call me Aziza. I am keenly interested in the dig, you see—and then when I heard that Sayed—your Dr. al-Rashad—had discovered a hidden storehouse from the ancient Library of Alexandria, you can imagine my excitement. It has been the talk of our circle, I can assure you—far more intriguing than the usual chatter among the members."

Robyn cringed at the thought of society gossip and knew that Huntley Saunders had found a fertile field for spreading his version of Sayed's work. "It's not all that fascinating," she demurred, "and it may take months or years to fully examine the papyri found in the excavation. There is still no real evidence that any of it came from the library, in spite of what you may have heard." She tried to sound authoritative.

Madame Atef looked her over. "Quite a serious person, aren't you? Dr. al-Rashad needs your sort in this work. Heaven knows, he has had his troubles with foreign assistants lately." Her laugh was light and chilly. "If I weren't so very busy I should like to poke around in the dirt and look for treasures, too, but I have to be content to hear about it from others' lips."

Robyn couldn't picture this slim, pampered creature ruining her long fingernails in the desert grime, but she could picture her leaning close to Sayed over a candlelight supper at a fine restaurant, listening to him tell her about the dig. She stopped herself. That didn't matter anymore, and she merely wished to be rid of Aziza Atef's probing conversation.

The woman had to be close to thirty, and her speech was well educated. Probably English schools, Robyn guessed. "I'm glad you appreciate the problems of archaeological excavation," she said as blandly as she could, "but the work has no real glamour to it. Dr. al-Rashad must have told you."

Madame Atef raised her teacup and watched Robyn over the rim. "He wants your university to continue its sponsorship."

"Yes, I am aware of that. That is why I'm here in the first place." Robyn resented the woman's tone.

"We—all of his friends—would very much appreciate your sending a good report to your superiors, my dear. Sayed would be impossible to live with if he couldn't finish work on his little library!" She laughed again. "He's hardly been civilized in weeks!"

"If Dr. al-Rashad's friends can wait a short while, I'm certain that he will regain his good humor," she said tartly. Why did this person annoy her so intensely, she asked herself.

"Have I offended?" she was inquiring with a worried expression. "Oh, my dear Miss Douglas, I am so very sorry. That was not my intent at all. I merely wished to meet you. I thought it best that we be aware of one another. I wanted to extend my best wishes for your brief stay in Egypt."

"Thank you." Then an impulsive urge made her say, "But I may stay in Egypt indefinitely—I don't know yet."

Aziza Atef's face changed swiftly, revealing deep creases at the sides of her mouth. "Then we shall say goodbye for now." She reached out her hand to take Robyn's. "I suppose you know that Sayed has his little pleasures when it amuses him, and lately it is American girls that amuse him most."

"I wouldn't know," Robyn said icily, standing rigidly while her visitor walked away from the lounge. If Madame Atef was congratulating herself for planting her vicious little seeds and upsetting the young American, she was mistaken, Robyn thought. The well-coiffed woman didn't know that she was no threat to any designs on Sayed—none at all. *He's all yours, Madame X.* She smiled darkly at the fast-disappearing figure in the lobby. *Maybe you are devious enough to understand his labyrinthine self; I certainly am not.*

She looked at her watch and realized that she would have to hurry to get cleaned up and changed in time to meet Sandi in town. A banquet in her honor was the last thing she wanted. Why had Sayed done it? Just politics? *He needs me the way he would need Dr. Wayland,* she answered herself, *and the protocol* for the university observer is the same—no matter who wears the title. She sighed. Maybe she was being unfair to Sayed....

An evening with Sandi might lift her mood of futility a bit. She would like to laugh again and feel like herself, without the awful nagging pull at her emotions. She felt slightly sick to her stomach. It wasn't from something she'd eaten, it was just what happens when you plunge a yearning heart into ice and leave it there.

Suddenly she realized that she hadn't mailed her mother's postcard yet. How much her mother didn't know about her only child! Maybe she should make the old dear happy and marry some predictable, boring man—her life couldn't be more unhappy that way than it was right now.

As soon as she got out of the elevator at the fourth floor she heard the raucous sounds coming from Huntley Saunders's suite. He was having a party, and his voice was unmistakable above the other voices. She hurried past his open door and was positive that she smelled the sickly sweet odor of hashish wafting into the hall.

She wasn't so naive as to think he was burning incense for his guests. *Dear God, let me just finish up my work and get out of this madhouse,* she thought as she pulled her own door closed behind her. *Is everyone half-crazy, or am I?*

She picked up the phone and dialed the hotel switchboard. "Suite 408, please."

The phone rang several times, and then the familiar drawling voice came onto the line. "Mr. Saunders, this is Miss Douglas," she said loudly, making sure he could hear her over the noise of his party. "If you don't want to get all of us thrown out of Egypt you had better flush whatever you are smoking down the toilet right now! Do you understand?''

"Now, honey..." he soothed.

"I'm in no mood for words. Just do it...or I'll come and do it for you!" She slammed the receiver down. Damn all men! She stalked across her room, yanking the band out of her ponytail. From outside the hotel the evening call to prayer sounded and Robyn thought of the irony of a world where prayer and foolishness were called out into the same night air, each attracting its own followers.

Under the shower she began to return to normal, washing much of her irritation away with the desert dust. It was almost seven when she found a taxi that would take her to Mohammed Ali Square. It felt good to be in the cool evening air, driving fast and alone in the back seat, without a disturbing masculine energy in the seat next to her. The taxi driver was an older man, silent and respectful.

Alexandria looked clean and sparkling with its night lights twinkling in the onshore breeze from the harbor. She was looking forward to exploring the suqs with Sandi and shopping as the women of Alexandria do, not as a tourist. She made sure she had remembered to bring her Arabic phrase book. Tonight she wouldn't be asking for *khass, aish baladi* and *foul*, words for food, which was about all she could say in Arabic. And she really did plan to buy her mother some of the fine cotton cloth that Egypt was so famous for.

She gave the driver a pound note and got a sober smile in return as he left her at the entrance to the bustling square. She wanted to walk by herself for a while and meet the city on its own terms. As she passed a Christian church she almost stumbled over a woman and her baby, who were sitting in the shadows of the building. The woman was young and old at the same time, a look Robyn had noticed in many places in Egypt, and her hand was extended in the begging gesture. Robyn stopped and put several coins into the hand. A blessing rolled from the quiet woman's tongue, and Robyn answered with *"Afwan."* The face was haunting, almost serene, as if she trusted that all would be well. *Inshallah,* Robyn said to herself. It was something she had yet to learn.

In the middle of the congested square was the bronze equestrian statue of Mohammed Ali, the great nineteenth-century hero who took Egypt back from the British and Turks and gave the people a sense of national purpose once again. Her mind was quoting from her cultural guidebook. What had the bronze figure in the square really been like as flesh and blood? Probably just a normal human being with problems, strengths and frailties. She was beginning to be quite a philosopher about life, something that she had not really pondered before. In the past there had never been any real reason to try to figure out the deeper streams of human motivations . . . not before Sayed.

Robyn enjoyed being a small speck in the crowd of rushing cars, carts, trams and pedestrians. Her skirt and khaki poplin coat were of modest length, and she knew that aside from her light-colored hair she didn't call special attention to herself. That was the way she preferred it.

As her eyes drifted to the faces of the stone turn-of-the-century buildings around her, she could begin to understand the changes that had taken place in the city. This square had once been the financial center of Alexandria—the banks, the exchange houses. Now laundry hung from the ornate balconies, and some windows were black and empty.

At the risk of her life she crossed the main street to stand on the little island in the center that belonged to Mohammed Ali's statue. Sandi was nowhere in sight. As the minutes passed, Robyn tried to look as if she had good reasons to be standing there. She walked around the statue, examined it from every angle, opened her guidebook and finally just stood with her back to the bronze hero, peering into the crowd of faces that surged past her.

She checked her watch: seven forty-five. Sandi wasn't coming, she knew. A white-uniformed police-man offered his assistance. She explained to him in slow and careful English that she wanted to shop in the suqs for galabias, and he wrote an address on a small piece of paper. "That way, miss." He pointed toward the far end of the square. "Turn right at the vegetable market and you will be there." He saluted her smartly and walked away.

She followed his directions and found the market. It was invitingly arranged with displays of vegetables, melons and many other fruits. She smiled at the marking on one crate of apples: Washington Deli-cious. Imported fruit for those Egyptians who could afford it.

When she turned into the narrow lane, the atmo-sphere changed abruptly. Arabic music blared from a radio somewhere, and bare light bulbs from tiny open shops on both sides of the busy lane swayed in the night breeze. She joined the jostling bodies and let herself be moved along. Shoes and children's clothing were piled high on counter tops, and the proprietors' alert eyes watched for any interest from the crowds, springing up with rapid words at the first sign.

That wasn't what she was seeking, and she searched among the displays of merchandise until she found a face that looked affable enough to show her address to. A young man met her eyes with a wide smile of helpfulness and pointed to the end of the lane. Some rapid Arabic words indicated which way to turn from there. She didn't want him to think his good directions were not understood, so she said *"Shokran"* and walked deeper into the confusing marketplace.

At the first corner she had to jump quickly out of the way to avoid being trampled by a horse carriage that was moving at a fast trot among the shoppers. Then a bicyclist made a mad dash between the carriage and the curb, honking and weaving, sending a spray of muddy water against Robyn's coat and legs.

She stopped to dab at the mud with a handkerchief, then continued to the end of the little winding lane. There she found herself looking down an alleyway lined on both sides with dazzling displays of golden jewelry. Chains, thick bracelets, fantastic designs in gold hung in the shop windows.

It was almost fully dark now, and this new street was deep in shadows, the only illumination coming from inside the jewel shops, whose interiors looked like gleaming golden spider's webs. The kindly policeman had written the address of the galabia shop in Arabic and English for her, and she strained to find a street number over the doorways. Rounding another corner she proceeded into the mazelike interior of the suq, leaving the jewel vendors behind her.

In places there were only a few feet separating the two sides of the twisting, overhung walkways, and she began to slow her pace and enjoy looking into the silver shops, the thread merchants, the lace makers and the tapestry factories—where one proprietor suddenly unfurled a large, beautiful woven rug out under the feet of passersby.

Music was everywhere, rhythmic and tinny from transistor radios, and the voices of haggling shoppers raised the level of sound to a numbing pitch. But Robyn was fascinated. This was the real Egypt. There were no tourists around, and every face belonged here except hers.

A man suddenly moved close to her and took her arm. When she pulled away in surprise he smiled and shouted near her face, "Best galabia! My place!" She shook her head and walked briskly away, but he followed her. "Cheap! Best galabia!"

A tingle of fear ran up her spine and she tried to look stern. *"Emshi!"* she said firmly, remembering the word for "go away." *"Emshi,"* she repeated when the man continued to dog her steps. A second man fell into step beside her, his black eyes sparking.

"Galabia! No monkey business!" He tugged at her arm.

She turned into a rug shop and the men stayed outside. But she couldn't browse all night and she was growing angry that her one free evening in the city was being ruined by importuning hawkers. She decided to face them. *"La', la'*—no!" she said. *"Emshi!"*

She tried to ignore them and pretended to be doing

leisurely shopping, but they wouldn't be dislodged. She was like a fish on a line, a potential customer, and they were not going to let her get away.

"All right, gentlemen," she said, stopping to deal with them once and for all. "I'm calling the police. You understand? Police!"

They grinned broadly. "Galabia, lady? My place! Cheap!"

"Please!" she finally begged. "*Emshi*—please! I'm not a tourist... *la'* tourist!"

Nobody in the suqs seemed to be paying any attention to her predicament and she suddenly felt cut off, helpless. Then the lights in the shops flickered out and the lane was plunged into darkness. Real fear gripped her for the first time.

She started to run, bumping past people and pushing against carts and wagons. This couldn't be happening to her, she thought desperately. She had always felt safe in Egypt.

Oil lanterns began to appear in the shops, giving a gloomy, surreal light to the many dark faces around her. She ran, stumbling and frightened, into an incense-laden alley and found herself stopped by a dead end. She was trapped, and the two men were close behind her, their long robes flapping ominously as they approached.

"Please!" she cried, and a strong hand seized hold of her arm and pulled her into an antiquities shop. It was Sayed. Robyn almost wept at the sight of him.

"It is not wise to come here alone at night," he said evenly. "Are you all right?"

"I guess so. I need a moment to stop shaking," she managed to say. "How did you know I was...?"

He shrugged his square shoulders. "I didn't. I only

knew that a woman was having problems—and there you were. I think you should have a cup of mint tea while I conclude my business here." He handed her his own cup and turned away to the shop owner.

She accepted the tea gratefully and looked outside to the alley where the two men had disappeared from view. She realized then that she still carried the piece of paper crumpled in one fist. She opened it slowly and Sayed noticed.

"An address?" he said, as he finished his transaction with the man.

"I was trying to find a galabia shop." It was important to her to seem self-possessed, especially after he had seen her in full flight from those two men. "When the lights went out and I couldn't get rid of the men who were following me, I was sure their intentions were not good ones."

"And you fell?" He was noticing her mud-splattered coat. He had a half-smile on his lips. "Rather an adventuresome evening, I daresay," he said dryly, but not unkindly. "The suqs don't usually have such a dramatic effect on tourists."

Robyn couldn't tell what he was thinking. How could he stand there so calmly and have that indulgent smile on his face after the previous night? Had he pulled a mask over the passionate lover who had punished her and detested her feminine weakness? Was he now simply the amused director of the excavation, a man who had no connection whatsoever with the other Sayed?

He was welcome to his cool facade. She was past caring what he thought of her. If Sayed could regard her with an unflickering expression, then she could do the same.

She looked into his lapis eyes. "Thanks for being here. Your timing was perfect," she said, with a little laugh that she hoped sounded plucky and independent.

"That's my function, isn't it—to rescue maidens from the consequences of their own folly."

There was a tinge of acid in his words that she was not going to accept. "Maidens should not have to be pursued when they are innocently going about their own business," she answered his double meaning.

He threw back his head and laughed. "Did you think those men would have harmed you?"

"Why should I think otherwise?" she demanded.

"You *are* charmingly naive, Miss Douglas!" Her skin crawled at his patronizing words. "They wanted nothing more than your presence in their shop. They get a commission for every customer they bring in. Your own fervid imagination made them into monsters lusting after your flesh."

"What a delightful way you have of putting things, Dr. al-Rashad," she retorted. "Thank you for the tea and for the brief respite from my follies. I'll be going now." She put the cup down decisively on a counter top and started for the door. The familiar strong hand stopped her with a light pressure on her shoulder.

"I apologize. You need not punish me further, and I insist upon escorting you to your little galabia shop."

She turned around slowly. "Then you are concerned for my safety, after all?" she couldn't help saying. There was so much she wanted to throw back at him after last night, so very much more she wanted him to apologize for.

"Not at all," he said easily, as he led her outside into the lane and started walking back toward the suqs. "I don't want a nervous wreck showing up at work tomorrow when it can be avoided. Your shop is not far from here."

The electricity returned to the streets and shops, giving them back their carnival atmosphere. Robyn decided to be agreeable and accept his offer. "I'm buying a dress for tomorrow night's banquet," she said.

"Oh, yes. The last time Dr. Wayland was here he found the affair quite boring, but maybe you will enjoy it. The timing is bad. The governor's office arranged it to fit their convenience rather than mine."

Robyn brooded silently for a while, not noticing the street of the silversmiths she was passing through. If she had hoped Sayed was honoring her with this banquet she could forget that piece of whimsy. It was only an irksome evening of protocol for him, having nothing at all to do with any personal respect for her.

She looked at him out of the corner of her eye. She had never known another human being who made her feel like murdering him and begging for his embrace at the same time. She knew he was capable of loving, of drawing a wildfire of passion up from her very roots, and she knew she had the power to bring him to the threshold of ecstasy. Dear God, what went wrong? Her stomach had not relaxed its hard knot since last night. Maybe it never would.

He stopped her forward motion with a restraining hand at her elbow. "Unless you just want to continue walking at the same breathless pace, Robyn, we have arrived at your shop." There was amusement in his voice again, which she found extremely irritating.

"Don't you want to know the name of this particular suq, so that you can tell your friends in California where you had the narrow brush with Egyptian white slavers?"

She fired a glance at him that spoke for her.

"No? Then I'll tell you anyway. We are in the very midst of the Women's Crush. A descriptive name, don't you think?"

She walked silently into the crowded little shop. In the lighted window was a black cotton galabia with brightly colored embroidery on the bodice and down the skirt. The cut was simple, like most galabias she had seen, with a slit opening from the plain round neckline and a straight A line flaring from the shoulders. The sleeves were wide and long.

The proprietor greeted Sayed with deference and asked to be of assistance. His answer in Arabic brought a smile to the man's lips, and he bowed to Robyn amiably.

"What did you say to him?" she asked warily.

"You will get good service from him," Sayed answered cryptically.

Robyn cursed her inadequacy with Arabic and pointed to the black dress in the window. The man looked at Sayed first, then brought out an identical dress from a pile of folded garments. Robyn stepped into a curtained dressing area and tried it on. She liked it—the way it flowed away from her body, the softness of the cotton. Her hair shone honey colored next to the black of the fabric, and she felt at ease in the classic style.

"I'll take this one," she said, and Sayed translated for her.

When she had removed it the proprietor brought

out another galabia from behind his counter. He held it up so that the light would catch the heavy crystal beading on the bodice of the golden-toned dress.

"He says an old man brought it in this morning. His wife made it and it is very finely sewn."

"It's lovely," Robyn said in admiration.

"Then try it on," Sayed coaxed. He actually seemed interested in her selection, a fact that puzzled her.

She retreated to the dressing room and held the golden galabia up in front of her, then let it slip over her head and down around her body. It was like a warm caress. The cotton was finer than the first dress, heavy and soft like the most supple woolen fabric. In the mirror she saw that it made her eyes look clear blue. The buttery glow of it was almost magical. It was cut lower in the bodice than the black dress, exposing the first gentle curve of her breasts, and the long sleeves were weighted at the bottom with heavy encrustations of slender beads. She stood staring at Sesha Neheru, the romantic wide-eyed woman who imagined in that moment that she really was Egyptian.

"Well?" Sayed called to her.

She stepped through the curtains, a little hesitant to reveal herself. She knew she looked beautiful, and she really didn't want Sayed to say something hurtful and mocking when he saw her, as she expected him to do.

Yet when she faced him she couldn't read the expression in his eyes. He was silent as the shop owner broke into a torrent of admiring Arabic words. "You should have it," Sayed said finally. "It becomes you."

She touched the beaded bodice softly, loving the feel of it against her skin. It was completely impractical, she mourned, and probably incredibly expensive. "I'll take the first one only," she said in a small firm voice, and disappeared back into the dressing room to remove the wondrous golden confection.

Sayed stood aside while she paid for the black galabia, then he took her arm and walked her to his car just outside the suqs. "Why did you decide against the golden dress? You should have had it," he said, as he opened the door of the Fiat for her.

"Where would I ever wear such a thing?" she said lightly. "My life doesn't include fairy-tale balls."

"Hmm." He looked straight ahead and moved the tiny sports car through the traffic and onto the corniche. She had forgotten all about having dinner, and wondered if Sandi ever showed up under Mohammed Ali's statue. She certainly wasn't going to tell Sayed she was hungry.

"We have found a good motor for the drill," he said. "It will take an extra day to set it up, but then...." He glanced at her briefly.

"That's good," she replied.

"Yes, tomorrow we start removing the cataloged material from the workroom. I should have been taking it to the museum at the end of each day, but I have been too distracted by the problems with the drill. I trust you and Rafica will be finished by then?"

"We'll try." She was feeling more and more awkward sitting next to him. The very atmosphere of the car was filled with recriminations from last night. The tan leather on the seats had the same cool feel against her body as when she had sat shivering with

outrage and love after they almost—she tried to stop
the thought—after they almost made love on the
warm desert sand by the pyramids. It was unbearable
to be so close to him again. Too many memories
crowded between them. It would not be possible to
behave as if nothing had happened. Her throat was
heavy with an aching hardness, and she was glad that
there was no conversation between them.

Sayed's eyes watched her as she quickly let herself
out of the car at the big turnaround in front of the
hotel. She stopped before she closed the door and
forced a smile to her lips. ''Thanks,'' she said softly,
and walked hurriedly away from him. She didn't
look back.

He sat for a long time in his car before starting the
engine and driving off at high acceleration.

CHAPTER TWELVE

SAYED'S WARM HAND *brushed the fine sand from her brow. She opened her heavy eyelids and saw his face, full of love, smiling down at her.*

"You have been dreaming, my lovely one," he said huskily, and bent to leave the most tender of kisses on her kiss-weary lips.

"Oh, Sayed, I dreamed that we lost each other! It was so terrible, and then I opened my eyes and you were here." She reached her bare arms up to draw him down to her once more, as they had done so many times during the endless, heavenly night of love on the cushioning desert sand.

"I am here, little bird—Sesha Neheru. I will never leave you...and I love you." His lips drifted lightly and possessively over her smooth nakedness, and she moved against him with each new awakening of delight....

ROBYN KNEW that when she opened her eyes the dream would vanish, like a cloud blown apart by harsh winds. Tears rose hotly beneath her closed eyelids and squeezed past them to roll down her cheeks.

It was morning. She was in Room 406, alone, and she would do well to forget the futile dream. Then why did that other reality seem more real than this one, she wondered painfully. *Because you want it to, silly goose, and you don't want to face life as it really is.* That unsatisfactory answer brought back the heavy knot in her heart, as if it were a concrete block of hopelessness, stored there until she could find some way to dispose of it without hurting herself more.

She wondered darkly what the half-life of misery was—how long it would take for her to feel half as wretched as she did this morning.

She dressed slowly, like an invalid, easing one arm into its cotton sleeve and then the other, making her body behave and cooperate. It wanted to stay in bed, to sleep, to wake only in time to meet the plane that would take her home.

Rafica was waiting in the lobby for Mohammed's car. She looked small and alone, Robyn decided when she first caught sight of the young woman sitting in one of the lobby chairs. But didn't they all?

Rafica rose and came toward her. "Tom and Sandi aren't coming out with us," she said. "He's staying in Alex with Dr. Gaddabi to prepare things at the museum. They have given us space in their restoration laboratory so that we can continue our work with the fragments there. I shall be so relieved when everything is safely stored."

"And Sandi?"

"Tom said she needed to be alone today." Her eyes showed concern.

"Just two of us, then," Robyn said quietly.

Rafica looked at Robyn for a long moment. "My sister, is everything good for you? Or are both of us making pleasant faces over problems?" She smiled sadly.

"Life goes on," Robyn said, trying not to tip over

the edge of control into the engulfing emotions that were so near.

"*Inshallah,*" Rafica said.

SAYED'S TALL FORM was visible in the distance near the workroom as their car came over the last little hillock and into camp. Several men were with Sayed, and the Bedouin workers stood at a distance watching. Robyn's nerves tensed. Something was wrong.

"What is it?" she asked Rafica.

"Antiquities police, I think. They are the only ones who dress in heavy brown suits on a desert dig."

They hurried to the workroom, where the door was standing open. Sayed stepped forward to intercept them. "Antiquities police are here. There has been anonymous information that some of our papyri have been stolen from the site." He spoke loudly, as if for the benefit of the three sober-looking men nearby. "I have checked the catalog and found nothing missing. It was just another prank, I am sure."

Hassan Tarsi walked out of the workroom. "Are you certain?" he demanded of Sayed. "What about the ones that were not yet cataloged?"

Sayed's face darkened quickly. "I am sure. There is nothing missing." He walked with commanding strides back to the men, speaking in Arabic. Rafica strained to hear and translate for Robyn. "He is telling them that if he has more information he will let them know. He apologizes for the incident."

The brown-suited men then shook hands with Sayed and drove away in a cloud of dust, leaving the tall Egyptian glowering after them. He turned angrily to Dr. Tarsi, Robyn and Rafica. "We must talk immediately. Follow me."

He strode into the workroom and, when everyone was inside, closed the door. "Now," he said, with his hands folded across his chest, "I want the truth about this. Just now I lied to those men—something that goes against every fiber of my beliefs. But I had to. Their information was correct; some of our finds *are* missing. If the antiquities police knew this they would shut us down today and begin a lengthy investigation. The Bedouin are already terrified of being accused. I have assured them that I do not blame them. But there has indeed been a theft and I must have an answer to this—right now!"

His eyes raked the faces before him. "Well? Have you nothing to say that will illuminate our mystery?" His face had taken on an ashen pallor, and a heavy energy emanated from his angry eyes.

Robyn's legs were suddenly weak and her hands had turned to ice. Was he accusing her? His eyes stayed on her coolly, as if she were just another worker who might as easily have stolen his antiquities as any other person. How could he even think...!

"I anticipated this situation," Hassan Tarsi said ominously. "From the start your methods of security were lax. You were too trusting."

Rafica cleared her throat. "What is missing, Dr. al-Rashad? It might help us to know."

Sayed reached over to pick up the catalog notebook. "Two things that I have been able to discover with cursory examination: number 163, a large papyrus fragment with the notation in the book that it bore a Greek signature of a man named Apollonius, and number 304, a partial scroll of papyrus with the notation that it was in demotic script, probably Eighteenth Dynasty Egyptian. The two papyri were cataloged by the same person." He looked up and caught Robyn's unhappy eyes. She knew what he was thinking.

"Yes, by me," she said firmly after a swift breath to steady her nerves. "I remember both papyri and the latter one was in good preservation."

"And what else?" he coaxed in a dangerously soft voice.

"What do you mean? That's all. I saw them, I cataloged them and I never gave them another thought after that."

"Hmm," he said to himself, flipping through the list of fragments in the notebook. "And what would I find if I checked on each of these numbers?"

"You would probably find them exactly as I noted them." Her composure hung by a thread. Everything was happening too fast. "I resent your implication and I resent the fact that you are questioning Rafica and me. What do you think we are, common thieves?"

"Nothing of the sort, Miss Douglas. But a most serious thing has happened here and I must get to the bottom of it. Anger is often a cloak for knowledge, is it not?"

Robyn was burning with fury. Her face flushed red, but she didn't care. "Accuse someone else, then! How do I know it wasn't you who took them? I have as much right to question *you*, since I represent the university that is funding your precious dig!" She stormed past him and pushed open the door. Sayed's footsteps were just behind her, and he swung her around roughly to face him.

"Don't be infantile, Robyn; listen to me! I'm not accusing you or anyone else. A serious crime has been committed and I don't know what else to do but start with the people who were closest to the things that were taken. Be reasonable!''

"Take your hands off me," she cried, tears running down her face. "I have had enough of your overbearing ways. Now, get Mohammed to drive me back to the hotel. Do you hear me?"

He stepped back from her, startled. "If you wish," he said. "I ask only that you keep this whole affair in secrecy until I determine otherwise. Rafica can return to Alex with you. I'll get as much of the papyri to the museum as possible today. It would only be an impediment to have upset women on the dig right now."

She sat in the station wagon for what seemed like an eternity before Rafica joined her. Robyn didn't offer to talk as they drove the bumpy, unpaved roads back across the desert to the highway. Rafica held her silence for a while, then turned a serious face toward her.

"My sister, you have to understand Dr. al-Rashad's ways. He meant no accusation of us, but is badly hurt that anyone would intrude on his work and do this. To him it is like a desecration of holy things. But I am not explaining myself well."

Robyn looked straight ahead at the barren landscape. "Don't try to explain, Rafica. The problem with Dr. al-Rashad is deeper than this one incident. He. . .he needs somebody to hit out at." Her hands were twisted into a tight ball in her lap.

Rafica said nothing more until they were on the smooth paved highway near Alexandria. "The scroll of the blue-eyed god was not taken," she said gently. "He wished me to tell you that."

Robyn leaned her head back against the seat and closed her eyes. "If I were his thief I would have taken that one scroll and left the others."

"I think he knows that."

"But I have no interest in the blue-eyed god anymore, none at all. I wish him well in his translation. Maybe he will learn something about human warmth and trust."

A comforting hand reached out to touch her shoulder. "Robyn, come with me to my village today. I want you to meet my family; and I think you should see Egypt the way I know it. Please."

Robyn dragged her eyes open and smiled. "I'd like that. I'm sorry to be acting this way, and I'm sorry to run out on our work. Sayed can't possibly do it all himself, and that means he will have to leave some papyrus in the workroom tonight. It isn't safe. And what about the vellum scrolls? He will need help to move them." There was a look of understanding in Rafica's eyes. Robyn didn't realize that her use of his first name had told the Egyptian woman what was bothering her.

MOHAMMED AGREED to drive them directly to Rafica's village, which was about thirty miles outside of Alexandria, just off the delta road.

"We can take the bus back to Alex," Rafica said. "There's one that stops in the late afternoon on its way from Cairo."

Robyn was still steaming inwardly. It would probably do her good to get completely away from anything that reminded her of Sayed. The desert scenery was a mirror of her mood, barren and bleak. She watched numbly as the landscape around her changed to the lushness of the delta. From time to time she caught glimpses of narrow dirt roads leading away from the highway, and sometimes she noticed earth-colored villages in the distance, sitting in the midst of cultivated fields.

Mohammed turned off a paved road and for several minutes followed the high dirt bank of a canal. On either side the soil was black and moist, the dark green crops tall and ready for cutting.

"We are proud of our fine road," Rafica said at length. "We paved it with the first profits of the village after the land was given to us by the government. We were also one of the first villages to have electricity."

Robyn was curious, for she knew next to nothing about this part of Egyptian life. "Did you go to school here when you were small, or did you have to leave home for your schooling?"

"School is compulsory up to the age of twelve. We have a school and two teachers here. Their salaries are very meager, and that is another reason why my father objects to my love for Karim. The daughter of Samir Sadawy al-Wahab should not depend on the salary of a poor teacher when she could be cared for comfortably by the son of a well-to-do man of our village. There is so much pride and stubbornness involved in my father's views."

Robyn imagined Rafica's father as a man like Sayed, dominant, unreasonable and without heart. "He should be proud that you have chosen a man of education who loves you."

"It isn't only that, my sister," the other woman said wearily, "it is the debt my father feels he owes to his brother, the father of Mustafa. Many years ago, when President Nasser's government seized power from the fat king, my father and my uncle were each given shares of land to farm. It was a very good thing for our families, but then my father developed heart trouble and he was unable to cultivate his piece of land. We had no money to hire workers and my brothers were just babies at the time, so my uncle offered to farm the land for us. He gave us the profits that came from the crops year after year, working with his sons, who were older than my father's.''

"He sounds like a good man. But why is there still such a feeling of indebtedness after all these years?"

Rafica sighed heavily. "It is nothing but pride, since my uncle is not the kind of man who demands reparation. My brothers have worked our land for more than ten years now and have given part of our profits each year to our uncle. There is no financial debt anymore and everyone is satisfied—except my father.''

"If there is no more debt, then I can't see why—"

"I cannot explain it so that you, an outsider, will understand. Just know that I am bound by my father's sense of obligation, and have been bound by it since I was a child and he promised me to my cousin Mustafa. My two younger sisters are waiting for me to marry so that they in turn will be free to wed. I cannot be so selfish as to deny them their chance for happiness. My sister Aisha is already miserable; she cares deeply for a young man and is afraid to tell our father—or even to tell me. I have no choice anymore but to accept Mustafa. He is a pleasant man, and I suppose I should be grateful for that, at least.'' She turned her face away.

Robyn's sense of justice was stirred up once again.

She longed to protect her friend, but was frustrated by Rafica herself. How could she just sit there and accept the marriage to her cousin as inevitable...? She was baffled by the intricacies of Egyptian behavior. At least in America she knew how the game of life was played, even if she didn't always approve of it.

Mohammed slowed the car as the road turned and led past several neat, square mud-brick buildings. He drove carefully through the narrow lanes of the village. Animals browsed in their path; goats, cats, straggly-looking dogs, chickens and geese. Small girls scolded the geese into line and grinned as the car passed. Rafica waved to them and smiled back.

The lane through which they were winding ended at an iron double gate set into high walls that enclosed a small garden. A tall young man was just shutting the gates behind him, then started to walk quickly away. His face and his body movements showed that he was agitated.

"Karim!" Rafica opened the door before Mohammed had brought the car to a full stop. "Karim!" She ran to the man, who turned immediately and stretched out his arms to embrace her.

Robyn's throat constricted with sympathy as she watched them. They were so clearly in love. Something had to be done for them. If this was her only reason for staying on in Egypt, it would be enough to keep her there, she vowed. So much was unfair in this strange land, but her friend's happiness was one thing she couldn't turn her back on.

Rafica brought Karim back to the car, where she introduced him. Mohammed discreetly excused himself, saying that he would have a drink in the nearby teahouse before starting back to the desert.

Karim was handsome, with large dark brown eyes that showed a carefully controlled intensity beneath their natural warmth. He greeted Robyn with a soft resonant voice and sat down in the front seat of the station wagon, turning around to face Rafica and holding her hand tenderly. His accent was heavy as he spoke. "I have just seen your father, Rafica."

"But we agreed that you would not!"

"It was necessary for me as a man to explain our feelings to him face to face. I could not let you go without meeting the man who denies me the happiness of this world." His face was set in lines of determination, making him look older than his probable age of twenty-three or twenty-four.

"And did he tell you what you wished to hear?" she asked—almost cruelly, Robyn thought.

"He did not meet my eyes, but spoke as if I were a piece of the furniture in the room. He said that honor cannot be played with by the whims of children. I could not stay a moment more in his presence. He was like a locked door and I did not have the key. It is now up to you, Rafica."

Rafica began to tremble. "No, Karim, don't ask me. There are too many others who would be hurt if I went with you." She put her hands over her face and shuddered silently, weeping.

Karim's eyes caught Robyn's. "Honor," he said in a breaking voice. "You are seeing the dark side of honor, Miss Douglas. And I am helpless to set it aside." He opened the door and let himself out. "I have three more days before I return to my unit in the Sinai. I will not see Rafica again...until after her marriage to Mustafa." He said the last words with real agony in his voice, walking away from the car with the same agitated stride as before.

Rafica raised her head to watch Karim disappear around a turn in the lane. "That is the end of it," she whispered.

Robyn reached for her hand and held it firmly in her own. "Don't say that. Karim is upset right now, but the situation will change, I know it will."

"Thank you, my American sister, but you still don't understand. All the good intentions of your kind heart will not alter what must be. It is kismet—my fate and Karim's—and it cannot be made otherwise, I know that now." She sat up straighter. "I do not wish to visit my family today, if that is all right with you." She managed a little laugh. "This was supposed to be a day that would cheer you up, and see what I have done to it!"

"Nonsense," Robyn retorted. "I still want to see your village. As long as we're here I insist on seeing where you went to school, and maybe Ahmed's little teahouse."

Rafica looked at her quizzically. "You know about Ahmed? Who told you?" Robyn's face held the answer. "Dr. al-Rashad?" Rafica continued. "He told you about his childhood and his family, then? That is good. We shall go next to see where old Ahmed serves his delicious tea to little boys and large men."

They walked together between the rows of low buildings and past open shops whose proprietors were talking animatedly with village neighbors and customers. Ahmed's establishment was nestled between a cloth seller's and a store that displayed a variety of brooms, pots and pans. Mohammed was sitting at a small table in the open front of the shop, puffing on a water pipe and laughing with two other men. There were no women customers and Robyn felt awkward about entering. Rafica walked toward the back of the little shop, however, where a stooped, gray-haired man was tending his counter.

Ahmed's smile was broad and kindly. Rafica explained in Arabic that Robyn was a colleague of Dr. al-Rashad's, and immediately two steaming cups of carcady appeared on a tray with the compliments of Ahmed. They sipped with pleasure at the brew, which once again seemed to have a restorative effect on frayed nerves. Even Rafica was relaxing the hopeless expression that had haunted her eyes since Karim left.

Looking around at the dark, pungent-smelling teahouse, Robyn couldn't help seeing the little boy who had come here so long ago for his morning tea. It was painful to feel so close to Sayed's life and know that she was forever shut out of it. Was that kismet, too?

She smiled a little at her melodramatic thoughts. Fate had nothing to do with it. She and Sayed had each built their situation at every step of the way, with no help from blind fate; he with his bitterness and distrust, wherever it sprang from, and she with her naive eagerness, which made her jump into strange waters that she knew too little about.

They thanked Ahmed for his hospitality and shook hands with him. As they left, Mohammed offered to take them back to the dig with him, since he had to be there soon to pick up Sayed.

Robyn had no wish whatever to return to the dig. "We can take the bus," she said. "I must get back to the hotel, but thanks anyway."

He smiled and wished them a good day.

"The school is this way." Rafica pointed down the

bright sunlit village street. Robyn expected to see a free-standing school with classrooms, but instead she was shown what appeared to be another shop at the end of the short lane. Inside, with light bulbs moving lazily in the breeze and benches facing forward in a semicircle, the room was full of young children reciting sums for the teacher at the chalkboard.

"We will go first to the older class," Rafica whispered, as she drew back from the doorway and headed toward the rear of the building. There another group of children was seated on the earth, listening to their teacher read to them. The outdoor class was situated in a grove of palm trees, sheltered from the noon sun and heat and made pleasant by a soft breeze that carried with it the scents of the cultivated fields.

The teacher, a young woman, smiled as she recognized Rafica. She stopped reading and the children stood up quickly. Rafica introduced "Miss Robyn Douglas of the United States," to the delight of the students, who craned their necks as politely as possible to get a good look at the American visitor.

"You are not our first guest today," the teacher said, gesturing toward the edge of the circle of palm trees.

A very clear British voice said, "What a lovely coincidence!" and Daphne al-Rashad stepped forward, clasping Rafica's and Robyn's hands in turn. "I was on my way into Alex on some business, and it was such a beautiful day, I decided to visit the village. Come, let's leave the children to their lessons. We've given them quite enough excitement for one day!" she said, laughing.

The no-nonsense, cheery presence of Madame al-

Rashad was like a knife cutting through the accumulated darkness of Robyn's heart. "Just the girls, is
it?" she questioned perceptively. "Are the men still
at the dig?"

Robyn spoke first. "There was a little problem this
morning, and Rafica was kind enough to offer to
show me her village while the men straightened things
out." She detested half-truths, especially when she
said them to this fine woman, but she didn't want to
start listing her real problems.

"And have you seen enough, or would my offer of
a lift into Alex break up your day here?"

"Thanks," they both answered at once, with
Rafica finishing, "I have shown Robyn everything
that is interesting. However—" she looked at Robyn
intently "—would you mind very much if I didn't
join you? I am most uncomfortable leaving without
seeing my family."

Robyn tried to read her eyes. "You're sure?"

"Yes. I cannot remain silent now, not after
Karim's visit. I must know what they are thinking,
and I want them to know that I still love them, even
though I do not agree with the way things must be. I
will take a late bus tonight and see you in the morning. Please give my excuses at the banquet tonight.
And thank you, Madame al-Rashad."

Daphne al-Rashad embraced Rafica warmly.
"Take heart, my dear."

Robyn walked with the older woman to the familiar blue Peugeot sedan. "I'm one of the few women
in Egypt who drives a car," she said, smiling. "I'm
so glad I found you here. It gives us a good time to
chat."

She deftly steered the car through the village streets

and back along the canal road to the delta road, where she turned north for the last thirty miles of her trip to Alexandria.

Robyn started to say something about the other night, how much she had enjoyed being at her home, but she was interrupted. "Nonsense, my dear, you belong there. I want you to think of it as your home away from home. Now you must tell me, what on earth has happened to Sayed to make him so out of sorts since then? I suspect you have the answer." She glinted a smile in Robyn's direction and kept her eyes on the road.

"Well..." Robyn began, her mind racing for a response that would stop further questions.

"Be direct with me, Robyn. I have never known Sayed's tone to be so abrupt with me as on the telephone yesterday evening. Is there something I should know? Has he been just as beastly with you?"

"Madame al-Rashad, I'm afraid the problem is a very personal one," she said softly, looking at her hands in her lap.

"I see," she said quickly. "Forgive me, I am intruding where I don't belong."

"No, that's not the reason. I just don't know what to say. Sayed should tell you himself, that's all. I'm not really involved anymore." Her voice was a whisper as she ended.

Daphne al-Rashad said nothing for a long time. Finally she asked, "And what about dear little Rafica? Things are not going well there, either, I take it."

Robyn told her about Karim's visit to Rafica's father, and about the older man's pride.

"Men!" the Englishwoman exclaimed suddenly, turning her clear blue eyes toward Robyn. "They can be so obtuse. Let me do a little scouting on my own about this matter. Sometimes a woman can find out things that a man would never even think to discover.''

''If only I could leave Egypt knowing that at least Rafica and Karim would be happy!'' Robyn said before she thought.

''And no one else, my dear?'' Madame al-Rashad asked with an arched eyebrow. She turned the car into Montaza Park and followed the winding garden road to the hotel. ''Promise me one thing: that you won't leave Egypt without paying me a last visit.'' She leaned over to kiss Robyn's cheek. ''Is it a promise?''

Robyn nodded her head, her voice too full of emotion to say anything more. Her lips formed the words, ''Thank you,'' and she let herself out of the car.

The banquet was to start at eight o'clock, and Robyn realized suddenly that she had missed lunch again. The dining room was closed, but she was just as happy to order room service for herself. The idea of being with a noisy crowd of people didn't appeal to her very much today.

In fact, the last thing she wanted to do was to get dressed up for a banquet and smile sweetly at the governor's staff, knowing that Sayed would be there. She was in no condition to deal with his presence, or the presence of any man.

What would Sayed be thinking right now? Was he wondering how he could get through the evening, sitting next to a possible thief and a temptress, a fallen woman who was a perfect example of everything he abhorred in her gender? Robyn decided that she would make it easy for him and sit as silent as a sphinx, impeccably modest in her black galabia.

As she watched the little brown birds darting and hovering around her balcony, the phone jarred her thoughts. Sandi's voice spoke through the receiver. "You're home? Can you spare a minute for a sick friend?"

"Do you need a doctor?" Robyn asked.

"That would be a breeze. No, I'm not sick that way. I'll be over in a sec."

Sandi stood forlornly at the door, ready to knock as Robyn opened it. "Just me," she said, shuffling inside. Her hair was disheveled and she had a thin kimono wrapped carelessly around her. "I wanted to apologize for not showing up last night."

Robyn waved a hand. "That's all right. I knew we'd got our signals crossed, but I found the suqs anyway."

"I probably should have gone there...instead of what I did...." Her voice trailed off and Robyn saw that her eyes were swollen and red. "The reason I didn't meet you was that I bumped into Tom at the museum, where I was meeting that gal from *Town & Country*. We took it from there—I mean he walked me down Shari Sherif, the Rodeo Drive of Alex, and we stopped for coffee at the Cecil Hotel. We just kept talking until I forgot about you standing under the statue. When I remembered it was already too late, and I thought, I've done it again...and I offered to treat Tom to dinner at the Santa Lucia." She wiped her eyes and took a pack of cigarettes from her kimono pocket.

"Didn't you have a good time with Tom?" Robyn needn't have asked, the answer was all over Sandi's miserable face.

"Oh, sure—for the first couple of hours. But then things got serious and he started lecturing me about my life-style, just like a father. I didn't mind all that much, because I could tell he really cared or he wouldn't have bothered." She held up the pack of cigarettes and then put them back into her pocket. "Like smoking. I'm going to try to stop again, for him. Anyway, I even thanked him for saying what he'd said and we held hands over the little table in the corner, just like two high-school kids."

Robyn could picture the Santa Lucia and the table in the corner—probably the same table where she and Sayed had had their dinner that first night.

"Then we came back to the Palestine and walked out on the little pier. I couldn't control myself anymore. I just turned to him and said to his face, 'Tom, I love you!' And then we were kissing out there under the big fat moon. I've never felt like that before—ever!"

Her voice choked and she stopped talking as two streams of tears started down her cheeks. "He kissed me like he meant it, but my God, do you know what he said then? He said he wished he could believe me! What could I say to a thing like that?" She fumbled again in her pocket and drew out a loose cigarette, lighting it and taking a deep drag. "To hell with him." She gave a bittersweet smile as the smoke curled around her face. "He wants a sweet untouched kid like you. I've been around too much. But tell me how I undo *that*—I'm no time traveler, for God's sake!"

"If I smoked I'd have one with you," Robyn said grimly, "but it would just make me sick. Maybe you did the best thing. At least you were completely honest with him. Tom can't help but respect you for that. It must make a man feel good to be told that someone loves him.''

"Terrific! He probably thinks I say that to everyone.''

"Give him time,'' she said, sounding to herself like a wise woman. "I think he cares about you very much.''

"Hey,'' Sandi said, jamming the cigarette out in the ashtray, "how come you escaped without a close call? Sayed and you, I mean. . . .''

"Because I know the secret of invulnerability,'' she answered, feeling a terrible urge to be silly.

"That's some secret!''

Robyn looked into Sandi's believing eyes and started to laugh. Tears were close behind and soon Sandi was laughing with her and they were both out of control. When at last Robyn could stop herself she said, "I'm an awful liar. I have no business giving you advice when I just made a complete mess of things myself. I'm so vulnerable it hurts. And the only amazing thing is how simpleminded I was to keep coming back to him for more.''

Sandi swept Robyn into a bear hug of sympathy that broke the last shreds of control over her tears. They both wept unashamedly, until Sandi pulled away and wiped her face with the back of her hand. Her mascara was streaked and blotchy, but she was grinning.

"Well, that's enough of that, girls. We're going to put on our best duds and knock their eyes out downstairs tonight, right?''

Robyn looked at her without enthusiasm.

"Sure we are, honey. May I have the honor of escorting you to the banquet, *mamsell*?''

Robyn couldn't help smiling at Sandi's low bow. She gave her a grateful squeeze. "I'll be the one in the black galabia and the briefcase," she quipped.

"And I'm the one who dresses all wrong and needs a keeper." She hitched up her kimono and walked jauntily to the door. "Eight o'clock in the lobby?"?

Huntley Saunders's face peered around the open door as Sandi departed. "Good evening, Miss Robyn. I hear there was more trouble at the dig today." He didn't make a move to enter the room, but stood with a cocktail glass in one hand, sipping at it.

"I'm sure you know as much as I do," Robyn answered tersely.

"A real shame. Sayed must be feelin' bad, but these things happen, I hear. Anyway, there's lots more stuff where that came from!"

"You don't sound very upset, Mr. Saunders. It's partly your dig, too, remember? That's what you're always saying."

"Sure, honey," he drawled, "but that's chicken feed compared to what we're gonna find when we get to drillin' tomorrow, right?"

"I trust so," she answered in a flat tone. "Now I have to dress for the banquet, so please excuse me." She started to shut the door but he stood there unmoving.

"Dull, dull." He shook a finger at her. "I'll be at the yacht club if you want to get away from all the boring talk, little lady."

She gently closed the door in his face, not bothering to feel ungracious. She was beyond that with him. It was getting late and she needed to make herself look half-decent, considering the way she felt. Her eyes were a fright and she wished she had some ice cubes to press against them. It angered her to think that Sayed might notice she had been crying.

The galabia felt cool and comfortable against her skin. Its blue, red, yellow and green embroidery trailed along the simple high neckline and down to the hem like a tumble of blooming flowers. The dress had its own special kind of self-assurance. It was important to Robyn that she appear—what was the word she always loved—insouciant. Indifferent, unconcerned. That was the theme for tonight. She would make yet another attempt to build up a shell of unconcern around her. Let Sayed believe what he wanted about her, she thought; it wouldn't matter now anyway.

Egypt had no more pull on her, she lied to herself. As soon as she returned home Egypt would fade back into the dry textbooks and stay there. She took one last look at her wistful face and sad eyes before snapping her evening bag shut and leaving the room. She took a deep breath and let it out with an exasperated burst. "Humph," she said about nothing and everything as she entered the empty hallway.

CHAPTER THIRTEEN

PART OF THE HOTEL'S PUBLIC DINING ROOM had been partitioned off for the banquet. A single long table had been set, with place cards at each seat. Sandi did a quick scouting trip and returned to the reception area to say that Robyn was seated between the governor's chief of staff and Dr. Gaddabi.

"They put me as close to the kitchen as possible," she said with her usual flippancy. "I'm sitting next to two men who probably shine the governor's shoes. And Tom has charge of some Egyptian woman named Aziza somebody-or-other."

Robyn smiled. "Don't worry about her, she's not Tom's type. Strictly dragon lady, long claws and all." Still, it bothered her that Aziza Atef had somehow arranged an invitation for the evening. Or had Sayed invited her himself? She looked around unwillingly to find him. He had made no effort to greet her so far, and he was talking now with several well-dressed older men, probably of the governor's staff.

Dr. Gaddabi came up beside her. "I'm sure Dr. al-Rashad has already mentioned it, but it would be best to say nothing at all about the status of the dig tonight. There will be members of the press attending, and they are clever about extracting statements. We must keep to pleasant generalities." He smiled with a long-suffering sigh. "The continuing struggle between the creative scientists and the bureaucrats and press... we have to keep our little secrets until we have a chance to finish our work."

Robyn brightened in Dr. Gaddabi's kindly presence. If he knew that something was wrong between herself and Sayed he said nothing—but she suspected he did. "Thanks," she smiled, "I'll talk about the weather and keep away from controversial subjects." Her glance drifted around the reception area and caught Aziza Atef's entrance. The woman, dressed in billows of sea-green chiffon, made a beeline for Sayed's circle, becoming for a moment the focus of a flurry of introductions.

"Good Lord," Sandi was beside her again. "Is *that* Aziza?"

Robyn grunted softly. "I think they make a nice couple."

"Don't kid about it. She's awful! You don't think Sayed's dumb enough to go for all that dazzle?"

"Who knows... and who cares?"

"Well, I do, for one. I don't want her around Tom. I can smell her sexy perfume from here. Excuse me for a sec, I want to make contact with the guy before he sits down with *her*!"

Then Hassan Tarsi was making a small bow and smiling at Robyn deferentially. "Ah, Miss Douglas, how lovely you look tonight."

Robyn instinctively pulled into herself at his approach.

"What unpleasantness we have," he said, his voice dropping to a whisper. "I have wished to speak with you about it—"

"I don't think this is the place, Dr. Tarsi."

"But I want you to know that I have no suspicions, none at all, that you are the thief." His face looked concerned and his eyes were full of sympathy.

"Thank you very much," she replied ironically. "It's a relief to hear that."

"... and I am doing all in my power to convince Dr. al-Rashad that you are not guilty, that he must look elsewhere to place blame. I'm sure it was the Bedouin. I never trusted them."

Heat flared through Robyn's body and into her face. "You're very quick to judge who is guilty and who isn't. What do you have against the Bedouin, Dr. Tarsi?"

"You have no knowledge of my continuing problems with them, Miss Douglas. Someday I will tell you more about them."

"I know ulterior motives when I hear them," she shot back, "and please, don't take my side in this matter. If I need an advocate I'll choose one myself!"

"Of course, you are upset now. I understand completely—"

"My final report to the university will make it perfectly clear what's happened here," she said. Her voice had risen and a few heads were turning toward them.

"Please, Miss Douglas, let us speak softly. I merely wanted you to know that Hassan Tarsi is still a faithful colleague, one who would very much like to know you better. Perhaps for dinner tomorrow evening?"

"I think not. If you are concerned about my report, I will make sure you get a copy of it... so that you will know just where you stand." She looked

sternly into his black eyes, a look that discouraged
him from going on.

"Then I will say good evening. And thank you in
advance for your favorable description of me and my
work." He managed a wary smile, bowed again and
moved off.

Robyn could have spit fire. How dare that miserable, fawning man cultivate her favor like that! How
dare Sayed judge her guilty! She crossed her arms
tightly in front of her, feeling like a fort under attack.

The banquet passed in a haze. Her mind feverishly
occupied itself with cataloging the hurts that she
had endured since she met Sayed, starting with the
very first day. She emerged only when she had to
acknowledge an introduction or a complimentary
reference to her university or herself. Even Sayed
made a short speech lauding her helpfulness on the
dig. How could he? His praising words should have
stuck in his throat. What hypocrisy!

Afterward, as the party was dispersing, she escaped quickly to the elevators. Something was reaching an explosive level inside her and she didn't know
what to do about it. She wanted sanctuary—but
where? Not in her lonely room, bereft of comfort,
and not in Sayed's arms, cringing before his attacks
on her integrity.

The elevator was delayed, so she turned to walk up
the stairs instead. At the same moment Sayed came
striding swiftly out of the dining room. She couldn't
avoid him.

He seemed taller than she remembered, looming
over her with a questioning expression on his face.
She raised her eyes to his, but couldn't think of a

single thing to say to him. So much was dammed up within her, needing to be expressed, yet she was speechless before his paralyzing masculine energies.

"Four flights is a very long way to climb," he said with that slight invitational quirk of his lips.

"The elevator...I...." The words wouldn't come out. In total frustration she just looked at him, then said very clearly to his face, "Damn you, Sayed al-Rashad! Damn you!" She wheeled and ran up the stairs, leaving him, in turn, speechless.

The last thing she saw out of the corner of her eye as she left him was a blur of green chiffon. Aziza Atef was joining him at the bottom of the stairs. The fragrance of her heavy perfume followed Robyn to the first landing, where she stopped to catch her breath before trudging miserably up the remaining flights.

The telephone was ringing as she opened the door to her room. No matter who it was, she didn't want to talk, but she obediently picked up the receiver.

Sayed's voice was gentle. "Robyn, I'm sorry if I upset you in some way."

She stared at the telephone in her hand. Why should she accept that sort of apology? "If you don't even know how, I shan't tell you! Yes, I will: I'm sick and tired of being told I'm something less than decent—a liar, and a common thief, and all the rest! I can't live with the kind of undeserved guilt you so neatly put on my shoulders. There's more, but I won't bore you. And I apologize to you, also. My father taught me never to use profanity, and if I could have found another word I would have said it. I did *not* take the scrolls, no matter what you believe. It would be the last thing in my mind, the very last!"

She didn't know from the silence whether he was still there. "Robyn, this is a futile conversation. Obviously I have failed to follow your line of thought. But about the scrolls—I can understand someone taking them. Strange things happen when we love something, desire something." His voice was smooth and coaxing, almost humoring, she thought. "It's really not such a criminal thing, wanting to hold onto something beautiful and precious...."

"What is that supposed to mean?" she demanded hotly. "What are you saying?"

He chuckled softly, which aggravated her condition further. "I'm saying good-night, small b... Robyn. We can talk tomorrow when you are more in control of yourself."

She heard the click as he gently hung up on her, and she stood there looking helplessly at the phone. He couldn't possibly have sounded more condescending. Small bird, indeed! Well, he could save his sweet words and his little games. It seemed incredible that this was happening to her. Did he think he was giving her a chance to return the stolen scrolls without punishment?

She brooded for long hours, sitting disconsolately on one of the leather chairs on her balcony. The sky had a hazy cast to it, making the stars shimmery and the huge moon bright orange. She felt utterly alone. This whole thing was a matter of honor—her own and her father's.

What she tried not to admit was that she wanted Sayed to regret his accusations as much as she was hurt by them. Love and hurt twisted painfully in her as she pondered what to do next.

Where had all the misunderstanding over the

scrolls begun? She tried to think reasonably and with neutrality. Sayed had no one to blame except those who were working nearest to the scrolls. And the one person he knew the least about—and had other reasons to doubt besides—was herself. It was simple.

So all she had to do was use her brain to figure out who had the opportunity and the motive to take them. "If I were the real thief, what would I do?" she said aloud to the air, and immediately had her answer. The thief would go to the dig at night, somehow get rid of the Bedouin guards or sneak past them, pick the lock to the storeroom and *voilà*!

He was probably there right now, choosing the best papyrus fragments at his leisure. She was sure that Sayed hadn't been able to remove all of them to the safety of the museum, so plenty must still be out there in the flimsy workroom....

How stupid of Sayed to think that she or Rafica had taken the scrolls, when it could have been done anytime during the night! Robyn was starting to feel exhilarated. The thought of catching the real thief at work was growing so appealing that before she knew it she was shedding her black galabia and slipping into her khaki shirt, pants and poplin coat.

She hadn't thought it through past her intense need to prove something to Sayed. She didn't even stop to consider that what she was about to do was dangerous. A few minutes later she was tying a scarf tightly around her head as she approached the hotel desk to arrange for a taxi.

"I'm sorry, miss," the deskman said, "it will take a little time to find a driver who wishes to trust his car to such a trip. But, *Inshallah*, I will find him."

Robyn cooled her heels for half an hour while several drivers negotiated with the clerk. One finally agreed to take her for a ten-pound fare. She felt she had won a little victory, and after tipping the desk clerk generously, she picked up her purse and flashlight and followed the driver to his car.

It was two o'clock in the morning. The streets of the city were still busy with traffic. What everyone was doing up at this hour Robyn couldn't imagine. The driver spoke little English, but he had once been hired by Tom and George to transport supplies to the dig. So far, luck was with her. At least she wouldn't have to describe where to turn off onto the unmarked desert road.

If she had been more experienced with Egyptian weather she would have realized that the red glow around the moon meant that the winds were stirring up dust clouds in the desert and blowing them toward the coast. But she was filled with an emotion that blocked her usual ability to think clearly.

She was going to hand Sayed his thief on a platter and watch while his cool lapis eyes filled with remorse. It hadn't occurred to her that she was acting like a woman desperately in love.

"Stop here, this is as far as I want to go," she said to the driver after they had been bumping over the unpaved road near the dig for several minutes. The headlights barely pierced the thick swirling sand and grit ahead of the car.

"No, lady—" he shook his head emphatically "—I not leave you here."

"It's all right. I know my way," she said with authority.

"Khamsin is blowing, lady," he warned.

"Don't worry, I won't have trouble. I'm meeting

someone here. Please return to the city now. I will be fine.'' She stepped out of the car, and immediately felt as if a warm hand was pushing her back against it. The wind was stronger than it had been in any of the previous days.

She experienced a little tightening of her heart as the taxi slowly turned around and left. She watched its blurry taillights until they disappeared, then started walking over the last little hill to the camp.

The wind blew steadily, sounding in her ears like a chorus of medieval monks singing a litany. At the edge of camp the night fire of the Bedouin guards burned, protected from the wind by a barrier of oil drums, and she heard their laughter. They were playing a game of some sort and didn't see her approach. She congratulated herself on her theory that the thief could easily manage to avoid them.

When she was in sight of the workroom and the excavating site, she pulled her coat closer around her and sat down on the singing earth, like a rock in the shadows. She was prepared to wait a long time if necessary to catch the thief in the act. But what would she do with him—or her—after that? She had enough sense not to try to confront him alone. She would rouse the guards and that would be that, she decided, smiling confidently as she strained her eyes on the door of the workroom.

For an hour she sat there, almost willing the thief to appear. Her concentration was focused completely on that, and when a rusty-sounding voice spoke next to her ear she almost jumped out of her skin.

''Not good for small bird to be here,'' old Bahiya rattled in a whisper. ''You not believe Bahiya when she say things.''

Robyn's heart was beating almost loud enough to be heard above the wind. The old woman sat down beside her in a heap of skirts and flashed her wrinkled grin at Robyn. "I say you have tears if not see clear. You not believe Bahiya. Now you make more tears for small bird in flowers. Sand not tell lie, *sitt*."

Suddenly a howl of gale winds roared over the campsite with ominous force, and Bahiya's next words were blown away before they reached Robyn's ears. All she heard was "khamsin."

The moon and stars disappeared from the sky, and the choking gusts blasted fine particles of sand into Robyn's ears. She reached out for Bahiya's hand. "I have to save the scrolls!" she shouted.

She could see the walls of the little work building starting to sag against the savage battering of the stifling hot wind. The Bedouin had been galvanized into action and Robyn could barely see their shadowy forms as they rushed to batten down the camp.

She leaned hard against the wind and made her way to the door of the workroom, where she had the sinking realization that she didn't have a key to the lock. The small structure was shuddering and making cracking sounds at its corners. Robyn knew it was just a matter of minutes before it would be blown flat, the boxes and trays of scroll fragments with it.

Picking up a large stone, she hit the small window several times to break it. The glass shattered around her, flying off in all directions in the wind. She paid no attention to the small cuts on her arms and hands, where slivers of glass had been driven into her unprotected skin.

As she squeezed her body through the jagged opening she tore her coat and pants, but managed to get inside. There she jammed a heavy packing crate against the window frame, securing it with two cases of water bottles that she dragged up onto the work-table.

The vibration inside the little room was deafening, as if a giant were leaning against the walls, banging and growling. With the help of her flashlight she was able to find what she was looking for. Sayed had not been able to clear out all of the papyri; even the large vellum mass was still resting under its cover. But it wouldn't be for long if she didn't do something quickly.

Where would be a safe place in this wind, she puzzled. She heard voices outside the room and knew that the men were piling sandbags against the walls of the shed. Immediately it began to feel more stable.

Bahiya's penetrating voice cut through the howling din, shouting things in Arabic as if she were the boss of the operation. "You open window, *sitt*!" she commanded Robyn from outside. "I help you!"

Robyn moved the crate at the window aside and saw that Bahiya was ready to push a heavy tarpaulin through to her. "Thanks!" she cried, "that's just what I need!" Bahiya vanished from sight and Robyn pulled the tarp the rest of the way through, then blocked the opening again.

The shaky building just might hold if the winds didn't get any stronger. The sandbags were already muffling the sound of the gale and absorbing the whipsaw force on the walls.

After Robyn braced the flashlight to shine on the work area she dragged several rolls of the padded plastic to the table and started cushioning the loose fragments in their trays. She had no feeling for the length of time she feverishly gathered the fragile pieces into their plastic blankets, but at about the same time her flashlight began to grow dim she was setting everything beneath the table. Easing the tarp over top, she made sure that all sides were covered before she anchored it in a dozen places with anything she could find that was heavy—the stools, the two folded cots, more packing boxes. She even managed to lift the massive table a few inches so that she could kick the corners of the tarp beneath the heavy legs.

As her battery finally gave out and she was left in darkness, there were tears of relief in her eyes. The wind outside the hot workroom seemed to be subsiding a little; but even if it worsened, she had been able to save the precious papyri.

She hadn't thought of Sayed once in all the time she was here, and when she suddenly remembered him she was shaken out of her victorious feelings. *Well,* she said to herself, *even if I didn't produce the thief, at least I proved my dedication to the dig.*

She pushed the crate away from the window, to see headlights of a car beaming toward her. The air between herself and the vehicle was a brownish yellow from the millions of dancing particles swirling in it. Moving almost in slow motion in the surrealistic light, shadowy people were getting out of the car. Then she heard voices. Tom was the first recognizable figure she saw. As he came into the car's headlight beams, she called out to him.

He stopped. "Robyn! What in God's name are you doing here?"

She gestured behind her into the room, not realizing he couldn't see her clearly. "I covered the scrolls...just in time!"

"You what?" He was moving toward the window where she stood. Rafica was with him.

"Get me out of here, will you? I don't have a key to the door and I don't want to climb through the window again." She felt overjoyed to see familiar faces and was eager to tell her co-workers of her accomplishment.

The door rattled and then opened, letting in a rush of dusty air with it. Tom stood with his arms akimbo in the doorway. "When Sayed called to tell me we had to get out here fast because the khamsin was blowing, I didn't have the heart to wake you, too," he laughed. "And you were here already! I'm impressed!"

She rushed toward him and gave him a hug of relief, then hugged Rafica. "I put everything under the tarp while the Bedouin were sandbagging the building. The whole place was falling down in the winds...I was sure it was going to collapse on the trays," she said breathlessly. "I got it all under the table. It was the only safe place!"

Tom snapped on his flashlight and played the beam around the room, letting out a low whistle. "You sure did, all right! Sayed! Hassan! Come in here! You've got to see this!" he called from the doorway.

Two more flashlights waved crazily into the room and Robyn's eagerness froze. Behind one of the lights was Sayed, she knew, even though she couldn't see him. "Guess who came out here ahead of us and saved the fragments?" Tom said loudly.

Sayed's face appeared in the dim light. "So I see," he said unnervingly. "That was a rash thing to have done, Robyn, very rash. You might have been injured, even killed, and no piece of papyrus is worth that.''

He was scolding her! How could he, after what she had done for him? "I did what I felt I had to do," she retorted, not able to see his shadowed eyes. Why wasn't he thanking her?

"Good Lord, Sayed," Tom said, "give her a break! She's the heroine of the day."

Hassan Tarsi's voice spoke from behind the other flashlight. "Very commendable, Miss Douglas. You have done our work for us. But one wonders what really brought you out here in the middle of the night. I think Dr. al-Rashad is wondering that, as well."

Robyn instantly regretted insulting the man at the banquet. He carried venom just as Huntley Saunders did. "Dr. Tarsi, I did what nobody else seemed able—or willing—to do: I came out here to catch our thief, to be here when he came. And I believe I would have if the khamsin hadn't suddenly blown up."

She could feel the circumstantial evidence of her guilt hanging heavily over her, like the murky sand that still hovered in the electrically charged air. How must it look to find her here?

Sayed said nothing, forcing Robyn to explain herself further. "I figured that the thief must come at night, when Rafica and I were not with the scrolls. I wanted to prove that it was somebody else who was stealing them."

"Poor kid," Tom said softly. "Why did you have to do that?"

Sayed cut in, "Because she believes that there has been doubt about her innocence, is that not so?"

"Yes," she answered strongly.

"And for that bit of misguided vanity you put yourself in danger."

"Not vanity, Dr. al-Rashad—honor. At least you can't blame *that* on vandals and thieves!" She waved her hand toward the wreckage of the camp, visible just outside the door.

"Listen, Robyn," Tom offered, "why don't you get comfortable in the car? Mohammed has a thermos full of coffee. We'll just check things over and be there in a jiffy."

"Yes, my sister," Rafica said gently. "You have done a wonderful thing and now you must rest."

The Bedouin workers were piling more bags at the corners of the workroom outside and laying tarps over the niches of the dig, anchoring them with huge stones. Robyn, walking past them to the car, couldn't have felt worse.

"We do good, *sitt!*" Bahiya's crackly voice came out of the darkness through thick gritty air.

Robyn kept on walking, conscious that the old woman was walking just behind her. "He doesn't believe me," she said almost to herself. "He thinks I took the scrolls from the workroom...even now."

Bahiya came closer and put out a hand. "I know man who take scrolls."

Robyn stared desperately into the wise glinting eyes. "Then for God's sake, tell them!"

The old woman smiled serenely. "It not time yet. Afreets still fly in winds. You not listen to them, *sitt*. Afreets tell lies to blue-eyed god and his bird in flowers." Silently she walked away.

Robyn, left standing next to the demolished cooking area, felt unreal and disoriented. Whenever Bahiya spoke to her the words carried something strange with them, like promises of things that could never be. She remained motionless for a moment in the brownish light from the lanterns and headlights. Voices sounded in the distance, distorted by the low groaning of the slackening winds.

What was she doing here, when all she wanted was for Sayed to hold her in his arms and love her? But he was somewhere in the whirling dusts, checking on his beloved scrolls—scrolls he thought she had come to steal!

She didn't want to go back to Mohammed's car and sit alone, waiting for Sayed to return and rekindle her misery. Her heart was beating heavily and unevenly and she had a sudden urge to be with old Bahiya. It was obvious that no one else understood her, she thought in self-pity.

She started walking aimlessly in the general direction of the village, stumbling over stones as she retied her scarf around her blowing hair. The wind was starting up again, sending hard blasts against her back, forcing her to walk faster.

The murky sand swirled around her, obscuring everything, and all at once she had no sense of direction. Her sense of timing was distorted, too; her long night of excitement was ending in a terrible aching fatigue and a letdown feeling. Nothing was real anymore except the hot rushing forces of the earth and air.

A little scene with her father flashed into her mind. He had been unpacking some pottery shards once, and in the box was a residue of reddish earth. He had stirred it gently with his index finger and said, "See, Robyn, the red earth of Egypt." She remembered touching the grains of sand and hoping against hope that she would see Egypt one day when she grew up....

Well, here she was, trapped in the very essence of Egypt's earth, and she couldn't recall a single moment when her heart had hurt so much.

"I want to go home," she moaned aloud. The words sounded muffled and dim and gradually a realization filtered into her tired brain: she was lost, turned around.

But she couldn't have gone far. If she continued walking in the same direction she would certainly find the village. It wasn't so small that she could easily miss it.

A sound startled her. A small uncertain bray came out of the dim haze, and then a dark shape loomed ahead of her. The next moment she collided with something warm and furry. A sad little donkey's face looked into hers, its eyes squinted against the dust. It was panting, trying to breathe in the dense air. With a murmur of sympathy Robyn put her hand on the shaggy gray head, and the animal nudged closer to her.

"Hello, you're lost, too?" A rumbling grunt answered from deep in the animal's throat. "What shall we do about it?" Robyn couldn't maintain her own growing fear with this needy companion at her side. She felt suddenly better for the patient little beast's presence.

Her face was burning and her nose and mouth were uncomfortably parched as she began to walk again. The donkey stayed beside her, so she put her arm around its warm neck. It didn't take long for her to realize that walking was not the solution. They weren't getting anywhere, and Robyn couldn't see two feet in front of her hand.

She remembered an old adventure story she had read as a child in which the characters, lost in a sandstorm had sat down with their backs to the wind and close to their animals. They had put cloths over their faces so that they could breathe.

She looked at the donkey, which was puffing pitifully. As they struggled up a slight rise in the ground Robyn made up her mind. "We'd better give it up, my friend," she said to the long gray face. The far side of the rise offered a degree of shelter from the worst blasts of the khamsin, and just below the crest of the slope she dropped to the ground. With little persuasion the donkey folded its thin legs and sat beside her.

"You're no fool." She scratched its soft erect ears and the little beast put its head down close to the earth. Robyn curled up against it. It was still almost impossible to breathe. She pulled the back of her coat up over her face and the donkey's snout. Together they breathed into the tiny tent formed by the fabric.

The sharp sting of the gusts beat against them, but soon the sand had built up like a light blanket and removed much of the force.

Robyn felt the steady heartbeat of her newfound friend as she rested her head against its furry, comforting neck. Gradually her mind ceased to function. She was drifting off, lulled by a feeling of acceptance that came from the solid strength of the earth and the vitality of the warm life beneath her head. She slept heavily, dreaming that she was running along the canal to find the blue-eyed god. He wasn't there, so she crouched in the dried grasses and wept. Then she heard his voice calling her name, and her yearning for him flamed through her sore heart.

"Robyn! Robyn!" Sayed's anxious voice was close to her and she felt hands brushing the sand from her back. She pushed the enveloping coat from her face, trying to move from her cramped position. The donkey suddenly scrambled to its feet, and she was drawn rapidly against another warm body.

"Praise be to Allah!" Sayed said huskily as his strong arms pulled her against him. He was kneeling in the sand, his eyes red rimmed and his hair filmed with tawny dust. She let herself be drawn tightly into his embrace, still partly lost in her dream of the canal and the blue-eyed god.

Then she blinked her eyes and saw that the air was clearing. The pale light of early dawn was on the horizon, and the wind was now only a steady breeze.

He held her close, murmuring words in Arabic that could only have been endearments. She pressed against his sandy shirt until he lifted her face and his eyes searched into hers.

"You are all right?"

"Yes," she said dazedly, "my little friend took care of me."

"I've been out of my mind looking for you—worrying about scorpions and the small serpents that live out here."

His voice sounded beautiful to her ears, and she clung to him, unable to muster any feeling but gratitude. He was still talking to her, and she knew he was distressed. "Why did you leave the dig? Surely you knew better than to go into the wind. . . ." His hand was gently stroking her gritty hair away from her forehead.

She looked at his tired face and all at once came back to reality. "I felt so terrible," she blurted honestly. "Everyone thought I had stolen the scrolls, and I just had to get away. I didn't care anymore." Easy tears sprang up in her eyes.

Sayed's deep blue gaze seemed to look into her soul. "Robyn, Robyn! I have not handled things with any perception! I know you would never take the scrolls, or did I make it seem that way? I beg your forgiveness, sweet small bird. I had no intention...."

He bent his head until his cheek rested against hers, and then his lips were seeking her mouth in a kiss that was long and gentle and infinitely sweet. There was soft passion in it, but also an essence of protection and caring. Robyn felt her very soul respond, her love for him flowed from her lips to his.

"My treasure," he said in a whisper, as his mouth returned to hers. "If anything had happened to you...!" His voice grew rough and his kiss deepened with his need. Her heart was spinning....

Suddenly a cold fear rose in her and she put her hands against his chest, pushing herself away. She couldn't betray her weakness for him again.

He looked at her, surprised. "What is wrong? Are you in pain? Oh, my dear little love...."

The last words flowed like warm honey over her bitter heart, but she couldn't respond. He was only saying the things that a man was supposed to say to comfort a woman.

"I think I'd better try to move," she said, turning away from him quickly. Just then the donkey gave a dusty shake and raised his bony face toward the rising sun. His flanks heaved and he wheezed out a long bray into the morning light.

They both had to laugh. Sayed lifted her onto her

feet, and one leg buckled beneath her. There was a dark stain on her pant leg where she had fallen on a sharp stone. He knelt swiftly to examine the cut.

"You can't walk until this is bandaged. Poor Robyn! And you didn't tell me."

"I...it isn't anything. I must have fallen in the storm."

He reached out and lifted her in his firm arms, easily and without strain. "Don't—I can walk!" she insisted.

"Be quiet, Robyn. I'm going to carry you to camp. You wandered way past Tarsi's dig...it's too far for you."

He started walking over the uneven ground with long strides. She could feel the ripple of his muscles against her, and her arms slipped naturally around his neck. She rested her head blissfully on his shoulder and shut her eyes in order to feel the full impact of their closeness. This was the way love was supposed to be, she knew. The sight of his crisp curling hair and his beautifully shaped ear, so near her own lips, roused a painful desire to kiss him, and she fought it down with effort.

"You needn't be so stiff. Relax, Robyn!" His voice had a teasing laugh in it.

"I'm not used to being carried."

She felt him chuckle. "We must do this more often, then."

She looked down to see the donkey trotting happily beside them.

A distant shout brought with it running figures, and in a few moments Tom panted up to them. "Thank God," he said. "I just got back from searching in the other direction. You gave us an awful scare!"

Robyn wanted to apologize for causing trouble, especially when Rafica, too, reached them, searching Robyn's face anxiously. "Praise be to Allah!" she exclaimed.

"I'm all right, really," Robyn protested uncomfortably. "The donkey and I curled up together... and breathed through my coat...."

"You're a regular girl scout," Tom exclaimed in a joking tone that covered his relief.

"She hurt her knee in a fall and cut herself in several places from the glass, as well," Sayed said in a brusque voice. "Rafica, will you go ahead of us and get the first-aid box?"

The girl had just sped off toward the camp when a colorful figure intercepted them—Bahiya. She moved close to Robyn and whispered, "It is time, *sitt*."

Her mysterious, complicated eyes turned to Sayed. "I have words to say, but I wait for you at camp." She walked ahead of them.

The odd procession strode into the dig area, where the Bedouin men were already starting to repair the wind damage. Rafica was waiting with a bowl of water and some bandages.

Dr. Gaddabi rushed to take Robyn's hand as she stood shakily beside Sayed. "My dear girl, we were so worried." His fatherly face showed concern, but his eyes darted between Robyn and Sayed.

Sayed supervised the dressing of her cuts. As they finished, Hassan Tarsi came up and stood nearby. Huntley Saunders was behind him, disheveled and rumpled in his cotton leisure suit. In the distance Robyn saw his white Mercedes, and she wondered why he had bothered to come. It must have given Tom pleasure to wake him out of his party stupor and tell him that his expensive investment in fame was being blown away by the khamsin.

Bahiya's face was a glaring mask as she looked from Hassan Tarsi to Huntley Saunders. Tarsi shifted nervously and said, "Why do you let that old witch stay around here, al-Rashad? She had reason to steal our things."

"Sirsir!" she hissed at him.

"Cockroach," Tom translated to Robyn. Sayed turned and met three pairs of emotion-charged eyes, then Bahiya stepped forward, her colored skirts swirling angrily. She shot out a long dramatic finger, first at Tarsi and then at Saunders.

"Oh, boy, now we're going to hear something," Tom whispered.

With a slight bow to Sayed, Bahiya spoke in a vibrant tone. *"Ya ustar,"* she began, then launched into a flow of rapid Arabic.

"That's a formal salutation meaning 'Oh, professor,'" Tom said softly. "What a great old gal!"

Sayed was listening, his face carefully neutral. Sometimes he commented with the word *wallah*, which Robyn knew meant "really."

Tom was trying to keep up a running translation for Robyn. Rafica filled in from time to time, but she hesitated at the names the old woman was calling Hassan Tarsi and Huntley Saunders. Tom eagerly explained a few of them, having to do with camel dung, rats, and human excretion. "She says that Saunders paid Hassan to help him steal the scrolls for his personal collection, and gave money to the guards to stay away for a night. Someone made a duplicate key to fit the lock," Tom related. "She has hidden with some of the village women and young men, who saw it all. She will testify. She says Hassan committed the vandalism because he hates Sayed."

Hassan Tarsi was obviously in a rage by the time she finished her singsong account. He was calling her a diseased old hag, Tom explained as the scene progressed. Huntley Saunders, red in the face, was in vain trying to find out what was being said, since his name frequently stood out from the flood of Arabic.

Bahiya ended her tirade at Tarsi by calling him a disgrace to Egypt and Islam, punctuating her words with a well-aimed spit. Then she turned her barbed English toward Huntley Saunders: "Fat dog! *Ya sitàn!* Rascal you!"

Tom rumbled with suppressed laughter at the ludicrous picture in front of him, and even Dr. Gaddabi grinned. Bahiya was choosing her words carefully. "Fat dog, only for pride you do this thing." She waved at the excavation. "You have no caring for old treasures...only to say you own them! Bahiya see you carry off under coat on top of big belly, scrolls belong to people of Egypt. I testify—so do men and women of village."

Goaded beyond caution, Huntley Saunders began to bluster in a loud voice, "Without all the money I've given you wouldn't have this lousy dig! This damn government is just plain greedy. They plan to keep everything—now what kind of deal is that? A couple of little ol' scrolls can't make a difference. Nobody'll miss two out of thousands. Anyway—" he wiped his sweating face with the back of his sleeve "—it's better I take care of them than sneaky darkskinned thieves who would probably have taken them anyway. Then they'd just sell them to me on the black market. This way I'm eliminating the middle

man.'' He forced a hearty laugh into the sudden silence before he realized he had made a confession.

Bahiya looked triumphant, but Hassan Tarsi was
muttering and growling in his throat. In a rush the
Iranian sprang at Saunders, who was taken off balance by the impact and crashed to the ground with a
surprised yell. Tarsi knelt on his bulk, pummeling his
face with his fists.

The group erupted for a few moments as Sayed
and Tom tried to separate the two men. Tarsi's wiry
body writhed in their grasp, and he managed to land
a heavy kick on Saunders's leg as he was pulled away.
Saunders was helped to his feet by Dr. Gaddabi and
George, who had run from the dig, and he stood
swaying and moaning.

A look of shrewd righteousness spread across
Hassan Tarsi's face. ''I must apologize to everyone,''
he said in a noble tone, ''but I have been outraged
and called a liar—deceived by a man I thought was a
friend. I ask that all of this be put before the Antiquities Department for judgment. At least they won't
take the word of a demented old witch.'' He shot the
word at Bahiya.

She said nothing, only swirled her skirts and spit
eloquently in his direction. Sayed and Dr. Gaddabi
had an impromptu conference, then Sayed raised his
hand for attention.

''Dr. Gaddabi and I are agreed that this is a matter
for the antiquities police. We shall file a formal
report tomorrow. Until then, Dr. Tarsi, you are forbidden to come near this dig. I guarantee you will be
given a fair hearing.''

Tarsi's face drew into a wrathful glare. Then Bahiya
spoke again, ''My village give judgment on the guards

who take bribe. We show money to police.... We testify!''

"Shokran, sheikha," Sayed answered, causing the wrinkled face to fold in delight. "As for you, Mr. Saunders—" Sayed's eyes held cold blue ice "—you will stay away from here entirely unless invited. I will not press charges because you are a sponsor of this work, and a foreigner who does not know better. But you will return the scrolls to Dr. Gaddabi when we get back to Alexandria. You will keep your mouth shut and engage in no slander or false statements. You are fortunate this is not a society where fools and thieves are publicly whipped."

"Hell's fire, who do you think you're talkin' to?" The Texan's bloodshot eyes bulged.

"He's going to have a black eye," Tom whispered to Robyn and Rafica.

Sayed's face was unmoved. "I am the director of this project, need you be reminded? I have every right to protect the findings here."

"I'll take my borescope, sonny boy, and leave this stinkin' incompetent country...as soon as I can get reservations."

"That would be unwise, Mr. Saunders." Sayed looked grim. "If you take the borescope you will be removing university property." He turned to Robyn. "Do you confirm my judgment?"

Robyn stepped shakily forward, anger making her forget her knee. "You know very well who owns the borescope, Mr. Saunders. If you touch it, Dr. al-Rashad will alert the police." She looked at the baggy face, on which a suggestion of blue was already appearing around one eye. She felt a perverse pleasure watching it swell up. "You have to live with yourself," she said, "with your lies and innuendos."

Sayed put a steadying hand on Robyn's shoulder. "I'm sure Miss Douglas doesn't want her university and her national image held up to scrutiny because of this. For your sake and ours, I pray it can be kept from the press. All you have to do is return the scrolls, and tell the truth to the antiquities police. You'll get full credit for your contribution when the results of the dig are announced."

"You'd just better see to it, hoity-toity!" The man explored his bad eye with a gingerly touch. "Okay, okay, I'll stay out of your way." He turned and lumbered off toward his car.

At the same moment, Hassan Tarsi was leaving the camp, his loping, goatlike walk changing to a swift run after a few yards. *As if to outrun his devils,* Robyn thought, watching him head toward his dig. Maybe he could soothe his losses there among his own ruins, dreaming of Cleopatra's villa.

Rafica sighed, "What awful men! At least the wind blew things out into the open."

Sayed turned to Robyn. "I have to stay here. With the winds starting we must get the drill ready for use right away, today. Now that these dark secrets are out in the open we have a good chance of succeeding with the discovery of the lower chamber."

Robyn started to search his face for signs of love, but stopped herself. What had happened in the winds with him wasn't love, it was something out of context with reality. She would be unwise to make of it anything more than what it was: Sayed's way of showing his relief at finding her. After all, she thought a bit cynically, whatever would he say to Dr. Wayland if he lost the university's observer in a khamsin storm?

"I will send you back in one of the cars, Robyn," he was saying. "You must get to bed and rest." His eyes surveyed her bandaged hands and knee. "My poor Robyn, I don't know how to say the right words to you...how to apologize. You did save the scrolls, I know that, and as for my clumsy accusations about the theft, I can only plead stupidity. It was Tarsi I was after; I thought you would have known that. I had to make him think I didn't suspect him. But I only made you suffer, and now you think me cruel and heartless." He touched her face with his fingers in a gentle caress.

"Dear Robyn, I never suspected you of anything more than being stubborn and a little naive. I intended to apologize to you in front of everyone—even before we heard Bahiya's revelations." His eyes were without their usual protective armor and Robyn might have convinced herself that she saw a mist of tears in them, but she couldn't let herself slide into hope again.

He cradled one of her hands in both of his, flooding her with a desire to believe him. "Two of the names of Allah are *ar-Rahman*—the Merciful, and *al-afuww*—the Forgiving. Will you forgive?"

Robyn fought down the urge to throw herself into his arms. "Of course," she said softly. She was at a loss to say more.

Dr. Gaddabi interrupted. "Robyn, I'm going to tell Dr. Wayland what a heroine you have been to us. Sayed, this lady looks exhausted. Let's get her to her comfortable bed at the hotel."

Sayed picked her up again and bundled her into the back seat of Mohammed's car. "We will talk later," he said gently.

Bahiya's face appeared at the car window. "Not worry, *sitt*. Wind blow away lies. Now moon bring up lost thing." Her eyes glittered brightly. "Be wise, shy bird. Troubles go. By next moon you have joy." She moved away with her usual regal air.

"Sheikha," Mohammed said. "Wise woman!" He gave a gold-toothed smile.

It was midmorning by the time she finally peeled off her torn and dirty clothes, bathed her bruised body and slipped into bed. She hugged to herself the few words that Sayed had spoken when he found her: "My treasure... if anything had happened to you... my dear little love."

CHAPTER FOURTEEN

WHEN ROBYN WOKE from her enveloping sleep it was dark outside her windows and the bright crimson-colored moon was just rising over the horizon across the small bay. She blinked her eyes at the sight, trying to remember why she was in bed and which end of the day she was seeing outside her windows.

The message light on her telephone was flashing silently. Her entire body ached as she reached over to call the desk. It seemed impossible that she had slept through the day and into the evening, but she had. The luminous dial on her travel clock said seven-thirty.

"Is there a message for me?" she asked the hotel operator in a voice made rough by long hours of sleep.

"The gentleman asks that you receive the package that has been left at your door. He did not wish to wake you."

"What gentleman?" she questioned, but the line went dead.

She slowly eased her stiff arms into her terry-cloth robe and went to the door, where a foil-wrapped florist box was resting on the threshold. Her heart leaped with anticipation. There was no card on the outside of the box, yet it had to be from Sayed.

She half expected to find a blue lotus flower as her

romantic mind followed its breathless scenario, but when her fingers lifted the shimmery silver top from the box she saw the red carnations and then the card with Tom's large signature on it. Her heart dropped from its soaring path as she read:

To my favorite girl scout. If you aren't too tired, join me for dinner. I'll be eating alone in the dining room at eight-thirty.

Cheers, Tom

It was the best offer she'd had and Tom had been very sweet to send her flowers. She smiled at his off-hand invitation and decided to accept. The carnations gave off a spicy fragrance that helped her regain some clarity, and she shook off the momentary disappointment at not finding a blue lotus instead.

Her skin was so bruised and sensitive that she couldn't stand the thought of getting dressed in anything but the softest cotton. The black galabia was the answer. It hung lightly from her shoulders and weighed almost nothing. Yet even its smooth fabric reminded her painfully of the many tender places on her body.

A glance at her watch told her that she would have to hurry. The first pangs of hunger in days were starting in her stomach. She knew she had been losing weight, and it wasn't because of the usual tourist maladies. Her insides had been tied in a knot for longer than she cared to recall.

Tom was at a table for two nursing a drink when she joined him. He stood up gallantly, then called the waiter. "I'm glad you came, Robyn."

"The flowers were beautiful. Thanks."

"The least I could do. Anyway, I had to lure you down to dinner with me. They say that flowers will do it every time. You look great," he added, smiling impishly and gulping down the last of his drink. "What are you having to drink?"

"Nothing for me. I haven't eaten for a while and it would just go to my head and make me silly."

"And why not, for a change? You deserve to let go and have a good time for yourself, especially after this morning's fiasco. My God, it was like watching a 1930s movie, dark dealings in the mysterious desert. Sayed and I worked all morning getting set up for the drill. If we don't get that blasted thing into the ground tomorrow I'm going to start believing that old Bedouin fortune-teller."

"Afreets, the tricky demons?"

"What else? I've never been on a project that had so many things go wrong. Let's order; I haven't been eating too regularly myself." He turned to the menu, accepting the waiter's recommendation for the special of the day. Then he leaned back in his chair and looked at Robyn. "I have a confession to make."

"Not you, too?" She laughed.

"No, not about the dig...about why I had to see you."

Robyn felt a prickle of apprehension. All she needed was for Tom to start acting like a courting male. It would be the end of her fragile sanity.

"Give me a straight answer, my friend, will you?"

"I'll try," she said tentatively.

"What am I supposed to do about that damnable woman?"

Robyn set her water glass down and looked quizzically at him. "Who?"

"Sandi. We're running around each other in circles. Every time I start to say something romantic to her it comes out like a lecture, and when she gives me encouragement I find myself getting mad at her. What's the matter with us?" There was real pain in his face. "And now she's so moody I can't even start a conversation with her. We always get tangled up and one of us ends up storming out. I'm not usually that kind of a guy. Tell me what's happening, Robyn—you're a girl. . . ."

She reached for his hand, feeling like a big sister even though Tom and Sandi were both older than she. "It could be love." She smiled, looking into his worried eyes.

"If that's what you call it, it's the weirdest thing I've ever known. But she did tell me she loved me. . . the other night."

"And. . .? What did you say to her then?"

"Something rotten. Then she cried and it was a mess between us again."

"You were with her today at the dig, weren't you?"

"She didn't show up. I don't know where she is right now—maybe playing with that Texan cretin." He ground his teeth gloomily.

"That's what's wrong, Tom," Robyn said firmly. "She told you she loved you and you didn't believe her. She doesn't know how to change the past and you won't give her a chance in the present. Kind of tough for a girl who loves someone."

"I'm no green kid. . . I've been around. But when I think of Sandi with another guy my blood boils. I'd love to trust her, I really would, but. . . ."

"How do you know until you try it? She does love

you, Tom, I know the signs." Robyn didn't admit that she had studied the signs of love in herself, and that was how she knew.

Tom brightened, then bent with an elegant flourish to give her hand a kiss. "If that's what it takes, I'll try being a lovable guy—and I'll let you know how it turns out. That's one lady I don't want to lose. Don't ask me why...."

He changed the subject, making some lighthearted jokes about the people involved in Sayed's dig. "This whole thing must seem like a soap opera to you instead of a serious archaeological expedition," he said.

"Sometimes I wonder," Robyn answered, with a quirk of her lips. "The only one who isn't lost in the midst of emotional upheavals is sweet old Dr. Gaddabi."

"And Sayed—he's free as a bird if you don't count all the females trailing at his heels."

"Yes... I forgot," she said, and lowered her eyes, then raised them quickly. "Tom, would you do something for me?"

"Sure. Just don't ask me to steal manuscripts and we'll get on fine." He laughed.

"I'm serious. Would you take me for a walk after dinner? No strings attached, I promise. I just want to stand for a while under the Egyptian moon with a normal, wholesome companion—and no male-female complications."

"Can't be any harm in that. Sure, I'll walk you anywhere you want to go." He signed the check and they left the dining room.

"Thanks for not asking me why," Robyn said as they walked across the garden. "I need to have a memory of this place that leaves me feeling good inside and not shattered into a million little pieces. Every time I've taken a good long look at the moon the past few days it's been hard on me.''

"Don't tell me anything you don't want to," he said. "I just didn't realize that you were involved with someone here. And I'm not about to start guessing who."

"You're a friend," she said, smiling. "And we both needed each other tonight. . . believe me."

They strolled out to the white crescent of beach that followed the curve of the quiet bay. The moon was still low in the sky and very red from the khamsin in the desert. The top of its disk was flattened; soon it would be a half-moon, like a huge rosy cradle gliding soundlessly among the heavens. Robyn thought of the ancient Egyptian sky goddess and could have easily believed that there were greater beings that inhabited the heavens.

Tom linked his arm with hers. If she could have asked for a more sympathetic friend she wouldn't have found one. They stood for a long time before Tom said anything.

"The winds will probably keep blowing for another day or so, but Sayed is determined to drill tomorrow—even if they have to tie the workers to the drill to keep them from blowing away."

"I wouldn't miss tomorrow for the world," she said. "It means so much to everyone—especially Sayed."

"He's staking his career on this. With the investigation coming up by the Antiquities Department, he'd better have something to show them that takes their minds off the irregularities and problems at our dig. Lately they've been getting nervous about having foreign participation, and this Saunders thing will give certain officers of the department a lot of ammunition. All Sayed can do is show them that *because* of the foreign involvement—and only because of it—he was able to make a magnificent discovery. That's what tomorrow is really all about. Let's go out on the pier and see if we can spot any fish."

One other person was standing at the end of the pier when they approached, a woman with a scarf over her hair and her hands thrust deeply into the pockets of her coat. She didn't turn around and Robyn and Tom didn't really notice her, although they were only a little distance away.

"See—I knew there were little schools of fish here." They looked down into the still water and saw phosphorescent gleams and flashes beneath the surface.

Robyn leaned her head against his shoulder. "This is exactly what I wanted to do. There's the moon, the perfect little bay, the perfumed air of Egypt on my face. It's the kind of memory I should have been collecting instead of—"

"Don't think about anything else. At a time like this we could both benefit from a walk under the moon." He leaned close to her ear and whispered impishly, ". . . and not have romance rearing its ugly head to complicate things."

She couldn't help smiling. "You're a mind reader."

"Mmm," he agreed, pulling her closer with a brotherly hug.

The woman at the railing nearby suddenly turned and started back along the pier, almost pushing past them on the narrow walkway. As they saw who it was, Robyn pulled back from Tom's arms. The look on Sandi's angry face was murderous, betrayed.

"Sandi..." Tom started to say, reaching out to stop her.

"Forget it!" she fired back at him, and started to run.

He caught up with her in a few strides. "Damn it, Sandi, don't do this to me! Whatever you thought you saw, it wasn't—"

"I said forget it!" She wrenched away from him and ran the rest of the way down the pier. Tom broke into a trot after her, leaving Robyn alone.

She felt awful. Did everything have to be misunderstood? Every time?

She stayed out on the pier for a while before walking slowly back toward the hotel, and she prayed that Tom was finding the right words to explain himself. Maybe they were making up right now, holding each other tightly and admitting that they couldn't live without each other....

The lobby was nearly empty and the desk clerk shook his head when she asked for messages. She let herself into her room. There was no florist box at the door, and she smiled at herself for even thinking that there might be.

In the morning she woke at the usual time for work and dressed gingerly in her extra pair of khaki pants and a cotton shirt. She still felt vulnerable, more from physical traumas to her body than anything emotional, she assured herself.

Down in the lobby there was no sign of the crew. She checked at the desk and was handed a note.

"They departed very early and left this message, miss," the clerk said impersonally.

She read it as she walked away from the desk.

Thanks for last night. I don't know if Sandi believed me, but I tried. That's a switch! Anyway, Sayed called late last night. He wants Sandi, Rafica, George and me out at the dig at the crack of dawn. He said not to wake you—he'll send a message if we actually start to drill. See you later.

Tom

PS: Sorry I left without saying good-night.

She crumpled the note. What was Sayed thinking? He knew how much it meant to her. When had she ever shown a lack of interest in the dig? She should be there right now.

Outside she found a taxi and negotiated a fare out to the desert. She fully intended to charge it to Sayed's expense account. Had she become an expendable member of the team now that most of Sayed's problems were cleared away? She was not going to let him treat her, and the university, with such cavalier disregard.

The first thing she saw when the car drew up to the camp was other cars—lots of them. And strangers walking all around the dig area. Robyn quickly let herself out and paid the driver. She thought at first she had come to the wrong place. Well-dressed men and women were chatting loudly and wandering around, laughing with each other and looking very much out of place in the blowing, hot desert air. The women were holding onto their hairdos, and some were breathing through their handkerchiefs.

Where was Sayed? For that matter, where was anybody she knew? A man came up to her with a note pad in his hand. "Do you have a statement to make, miss?"

"What about?" she said anxiously. "Has something happened?"

"The hidden Library of Alexandria, of course!" A photographer stood next to him and aimed his camera at Robyn.

"I don't know anything about it," she said brusquely. "Ask Dr. al-Rashad." What were newspaper people doing here? All at once her temper flared. Did Sayed really want publicity, after all? It couldn't be, she thought more steadily. Then she caught sight of Tom walking toward her. "What is this all about?" she demanded.

He shrugged his shoulders. "They just popped out of the rocks a little while ago. Huntley Saunders, too."

"Where's Sayed?"

"Over there, with all those women, trying to be polite. Robyn, I'm sorry I took off so fast last night, but I had to."

"I understand. How's Sandi?"

"I'm getting the silent treatment today. She's doing her work and that's it. Not a word to anybody."

"I'm sorry."

"Me, too. But the good news is, the drill's ready to go. The A-frame's steady, and we're right over the center of the lower chamber. I'm glad Sayed sent Mohammed back to get you."

"He didn't. I came by myself in a taxi. And I must

say, I'm good and fed up with his disregard of me as the official observer!''

"Then you'd better talk it out with the man himself. Somebody's got his wires crossed here.''

"Exactly,'' she said hotly. "Sayed al-Rashad's game of musical chairs has gone on long enough!''

"I don't know if this is the best time to straighten out a personal problem with him, Robyn, he's pretty busy....''

She stormed off anyway and pushed through the group of admiring women to find Sayed with his arms folded across his chest and a tolerant half-smile on his handsome lips.

"We have to talk, Dr. al-Rashad. If you'll excuse me, ladies....'' She grabbed his arm and pulled him out of the circle. He let himself be led away, then stopped her with an amused look.

"Good morning, Robyn. This is rather an abrupt greeting for my small bird. Everything is going perfectly for the drilling—except for my newly arrived audience. But today not even that is going to mar my pleasure.''

His calmness was galling. "You know very well what I'm about to say,'' she said carefully, trying not to sound like just another angry female. "You excluded me from the discovery of the lower chamber. You brought these...people...out here and kept Dr. Wayland's designated observer away. I demand to know why! When were you planning to inform me of your discovery—next week?'' She met his eyes with smoky blue sparks of her own.

"I see,'' he said gently. "And why would you think me capable of such action? It was your Mr. Saunders who made a carte blanche invitation to his society friends to look over my shoulder today—and to the press. Look at me, Robyn; I'm a tired man, a very tired man. I no longer have the strength to direct this project and waste my energy on the fools around me, as well. Let the curious ones come—I don't care anymore. And the press—if I send them away they will only go home and invent stories anyway. Is that satisfactory to you, or do you want me to whimper and beg forgiveness all over again?''

He was meeting her eyes with his unwavering lapis gaze, fully in command once more. She would never learn to withstand those powerful, beautiful eyes.

She took a steadying breath and lowered her voice. "Why didn't you send me a message that you were about to start drilling?"

He looked at his watch. "Mohammed is probably at the hotel right now, wondering where you are. I sent him to fetch you. Now that that is settled, I must see to the drill. The foreman is ready to start... *Inshallah*, Robyn, *Inshallah*!''

He walked away before he could see the red flush on her cheeks. He had taken her anger and turned it around until she had nothing to be angry about. She was left feeling angry anyway.

She walked quickly toward the workroom, considering it her refuge until she could get a better hold on herself. On the way she saw Huntley Saunders strolling around as if he had done nothing—jolly and insufferably innocent. Rafica fell into step beside her and smiled a greeting.

"Did Sayed permit *him* to come?" Robyn asked, still burning from Sayed's easy dismissal of her.

Rafica nodded. "Dr. al-Rashad is a kind man. He didn't have the heart to deny the poor man the experience of seeing the borescope put to work at last.''

"Humph!" Robyn grunted, as she retied her scarf against the gritty wind. "He took unfair advantage, inviting all of his idle cocktail-party friends."

Rafica laughed at her friend's expression. "In Islam, a *musfid*—an evil one—who bears *hasad*—a grudge and envy—is best left to the teaching of the greater law of Allah."

"I agree it was very forebearing to let him come." Robyn's voice was flat. "How nice it would be if the best meaning of all religions was practiced."

"*Ya rit!*" Rafica said, smiling.

"Don't tell me...." Robyn held up her hand. "I'm picking up a few Arabic words. That means 'I wish it were.' "

"*Kuwayyis!* Good, you understand. Now I must go to the dig with Dr. Gaddabi. It is starting now, at last."

Robyn felt left out. She watched Sayed from afar. Even kindly Dr. Gaddabi was too busy to talk. The circle of workers was drawing tightly around the drill, and anyone not actually involved in the process was extraneous. She could only wait.

She sat on the steps of the work shed and watched the huddled cluster of workers at the dig site, while drifts of conversation floated to her curious ears. What she heard most clearly was the chatter of the visiting women, who were standing a respectful distance from the work.

An age-ravaged woman with mournful eyes and heavy makeup was speaking to another woman, whom Robyn quickly recognized as Aziza Atef. "What a handsome man Sayed is!" the first one said. "How do you expect to keep his attention,

Aziza, my dear, when he has a heart like a khamsin? It blows and then it doesn't blow.'' The strident voice had a strong British accent.

Robyn couldn't hear the reply and she didn't want to. A heavy painfulness cramped her chest, and she decided to go into the workroom and continue to clean up from the wind. Rafica had done a lot, but more needed to be done.

Her mind grew busy with doubts. What could she expect from Sayed? She wanted to believe him...but what could she believe?

Most of the papyrus fragments had been removed to the museum, but the large mass of compressed vellum scrolls and fragments was still bundled in its cloth and plastic blanket under the table. She ducked her head to reach down and draw it out. Awkwardly but gently, she pulled the edges of the plastic wrapping toward her.

She intended to pack the vellum into one of the large boxes and seal it for shipment to Alexandria, but as she pulled, part of the plastic snagged on a rough place and the vellum spilled out onto the floor. To her dismay, bits of vellum cracked off of the scrolls, and she spent a long time gingerly picking up the brittle pieces with padded tweezers. Then she prepared the box, cushioning its sides with more soft plastic. The main mass of the scrolls was stuck stubbornly together, and she lifted it carefully to set it in the container.

As she did, however, one scroll suddenly became detached from the bottom of the mass and fell back to the floor. Thank God it stayed intact. She couldn't bear another scolding from Sayed. The center of the scroll was still wound tightly, but the outer edges were looser. The last inch of vellum stuck out dry and crisp; the wooden winding rod at the bottom was gone.

Robyn crouched on the dusty floor before it, picking it up as delicately as she could, before she noticed the writing. It was more faded than that of the papyri had been, but it was still legible—ancient Greek.

A line at the very end caught her eye because it was written in different ink and not in the Greek alphabet, and the writing was much smaller. In Latin, it was like a clerk's notation. It read: "Pergamum—Scroll 708. Gift of Marcus Antonius, Imperator."

As she turned the scroll toward the light to see more clearly, something round and hard fell against her hand and down to the floor. Her heart almost stopped. She set the scroll gently in the box and picked up the fallen object. Almost before she looked she knew what it was.

It was a small flat ceramic disc, a tag with a chip off of one side. Obviously it had hung from a leather thong, a part of which still adhered to a hole made for it. She turned the object slowly in her hand and saw in clearly printed Greek letters: *Museion Alexand* . . . .

"My God!" she whispered, "Oh, my God!" This was a scroll from the huge Library of Pergamum, one that Antony had given Cleopatra as a gift. So it had become part of the Library of Alexandria. This was Sayed's proof! And she had found it for him!

She rushed out of the door to tell him her wonderful news, then stopped in her tracks. Not far away Sayed stood, Aziza Atef clinging to his arm. He was inviting people to move closer to witness the drilling.

For a moment Aziza stopped him from returning

to the drill site. She was looking adoringly into his eyes. "No matter about propriety, darling, I must give you this for luck." She left the print of her crimson lips on his cheek. He smiled slightly and led the way to the waiting drill. He hadn't noticed Robyn.

Clutching the tag fiercely in her hand, she followed. No matter what, she couldn't miss the great moment of discovery. Two women were walking near her, talking in English. "They look as if they are married already," one said in a sour tone. "What a catch! I gather that there will be an announcement in a matter of days."

"Aziza is clever," the other one answered. "I hear that his mother—you know what a dragon she is—really dislikes her."

"Trust Aziza to get her way...."

Robyn's feet continued walking, but she felt nothing, not even excitement about the precious tag in her hand. A sick tide of misery began to rise in her heart. That was the end of it, then.

The finality of her loss hit her hard, and she realized that she had never truly stopped hoping, in some hidden corner of herself, that Sayed would someday love her.

Dr. Gaddabi motioned her inside the fence. "Our great moment, Robyn; you must be very proud."

She dredged up a smile. He couldn't possibly imagine what a great moment it was—both good and bad. Sayed would get his heart's desire: the long awaited proof of the library, and the woman of his choice. She wished him well, but her sore heart still had questions unanswered.

Why had he blown hot and cold, like the khamsin, as those women had said? Was he really cynical and cruel, amused at playing with the emotions of a naive young American? Had he fed her little morsels of hope and pleasure because he needed her help and wanted to keep her happy?

Surely she had been an open book for him to read. She cringed, remembering how easily he could sway her with a touch or a word. For one icy moment she was tempted to keep the little ceramic tag and cheat him of the final proof. But her love burned through her anger. He must have this last gift from her and then go to the sophisticated woman who could match his temperament. . . .

A silence had fallen over the dig. Rafica came over to stand beside Robyn. *"Ya Salam,"* she whispered. "Isn't it wonderful? We're going to finally do it."

Sayed and the drill crew hunched over the engine. It began to chuff and pant noisily, and the heavy drill drove into the flat stone paving on the floor of the excavation. There was a cracking sound and Sayed gestured for the drill to stop.

He was about to step down to investigate when a strange sighing sound came from the flooring. Little eddies of dust puffed along a joint in the flat stones, which seemed to have moved slightly under the pressure of the drill. Air was rushing into the chamber.

The sound ceased and both Sayed and Dr. Gaddabi knelt down for a closer look. After a moment Sayed climbed back out of the drilling area to report to the silent spectators.

"The drill has moved a stone slightly." His voice was controlled and tense. "The sound we heard was from a vacuum being broken. Whatever is in the room below was put there in the same way as the sun boat found near the Great Pyramid—cleverly preserved in a vacuum.'' He drew an excited breath. "We should find our chamber in good condition, and surely containing things of considerable historical value.''

Exclamations broke from the watchers. Rafica clutched Robyn's free hand. "We are right...the room will be full of scrolls!''

The drill was started once more, and its chugging voice echoed off the high walls of the enclosed dig area. It seemed endless, waiting there while the bit whined and ground. Then suddenly there was no resistance and the drill was hastily stopped. When it was withdrawn, a neat round hole remained in the stone flooring.

Robyn forgot her own personal emotion, looking at that dark little hole, like an eye into the past. The fears and hopes of the men who had hidden their treasure with such urgency and care were very tangible for a moment, and she realized that the vision she had seen on that first day here was a true one.

The borescope was brought and set into place near the drill hole. Huntley Saunders waddled to the edge of the dig, obviously with the intention of climbing down, but a sharp look from Sayed stopped his descent.

Slowly and with great caution Sayed guided the machine's arm, with its light and mirrors, as it was lowered through the hole into the darkness. He put an eye to the viewer and stood quietly, rotating it almost imperceptibly for what seemed an eternity.

Finally he straightened his back and looked up. He didn't smile, but his eyes were burning with blue light. The steady low hum of the wind wound down at the same time, as if even the afreets had respect for this moment of discovery.

As he cleared his throat roughly, Robyn's heart ached in sympathy for him. She knew how moving that first glimpse into the past must have been.

"We have found a room, perhaps ten by fourteen feet. It is filled with scrolls on shelves and in boxes. From this small first look they appear to be in excellent condition. It is undoubtedly the greatest number of manuscripts from ancient times ever to have been discovered."

Cheers and clapping exploded around him. Robyn felt an almost irrepressible urge to rush to him and hold him with all her strength, to join with him in every way possible. What other person here knew so intimately what he was feeling? Who else could share without need for words the enormity of this discovery?

"Allah be thanked!" Rafica's eyes were wet with tears. "I'm so happy for Dr. al-Rashad; he deserves his good fortune."

Robyn hastily tucked the ceramic tag into the breast pocket of her shirt before she was folded into an embrace by Rafica and then by Tom. She heard Sayed's voice calling her name.

"Come down, Robyn." He was smiling. She stood immobile for a few seconds, not sure that he was really speaking to her. Then he raised his voice and addressed the people who stood around the edge of the dig. "Miss Robyn Douglas is the official representative for our university sponsor in the United States. She is also the daughter of one of my best-loved teachers—the famous and unexcelled expert on translations of ancient manuscripts, the late Dr. James Arthur Douglas. Miss Douglas is herself a very competent translator. As the university's representative, Miss Douglas should be the next person to look into our room." He looked calmly into Huntley Saunders's angry glare, then back at Robyn, his hands extended to her in welcome.

Rafica gave Robyn a push. "Go!" she ordered.

Her feet slipped and stumbled down the pebbly steps into the dig. She felt Sayed take her hand and lead her to the borescope. His touch flamed along her hand and arm, only serving to remind her of her confusion and misery, but she fought to appear calm.

Dr. Gaddabi was smiling at her and Sayed's eyes had a gentle and tender look that made the threat of tears rise up and constrict her throat. With his help she looked into the eyepiece, gradually focusing on the lower chamber. A sense of awe brought an involuntary shiver.

The tiny circle of light was enough to show some extent of the find. What lost treasures of thought lay there—the salvage of the greatest library of the ancient world!

"Are you happy, small bird?" Sayed whispered close to her. "There is so much we must talk about." She thought she felt his lips brush the tip of her ear, but she had enough sense not to respond this time.

She looked into his lighted eyes for a moment. "I'm glad for you—very glad," she managed. She knew her eyes were not warm or happy. His expression changed, but he was flooded with the excited press of people waiting to look through the borescope, and his attention left her.

Reluctantly she moved away to give others a chance—Dr. Gaddabi and Tom, Rafica and George, and finally Huntley Saunders and a few of his guests, including Aziza Atef.

Sayed attempted to wave everyone to silence. "One more announcement, my friends," he said urgently. "There will be a formal press conference and dinner tomorrow night at the Palestine Hotel. As difficult as it is, I must ask your cooperation in not speaking of this day's amazing events until then. I will give those members of the press who are here today the opportunity for interviews, but there must be nothing released to the public until after the press conference. I know I can count on your cooperation."

The antiquities police moved into the area with the intention of sealing it off to visitors. This was no longer going to be an easygoing dig, but a well-protected national treasure.

Robyn eased herself out of the crowd. Some people, sensing that she was of more consequence than they had thought, tried to stop her to talk. She pressed past them as politely as she could and got back to the workroom, where she put the tag into an envelope and then in her purse.

She would give it to Sayed at the press banquet and then leave for home immediately. She didn't want to be around for the announcement by Aziza Atef.

With all her heart she wanted to stay and help with the translation, to be close to Sayed while he moved back into the wonders of the past. If only her brief dream that he might love her had been a reality! Now she would never stand by the lotus pool in the garden so close to paradise, never know the ending to the scroll of the blue-eyed god. She had a dizzy feeling, as if life had slapped her down.

Rafica came and took a last look at the workroom, and Robyn showed her the box with the vellum. While she entered the box number in the logbook,

Robyn went outside. The late-afternoon sun was setting fast, swallowed up above the horizon by the far-off shroud of blowing sand. For some strange reason the winds at the dig had stopped.

The flock of visitors were driving away in their sleek Citroëns and Fiats when Robyn felt a touch on her shoulder. She turned to see Bahiya's face crinkled into a big smile.

"Good luck!" She peered at Robyn. "You become happy, lady. Moon give blessing; wind finished. Only few tears more to wash away dust of not understanding." She brought her face close to Robyn's. "All not told yet, you have secret. Other secrets come soon. Tell man who has the blood of pharaohs, Bahiya bless him. Bahiya bless bird on shoulder of prince. Not fly, little bird—wait."

She turned with her usual swirl of skirts and strode toward her village. Robyn looked around at the camp. It seemed desolate now, not welcoming. She would never forget this isolated dusty place, never.

She rode back to Alex with Rafica. The others were staying behind to work at securing the site, now that the find was known. But she wanted only to get to her room. Bahiya was right—there were more tears to weep. She wondered if she would hear from Sayed again. It was best if she didn't.

Rafica walked with Robyn to her room and came inside with her. "You are so quiet, Robyn. Are you all right?"

"Just still tired, I guess."

"You didn't tell me how expert you are in translation, my sister." Rafica's voice carried a certain sadness under her words.

"I'm sorry. I learned from my father and never

thought of myself as a professional. Dr. Wayland felt I should keep my father's identity a secret. I didn't want to trail along in his glory, anyway. Dr. Wayland was also worried that I would have problems with the Islamic attitude toward women. I can see now that it didn't matter."

"You have love for your father and pride in him. The parent should be honored in the child."

"I've learned a lot since I've come here. You have shown me how fine the women of Islam are and how much is possible for them."

To her distress Rafica burst into tears. She sat huddled on the end of Robyn's bed while her thin graceful shoulders shook with sobs. Robyn put a comforting arm around her. What could she say to the sad and patient eyes that had such a deep look of love denied?

"Have you talked with Karim again? Is there anything I can do?"

The smooth dark head moved from side to side, and a muffled voice wavered, "I can't go on without him. After a while he will marry—he's a healthy man and needs a woman. I couldn't bear it. I think I'll die if I have to marry Mustafa, even though he is a good man."

She groped around in her purse for tissues and blew her nose, then looked up, again pulling on her mask of calmness. "Forgive me, I shouldn't give you my burdens. I see in your own eyes a hurt that is deep, my sister. I know it has to do with Dr. al-Rashad; do not deny it."

Robyn walked to the window. Outside, the lights of the hotel across the bay gleamed on the water. She said quietly, "I've been very foolish, Rafica. Sayed is a remarkable man and I've let myself be drawn to him. I even imagined that he really cared for me. Someone told me that men of Islam don't feel the same responsibility for foreign women as they do for their own. They think we are all permissive and not quite respectable, and so we can't expect them not to take what they can get.''

Rafica sighed heavily. ''That is true, in part. I have seen the foolish actions of American and European women toward even the guides and drivers. But Dr. al-Rashad is a gentleman. He could not think that about you.''

''I don't know what he thinks. I overheard today that Aziza Atef is soon going to announce her engagement to him. You saw her hanging on his arm this afternoon.'' Her throat constricted. ''As soon as the banquet is over tomorrow night I'm going home. I'll be better off when I can't see him.'' She gave a trembling laugh. ''Egypt weaves a spell over people, you know. Maybe I'm fascinated with Sayed because he looks so much like one of the nobles of the Old Kingdom. I've been in love with the old Egyptians ever since I was a child...but it's time to go home and be sensible.''

Rafica gave Robyn a quick warm hug. ''I pray to Allah that our hearts will be healed.'' Then she drew away, frowning. ''But Aziza Atef! That manikin! It can't be true. Poor Madame al-Rashad—it would kill her.'' She looked earnestly at Robyn. ''Wait, my friend. Don't believe until you hear officially. The Dr. al-Rashad I know couldn't possibly want that woman for a wife. *Subhân Allâh!*''

''Thanks, Rafica. Don't worry, I'm not going to be a romantic dreamer, anymore. Sayed only meant to be kind to me. His real life and friends are here.''

They hugged again without words and Rafica left.

Robyn forced herself to sort out her notes and papers. Tomorrow she would get everything in order for Sayed and Dr. Wayland.

Her phone didn't ring and there was no tapping at her door. She had no appetite for dinner, even with room service, and she hurried to bed. There was a storm of tears gathering in her heart. She pressed her aching head into the pillow and let it break.

How little she had known about life when she had cried over stodgy John—was it less than a year ago? Now her feeling for him seemed like childish nonsense beside the reality of her love for Sayed. The Library of Alexandria, the ancient ceramic tag in her purse, the little statue of Ptah—why did they have to be so important to her? It would have been better if she had listened to her mother, had learned to cook and sew and be like other women. Where did she belong? Without Sayed she was stranded halfway between two worlds, and not really living in either one of them.

CHAPTER FIFTEEN

ROBYN WOKE RELUCTANTLY the next morning, her eyes still hurting from last night's tears. She dashed cold water on her face and went to the balcony to look out over the bay. The little brown birds, which had grown used to coming for their morning crumbs, fixed hopeful bright eyes on her.

She ordered breakfast as usual, enjoying her toast, coffee and salty Egyptian cheese with honey out on the balcony. And as usual, she shared the crumbs with the birds.

Today would be for tying up the loose ends of her work. If she ever planned to be a career woman she would have to pull the shreds of her resolve together. She should be looking forward to home; there would be a good job waiting for her at the university.

Someday she and Sayed might meet at some learned seminar. By that time she would have an unchallenged reputation, she daydreamed. Someday... perhaps... she wouldn't even care about proving herself to him.

The morning flew by. There was a pile of typing and organizing and duplicating to do for her final report. By two o'clock she had finished; there was one copy each for Sayed and Dr. Wayland. The reports looked dignified and official in their covers. And they were good—she knew that and was proud of the fact.

One more thing had to be done, and she resolutely picked up the phone. She had to make reservations for her flight home. With an airline clerk she made arrangements to leave the next afternoon, after driving to Cairo in the morning.

Her back ached from all her typing and concentration, and she was glad to leave her room to stretch her legs and have a sandwich in the quiet hotel coffee shop. This was her last full day in Egypt and she hadn't said goodbye to any of the places that had meant so much to her. But that would probably just make it worse, she mused.

On the end of the little peninsula where the hotel stood was a grove of pine trees. There were places to sit overlooking the sea. Below the low cliff the water foamed softly around fallen boulders. Robyn walked past the gift shop and out to the observation point, where she found a nook to sit in.

Sighing below her, the sea mingled its fresh scent with the warm perfume of pine. She wanted to remember the essence of the ancient Mediterranean, to absorb the smell and energy of it.

A measure of peace came to her, an acceptance of her situation, as she sat there. It was no use pretending that she didn't love Sayed. She would love him for as long as she lived. There would always be an empty place in her heart—but no doubt the ache would grow less with time.

She was glad that she had been able to get to know him. At least he would be somewhere in the world and she would hear about him from time to time. Words of her father came back to her: "Wait until you go to Egypt, my darling. You will not be the same; no one ever is. There is something in Egypt that brings you face to face with your own self, like a catalyst that rearranges your inner necessities.''

Well, Egypt had done its work. She was no longer innocent, untried. But she still had to answer the riddle that the great Sphinx's farseeing eyes had seemed to demand of her: ''How will you understand love?''

After sitting and looking at the sea a long while, she went for a walk along the pleasant paths of the surrounding park. The banquet and press announcements were still to be endured, but she felt better. She would be able to meet Sayed's amazing eyes without shaking inside.

When she returned to her room a large box was resting against her door. It was not from a florist, and Robyn assumed it had been left there by mistake. She picked it up and let herself into her room, then noticed that the box was tied with ribbon, like a gift. A small envelope was tucked into it.

Before she could stop it a knot of anticipation sprang up into her solar plexus. She lifted the flap of the envelope and pulled the card partway out. Sayed's swift black writing swam before her eyes for a moment. ''Wear this tonight,'' it said—nothing more.

She felt heat flooding into her cheeks as she laid the box on her bed and opened it. Inside, folded in layers of tissue paper, was the golden galabia. Delicate traceries of fine beads flowed over the shimmering gold ocher cloth. It was even more beautiful than she had remembered.

Irresistibly her hands drew it out of its wrappings and she hurried to the full-length mirror on her closet door. As she held the lovely gown against herself the same strange feeling of ownership came over her that she had known in the shop. The galabia belonged to her.

The golden color accented the tawny lights in her soft cloud of hair, now almost blond from the desert sun. It brought out the amber flecks in her gray blue eyes and reflected a sheen of gold on her skin. In this magic dress she could only be beautiful.

Her knees grew weak and she laid the galabia back on the bed, as if its fascinating smooth touch would seduce her into Sayed's arms. There was a feel of him clinging to the garment. Why had he sent this lovely gift? Was he repaying her for services rendered, an elegant goodbye... or was there another reason, one that had to do with man and woman and the excitement that tugged between them?

She stood looking at the galabia, her heart warring against itself. More than anything she wanted to wear this beautiful dress. In it tonight she could look lovely and poised. She could be more attractive than she had ever been in her whole life, and she wanted Sayed to remember her that way.

She would carry it off, she decided abruptly, would show him that she was not a wide-eyed, easy-to-get American girl who could be swept off her feet by an accomplished Egyptian male. She would accept his gift in a sophisticated way, with a cool smile and pleasant thanks.

Darkness settled over the sky outside. Robyn hadn't heard from anyone—except for the dress. Slowly she made her careful preparations for the evening—bathing luxuriously, brushing her shining hair into an upswept coil on her head. Makeup came next, more than she normally used, but still subtle. Then she let the cool weight of the galabia slide over her head and settle in long folds over her body.

The mirror reflected a woman with deep glowing eyes and a mouth that obviously was not a stranger to kisses—or to pride, either. For one night at least she would be a secure woman who expected the admiration of men as a matter of course, one who could deal with it easily.

Fortunately her evening purse and dress sandals went well with the dress. There was a small scratch on one of the smooth heels, but no one would ever notice. Her mind cringed from the happy memory of her night with Daphne al-Rashad and Sayed; she had scuffed her shoe as they had stood at the top of the tower, looking over the fairy landscape of Cairo below.

She stopped the flow of her thoughts before the longing and the sense of failure could claim her. Deliberately she picked up the lapis Ptah on its delicate chain and fastened it around her neck. Its deep blue shone against the soft fabric of the golden dress.

The small necessities went into her purse, then she found a fresh envelope and a piece of official university stationery. She wrote Sayed's name on the outside of the envelope, giving his full titles—doctor, professor...director, the Desert Manuscript Project.

Then she typed her last message to Sayed al-Rashad:

This tag fell from the scroll that became separate from the larger body of vellum (see entry in logbook No. 331). The scroll is in Greek, with a notation in Latin at the end. The Latin reads, "Pergamum: Gift of Marcus Antonius, Imperator.'' The tag, despite its missing chip, is easily read, "Museion Alexand...."

It is my belief that the scroll and the tag identify the material beyond doubt as coming from the Library of Alexandria—part of the material taken from Pergamum by Antony. It was found yesterday afternoon. My only excuse for not giving it to you immediately is that you were extremely busy with the drilling and with your guests. Also, since I found it, I wanted the pleasure of giving you the proof that you have wanted.

As representative of the university, I congratulate you on the wonderful treasures your fine deductive work has brought to light. I am sure that more proof lies in the underground room.

Dr. Wayland will be delighted, and I will give him full details when I see him in two days. I wish you the best of luck in the translation and preservation of those marvelous manuscripts.

Sesha Neheru Douglas

As she folded the paper she longed to put a personal word at the bottom, but hardened her heart. Everything must be businesslike from now on.

She sealed the flat ceramic tag into the letter and put it in her purse. Her travel clock showed her that she had dressed too early. The dining room didn't open until eight o'clock, and she didn't want to risk seeing Sayed before the crowd had gathered.

She paced around her room. If only time could have stopped at that moment of dawn by the canal. If only she could have kept that one moment of bliss as her own, gazing into Sayed's lapis-blue eyes and sharing the joy of the morning light as it roused the energies of the sleeping earth. She would have been satisfied with that one kiss by the canal.

But time had been her adversary. Time had made him doubt her, when maybe he would have loved her. If only... if only....

She sighed and straightened her back. Time had taught her too much about the illusions of love and its fragile connection to reality. She would probably never again allow herself to love like this, and it would always be deeply painful to think of Egypt.

It was time to go down to the banquet. She took a last look in the mirror and practiced a sophisticated smile. She was going to project the image of a charming woman who moved easily among men and could take them or leave them.

While waiting for the erratic elevator she breathed deeply and slowly several times to calm her rapid heartbeat. In the lobby she could hear the ebb and flow of voices from the dining room.

Once again the banquet was being held in the main dining room, but this time a folding partition divided the area in two. Robyn approached the milling crowd with as much self-assurance as she could muster, trying not to look uncomfortable. The long main table was splendid with flower centerpieces, and smaller tables were clustered before it. There were dozens of faces that she had never seen before—the press, no doubt, and political dignitaries.

Her eyes picked out Tom, who looked handsome in evening dress, and Dr. Gaddabi in the midst of a group of people. To her surprise, a regal-looking Daphne al-Rashad was seated at the long banquet table, with Aziza Atef gesturing and smiling beside her. Madame al-Rashad's expression was one of cool patience.

Robyn turned a little and saw Sayed with Huntley Saunders at his heels. Her heart did a few alarming gymnastics under the golden finery on her breast.

Fortunately, Dr. Gaddabi noticed her and came quickly to offer her his arm. He piloted her from group to group, making introductions. She was grateful to him. He was setting a tone for her as a respected member of the team. Some of the society faces she remembered at the dig this time greeted her with gracious and curious smiles.

After a little while she found herself forgetting her shyness and talking easily about the university and the project. Tom caught her eye to give a silent okay sign with his thumb and forefinger. At his side was Sandi in a white galabia embroidered in pale pink. Her blond hair was brushed back into a classic twist and her makeup was unobtrusive. The only part of the old Sandi still evident dangled from her ears in the form of elaborate silver Bedouin earrings. She gave Robyn a big smile and leaned her head against Tom's arm for a second. Robyn felt delighted for them.

Then Dr. Gaddabi's fatherly hand urged her toward the main table, where Daphne al-Rashad's elegant silver head was turning restlessly from Aziza Atef to an Englishwoman, the same one whom Robyn had overheard gossiping at the dig.

"You are a lovely woman, Robyn, very lovely," Dr. Gaddabi said quietly in her ear. "I envy Sayed's youth and his privilege to sit beside you this evening."

Robyn gazed into his calm, uncomplicated eyes and noticed odd sparks of amused admiration glinting there. It was almost as if he knew something that she didn't.

As they approached Madame al-Rashad, the older woman rose with an exclamation of pleasure and pulled Robyn into a scented embrace. "My dear, I've waited impatiently to see you. How radiant you look! Sit here beside me now. Later Sayed will be between us."

She turned to Aziza and her friend, "Of course you have met Miss Robyn Douglas from the university, who has been such an invaluable help to my son." Two empty smiles came toward her, and Aziza's eyes shot shafts of such dislike that Robyn was glad she had the golden galabia as armor.

Madame al-Rashad sat down, turning a determined back to the other ladies, her insistent hand drawing Robyn down beside her.

The two other women left immediately, gushing some insincere flattery, but not before Aziza bent over to place a kiss on the stiff British cheek.

"Phah!" Madame al-Rashad sniffed, watching them go. "Such cloying perfume—a perfect match to her personality!" She turned to Robyn again. "Lovely, lovely, my dear. Be happy—this is your night."

Robyn mustered a smile. "It's Sayed's night, and I'm happy for him."

"Yes, a culmination of his years of dreams."

Robyn felt the envelope like a hot coal of expectancy in her purse. If only she could just set the envelope at Sayed's place and leave the banquet. Madame al-Rashad's penetrating eyes weren't helping the tide of misery that was rising in her.

"Don't be nervous," the clipped English voice advised. "You won't have to make a speech."

People were beginning to take their places. "I'd better move," Robyn said.

"Wait, my dear; Sayed will seat you when he comes."

Dr. Gaddabi took his seat on the other side of Daphne al-Rashad and they conversed warmly. Robyn was left to her lonely tension.

She saw Tom and Sandi take their places at a nearby table, then Sayed moving toward the main table with two dignified-looking men. "The governor of Alexandria and the head of the University of Alexandria," Madame al-Rashad said discreetly to her.

Robyn rose and stood back from the table. As he saw her Sayed's face lighted into a smile that made her tremble and the blood rush to her cheeks, ending with a single look the composure she thought was hers.

"You look beautiful tonight, Robyn." He took her chilly reluctant hand and cradled it in his warm one, while tremors of response raced through her traitorous nerves.

With an especially gracious word he introduced her to the two men. He was more than handsome in his white evening jacket. His ruffled shirt was fastened with tiny lapis studs, and blue color flashed from his lapis-and-gold cuff links. She pulled her eyes away from him to see the results of her newfound elegance in the dark, attentive eyes of the smiling men.

Sayed seated her to his left, and the table filled quickly with other people of importance to the project. There were more introductions, most of which went flying past Robyn. Sayed's nearness was melting the wall that she had built so carefully.

The head of the university engaged her in expert social chitchat from his place on her left, and she began to pull herself together again, despite the disturbing feel of Sayed's warmth next to her. It was like a fire that threatened to engulf her the moment she let down her guard.

Two people entered the banquet area at the last minute, just as the waiters were pulling the screen completely across the dining room, and Tom raised a beckoning hand to them. Rafica, lovely in a soft peach flowing dress, was holding tightly to the arm of a tall man in an army uniform—Karim! Robyn could only stare.

They seated themselves with Tom and Sandi. When Rafica's eyes found Robyn's she smiled broadly.

What had happened? Robyn's curiosity made her temporarily forget her own distress. She looked past Sayed to his mother, and saw an expression on that aristocratic face almost like a cat who had just eaten the best cream and was rather pleased with itself. Robyn didn't doubt that she had something to do with the glowing look of happiness on Rafica's face.

As the food was being served and general conversation buzzed in the room, Sayed turned to her, his voice low and vibrating. "Thank you for wearing the dress. It becomes you perfectly and you honor me in it." He half smiled, holding her eyes for a long moment until she colored and looked away.

"I shouldn't have accepted it," she said stubbornly.

He made a sharp sound in his throat. "It is my gift of gratitude." His eyes narrowed, and she regretted her words as she watched his brows draw into a frown.

"Then, thank you. I have never owned such an elegant dress."

"Hmm." He was still looking dark.

The weight of her evening bag in her lap stabbed again at her sense of guilt. She made a quick decision and fumbled with the catch, drawing out the envelope. With a shaking hand she held the white oblong toward him.

"What is this?" His eyes probed hers, the familiar smoldering blue flame in their depths.

"I want you to read it, uh, before you announce the work on the dig."

His brows lifted in surprise. She watched the lean hardness of his hands open the seal, and she wanted to lean down and press her lips against their supple strength. With a sharp pang she remembered how those hands could arouse passion in her body.

He pulled out the folded paper, and with it the thin ceramic tag. As he did she released her pent-up breath in a long sigh. There was no going back now. His eyes read the note swiftly and then he looked carefully at the tag in his hand. *"Subhân Allâh!"* His eyes flared with excitement but he looked suddenly angry. "What do you mean, you will see Dr. Wayland in two days?" he whispered harshly to her. "You haven't my permission to leave Egypt."

"I have plane reservations for tomorrow," she said through trembling lips.

"They will be canceled. Do not argue with me now, Robyn." The command in his voice, instead of making her angry in turn, sent a ripple of excitement up her spine. His face softened with a glint of a smile. "So you wanted to give me the news? You realize it is an illegal thing you have done—removing an artifact from its site and concealing it?'' He gave a short laugh at her expression, while the look in his own eyes was so intimate that Robyn could only stare at him mutely. ''You'd best tell me about the circumstances of finding this tag—in detail, and quickly.''

His rapid questions drew the story from her. ''You are sure of the Latin notation at the bottom of the scroll?'' he asked in a flowing, modulated voice that scattered her concentration dangerously.

She nodded. ''Very sure.''

His vitally charged hand found hers and held it for a moment. ''Small bird, you always bring me the best of all gifts.'' Turning to his mother, he spoke swiftly for a moment and put the tag into her hand.

''My God—you have the proof!'' Robyn heard her soft exclamation. Daphne al-Rashad leaned around Sayed with tears in her eyes. ''Bless you, my darling girl!''

The waiters were whisking away the dinner plates, and Robyn realized that she had eaten practically nothing. In fact, she couldn't even remember what had been served. She watched as a creamy dessert of many delicate layers of pastry was set before her. A tiny steaming cup of thick Egyptian coffee came with it. Robyn could only sit and look at the dainty confection.

Sayed had handed the tag to Dr. Gaddabi and was talking animatedly with him, leaning past his mother. Undoubtedly he was delighted with the proof—but where did that leave her? He had his back to her as if she no longer existed. Her eyes traced the line of his face, clear and strong, and the antique shape of his fine head with its energetic curling hair. The shadow of his amazing long lashes moved across his cheeks as he gestured vigorously. The sensual curve of his lips sent magnetic signals to her emotions. Memory of the passionate demand of those lips on hers flooded her body with unwanted awakening. She had an almost desperate desire to touch him once more before she left him.

But she had no intention of changing her plane reservation. Even if he insisted that she stay to testify at the Antiquities Department hearings, she could write a deposition at home and mail it to Egypt. She knew now that this was no brief foolishness on her part—she truly could not stand to be near him much longer, not while she wanted him with such urgency. She couldn't be just a friendly colleague.

She picked at the *gâteau* and sipped at the bitter, bracing coffee. The head of the University of Alexandria smiled benignly. "It won't be long to wait for our announcement now," he said, chuckling. "I see our press and even some international reporters waiting with their cameras and note pads at the back tables. This may be one of the greatest finds in recent history, don't you agree?"

"I think it will rival King Tut in value." When he looked surprised she raised her head in an unconscious gesture of pride. "The manuscripts may contain some of the lost works of the ancient world, a priceless addition to human history. Dr. al-Rashad's work will have made an immense contribution to Egyptian archaeology and the literature of the Ptolemaic Dynasty."

"I hope you are right." He looked at her more seriously.

Sayed turned away from Dr. Gaddabi and rose to his feet, his untouched dessert and coffee forgotten.

He tapped on his water glass for attention until the level of conversation dropped and the roomful of faces waited attentively for his speech.

Sayed smiled at the crowd. "I will not delay the announcement you have come to hear." There was an undertone of controlled excitement in his smooth dark voice. "But first let me tell you that if it were not for the many people whose love for the past motivates them to dig forever in the dust, I could not bring this announcement to you." He paused. "We have uncovered a large cache of ancient manuscripts—the largest single discovery of written material so far in our records."

He went on to describe the upper room, and then to speak about the wonderfully preserved scrolls in the lower chamber. His words were brief, but full of the wonder of his search into the past. He made no effort to claim credit. He praised the American university for its help and even briefly introduced Huntley Saunders. He spoke of Dr. Gaddabi's support and gave the crew full recognition.

Robyn saw the reporters busily scribbling as flashbulbs flickered. What was he going to do, Robyn wondered. Wouldn't he mention the proof? She drifted into a dark place of misery again, listening to the flow of his beloved voice.

Dimly she heard Sayed saying, "There is one person who has made invaluable contributions, whom I have not yet introduced to you. This person is the accredited representative of the university in the United States." He smiled down at Robyn and went on to describe how she had protected the scrolls in the khamsin.

She wished he wouldn't do this. The curiosity of

many eyes turned on her tightened her already over-loaded nerves. She tried to look calm and business-like, like the woman Sayed was describing. Tom winked at her and Sandi and Rafica smiled. Sayed's voice went on, praising her for following in her father's footsteps.

"But now," he said, "this lovely young American has found for us the proof that I have been hoping for." His voice was deep with feeling as he held up the ceramic tag. "This small object fell from a mass of vellum manuscripts that our expert young archae-ologist was carefully packaging. It was lying unseen in a loose scroll, the bottom lines of which were legi-ble." He set the scene for the attentive audience and repeated the Latin inscription she had found. "I be-lieve that scroll to be part of Marc Antony's gift of love to Queen Cleopatra—from the great library of conquered Pergamum two thousand years ago."

He lowered his voice dramatically, still holding the tag for all to see. "This is an identification tag from that scroll; one that we have dreamed of finding in-tact. This tag reads in Greek, *Museion Alexandria*!" A gasp went up from the audience as they realized its significance.

"You must know what this means. We now have the first real manuscripts from our ancient treasure house of learning. We believe we have verified the legends that some of the scrolls from the great library were hidden when wars moved across this city." The room erupted into cheers.

Sayed held up his hand for silence. "I want to in-troduce to you a very special member of our project, the one who identified the scroll tag and brought it to me." He smiled. "Her father, in a flash of insight at her birth, named her in the old Egyptian language that he so loved: Sesha Neheru Douglas. Small bird among flowers. For convenience she is known to us as Robyn, but to me she will always be my small sweet bird—the woman I am going to marry.''

A burst of applause and congratulations filled the room. Robyn sat stunned until she felt Sayed's hand urging her to stand up. She rose, trembling violently in the circle of his arm while cameras clicked and flashed.

From the midst of the din she heard Sandi's loud high voice exclaim, ''Now I've heard everything!''

Tom ran up and grabbed Sayed's hand, then leaned across the table to give Robyn a quick kiss. He went back to his table, and Robyn heard his laughing voice calling to Sandi, ''Just wait, my girl, you *haven't* heard everything yet!''

Through her bemusement she felt her hand being shaken by the various guests at the banquet table, and especially warmly by Dr. Gaddabi. ''I knew all along,'' he confided. ''It is a good thing for both of you.''

She was quickly caught up in a triumphant embrace by Madame al-Rashad, who whispered, ''I am so happy, my dear. Yours is the second marriage to be arranged tonight.'' She nodded in Rafica's direction.

Robyn's startled mind repeated those wonderful words, ''the woman I am going to marry,'' and a slow ecstatic warmth began to flood through her heart. This was no dream—not this time. Sayed was here next to her, people were kissing her cheek—it had to be happening.

Sayed was engulfed by the reporters. Press releases

were being handed out by George, but that wasn't enough for the hungry members of the media. They wanted more details, more excitement.

They filmed Sayed holding up the precious tag and in company with the city fathers and members of the academic societies. All the time he held tightly to her hand, as if he would take no chance on letting her go. She swallowed hard as the reality of her joy finally began to seep into her mind. She had lived for so long not being sure where reality ended and dream began.

After a while Daphne al-Rashad left her place and linked arms with Rafica and Karim. "These dears will take me home," she said, calling for Sayed's attention. "Rafica won't be back at work until the day after tomorrow. Karim is leaving for his unit again." Her manner was high-handed and imperious, but Sayed merely smiled agreement.

Rafica whispered to Robyn, "All is well, my sister. Thanks to you and Dr. and Madame al-Rashad. I'm so happy and I know you are, too." She looked into Robyn's still-bewildered eyes with an understanding laugh. "Ask Dr. al-Rashad to explain it to you."

At last Sayed dismissed the reporters politely, and with a strong hand on her elbow urged Robyn away from the crowd, out of the hotel and quickly onto a tree-shadowed path in the park.

They walked in silence a moment, then Robyn's pride took strength from the cooling breeze from the sea. How could he have been so sure she would accept him? What if she hadn't wanted to marry him—how embarrassing it would have been! It hadn't occurred to him that he would be refused.

She stopped walking and turned to him. At her offended expression he threw back his head and laughed. "Don't say it, my dearest little bird. It wasn't a very romantic proposal, but I had to make sure you couldn't run from me again. How do you think I felt, to read in your letter that you were going to leave Egypt immediately?"

She drew in a breath to speak, but the next moment she was being pulled close in his compelling, powerful arms. All thought left her except the wonder that surged into her whole being. His kisses were soft and gentle, then with a thirst that drew from her a passionate response, he expertly explored her lips and all the sweet hidden places within. She clung to him helplessly with no thought of reserve. His hands moved caressingly down her body and drew her hips close to his while she gloried in the vitality that flowed to her from his body.

When she could finally speak she whispered, "You never told me . . . there was Madame Atef . . . you even suspected me of taking your scrolls." Her breath came in shallow bursts. ". . . and at the pyramids. . . . Oh, Sayed, I never knew what to think!"

His hands cupped her face. "Stop your words, my darling one, and listen. I fell in love with a quiet and beautiful woman who captured my heart one morning at sunrise." He brushed his lips against her hair, then moved swiftly to kiss her eyelids, the tip of her nose, and then her lips again, until she thought she might faint from his love. "Don't you understand how much you taught me, how I had to learn to trust?" he murmured. "I had to forget what I thought I knew of women and learn all over again." His lips came down to hers again and drew her into himself with tenderness and possession.

He raised his head and smiled while his eyes glistened. "I think I shall have to spend a lifetime putting right everything that was hurtful between us."

"Sayed. . .I don't know. . . ."

"I love you, my darling Robyn; it's very simple."

"Should I be afraid to believe you?"

"Never again, my beloved." Tears shone for a moment in the darkness of his lashes. "I am finished with saying stupid words when I mean only to speak of love."

With a little cry she put her arms around his neck and held him tightly. She was sure she would not be able to stand without him.

His voice spoke huskily into her ear. "Shall I fly away with you to my desert tents on camelback to prove my love? Don't you know I was so afraid you would leave me, after my being such a grand fool, that I had to do something? I didn't know how else to ask you to be my wife except to tell the world. That way it would be more difficult for you to refuse me."

He kissed her deeply and she felt him tremble. "If I had lost you, small bird. . .! I can't even think of it. I told my mother that I had at last found the woman I could love for the rest of my life and never tire of. She warned me to move swiftly or I might lose you— so I moved swiftly." He held her away a little to look into her eyes. "Were you really going to fly from me, small bird?"

She nodded, biting her lip. "I was so miserable. . . oh, Sayed! I thought you didn't care, and I loved you! I love you so much!"

He pulled her close, and his kisses sent heat and desire coursing through her veins. After a timeless interval he sighed, "We can't stay here. Do you know what I'd like to do?"

She looked at him questioningly, her eyes shining in the shadows.

"Would you let me drive you to our place by the canal to see the sunrise? There is something I want to tell you there."

Her joyful expression answered him, and hand in hand they hurried back to the hotel. In her room Robyn quickly slipped off her evening sandals and putting on a pair of flat-soled shoes; then she grabbed up her warm sweater. The face that looked back at her from the mirror had eyes full of wonder and happiness.

In the lobby Sayed was waiting impatiently, and Robyn hoped fleetingly that he would always be so anxious to see her coming. He had put the top down on the Fiat, and they sped through the quiet city, past the lake of reeds and into the desert. As they went they spoke together softly.

"Do you remember the chief of the antiquities office in Cairo?" he asked, laughing. "He told me that day how much he admired you, and said I should think about getting married." When he leaned over to kiss her swiftly, she smiled at him adoringly, then looked away.

From time to time cars sped by them, turning on their headlights when they wanted to pass. The rest of the time they drove as the others did, in the light of the waning moon.

At length they turned onto the bumpy dirt road to the dig. The guards came to attention, but when they saw who it was they settled back to their card playing by lantern light.

All the way out, despite their quiet talk, Robyn had felt a growing sense of urgency. The excited thudding of her heart made her feel breathless, and the unnerving joy that she associated with Sayed's presence was like glorious music around them. She found it hard to meet his eyes for long, because she was afraid he would see how urgently her whole being was roused by him. She was caught up in a shaking confusion, and at the same time a feeling of utter sweetness, having Sayed beside her.

He stopped the car near the excavation site and they started toward the canal hand in hand. Suddenly out of the darkness there was a swirl of skirts and a figure rose from a hollow in the sand. Bahiya stood there smiling at them.

"I wait for prince and his treasure." Her voice was a resonant whisper. She held out to them two small envelopes of cloth sewn around something flat. "*Higab*—for your happiness." Ceremoniously she gave one to each of them. "Not lose...bring good luck. Made by blessed sheikh." She gave Robyn a light embrace. "See, little bird. Bahiya see clear... no tell lie."

Robyn kissed her wrinkled cheek. "Thank you, Bahiya. I want you for our friend always."

The old woman turned to Sayed. "Honorable son of Khalid, the past remembers your blood. Build new Egypt as wise as old...like circles of returning stars. Not worry now—I see you have time alone here...." With a rakish, knowing grin she backed away, murmuring something in her own language, and was lost in the darkness.

"She's a remarkable woman," Sayed stated under his breath. "Come. Sunrise will be soon."

They walked on feet made light by expectation, Robyn holding up the hem of her galabia. The canal glittered in starlight through the screen of trees that still held night in their branches. Along the canalside path they moved, their steps whispering on the pine needles underfoot. "This is the place," Sayed finally said gently.

Robyn realized for the first time that he had a light blanket over his arm. Now he spread the blanket on the little patch of browning grass and sat down in a graceful motion. "Come," he said as a prince would speak.

Robyn obeyed, a delicious tremor starting in her body. She sank down on the blanket and he drew her against him, then gently pressed her back until she lay with her head nested in the curve of his arm. "My darling," he whispered, "I have asked for and been given the scroll of the blue-eyed god to translate. But it is for both of us to do. In some way I can't explain, it belongs to us out of some past I can only dimly remember."

She wanted to agree with him, but she dared not speak and break the spell that had settled around them.

"We will read our scroll together, my sweet Robyn," his voice continued. "But I confess that when I was so fearful I would lose you I looked ahead to see the ending. . . to give me some hope, perhaps." He smiled down into her love-drenched eyes. "When the sun rises I will tell you what I have committed to memory."

He gazed intently at her, and she saw that his face was glowing with a light she had seen only once before. Then he sat up straighter, laughing on a deep note that sent shimmers of expectancy racing in her sensitive nerves. With one supple motion he got up from the blanket and removed his clothing as if it didn't belong to this man out of time.

For a moment he stood tall and beautiful, stretching his arms to the stars, his muscles rippling smoothly under tawny skin. In that instant he was the splendid ancient god, and his body seemed to flow and sway blissfully in rhythm with the energy of the starry darkness pregnant with morning. Then he held out his hand to draw Robyn up to him.

She rose, not knowing if this was past or present, and stood before him, held in a kind of enchantment. She felt his strong fingers pull the golden galabia up over her head in one smooth and insistent motion. He dropped it on the grass and removed her underthings, as well. When she was completely nude he gazed at her with such love that she felt no embarrassment. She was wrapped in his love and the sweet soft air.

"This treasure is mine—Allah's gift." He spoke on a note of whispered joy. "A star sent from eternity to shine in my heart and home." And then he was holding her body against his while the heat of his desire sent waves of fiery joy into her heart. He drew her down with him onto the soft blanket on the grass, and he kissed her, in a way that pulled her energy into his like two flames meeting. She gave herself, the essence of her being, to him with complete trust.

He was gentle and yet fiercely passionate. Her body met his with rejoicing, and the scents of the canal and the ancient earth became part of their bliss. Each touch of his lips and his hands was part of an ecstatic vibration that reached to some far eternity. In all her dreams she could not have imagined the sweet alarms of pleasure that her body now knew.

His warm searching lips on her breasts woke her to a complicated delight, while shivers of yearning pressed her to offer him more—everything. She wanted to hold his head close to her in comfort and joy forever, and at the same time she had a fierce need to be taken by him, to be mastered by his strength. Each nerve was being brought to a peak of pleasure, and his every caress sent rivers of indescribable urgency sweeping through her.

When she arched herself along his hard potent body, he lifted his head to look into her eyes for a long moment. Then, with a groan that was both passion and love, he came to her. The sharp swift pain she felt dissolved into an amazing ecstasy and she cried out softly. She felt the waves of his own bliss move deep against her, and she couldn't stop the tears of love that started in her eyes. Thought was dimmed in the ancient fire of their complete union. She had never believed such wonder and happiness could be possible.

At last the flames of their sensation diminished and they lay together in their own soft sea of fulfillment. Feeling perfectly at peace, Robyn opened her eyes, to see the rose and orange glow of sunrise on the horizon. Waking birds were calling joyfully to each other about the new day.

Then Sayed stirred, raising his head and kissing the soft shoulder it had been resting on. "It is dawn. This is the time, my love," he said, kissing her gently on her eyelids, then her lips. He rose gracefully and helped her up, as well, smiling when she swayed toward him immediately. As the light brightened into a mist of color he laughed at her disheveled hair and touched with a loving finger the stain of pink that dyed her cheeks. She in turn caressed the warmth of his bare shoulders and traced the hardness of his chest with open palms.

Then he gazed into her eyes and spoke with such a resonant tone that his words vibrated in his breast beneath her hands.

"In the dawn he kissed me at last, Mother Isis...while the stars wove their patterns into the night. The blue-eyed god taught me the bliss that Earth feels when the water of the great river makes it fruitful. He taught me that love is the circle of eternity and goes from darkness to dawn, from noon to sunset and back to dawn again—forever. For surely I stand upon the horizon of love wherever I may move, and I belong to the blue-eyed god forever."

She looked up into the blue fires deep in his eyes, and her heart melted with the full love that a woman gives to a man. She would love him and walk with him in honor always. Standing so close to him she was aware again of how tall he was, tall and arrogant and kind. And they had just played out the end of the scroll, she knew; that ancient enchanting story had fulfilled itself.

"And I belong to the blue-eyed god forever," she repeated softly to the loving face looking down at her.

His answering voice was a caress. "Am I forgiven for my stupid doubts, my own woman?"

She laughed and reached up to kiss his beautiful lips. "I think I have always loved you." She let him see the joy in her eyes.

"Praise Allah," he said to the little birds watching from a nearby shrub. "The light is growing. We mustn't shock these small ones in their respectable feathers." He gave a deep, satisfied chuckle. "Old Bahiya has done well, keeping everyone away. I must reward her with a gift."

He let go of Robyn just long enough to gather up his clothes. She reached down to brush a few strands of grass from the golden galabia, then settled the shimmer of beads and fine cloth over her warm body. While she rearranged herself into some semblance of dignity, Sayed was transformed once more into a twentieth-century man.

She helped him fold the blanket, then they found each other's arms again, standing for a long time in the most peaceful enjoyment of their love.

"Who could possibly be as happy as I am at this moment?" she asked him.

"Who indeed?" His voice had a hint of play in it. "I suspect that Rafica and Karim are asking the same thing."

Robyn raised her eyes to his. "How did you arrange it? It all seemed so impossible. Did your mother intervene?"

"She is very skilled at diplomacy—and at finding out what she wants to. Undoubtedly she scolded Rafica for knowing so little about her sister Aisha's secret love."

Robyn drew in her breath. "Mustafa?"

"Exactly. Aisha and Mustafa were afraid to say anything for fear of upsetting both families. My mother is especially good at unraveling tangles such as theirs, and she gave me my instructions. It was not difficult to speak to Rafica's and Mustafa's fathers and propose a more happy alliance.''

"You used your position as sheikh, after all," she teased.

"In a way, small bird, but I followed my mother's advice and made it seem as if they all arrived at their new solution without my help. That is what my own father would have done, and everyone's sense of honor is preserved.''

"That makes my joy complete." *Definitely Third Dynasty,* she thought, smiling to herself as she took the measure of his square shoulders.

"Oh, in case you still think me a hard taskmaster, I assured Rafica's father that she would not have to subsist on the pay of a poor schoolteacher. Rafica is permanently on my staff." He stopped further conversation with a long and breathless kiss, lifting her a little off the ground as he held her. When he set her down again he confessed with a smile, "I have told my mother that she has two weeks to arrange our wedding. I do not wish to wait longer.''

A ripple of laughter escaped her. She leaned against him, and letting her lips explore the warm pulse of his throat. "And what did your mother say?'' she prompted.

"She said yes, of course." He trapped her face between his hands and kissed her. "We must now arrange for your mother and your aunt to come, and Dr. Wayland, too, if possible. My mother will take care of everything on my side of the family. Then there is the matter of your wedding dress; my mother would be more than delighted to help with the selection. You must understand, she had given up hope that I would marry anyone at all—and surely no one she would approve of...."

Robyn's eyes had widened. "My mother isn't anything like yours, Sayed. She may not want to travel so far. She's afraid of strange places and long airplane flights...."

"But she *must* come! I will talk to her," the blue-eyed god said, on a note of unshakable decision.

"She just may come, after all." Robyn's joy bubbled up into another laugh.

"I think we'd better go," he said, his eyes luminous and clear. "People will be coming to water their goats and sheep, and they wouldn't know what to think of two lovers laughing and kissing at dawn by their canal."

Robyn nodded. Then turned a final time to look at the glorious sunrise.

Suddenly she seemed to hear again the whisper of the young voice from long ago: *Mother Isis, take my hand.* And she felt on her own lips the mysterious eternal smile of the goddess. *Each of us is Isis,* she thought musingly, *the mother, the wife and the beloved.*

The warm shafts of the slanting sun touched her head like a blessing from the ancient gods, and Sayed turned to look at her. "Your smile is a special one, my darling. Can I guess why?"

"It is because I have just understood how much I love you." She held out her hand to be taken in his.